GET ANOTHER SHAANTI TALE FOR FREE.

Sign up for the no-spam newsletter and get a free copy of Neil's short story THE PILGRIM, set in the world of the Shaanti.

Details can be found at the end of THE SCARRED GOD.

ABOUT THE AUTHOR

Neil has been writing since he could hold a pen, publishing for over ten years and still has most of his own hair. He is the author of many short stories, some of which are gathered in his collection *After The Rain* and some of which are available as individual eBooks. He has been previously published in a number of small press outlets.

Neil has lived all over the place including London, Bradford and Somalia but is now settled in his native South Wales where he spends his time running after small children (his own) and endlessly toying with the idea of retiring to a fishing boat.He makes his online home at https://www.neilbeynon.com. You can also find Neil on twitter at https://twitter.com/neilbeynon, on Facebook at https://www.facebook.com/neilbeynonauthor/ and you should send him an email at neil@neilbeynon.com if so inclined.

For Gemma, who was there at the beginning.
And Joseph and Anwen, who were there at the end.
And Muriel* and Ziggy, who I wish could read it.

*Obligatory disclaimer: not the Muriel in the book.

'In the dark regions of the forest, where the oldest trees stand, if you listen carefully enough, you can hear them talk of a time when the suns did not bleed and the night sky was full of flecks of light, like gold scattered through rock. You can hear them weep as they talk of the hairless apes who came from the sand, bringing strange gods with them, who knocked the stars from the sky until only three remained, and of the family they cut down as they spread across the world like a disease. While it is true that there is no evidence to suggest stars were ever as plentiful as these decaying and corrupted records claim, there is no doubt that our ancient distrust of the world of men is rooted in some calamity that coincided with their arrival in our lands and drove those trees mad.'*

\- Tream historian Jeylin

PROLOGUE

THE STRANGER CAME on the last day that Moluc was ever to call himself a priest. Moluc watched the man enter the stone temple with the rest of the small congregation and take a seat on one of the middle benches. They were smooth, polished pieces of rock that had been glazed to stop them leaving white stone dust on their occupants, the wider temple being made of matt white rock that was dusty to the touch, carved out of the hillside into a dome. The clever acoustics of the temple bounced sound around the chamber with ease, making even the smallest of gatherings feel larger, amplifying any noise from sacrifices. The arching ceiling made the place feel oversized. The extra space made the room cool and dry. The raised areas could just have easily served as a seat for a much larger being. There were no depictions of the stone god. It was forbidden.

That Moluc did not know this man was strange. These days, so few people believed, Moluc knew every follower by name. Every few weeks, the number of believers decreased. A new follower had not been seen since before the king had died. *Murdered*, thought Moluc, correcting himself, *the king was murdered by his son, the new king, Montu.*

The stranger was taller by a head than anyone else in the temple. The Kurah were not a small people. The man was as close to a giant as

1

Moluc had ever seen, and his wild curls fell in all directions. When Moluc squinted, the blurring of his vision made it seem as if the man had antlers. The man's face was what made the priest really stare. His skin was covered in the most elaborate of tattoos. They weren't the swirling, colourful ink of the Shaanti but the runes, glyphs and letters of at least four nations. When the stranger moved, the tattoos moved and flowed and reconfigured. Moluc could not read any of it, but he suspected the tattoos ran all over the man's body.

Moluc looked around for the high priest but could not see him. The welcoming of a new follower was a critical step in conversion, and so the job of greeting the giant fell to him. The stranger did not look approachable. He stared straight ahead at the glazed lattice of channels around the sacrificial dais at the front of the temple. The man appeared to be staring intently at something on the raised platform. Moluc could not decide what had captured the visitor's attention so. He approached the man slowly in case the stranger decided to leave or lunge at him. He had the bearing of a warrior, and Moluc had no desire to fight.

'Welcome, my son,' said Moluc.

The stranger looked at him as if he were an ant. It was the briefest of glances before the man returned his gaze to the dais.

'Welcome to the temple of the stone god, Ku. You are new here?'

The man raised an eyebrow. 'I have not been here in some time, but I am not new.'

His voice was deep. Moluc could feel the words vibrate in his spine.

Moluc smiled. 'But always welcome back. What brings you here?'

'Murder,' replied the stranger.

Moluc felt his stomach flip over. The view of the population was turning against the sacrifices, and he had been accosted before over the practice. But they had never been so bold as to enter the temple. Still, he might not mean to kill Moluc.

'I am sorry for your loss,' Moluc replied, hoping the stranger was not a priest-hater.

'I don't hate you, believer,' said the man. 'Quite the opposite. I love all you little monkeys who believe in magic.'

Moluc frowned. He had not spoken his fear aloud, but the man had answered his thought as if he had heard it.

The temple vibrated. The noise was low, almost imperceptible, and if it had not been for the dust from the rock above, they might have missed the sound. It wasn't a single crash but a repeating *thump-thump* that sent dust down. If the benches and the sacrificial areas had not been glazed, the dust would have risen up from the floor as well. The noise was growing louder as the *thump-thump* drew closer, until Moluc realised it was the marching of warriors.

'They are here,' said the stranger.

Moluc looked at the man. Up close his features seemed to have been carved from wood. His eyes were as piercing a blue as the sky outside. He was clearly younger than Moluc, and yet he felt but a child next to this warrior.

'Who are here?'

The stranger stood and moved past the priest, towards the entrance to the temple.

'No, wait,' called Moluc after him.

But the stranger wasn't leaving. The other four people in the congregation turned to look at the scene that was developing.

The stranger did not care. He looked at nothing but the door as he strode up to it, clasped the handle and pulled.

There was a king in the doorway.

Montu was dressed in leather leggings, a white tunic and a purple cloak. A simple bronze circle on his brow indicated his rank. The king removed his black riding gloves and adjusted his sword, Polestar, on his back. The king nodded at the stranger.

Moluc dropped to his knee. The priest's heart felt like it had stopped with the shock of seeing his monarch in the doorway. This was not good. The king was no friend of Ku.

'It is here,' said the stranger.

The king glanced around the room, taking in the occupants and the temple as if they were one and the same. He folded his arms.

'I do not see him, Cernubus. This is just a temple like all the others.'

Moluc looked at the stranger. 'Your name is Cernubus, like the Shaanti god?'

The stranger turned to the priest. 'You know your gods, believer. Most Shaanti do not remember that Cernubus was a god of their people when the world was young.'

Moluc could see gold flecks in the blue of the man's eyes. They looked like the pinholes of light that the sentinels gave off in the night sky.

'Cernubus, where is it?' asked Montu, moving further into the temple. Kurah warriors filed into the chamber behind him, swords drawn and eyes on Moluc and the stranger.

Cernubus looked away from Moluc and pointed to the sacrificial dais. He muttered in a language that Moluc did not understand but might have been that of the river worshippers in the icy southern continent. There was a grinding noise that made the priest and the king put their hands over their ears. It sounded as if the universe had been pulled apart. The warriors shifted and lifted their weapons.

Moluc turned to the dais.

The creature was gargantuan. At least twice the size of the stranger, the thing filled the end of the chamber in its seated position. The beast looked balefully at them. The being appeared to be made of rock that might once have been man-shaped but was now just a grotesque memory, almost featureless. A clumsy thing.

Moluc did not have depictions of Ku in his temple, but he knew what he looked like, and to see the god sitting across from him nearly undid the priest. *It can't be. Gods are metaphors.*

'The thing about metaphors,' said Cernubus, 'is they are based on something real.'

'Go on, then,' said Montu. 'Kill it.'

Moluc turned to the king. *I am going to die,* he thought. *His Majesty is going to sweep us away.*

Cernubus stared hard at the young monarch. Montu did not look away.

'Our agreement stands?' asked Cernubus.

Montu nodded. 'You get all of them.'

'And the forest?'

Montu nodded again.

'Give me your sword,' said Cernubus.

The king drew Polestar and passed the weapon to the stranger without hesitation.

'Now, Moluc,' said Cernubus, moving further into the room. Moluc did not know how he knew his name. 'I'm afraid I must reduce your congregation further.'

The stranger threw the sword in an arc that sent the blade spinning through the air, almost faster than the eye could see, striking the first parishioner, a tailor called Jeren, and beheading him. The man's arterial blood painted the ceiling of the temple crimson as the sword spun on, beheading an old woman called Jasmine, and cutting down the other two worshippers before returning hilt first to the stranger's hands. An impossible throw.

Moluc stared at the scene of the massacre.

'There is little you could have done,' said Cernubus, his voice soft. 'You don't really believe in this one.' He kicked the stone god's leg; the god looked mournfully at him. 'You know that it is all a trick. You have seen behind the veil.'

Moluc did not answer.

'Enough,' said Montu. 'Get on with it.'

Cernubus smiled. 'You must leave first.'

Montu frowned. 'Why?'

Cernubus shook his head. 'The god must be alone for me to kill it. It's complicated. You will have your proof.'

Montu looked at the god and then back at Cernubus. He pointed at the stranger. 'Proof, or no deal.'

Cernubus watched the king leave, along with the warriors, before he turned to Moluc.

'Would you like to see your god destroyed?'

Moluc did not answer. He thought he was going to die, and he very much wanted to live. There was so much he hadn't done yet. Why had he wasted his life here in this dusty temple? There was a whole world out there: beautiful women, handsome men and a plethora of sights he had never laid eyes on.

'I will show you wonder right here,' said Cernubus. 'And you will see it is terrible. I will give you a new faith.'

Cernubus snarled and leapt onto the stone god. The man's momentum carried Ku backwards to the floor of the dais. Cernubus lifted both his hands up and brought them together before thrusting them down into the chest of the stone god. Ku screamed. The high-pitched howl felt to Moluc like it had split his eardrums.

Cernubus looked at Moluc from atop the prone god, covered in dust and golden blood, and grinned at the priest. He withdrew his arms from Ku's broken chest, clutching a fistful of stone in his hand that he lifted up to the light. The rock was pulsing amber in a slowing beat, casting fire from the golden blood onto the temple ceiling. Cernubus crushed the heart into dust with his right hand, and the god stopped screaming. All was silent.

Cernubus spoke in Moluc's head. *Are you not awestruck? Behold, I have slain your god.*

Cernubus smacked his hands clean, leant over and grabbed the god's head. He strained until his biceps seemed as if they would burst through his jerkin. The god's head came free of his body, and Cernubus hooked it under one arm.

Proof, he explained in the priest's head. *Now go, out the back door, and tell the people how Cernubus has slain the stone god. Tell them I am returned.*

Moluc hesitated. Was this a trick? *Surely, if he lets me go, I could come back with warriors and kill him in the same way.*

No, you could not. I am already stronger than any other: my power does not come solely from the monkeys any more. Do my bidding. Remember, there is nowhere I cannot find you.

Moluc watched as the tattooed stranger, this scarred god, walked out of the temple into the light, with the head of the stone god under one arm.

CHAPTER ONE

THE KURAH CHASED the wounded girl across the hills towards the forest.

The path Anya took over the parched mud and sparse grass of the Barrens was anything but random. The Rift Forest offered a slim chance of survival if she could only make the treeline. She dared not look back, but in her more hopeful moments, she thought it sounded as if the number of men behind her had lessened. They were afraid of the forest. She pushed herself as hard as she could, her calves and knees burning with the effort, and her right thigh screaming with the wound she had taken when escaping.

An arrow slammed into the earth just ahead of Anya. She stumbled and fell. It was tempting to lie there, to let the men capture her, and face whatever punishment they deemed fit to issue. Another voice – the woman who had abandoned her – buried deep in her memory, whispered at her not to be so weak. She knew what happened to Kurah prisoners of war. She knew what would happen to the others if she didn't make it. No, she wouldn't think about that, just focus on the next step. *The Kurah probably think they are doing us an honour.*

Anya looked up. The forest was little more than a few hundred yards away. Another arrow flew. This one embedded itself in her hand. The pain was incandescent.

Howling, she pushed herself up from the ground with her good hand and ran with all the fury she had left. The arrow had done her a favour, woken her up when she was nearly ready to die. The pain had reminded her she was alive and had a job to do. Anya crashed through the wood without thought or reason, her gait loping from the thigh wound, and her clothes wet with blood that was not all her own. There were shouts behind her. Some of the Kurah had come into the forest despite the legends. They would brave the ghosts for a chance at revenge. Anya's only hope now lay in hiding. She felt the throbbing pain in her hand with acute irritation – if only she could climb. A wolf howled in the distance.

The trees seemed to have turned against her, determined to inflict more damage: their branches and undergrowth whipped her body. Moving her lead-like limbs was an effort that drew tears as she continued to pound through the woods. *Would the wolves make a better end of me than the Kurah? It would be quicker, surely?*

'And dying would make up for getting me killed, right?' The ghost of Fin looked across at Anya, keeping easy pace alongside her, as she ran for her life.

An arrow thunked into the wood of the tree next to her. She changed direction and ducked as best she could. There was thicker foliage in this direction. Faintly she thought there was also a smell of smoke on the air. Her stomach sank – had they set the forest alight?

Another wolf howled. This one sounded closer.

The cursing from the Kurah got louder. She didn't understand it. Anya ran on, as fast as she could, hoping they couldn't see her. Distracted, she missed her step, her foot catching on a knotted tree root and sending her sprawling.

In the darkness of this heavier part of the forest, she could hear men scouting, trying to find her. Whether because of her woodsmanship or the thickness of the undergrowth, the Kurah sounded as if they were going in the wrong direction. She put her hands out, ignoring as best she could the flame in her wounded right hand, and pushed.

Anya got up. Her ankle felt like the joint had exploded. She wobbled and fell down, striking her head on a rock. There was a moment – perhaps two – where she tried very hard to remain conscious, but the darkness came out from the pulsing pain and pulled her down into the black ...

... A VOICE *... No, that wasn't right. More like a moving picture in her mind. She was looking at herself as she called over to the guard, aware of what she was risking as she mocked him just enough to draw him in. As she pulled her hair over to one side, his interest was piqued. The others in the cage pleaded with her to stop. She refused. The stakes were too high. The two guards drew nearer, egged on by the others, who stood further away at the edge of the camp, where they could relax.*

The younger, brasher guard opened the cage. She watched herself wait until they had both come in, blocking the entrance from any help from outside. The two guards were too close to have been expecting what was about to happen. She had not yet taken the ink, and so there was no clue she was anything other than an Shaanti maid. She watched herself attack the younger one. He was stronger than she had expected. The fight wasn't a smooth kill like she had practised in sparring, when all had been pretending. It was untidy and impro-vised. She watched herself headbutt him, and his dagger slipped into her hand as he reeled in shock. She had taken two attempts to find the gap in his armour before she had been able to force the blade in between his ribs for the killing blow. He had called at her to stop. She had felt his heart yield against the blade before he slumped to the ground. He looked even younger in that moment ... a boy.

She watched herself blink once before her training kicked in, and she attacked the man's still-shocked companion, thrusting the dagger into his unpro-tected leg. She twisted the blade to prevent him being able to give chase and tried to ignore the woman's voice telling her she should have killed him too. Taking the men's swords, she emerged from the cage. She looked back, briefly, at the other cages – the ones where small hands were emerging from the darkness, their owners pleading for her to take them with her. The remaining warriors leered, drawing their own blades and making ready for some sport. She ran, fighting only where she had to, and emerged victorious each time as panic began to spread through the camp. She burst free of the tents, running through the Barrens, her mind still on the tiny hands she had seen reaching from the shadows ...

ANYA OPENED HER EYES. Her ankle throbbed in time with her heart, but she ignored it as best she could, standing with care. She tested her weight on the leg and found the limb held. She limped on slowly. The Kurah warriors sounded as if they had wandered further away, lost as to which direction Anya had run in. The memories of her escape threatened to return, her gut lurching almost as if she were back there once more, but she caught the unhelpful intrusion and pushed it away. Not now. There was only room for putting one foot in front of the other.

'There she is! Hey! She's over here!'

The voice cut through Anya's fragile hope. In desperation, she limped on as fast as she could, forcing herself not to look back at the Kurah warrior giving chase. She tried not to think about the sounds of him fumbling with his bow as he came, trying to let an arrow fly after her. He swore and discarded the idea, his pace quickening behind her.

The undergrowth pulled at Anya, and tree branches snagged her skin. One whipped clean across her body, badly bruising her ribs and leaving her gasping as she plunged on through the undergrowth. The dark of the forest was broken suddenly by sunlight. It blinded her. She had no idea where she could be, having never been allowed to come in further than the edge. Still half-blinded by the light, limping and near passing out again, Anya lumbered on, arms outstretched to prevent further falls. She had carried on a dozen paces before her eyes adjusted to the light, and she realised she was in a wide clearing like the ones in her grandfather's stories. The only difference was a log cabin at the far end, where smoke was gently wafting into the air from its chimney.

Anya did not have time to look for cover. The Kurah behind her slammed into her and sent her sprawling just as she noticed there was another person in the clearing. He didn't appear to be a Kurah, as he was too old to be in their army, and he was dressed in Shaanti clothing. He stared at her with intense blue eyes as she lay tangled on the grass.

He remained bent over his axe. The axehead was embedded in the wood in front of him.

Anya tried to scrabble away from the guard, but he had hold of her hair and was trying to get a set of chains on her wrists. Anya tried to lash out, but her body wouldn't cooperate. She could taste the copper tang of blood in her mouth. *I was right, I am dying.* In her mind's eye, the hands reached out to her from the cage; voices whispered to take them with her; and she could smell fear like piss reeking in her nostrils. She was about to call out to the strange woodsman when the guard let go of the manacles, his eyes trying to focus on the axe now embedded in his head. The Kurah warrior collapsed even as others appeared in the clearing.

The last thing she heard before she fell back into the dark was screaming. She wasn't sure whose voice it was.

CHAPTER TWO

THE KING WAS HERE.

The commander of the battalion guarding the prisoners stared hard at the note the messenger had handed him. The king wanted to see him. He felt dizzy and hyper-aware all at the same time. The cocktail of smells in the camp – the smoke, the men, the cooking food, the piss and the shit – they all poked at his nose. The sounds clambered at his ears from the forge: the men bantering and the prisoners whimpering and moaning. The entrance to his tent flapped in the breeze. He could have returned back inside, but there would be no avoiding an explanation for the king, so what was the point?

The Kurah lines stretched across the Shaanti territory for miles; Montu couldn't visit everywhere – it wasn't feasible – but now his warriors would be singled out. *He must know of the escape.* In a few short years, this young king, Montu, had made a name for himself every bit as feared and respected as his grandfather's. The commander necked a strong swig from his hip flask before he responded to the messenger.

'Tell the king I shall attend to him in a moment—'

'You can attend to me now,' replied the king, pulling his gloves from each of his hands.

The commander turned around to look at Montu. The king smiled without a trace of irritation. The commander couldn't help but glance at the man's sword; Polestar gleamed on the king's shoulders. Montu was renowned for his skill with the blade. The sword was the first to earn a name in its own right since the time of the last war with the Shaanti. It was the sword that slew the last king. *Will my blood coat the blade too?*

'What has one of my commanders so spooked? Have you seen the ghosts of the priests coming behind us?'

The commander shook his head. There was no sense in drawing this out. 'Sire, there has been an incident.'

The king's smile broadened out into a grin. 'No, my dear fellow, there has been no incident.'

The commander felt ice up his back. 'Yes, sire, there has—'

Montu laughed. 'No, there has been a monumental fuck-up. An incident would be "I've run out of potatoes" or "an unarmed prisoner was killed during an escape attempt", not "an unarmed prisoner managed to kill a guard, seriously wound another and fight her way out of the camp".'

The commander knew he was dead in that moment.

'Sire, I regret to report a prisoner escape in our camp. A single prisoner has managed to get free, killing a guard, wounding another and in all likelihood has led another three men to their deaths in the forest.'

The king's smile faded. 'You tell the truth too late. Had you dispatched to me at once, had you but told me as you saw me, things might have been different, but now ... you will be executed tomorrow at dawn. Bring me to where the escape happened, and have the men who were present and not maimed brought to us.'

The commander felt ice in his belly. His hands shook. *Perhaps I can still turn this around? I just need to be helpful.* He led the king through the network of tents to where the cages had been set up. They passed vast wheeled structures that had been erected to prevent the prisoners from looking on the rest of the camp. They stopped in front of the makeshift dungeon.

The defeated Shaanti were a bedraggled collection of adults, too young or old to fight in some cases, but the majority of the prisoners were children. No tattoos amongst any of them. No warriors had been allowed to live, and no Shaanti swordsmen or women would expect the Kurah to take prisoners. The Shaanti that had survived were frightened and confused at this deviation from Kurah practice, unsure if this meant they would survive, or if they would be slaves. If they should be happy, or anguished and unable to look away from the bodies of the dead. Many of the captured were crying.

'Which one got away?'

The commander looked at the king. He realised he did not know the name of the prisoner and that this admission was another nail in his coffin.

'From the reports, it was a girl, almost of age, who lured the guards in and then fought as well as a warrior.'

Montu held the commander's gaze. 'Rather better, given she escaped from the camp.'

The commander clenched his jaw.

'You're sure she had no markings?' asked the king, peering closer at the prisoners.

The commander nodded. 'We would have executed her if she had been marked.'

'Which cage was it?'

The commander pointed at Cage Ten. There were only a couple of other prisoners inside, all women in their sixties and all staring at the king with very wide eyes.

'Open the cage,' said Montu.

'Sire?'

The king looked witheringly at his commander. 'I can shorten your life further. Open the fucking cage.'

The commander moved to the lock, and it took him two goes to unlock the door, given the way the king was looming over him. Once it was open, Montu pushed past him into the cage, drew his sword and cut the head off the first of the three women. The other two screamed.

The king wiped his blade on the fallen woman's dress.

'You are to understand that I am serious when I say harm will befall you if you do not cooperate and tell me what I want to know,' said the king to the surviving prisoners.

'Who was the girl?'

The women stared at him, too terrified to speak.

He extended his sword, now clean, towards the closest one.

'Do not make me ask again,' he said.

'She was Anya, General Thrace's granddaughter,' said the woman nearest to the blade.

'She was a warrior?'

The other woman shook her head. 'No. Thrace forbade it ...'

The king raised an eyebrow. 'But ...?'

'I heard her talking to Fin ... you killed him ... saying she was going to run away. Our Evie says she thought Falkirk may have been training her.'

The king closed his eyes briefly. He left the cage and strode over to the commander.

'You're an even bigger fool than I gave you credit for. Did you interrogate the prisoners?'

The commander looked blank. *Why interrogate soon-to-be-dead prisoners? Wouldn't that further demean the enemy's warriors in defeat? They would say anything – true or false – to save their lives.*

'Promises were made, Commander, and one of the conditions was we hand over the prisoner your men allowed to escape to Cernubus. That promise has now been broken.'

'She was just a girl.'

The king moved so he was nose to nose with the commander. 'A girl whose grandmother was the greatest warrior the Shaanti ever produced and whose grandfather was a skilled general. Regardless of her heritage, we warned you about those Shaanti of fighting age.'

'Sire, she's a girl. How were my men supposed to know ...?'

Montu stepped closer to the commander, wrapping one hand around the back of the man's neck and whispering in his ear. 'We're not talking about your men, we're talking about you.' He thumped the commander in the stomach for emphasis, driving the air out of his gut.

The king moved back, wiping a small knife on the edge of his cloak before turning away. The commander coughed in pain. The blow had left a dull ache in his stomach that was growing, making him double over. Everything felt distant and distorted. He tried to move after Montu but found he could not; indeed, he felt like he was melting away into the grass. He looked down and saw blood seeping across the front of his tunic as his legs folded up underneath him. He was staring up at the sky now. His last thought was that he had finally seen the young king lose his calm. It was a triumph, of sorts.

MONTU LOOKED at the executioner getting ready to kill the men who had let him down. The temporary scaffolding looked only just sturdy enough to hang them. The suns were edging closer to the horizon in their slow waltz across the sky. The smell of the evening meal mingled with the dying embers of the forges they had set up to keep their supply lines running. He had picked every other man from the squad of guards who'd failed to secure the prisoner, and marked them for execution. In an hour, he would pardon those who had already proved themselves in battle, and execute the remaining three. Discipline had to be maintained. The lines would be stretched before they had control of the Shaanti, and Delgasia was only just under control.

I will not repeat the mistakes of my grandfather.

'That is reassuring,' said Cernubus.

Montu turned to look at the god. He was leaning against one of the cages, his hood thrown back to show his ragged curls, and he had wrapped his cloak around himself. The prisoners were staring at him with fear from the furthest corner of the cage. Their nightmare was a real and living thing: the banished god come amongst them to punish.

'I will not find myself abandoned as the stone god was, then?'

Montu flushed. *Did he suspect?* 'As long as you keep your side of the deal, I will honour mine.'

'But you have already broken your side by letting the girl go,' said Cernubus, not moving.

'The magic you described, the reason these dishonoured people were kept alive, does not rely on a single girl. There is no chosen one in Shaanti myth.'

Cernubus smiled. 'You are but a child in armour. A precocious and violent one, I grant you, but do not speak on matters beyond you. The girl has her value.'

'Where have you been?'

Cernubus stood up straight and walked closer to the king. 'I have taken the forest under my control. You will not experience any attacks on your flank.'

Montu felt his shoulders relax. 'The goddess has lost the forest. I wonder if the thain knows yet?'

Cernubus shook his head. 'There were no humans in the forest.'

Montu froze. *There were humans now.*

Cernubus tilted his head. The god had heard Montu's thought. He stared at the king. 'The girl ...?'

Montu nodded. 'And some of the men went in after her. The ones who fear us more than the old legends.'

Cernubus was silent.

Montu felt the god's anger. Rage vibrated deep in the base of his skull and crackled on the air as if he were barely holding in his power. The runes painted into his skin moved faster, changing with the beat of Montu's heart, or so it seemed.

'She's just a girl.'

'The problem is the forest is large and she may run into help.'

You said you had the forest under control, thought Montu.

'And I do. Where did she enter?'

The king did not like it when Cernubus listened to his mind. The mages had still to find him a reliable technique for blocking such intrusions.

Montu pointed north. 'She knew what she was doing. The southern belly of the forest is its furthest outcrop, due north of here and the fastest route to cover.'

'The forestal ...' whispered Cernubus. 'Well, that's a pretty twist.'

'Who is the forestal?'

Cernubus looked up as if remembering the king was there. 'Your men are dead or dying. The forest will not abide Kurah in its boundaries, I did warn you.'

'And the girl?'

Cernubus knelt and drove his hand into the soil.

'Most people think the Barrens were always this way, but when I was young, these hills and valleys were covered in trees. The soil is weak now, but still remembers the forest.'

Cernubus rubbed the soil over his hands and forearms. The runes pooled and poured over the dirt with the occasional flash of red and green. The god closed his eyes briefly.

'The girl is alive,' he said. 'I must go. While she is free, there is a risk I have not accounted for.'

Montu frowned. 'What of us?'

Cernubus looked around. 'You have taken nearly all of the Shaanti borders. You have them locked in, and they cannot out-siege you at this time of year. She has no choice but open battle, and as long as the battle is joined by the alignment, we will be fine.'

Cernubus stepped back from the king. He dropped his cloak to the ground and pulled his tunic off in one motion. Other people were looking now.

'Go, then. But do not stay away long lest I forget when you want the ceremony ...'

'Have faith in me,' said Cernubus, a little loudly. Montu knew he was playing to the crowd.

'I'm an atheist,' replied Montu.

Cernubus laughed. He turned and ran, shifting form to a stag as he went, and disappeared from view.

'He has too much power,' said the guard closest to Montu.

Montu looked at the guard. 'Why?'

The guard shrugged. 'He doesn't fear you, and so his promises are empty, and he has already left us half a dozen times when we needed him.'

'Good observation,' said Montu. 'And brave words. Are you prepared to speak your mind to me when you disagree, but follow my orders as if they were your own?'

The guard shrugged and nodded.

'Good. You're the new commander.'

'Thank you.'

'Don't. Do your job, that's enough. Now find out if anyone knows how to get rid of this god before this deal sours any further.'

The new commander nodded and headed off to the magi's tents.

CHAPTER THREE

THE HEAT WAS like a hand pressing down on the god as he made his way across the desert. The vast wasteland seemed to stretch away to the ends of the world, the ground a cracked and dried mud, broken only by occasional rocky deposits and drifts of sand at the bottom of shallow valleys where it could not be blown away. The forest seemed a distant dream. If he stopped for any length of time, Pan feared he would melt away, leaving nothing but a smudge of damp in the dirt. Each step took him further from the forest and from the Shaanti clan. His power was ebbing away. The occasional breeze just whipped up the dust and sand, forcing him to cover his nose and mouth with his cloak.

If he did not find water before his powers retreated altogether, leaving him as weak as the mortals, he would have to finally take the long walk across Golgotha.

The cry was so weak he almost missed it.

The sound repeated as Pan stumbled on, and brought him to a halt when it was issued a third time. Something was alive out here. He scanned the horizon, but there was nothing clear; he was at the bottom of a shallow dip that obscured his view. The cry had gone away, and he feared he was too late. He ran up to the top of the rise. There was nothing around, just a shallow collection of rocks that cast little shade.

The cry came again.

Pan looked closer at the rocks. *Perhaps ...* He broke into a run and skidded to a halt at the outcrop. Carefully he picked his way over the rocks, looking for a place of shade where sufficient moisture could remain. The sapling was hidden in the deepest recess of the boulders, barely surviving, but defiantly wrapping itself around the dribble of water. Pan was always astounded at how the trees would cling on even when the environment was almost impossible. He wrapped his hand around the sapling with the care of a man holding a thing made of glass.

Come home. We are under attack. Come home. We need all of us ...

Pan felt his heart lurch. Danu had sent the message, and the words felt as if they had been carried on a wave of pain. The message tasted of smoke and blood. A presence lingered in the background. Familiar. The tree was scared. Its fear was palpable. There was the pain of trying to survive in the desert; the tree did not understand why it was here or how it had been born. The forest had sung to the sapling in the dark of night, but the tree had been driven half-mad by loneliness and the heat of the suns. Now the forest was screaming. The only voice of friendship the sapling had known was in anguish, and the tree could not help.

Pan didn't know what to do to comfort the little tree. His own fear was a real thing in his belly, twisting and flipping like a trapped fish. *I must return.* That his quest was at an end already was a bitter disappointment, diluted by the dilemma of how he could get back in time to make a difference.

You know what you must do ...

'What do you know of it, little one?' replied Pan out loud.

You can fold the world. Make the distance like moving from one foot to the next.

'It will cost more than you know,' said Pan. 'If I am too weak to help, then I have done nothing.'

If you arrive in three weeks, you will be too late ...

Pan did not reply. The sapling was right. There was a reason Pan had walked for three weeks just to get to this point. He loathed the magic that would take him back in the blink of an eye. It would hurt as if he were dying and being born again. It would leave him as fragile as a mortal child. He rarely used that power when he was in the forest, where he was strongest. The idea of performing it here, where he was barely stronger than a mortal ... was laughable. He would need any strength he could take.

Pan looked at the sapling.

What are you going to do?

'Sorry,' said the god, thrusting his hand into the soil around the sapling.

PAN RETURNED to the forest on the wooded edge of the glade, where he would be hidden from view. The forest screamed, and Pan, utterly undone by the journey, was driven to his knees. The additional contact with the soil increased the volume of the screams, and he collapsed. He landed on his back, which was the only thing that saved the sapling he was cradling from being crushed. The young tree was whimpering in his hands. The sapling would die if he didn't get it into the ground soon.

This part of the forest was ancient. The trees were as wide as cottages and stretched so far into the sky that the canopy appeared like a roof in a holy place. The only daylight came from where the suns poked through the gaps in the foliage. The smell of smoke on the air made the whole place seem threatening in a way Pan had not expected.

The god forced the noise in his head down to a manageable level. The cacophony of voices was overwhelming, making it harder for him to stand. Pan took what felt like an eternity for him to will his body to move, and then he could only manage to get to his knees. He crawled, one-handed, the other hand cradling the sapling, to a part of the undergrowth where there was no sign of disturbance and the tree could grow. He dug the sapling in with his bare hands. He allowed himself a moment of indulgence as the sapling, despite its pain, sang with joy at the moisture in the earth and the proximity of other trees.

The soil on his hands helped. Pan could feel a little strength returning. He pushed himself up to his feet and turned in the direction of the smoke. The glade had been burned. He drew his short sword and began the careful journey to his sister's home.

He saw Bacchus first.

The god of wine had been decapitated by a weapon swift and sharp, but not a sword from the look of it. A spear, perhaps? Why was that familiar? His body, nearby, had a gaping wound where his heart had been, and the golden blood of the gods soaked the soil around him. Pan picked up his cousin's head and held his forehead to his own.

'Oh, Bee. What have they done?'

Pan's fury was a cold thing. He placed Bacchus's head by his body and added the god's scimitar to his own sword. He would not go down without a fight.

He made his way to the edge of the glade, passing body after body of minor and major gods and goddesses. Apollo had been nailed to a tree and skinned in addition to his heart being ripped out.

In the glade, the grass had been scorched away by the magic that had been cast in a battle that had been vicious in its ferocity. Danu was laid out on the soil, her chest rising and falling with ragged breaths. Her hair was matted with mud and blood. Her skin was pale as if she were sick, and her hands pawed at the ground. A cage made of ancient magic pulsed and vibrated, giving off an orange glow nearly the colour of the suns. She was a prisoner.

But of whom?

Pan looked around to see if he could see anyone guarding her in person, but there were no guards to speak of. He still felt shaky, weak. He gripped his swords in each hand and stepped out into the clearing.

Danu turned as soon as Pan's foot made contact with the glade. Her eyes were wide with panic, checking for the enemy – whoever that was. Pan sent his view into the forest but could see no sign of anyone else, just the pain of the forest at the slaughter of what had happened. Pan thrust his swords into the ground by the cage. He put his hands hesitantly towards the burning bars.

'Don't,' said Danu, sitting.

'I've got to get you out of here.'

'You cannot. This is beyond you. Do you think I would let myself be contained like this?'

Pan bowed his head.

'It's not your fault ...' said Danu. 'If it's anyone's, it's mine. I should have stopped him ...'

'Who?' replied Pan, placing his hands on the ground.

They both felt it.

The returning god was like electricity coursing through the soil. An alien thing, a corrupted and twisted presence that was almost unrecognisable from the last time Pan had felt it.

'Cernubus ...' whispered Pan. 'Cousin ...'

Danu shook her head. 'Not our cousin. He is no longer a god, he is something else.'

Pan could feel the god drawing near. He buried his own flickering power deep in his core, trying to mask his presence. Danu shifted and reached for him through the glowing bars of her prison. She clasped his right hand. Her grip was surprisingly strong.

'You must bring the woodsman.'

'The forestal?' Pan was surprised. He failed to see what the trained monkey could do to help that he, a god, could not.

Danu nodded. 'He can help, though I doubt he realises. There's someone else with him, a girl, Thrace's granddaughter. She can help our cause as well.'

Pan felt dizzy. The power approaching was like cancer made alive. The strength of the sensation was unsettling, but the real horror was the wrongness of it to the forest. The ancient soul of the wood twisted and coiled like Pan's stomach in response to the oncoming storm.

Pan had not thought of Thrace in a long time. Another monkey who caused nothing but trouble.

'The forestal cannot be trusted,' said Pan. 'He thinks only of himself, even when he purports to love one of us.'

Danu's eyes flashed with anger. 'Listen to me, little goat, you will do as I say, or we will lose all that we have worked for.'

Pan felt her grip digging into him.

'All right.' He nodded. 'Where are they?'

'On the edge of the forest,' she replied, her grip easing. 'But I cannot sense them clearly from in here.'

Pan's shoulders slumped. 'I have no power for another jump. I need rest.'

Danu let go of his hand and touched his cheek.

'I am sorry to ask this of you,' she said. 'You must send a message somehow. Hurry. He is drawing near.'

Pan let himself enjoy the touch of her hand on his cheek for a moment. He stepped back and plunged his hand into the soil, aware that he was lighting up his location for Cernubus, and let his message pulse through the soil and the trees in a wave. Only his allies would understand the instruction, but that would not matter to the scarred god. He would just want to know who had intruded.

Pan felt the last of his energy leave his body with the message, and the weight of his eyelids felt like the heaviest stone. Danu waved him away.

'Go, hide, far from here, and recharge,' she said.

Pan felt himself rise sluggishly, as if drunk. He bowed low and then staggered, swaying, back to the treeline, where he continued to move as fast as he could without making himself sick.

Crack!

Thunder rumbled behind Pan.

'Where is he, Danu?'

Cernubus's voice was still recognisable but had taken on a deeper, throbbing quality that made Pan feel like his spine was being rearranged by the timber. Pan moved as swiftly as he could up the northern slope leading away from the glade, sticking to the trees and avoiding any kind of path. Cernubus roared in anger at not getting an answer.

The howls started.

In an instant, the forest was alive with the sound of wolves all about. Cernubus had brought his servants with him to help in his invasion of the gods' territory. The god himself came bursting from the clearing in his stag form, antlers down as he caught the scent of Pan, and as he streaked up the slope towards him, the trickster god realised he only had one chance. Pan leapt off the ravine at the top of the slope before he could be seen, and plunged towards the waiting ground below. He was a god, but landing was still going to hurt.

CHAPTER FOUR

THE DAY HAD BEEN good until the girl appeared. Vedic had been chopping wood, which always cleared his head. The atmosphere spoke of a coming storm that would do the same for the humidity that had stopped him venturing further than the edge of the clearing. The feeling of the axe splitting the logs, the transfer of his will from tool to wood, was sublime in its simplicity. It wasn't like people. Thank the gods.

Vedic was a big, broad man standing at warrior height and had the muscle to go with it. Age was nipping at his heels: his closely cropped beard was greying in patches; a slight paunch hung over his belt; and the suns looked down on an ever-expanding pink canvas that had once been covered in golden hair.

He watched the girl, his hands still on the axe embedded in the wood in front of him, as she blinked and blundered in the sudden light. There was an arrow in her right hand. He would have known the weapon was Kurah even if one of their warriors hadn't followed her into the clearing. Vedic couldn't allow one of their kind in this place.

Vedic pulled the axe from the wood and threw it with practised precision that sent it into the man's skull. Vedic ran for the body, ignoring the girl as she folded to the ground, and pulled his axe free from the fallen Kurah.

There were more warriors in the forest. He could hear them. The trees were unsettled. He could feel them. Two more Kurah appeared on the treeline, in search of their mate and the prey. Vedic was forced to cover more ground, weaving out of the way of an arrow that grooved his left arm, before he was close enough to strike. He ducked under the blade of one warrior, burying his axe in the man's throat and stealing his sword in one fluid motion that allowed him to block the other's strike. The woodsman swept his leg out, taking the Kurah to the ground as if he were tussling with a small child.

The woodsman held his blade to the man's exposed throat.

'How many more? A full battalion?'

The warrior stared at him in confusion and terror.

'Who are you? Why are you helping her?'

Vedic felt himself relax. There was no battalion. The man's fear was too palpable, too alone. The woodsman plunged his blade into the man's throat, ending his life, and threw the weapon away into the tree-line. 'I'm not a nice man.'

The fourth Kurah caught him by surprise.

The man burst from the treeline, screaming a battle cry as he swung his broadsword. Vedic just about managed to get his hands up to stop the man from bringing his sword down on him, but the momentum carried them both down to the ground. The warrior's blade rattled away as they rolled over and over, trying to get into the other's guard. Vedic's strength carried him through, allowing him to pin the man's arms to the ground and freeing himself to headbutt the warrior again and again. When the man went limp, Vedic twisted around and broke the warrior's neck. Leaving him alive would've been too risky.

Vedic pushed away the body as if it were on fire. He lay on the grass, looking up at the sky. He hadn't killed anyone in thirty years. His entire body ached, and the cuts, which were now covered in the mud of the forest, throbbed and itched with the power that would heal him in a few hours. He didn't know why the magic worked. Right now, he didn't care. He just wanted to let himself catch his breath. He was getting old.

Not before your time, came the voice in the back of his head. He ignored it.

The forest was different. Vedic did not have the gods' sense for the forest, but he had worked with the trees long enough to know that the difference was wrong. The constant harmonious hum in the back of his mind, their communication in a language he did not understand, had become discordant and shrill. He forced the sense to the back of his head. What he needed to know was whether there were any more Kurah in the woods. He could not hear anything: the forest was unusually quiet, and even the birds were silent. Only a single fawn was visible, winding its way through the bush and bracken of the clearing edge. The fawn looked up under his gaze and refused to look away.

A wolf howled. Vedic smiled.

The pack would save him a great deal of digging. He rolled to his feet and tried not to think about when he would have been young enough to nip up. He picked up his axe and limped back towards his cabin. The cleaners of the forest could deal with the bodies.

What about the girl?

'Not my problem,' he muttered to the voice in his head.

She wouldn't like that.

'She doesn't see me anymore,' he snapped.

Whose fault is that?

The pain started slow. Vedic was hurting already, his body a topography of bruises from the short, sharp battle he had just fought. His left arm, the one he had used to break the man's neck, already hurt before the pain started to throb and grow. Agony extended up his arm and wrapped its invisible hand around his heart and began to squeeze. Vedic stopped. He was halfway across the clearing, and his cabin seemed miles away. There was no way he could reach safety. There was no one here to help.

Is this how it ends? She promised to keep me safe, he thought. *This isn't what I expected.*

The voice in his head replied, faintly. *Not yet.*

Nevertheless, the pain drove him down onto his right knee. His right hand went fist first into the ground to help steady him. His left arm had an angry welt, like a recently healed scar from an arrow. There was no one but the girl and himself in the clearing. *Was she even still alive?*

Vedic turned to look at her. She was prone near the first of the Kurah, but unlike him, her chest was rising and falling with ragged breaths. The pain in his chest subsided as soon as Vedic looked at the girl. Agony returned as he turned his gaze back to the cabin. He looked back. The pain subsided again.

Was the girl ...?

No, that was impossible. She was bashed up to the point where she would almost certainly die if she did not get any help. Vedic looked away again, and the pain returned once more. He forced himself to his feet and staggered back towards her, leaving his axe where he had dropped it. The pain subsided, and he started to feel good for the first time in a long time. He stopped. He retraced his steps back to the middle of the glade and was driven back down to his knees.

'Spell,' he hissed between painful breath after painful breath.

Would you respond to anything else? The voice in his head was too close to how he used to talk. Vedic pushed the thought away and staggered back to the girl. Wolves continued to howl in the distance.

Vedic scooped her up in his arms and made his way across the glade without being attacked by pain. The rain started just as he reached his simple porch. He kicked his front door open and took her into the kitchen, where he slammed her down on the table.

Vedic's arm and chest were aflame.

'All right,' he hissed. 'I am helping.'

The pain subsided to manageable levels but did not go altogether. The familiar smell of wood smoke from the oven fire and the sound of the wolves in the distance meant all Vedic really wanted to do was lock the doors and fall asleep until the pack had passed. Whoever had set the spell that was forcing him to help had put paid to that.

Vedic looked at the girl. She was not more than seventeen and had been beaten up pretty badly, and sliced more than once. Her thigh had an ugly wound from a sword strike that had gone through her trousers, which were made of the thick leather Shaanti cattlemen and women favoured. The leggings weren't as good as armour but a damn sight better than if she'd been wearing a dress – she'd have lost the leg and probably her life. There was another slice on her forearm. The right hand had a nasty-looking arrow protruding from it, and she was bleeding from somewhere on her back. Blood was pooling on the table.

Vedic rolled up his sleeves and washed his hands in the basin of water he kept for when he needed to get clean. It was going to be a long night.

... I AM IN A CITY, and it burns. The smoke from the fire wraps around me like some kind of enchanted wraith, pawing at my mouth, smothering my nose and clawing at my eyes as I move through the ruinous heat. I am Anya, but I am not Anya in this place. I don't know who I am, let alone where I am, although I am familiar with this place in some way – an echo I can't quite make out.

The sounds of the dying and the wounded hail my slow journey through the ransacked metropolis. I continue to walk. I don't appear to be able to stop myself or control my actions as my path takes me, inexorably, towards the centre of the city, where a large towered fortress waits with smoke billowing from one corner. I notice the heavy weight in my hand and look down to see one of the largest swords I have ever set eyes on. This one reminds me of another weapon, but I can't remember its name. It's a two-handed affair like the Kurah used to carry, and I have the sword held ready to strike. I can't help but notice the strange patterns on the blade that make it look, in the firelight, like it is made of water.

Shaanti men and women run from me as if I am the Morrigan come to take them down to the underworld.

What is this? It's clear I am in a dream of some sort. I have no control. I can only make out what the person I am in the dream can actually see. All around me is carnage. It's worse than the village. The sheer scale of ruin. Bodies line the street, and the smell is of smoke and blood and piss and shit and fear.

Kurah turn to talk to me in their language, and I can only understand a smattering of words, and little of it makes any sense. They do not address me by name. They are as scared of me as the Shaanti, only they either can't or won't run. I respond in words I do not understand. We are at a crossroads: the road ahead leads straight to the castle, and the road bisecting it leads out around the city in what looks like a circle. There is a pile of bodies marking the spot where the Kurah have attempted to keep the path clear for their troops.

I have placed my sword in the crook of my arm as if nursing the weapon, and I am listening to a nervous, sweaty warrior of around twenty years reporting to me. The man's attention shifts from me and moves to someone behind me.

I turn.

The king is on horseback, his purple cloak floating out behind him, dust-covered but the colour still clear, and his armour reflects the fire all around him. He is old and grey-bearded. This is all wrong. He pulls on the horse's reins to bring the animal under control and stop it cantering on.

The king speaks in tones that suggest he is happy with what he sees, but his eyes never move from me. He is testing me: the king wants to see if I brag and posture. I reply in an obedient tone, gesturing to the victory the men are delivering for him, the sole ruler of the Kurah, and I convince even myself.

The king mutters. I have enough understanding of their language to make out the word for 'god', but I do not hear my host reply, though I feel my shoulders tense. There is a cry.

I spin and see a boy break from the pile of bodies where he must have been hidden until the Kurah approached with flames. There is no threat to us, but I bark a command and follow with my sword. I have no need to run. He never disappears from sight, and I have long strides in this nightmare.

As the boy runs into the palace, I know it is a trap, and whoever I am in the dream knows too. The person whose head I occupy here chuckles to himself. The bass sound vibrates deep inside. I move through the doorway with my sword in the guard position, but the trap is not sprung. Instead, I can see the boy running up the stairs to the western tower. There will be no escape.

I try to will myself not to follow. I want the Shaanti boy to get away and live a long life far from here, but I can't control my host. I prowl up the spiral staircase like a tiger on the hunt.

I get the occasional glimpse of the boy ahead of me, but I do not rush. Both I and my host know if I run after the boy, up the stairs, it will be very easy to get me off my feet and tumbling back down again. I emerge into the light of the top of the tower with my heart pounding, and there is no sign of the boy.

There is a girl in his place, wearing armour at least one size too big. She has a sword pointed at me.

I speak in Kurah-inflected Shaanti. 'You have already lost. Give up, and thy life will be spared.'

The girl does not reply, but she adopts the guard position for an Shaanti. Her blade is shaking but she stands her ground. A formal challenge, and my host knows that.

He replies, 'Very well. I will pray for you.'

The girl screams a war cry and attacks.

She is good. I am impressed even if the warrior I am in this dream blocks with almost indifferent ease, and I am unable to look away, even if I could, when he disarms her. I ... he ... I am losing my sense of self ... sends her sword clattering over the edge of the parapet. She is at sword-point, pressed against the wall. I could let her go. I hear myself begin the Kurah prayer for the fallen as I press the sword into her belly. She gasps in pain, eyes wide, but she does not cry out. She doesn't scream even when I lift her on the blade and tip her over the edge to the ground below. I mutter the Kurah saying that I know from some-where – 'Kinah Filah, Shanelle Itai.' In pain, set free.

The boy screams as he bursts from his hiding place and loses his head with one swing. I do not look back as I walk past his body, feet slick with blood, and descend back into the palace, repeating the prayer as I clean my blade.

I am screaming silently as this awful creature I am imprisoned in goes back into the city, and the fading of this nightmare is a mercy that I would have welcomed the minute I saw the Shaanti running for their lives. My fear as I slip into the dark is that this is happening right now, rather than a muddled night-mare from the ransacking of my village. Am I too late?

IT WAS dark when Anya woke. The sky had been replaced by worn wood, and the grass had become a stiff bed with little padding. For a moment, she thought she had died and that they had placed her in a coffin, like the people across the ocean who followed the engineer. The notion was dispelled by the sound of rain on the roof of whatever building she had been placed in. Still, she struggled to move, as the sheets had been tucked in so tight they were almost a restraint. There were dressings on her arm, hand and leg, but she couldn't feel any clothes. That caused her to sit up fast, and immediately she regretted it – her head felt like it was about to roll off. There was no one else in the room.

Somewhere nearby a wolf howled.

The building smelt of tobacco smoke and mud and burnt meat. There was a copper tang to the air that put Anya in mind of blood. For the briefest of moments, looking round the dark room with only a bed and an old wardrobe, she thought she saw Fin in the corner nearest the window. He sported the ugly wound that had killed him and the faintly accusing look that demanded to know why she had stood her ground instead of listening to him. He'd be alive now if she'd only run.

Anya blinked and the ghost was gone.

Anya got out of the bed. She looked at the dressing on her arm: a leaf had been pressed closest to the wound before the bandage had been applied, and what looked like mud had been smeared between the makeshift dressing and her arm. Her instinct was to remove the dressing and clean the injury. Yet why go to the trouble of killing her by triggering an infection? She had been unconscious. Anything could have been done to her, and she was relieved that dressing her wounds was the only thing that seemed to have taken place. They itched. Her other injuries all felt the same.

Anya wrapped herself in the bed sheet and made her way over to the wardrobe in search of clothes and anything that could be a weapon. The door opened with a creak. She paused to see if anyone had come to check on the noise. Her heart was an angry fist in her ribcage, demanding to escape.

Inside the wardrobe, there was a selection of jerkins and leggings that were an amount bigger than anything that would help Anya. She tried not to think about the size of the person they belonged to. The bed sheet offered even less protection. She took one of the jerkins down and used it as a short dress that she tied at the waist with a torn strip from a pair of leggings. She wouldn't ordinarily be seen in a skirt for love nor money, but there was nothing to be done.

Anya took the other clothes out of the wardrobe and discarded them on the bed. She lifted the piece of wood that they had been hanging from out of the wardrobe and felt its weight. There wasn't as much heft as she would like, but – like the tunic – it was better than nothing. Armed, she listened at the door's edge.

Silence.

Anya opened the door a crack and peered through. A wolf howled again. She ignored it.

The room beyond was a living area almost as sparse as the bedchamber, with nothing but a couple of armchairs that had seen better days and a series of tools and basic weapons adorning the wall. The fire gave off the only light. There was no sign of her saviour.

Anya stepped into the room, not looking for any further evidence, because all she was focused on was the doorway ahead of her and the sound of the storm beyond. She could be up and away before anyone could stop her. She reached for the handle.

'I wouldn't do that if I were you.'

Anya froze. When she recovered, she gripped her club harder and turned.

The man stood in the other doorway, which led to a kitchen, judging from the smell and the light. A pipe was wedged between the man's teeth, and the smoke billowing from it made her want to cough, but she suppressed the reflex. Any coughing would give the man an opening in which he could attack.

'You can't hold me here.'

The man took the pipe from his lips with his right hand and gestured towards the door.

'I wouldn't dream of it,' he said. 'But that storm will end lives tonight, and that will include yours if you go out in it wearing nothing but my best tunic.'

Anya looked out of the window at the back of the room. The storm flashed lightning that briefly showed off the wet and swaying trees beyond.

'I have to help them,' she said, feeling her head spin. 'They need me to get to Vikrain.'

The man laughed. 'You aren't even going to make it to the Tream border.'

Anya lifted the club and pointed the makeshift weapon at the man.

'Tream are myths,' she said. 'You will help me.'

The man put the pipe back between his teeth and muttered, 'Put the wood down, child. You are only making yourself look silly. I couldn't hurt you if I wanted to, and you can't help anyone if you're dead.'

Anya thought on this.

The wood was really heavy. She dropped it. If the man had wanted her dead, then he could have killed her a hundred times by now. In her mind's eye, she saw the axe strike the Kurah warrior's skull.

'You killed them?'

The man's expression changed to one that approached regret.

'They left me no choice. They know they are not allowed in here. I had to protect the forest.'

'Who are you?'

'My name is Vedic, Anya,' said the woodsman. 'I am the forestal of the Rift Forest. I guard the last of the ancient trees on behalf of the gods.'

'How do you know my name?'

'You talk in your sleep.'

'Oh,' said Anya. She felt sick. Her head was still thumping. She sat down on one of the arms of the nearest chair.

'Someone is looking after you,' said the man, coming into the room and sitting on the other chair. 'I don't suppose you know who.'

Anya shook her head. 'No one is protecting me. If you knew what was going on beyond this forest ...'

Vedic tilted his head and took his pipe from his lips again. He began tapping out the tobacco into the fire and stuffing the bowl with a fresh supply.

'I do know,' said Vedic. 'You talked a lot while you were out. Besides, your story is hardly unique – lots of villages get sacked by the Kurah. Someone within the forest has your back. I would not be protecting you unless they did.'

Anya frowned. 'I am grateful for your generosity.'

'It's wasted,' said Vedic, shaking his head. 'I didn't want to help, and wouldn't be if I had not had the misfortune to be cursed by whichever god has granted you favour, to help you.'

Anya stared at him. 'You are honest. There's that at least.'

'I wasn't always a forestal. I am not a nice man,' said Vedic, folding his arms. 'Do not forget that, and we will get along fine.'

A wolf howled.

Vedic lifted his head.

Another wolf answered.

'They are getting a little close,' he said.

Anya did not respond: she had no idea what was normal, and she felt nauseous. She felt her skin moving and stitching and coming together over her wounds.

The woodsman put his pipe down on the crude wooden mantelpiece over the fire and took his bow from the wall. He paused at the door to the forest.

'Your clothes are repaired and on the kitchen table. There's stew in the pot over the fire. I will be back soon.'

The clothes were where he said they would be. Crudely stitched but bound secure, her tunic and leggings were on a makeshift hanger next to the fire. The table was pretty close by. At that moment, Anya had an urge to try and run, but she pushed the feeling away. Anya had shelter, and she'd be foolish to ignore that and die before the message could ever get there. She put the clothes to one side.

Anya filled her bowl with stew and sat at the table to eat.

You are taking time to eat? asked the voice in Anya's head that sounded so much like her mother. *An army marches on its stomach,* said her mother, continuing her theme. *But you need to be tougher if you're going to make it. Smarter. How do you know the stew is all right?*

Anya ignored the voice. It had been a long time since she had thought the voice was actually her mother and longer still since she had thought her mother might still be alive anywhere. Her grandfather had taught her that when you were at war, the two things you took whenever you could were food and sleep – you never knew when you would be without them. Seasoned warriors could sleep standing up. The woodsman could have killed her in any number of ways, and so the food would be fine.

After eating, dressed in her own clothes once more and feeling a little sleepy again, Anya looked for clues as to who her saviour was. The kitchen was simple: a fire was set into the right-hand wall as you looked from the doorway and was the only stone in the building. The table was rough but well made, as if created from driftwood or forest debris. There was a simple cupboard in the left-hand corner, leading up to the edge of the rear window, and the shelves were filled with just a few simple plates and bowls, all wood, and a few jars of herbs, pastes and ointments that were labelled in Shaanti.

There was no sign of any weapons here other than the bow the woodsman had taken. Now that Anya thought about it, there were no signs of any weapons at all. She returned to the main living area. The tools that hung from the wall were all related to working the woods and obtaining food. There was the gap where the bow had been; the axe he had used in the fight was just a woodsman's tool, not an actual battle-axe; and the rest was just a collection of hooks, ropes, saws and shears. The closest thing to a sword was a machete that looked hardly used. Anya lifted the blade off the wall and felt the weapon for weight and balance.

The door popped open and Vedic came back in. He was soaking. The forestal went to the fire and let the heat of it soak into his hands as he stood there, not speaking. Agitation was coming off him faster than the water on him was turning to steam.

'Who are you?'

Anya blinked. 'I am Anya. You already knew that.'

Vedic looked at her and held her in his gaze with ice-blue eyes. 'There are a pack of wolves combing the forest for you, and they are not alone – someone is helping them. So – who are you?'

Anya's confusion dispelled any feeling of sleepiness. 'I am no one. Honestly, I am just a girl from Anaheim. They ransacked my village and I escaped.'

Vedic held her in his gaze a moment longer, looking for deception, and then looked back at the fire.

'Nobodies do not escape a Kurah camp,' said Vedic. 'Not that I understand why they were taking prisoners in the first place.'

'Many of my family were warriors,' said Anya, unwilling to say their names until she knew this man a bit better.

'But you are not – you have no tattoos.'

Anya pushed a memory of her grandfather forbidding her from her mind. *The safest lie is the one that is closest to the truth* – another of his sayings.

'My trials were to be in the autumn.'

Vedic smiled. 'The Kurah didn't get the appointment time right. What aren't you telling me?'

A wolf howled. This one was very close. Vedic strode past her and looked out the window at the clearing beyond. He rested his head against the glass before letting the simple curtains drop back in place.

'It can wait. We cannot stay here.'

Anya wasn't sure she had heard him correctly.

The woodsman moved to the wall and began taking down every tool that could be a weapon. The machete went onto his belt first, then the axe over his shoulder, and the quiver of arrows went back on. The rope he wrapped round his waist.

'You will have to make do with one of my cloaks,' he said. 'It won't be perfect but will offer some protection. There is a knife in the kitchen you can use to cut the length. Be quick.'

Anya stared at him. 'But you said—'

'That was then, this is now. Our only chance is to get out of here. If we take too long, they will surround us and we will die.'

Anya ran to the front door and opened it. The clearing was dark, the lashing rain killing any visibility she might have had in the moonless black. As her eyes adjusted, Anya realised there were at least thirty pairs of golden eyes gleaming back at her. She slammed the door.

Vedic was staring at her from about a foot away.

'Do you want to live?'

Anya nodded.

'Then get the cloak and the knife, and let's go.'

The sound of claws on wood chased at Anya as she ran to the kitchen and back. On her return, she found Vedic bolstering the front door and the shutters with pieces of what had been his chairs.

'Ready?'

Anya nodded.

'We're going out the back,' said Vedic, leading her to the far wall of the living area. She got ready to push the window open, but Vedic stopped her with his hand on hers. His touch was dry and rough. She didn't like it.

'No,' he said, softly. 'They may expect it. I have an escape route.'

'Why?'

'Hardly the time, little one,' said Vedic. 'Follow me.'

The woodsman pulled up the rug and lifted a trap-door that dropped down to the forest floor below the foundations of the cabin. He scrambled away for the rear left corner of the building, where the trees were thickest. The sound of rain was so loud they could only just hear the howling behind them. Anya followed the woodsman's path under the cabin. He waited for her and only spoke when she was close enough for him to whisper in her ear.

'Follow me,' he hissed. 'Stay as close as you can until we hit the stream, then follow me into the water. We must lose our scent to stand a chance.'

Anya nodded.

Vedic sprang from under the cottage, oblivious to the weather and the wolves. Anya followed him into the night, praying she had made the right decision and the forestal could protect her. There were people whose survival depended on her.

CHAPTER FIVE

'THE THAIN HAS NOT PROVIDED any evidence that the Kurah would have any reason or capability to attack us. There has been no incursion since she defeated the Kurah king fifty years ago.'

The thain stared at Golan of the Shaanti council from her seat. The councillor's large frame seemed to draw his peers into his orbit. The council were in the war room that lay next to the main throne room, where the Shaanti court gathered on the increasingly rare occasions that the thain felt like socialising. The war room had always been the heart of this thain's reign, first because of the war that had made her famous, and then through habit. The chamber was light, the exterior-facing wall made of glass, painted with the named warriors of Shaanti legend. In the late afternoon sunlight, the room was cast in shades of deep red. An ugly hue, matching the mood of the council.

The council sat round a roughly hewn wooden table that had been gifted to the thain's grandmother by the now-vanquished Delgasians. Not a single member of the council met her eyes. The capacity for politicians and merchants to completely overlook the facts in the interest of personal gain of power and money was a constant disappointment. She could almost smell their fear ... No ... that was simply the nauseous collection of their perfumes.

'The Kurah have taken Delgasia,' said Bene, her chief bodyguard, from his place next to her. 'It is a case of *when,* not *if,* they invade.'

'Even if that were true,' said Golan, looking at Bene as if he were an ant, 'we have time. They cannot simply carry on marching – they must lay supply lines and wait for the spring or risk the same mistakes milady exploited.'

The thain's smile did not meet her eyes. The written reports of her scouts and spies were stretched out on the table in front of her. She could recite whole passages by memory. Would that help?

'This Kurah king,' began a councillor by the name of Kurn, who was more corpulent than Golan and usually a man to be relied on for sense. 'He killed his father to take the throne?'

The thain nodded. 'Montu didn't even hide it. Stood up in front of the lords and told them straight that if he had not, the Kurah would have fallen.'

Jeb shifted in his seat. The ancient warrior was an ally who had fought with the thain since she was a young girl, come to power too soon. His hair was the colour of snow, and his skin was cracked like dried mud, but his eyes were as sharp now as they had been pretty in his youth. The thain wondered when they had both got so old.

'That young king was right,' said Jeb, rolling his empty pipe in front of him. 'His father was a fool. There was a need for change, but his methods ... they are ruthless on a level we have not seen in these lands in a hundred years.'

'This is my point,' replied Kurn, thumping the table. 'This king is no fool. He must know that we only defeated the Kurah because his grandfather had overextended himself. He will not invade while he has to assimilate the Delgasians into his territories. At best, he gets held at the Barrens; at the worst, he winds up with two fronts on either side.'

The thain cleared her throat. 'While I welcome my friend's analysis of the last war, those of us who were there recall a slightly more complex set of reasons behind the enemy's defeat. Including the blood of many of our friends and relatives on the field of battle.'

The room was silent. Only Jeb was nodding in approval at her words.

'Even if we assume that your analysis is correct,' said the thain to Kurn. 'We are still talking about *when*, not *if*.'

'You can't know that,' said Golan, shaking his head.

The thain nodded. 'Yes, I can. The Kurah king is not doing this for glory. He pays close attention to the events beyond the sea, and he knows the Tinaric are looking at these lands. This continent is not unified. The Kurah look weak to them, and if he cannot subjugate us, then an invasion attempt is almost certain.'

'Why not form an alliance?' asked Golan.

'The Kurah do not negotiate,' said the thain. 'Have you not remembered your history?'

'When we formed this council, you promised to abide by our decisions. This is sounding like you have made up your mind.'

The thain stood. The room had frozen in fear. She had thought to raise her voice, but the sight of a portrait of a young boy hanging at the far end of the chamber stopped her. Such a beautiful boy. He was gone. She had hung the picture there for just this reason. *Think.* She placed her hands on the table and bent her head.

'This council exists for good reason,' she said. 'Though some forget that it is meant to serve for the people and not for the council's own sake. In time of war, the decisions are mine alone, and not for the sake of power but because war is ill-suited to decision by committee.'

'We are not at war,' said Golan, his voice soft, patronising.

The thain fixed him with a look that made him lean back in his seat. 'No, Master Tholop. We are not at war, and all I have made is a recommendation to muster the reserves and prepare for refugees.'

'You must see that will start a panic,' said Kurn.

The thain folded her arms. 'You judge our people with so little faith.'

'Is it a motion?' asked Ranth, speaker of the council, from the opposite end of the table. She said little despite the title. It was hard to tell who she favoured.

'I propose it as such,' said the thain. 'But I leave it to your consciences for now.' She sat down.

'Those in favour ...'

Jeb lifted his hand; Bene had no vote; and the speaker lifted her hand in support. Looking around the room and seeing no further support, she exchanged a look of apology to the thain.

'Motion fails,' said Ranth. 'To other business ...'

The thain heard little else of the council meeting. There was a series of motions from the merchants, who, to her at least, it seemed were increasingly over-represented on the council. She stared at the picture of her son. She wondered if this had ever been what he had intended when he had asked her, all those years ago, to form the council.

The suns continued to set as the council meeting dragged on, and the thain found herself glancing at the portraits of heroes gone by. Her own pane was the most recent. *Have I lived too long? Am I a useless legend that doesn't have the decency to die or disappear?* Her eyes drifted to the pane next to hers and a face she had not seen in thirty years. *Is that why you ran away?*

'... council meeting adjourned.'

The thain looked at her council, waiting for dismissal – a ridiculous custom, and she waved them away.

'They are such fools,' hissed Bene, turning to her.

She smiled. 'They think the world is logical and in their favour.'

'We are sleep-walking into defeat.'

The thain wasn't really listening. Jeb had not left the room – he was waiting for her to notice him as she just had.

'Yes, Lord Jeb? What is it?'

'Mistress,' he replied, standing and leaning on his stick. He seemed to be bent over more heavily than the last time she had seen him. 'I cannot but agree with your loyal servant.'

'About the council?'

'It was a noble experiment but a failure. They have not understood its purpose and will destroy us if we do not act.'

The thain sighed.

'And monarchy isn't a failure? Blood is no surer sign of competence.' Her eyes returned to the portrait of her son. 'Besides, I am too old to solve this problem.'

Jeb flushed. 'Forgive me, mistress.'

The thain laughed. 'I am joking with you, old friend. The council is not perfect, but we will find a way forward. The people will not fall while I live.'

Jeb bowed. 'I will leave you.'

The thain nodded and stood to leave herself. She whispered in Bene's ear before she left. 'Bring the generals to my chambers in thirty minutes.'

THE SWORD TOOK TOO long to unbuckle. The weapon was heavier every day. That was how it seemed to the thain as she allowed herself to relax for a few moments. She placed the blade on its stand next to her bed and placed the gold circlet from her head onto the dresser. She moved slowly these days: her hips ached with a hundred injuries and the birth of a child. She moved to the table that held the washing bowl, and splashed her face with the cold liquid. The water gave her a shock and reminded her that she still lived.

The coughing came again. Worse this time. Blood stained the cloth – bright and red like the berries she had picked as a girl.

'You are doing too much.'

The thain turned to look at the healer. He was young. Everyone was young these days. Yorg was twenty-five and one of the brightest students of his predecessor, Marakesh. The thain's old healer had promised that she would look after the thain even as she lay on her own deathbed. Truthfully, the thain had not wanted another healer, but it had been an offer she could not refuse.

'There is no time for me to slow down,' she replied.

The thain threw the bloodstained cloth into the fire and checked her lips and nose for stains before the generals appeared. Yorg came over to her side. He placed a hand on each shoulder and gently but firmly turned her to look at him. For one giddy moment, she thought he was going to kiss her, but then she remembered her age. He leant in and tilted her head to look at her mouth. She let herself be manipulated so he could get the best view possible in the candlelight. When he was done, he placed a glass against her back, and with his ear to it, he listened for heaven-knows-what.

'Breathe in,' he commanded. 'Breathe out. Again.'

On the third go, he moved away. He wiped down the glass and led her to the armchair next to the fireplace.

'You're dying.'

'This I know. How long?'

'You have a few weeks at most.'

The thain did not know how she felt. It was almost a relief to have an end, to know that she was not just marching endlessly on while everyone else fell. On the other hand, she felt angry. Why now?

'I cannot. I refuse.'

The healer bowed his head. Yorg was upset. 'I am sorry, milady. I have heard of this many times in the city and beyond – it is the lung fever. The disease never spares.'

He was right, of course. Lung fever was utterly fatal. She had watched enough warriors die from the contagion on various campaigns and expeditions. She had dispatched some herself to save the suffering.

'The universe is cruel,' she whispered. 'That I must leave my people in such dire circumstances.'

'I promised to look after you,' said Yorg as he kicked at the stone floor. 'I have failed. I am sorry.'

The thain watched actual tears fall down the man's cheeks. This was no good at all. She placed a hand on his shoulder and raised him up so that he was looking at her.

'You must not think like that,' she said. 'This was not your fault. I am old, and the old get sick.'

'But—'

'But nothing. I need you to listen to me. This is an absolute secret on pain of death. Not even Bene can know.'

The man stared at her.

'The council would take over if they knew,' she said. 'You understand what that would mean? Golan, in charge of the Shaanti. I must have time to sort this out. I must leave you all safe.'

The healer was scared. She could smell fear on him, but he nodded his head in acquiescence.

The thain held him in her gaze for a moment. Partly to make sure, and partly because he was so damned beautiful.

'Now go,' she hissed. 'Before the generals arrive. Come back when you have a way to slow this contagion down.'

The thain watched the healer leave by the hidden path. Satisfied she was alone, she placed the circlet back on her head and lit a pipe before sitting back in front of her fire. She found the heat helped her move like she used to. The door swung open, and Bene ushered her six generals into the chamber.

The generals – Hedite, Roathfort, Culino, Vort and the two men Ashnon and Yurn. The thain had forgotten when the people she commanded had started to look like children to her, but it still distressed her. Jeb entered from the antechamber and wordlessly sat down in the chair opposite her.

'As you commanded,' said Bene. 'The generals and Lord Jeb.'

'Apologies for the secrecy,' she began. 'The council has voted not to begin preparations for the coming war. I do not have time to debate the finer points of this decision with them or you. Instead, we will prepare on our own.'

'That could be dangerous,' said Vort. She arched her eyebrow as if the thought would never occur to her. 'If the council were to find out ...'

'They will not,' said Bene, his arms folded and his glare hard to look at.

The thain smiled. 'The council will see nothing other than a meeting between the military leader of the people and her generals. At most they will see normal drills and practice against the rising dangers of our world.'

'That's good,' conceded Jeb, nodding. 'Very wise.'

'Glad you approve,' said the thain. She fought down another cough by clenching the pipe between her teeth. 'Now, I need each of you to make your reservists ready – the usual: full weapons check, swords sharp, gear at the ready. I want the traps checked for readiness and all of the beacons between here and the forest checked for communication.'

'That will be hard,' said Hedite. She gestured east. 'The council had the beacons nearest the forest dismantled.'

The thain looked up at the ceiling in frustration. She had lost that vote as well.

'They weren't scheduled to removed until next year.'

'It was brought forward,' said Jeb. He shook his head. 'Stupid people.'

'Very well, we must increase the scout patrols to the border but without anyone appreciating we have done it. Use reservists you trust – no warriors' colours. I want to be in a position that if anyone passes wind on our border, I know about it within two days.'

The pain was lancing. It felt like someone had shot an arrow through her left breast. They all noticed, and that upset her more than the pain.

'Milady,' said Bene, leaning over her. 'Are you all right?'

'Yes, yes,' she said. She waved him away. 'I am just tired. Do as I have asked, and report to me tomorrow.'

'Milady ...'

'Go!'

The thain regretted shouting, but even Jeb left the room silently. The outburst had had the desired effect. As soon as she was alone, the pain drove her to her knees, and she found herself panting for breath. Blood dripped onto her tunic from her nose.

'Here.'

The shadow passed her a handkerchief that she took without looking up. The thain pressed it to her nose.

'You're late.'

'I got held up,' replied the figure, dressed in black. Her shadow. First amongst the order of shadows. A spy she had recruited when she was just a pretty noble-girl playing at picking her pocket.

'What news of our merchant friend?'

'He is confident of taking control of the council,' said the shadow, moving through the room like she was a ghost. 'Based on your current health, he may be right.'

'I still have a few tricks up my sleeve,' hissed the thain. 'What I need to know is who else is with him.'

'I do not know,' said the shadow, sadly. 'But I agree, there is more to our merchant than meets the eye.'

'I must know the extent of his betrayal,' she said, slamming her hand against the fireplace. 'Without that I cannot act with free rein.'

'If I could get to the border,' said the shadow, 'I could see what they are planning.'

'Others must carry that burden,' she said, not unkindly. 'You must hunt down this traitor that is working with Golan before it is too late.'

'As you wish.'

The shadow turned to leave.

'No,' the thain said, looking once more at the blood on her sleeve. 'Stay. For a little while.'

The shadow turned, pulled back her hood and looked at her with older eyes than the thain remembered. Without speaking, she strode to the thain, picked her up and carried her to the bed.

'For a little while,' her shadow whispered.

CHAPTER SIX

THE STREAM WAS MORE like a river in the torrential rain.

Anya was still limping from her beaten ankle and wounded thigh, keeping Vedic in sight more through force of will than any strength. She knew if she fell, the woodsman might not notice until whatever was wrong with his left arm flared up again. The first time she had lost sight of him, he had bellowed in pain and come back to find her, his left arm clutched to him. Each time after, if he got too far ahead, he returned doing the same thing.

They no longer heard wolves. The sound of the rain on the water and the leaves was overwhelming, but still the woodsman pressed on down the stream. Anya was soaked to the skin. She felt tired in her bones, and her lungs were burning with deep ragged breaths that felt like she might combust into flame at any moment. *At least I would be dry then*, she mused. She fell. The water gushing behind her rolled her over and over, and she thought she would drown. Large hands lifted her firmly from the onslaught, righting her onto her feet, and the woodsman clasped her head in his shovel-like hands. He looked her straight in the eye. The man's gaze was like the moon – all-seeing, cold, mercurial.

'You are at the end of your strength?'

She shook her head.

The woodsman frowned. 'Warriors know their limits, little one. Your death will help neither me nor the ones you seek to save.'

'But the wolves—'

'Are a danger,' said the woodsman. 'But they are unlikely to scent us this far downstream.'

Grasping her right arm, the woodsman turned and half dragged, half led her up the bank and out of the stream. Once they had clambered up, both becoming coated in viscous mud, they paused to listen for any sign of pursuit. The trees here were bigger than those near the cabin, large leafy branches attached to trunks twice the width of the forestal, and if Anya had ever known their names, she could not think of them now. The surrounding undergrowth smelt sweet in the rain.

The woodsman pointed up a slight incline that led north, away from the water, to where the trees grew closer together again and the light was minimal.

'Can you manage it?'

Anya wasn't sure but she nodded. The woodsman might be right about warriors knowing their limits, but she had yet to take the ink and could not afford the luxury. She knew as well as he did that they needed a hiding place to rest. She limped after the forestal.

They walked on until the trees grew more tangled. Anya thought every now and then that she could see Fin following, a ghost glimpsed out of the corner of her eye, seen between the boughs, head covered in blood. She was too exhausted to feel guilt. She just wondered if the blood would attract the wolves.

Vedic stopped periodically to examine the trees, always sloping and tangled. Anya thought that he was looking for a makeshift platform where they could rest without worrying about anyone stumbling on them.

The howl was like nothing she had ever heard.

Anya had time to half turn, half consider that the noise sounded vaguely vulpine before whatever it was bounded into her and sent her to the ground.

Vedic swore in a language she didn't recognise.

Anya rolled to her feet, searching for a weapon. The woodsman was on the ground. A tangle of hair and fur was wrestling with him, howling that god-awful noise and gnashing at him with teeth that looked all too human. The woodsman was holding the creature's hands, claw-like, away from his throat. He had not managed to draw his machete, and the two were now locked in a kind of stalemate.

Anya grabbed a branch of the nearest tree and broke it off. Vedic howled in pain. Anya swung the branch at the creature, knocking it from the woodsman. The thing scurried up onto the trunk of the nearest tree and leapt at her. The two of them tumbled end over end, Anya managing to throw the creature away from her once more.

'Anya!' shouted Vedic, throwing her the machete.

She caught the weapon by the hilt and swung without thinking as the creature leapt at her once more. She severed the creature's arm, causing the thing to scream and crash to the wet mud, where the animal hissed and spat at her. Anya pointed the machete at the creature's head. It looked just like an old woman, lined and grey-haired and with eyes that spoke of human intelligence. The woman's face had the same expression as the young guard had before Anya had forced the blade under his armour and into his heart. For a brief moment, Anya thought she was the guard, her stomach lurching and making her feel as if she were back in the Kurah camp, right in that moment where she had first killed.

Vedic stepped forward and broke the creature's neck with one swift twist of his hands.

'Never hesitate,' he said, taking the machete from her. 'You will die.'

Anya was still staring at the body. It looked like a collection of wet furs and skins.

'Banshee,' said Vedic, examining himself for wounds. 'I doubt she was with the wolves, but she'll have raised enough noise. We need to go up into the trees. Do you need a rope?'

Anya was about to say no, and then she remembered his words. He was right. She suspected he often was. She was exhausted. She nodded.

Vedic made no comment. He undid the rope around his torso, looped one part to him and the other to her.

'We'll go as fast as you can,' he said.

'What if the wolves come?' she replied.

'Then we will think of a new plan,' he said. 'Thinking about ifs will get you killed just as much as hesitation.'

They climbed.

IN THE END, it was Vedic who could not carry on. They had been climbing carefully for an hour or more. The morning light was occasionally visible above them, and the rain had slowed to a drizzle that they could hear more than feel. The forestal stopped at the end of a large flat branch and sat down as if someone had struck him suddenly on the head.

Anya limped up to him.

'Are you all right?'

Vedic looked worn and old and in pain. He pointed.

'This was its lair,' said the woodsman.

Anya could see the tree ahead of them had been partly felled. Its taller section lay hanging from a sinew; its top dug into the ground below. The exposed innards of the tree showed the fresh white of recently broken wood, and parts of the lower trunk looked as if they had exploded out. In the centre of the tree, the crystal had fractured and was dull.

'It's true,' said Anya, her disbelief obvious. Her grandfather had told her tall tales of the forest where the trees had diamond hearts and the Tream emerged from the dark green like wraiths.

'It is dying,' said Vedic. His voice was thick with emotion Anya couldn't place. It might be guilt. 'I should end it now.'

'Why can't you?'

Vedic looked at her. 'The wolves will sense it. Whatever is helping them would guess where we are.'

'Well, I can't do any more,' said Anya, sitting down next to him. 'I must rest.'

Vedic looked at her. 'I'm surprised you lasted this long.' He looked at the dressing on her arm. 'I think this stuff is keeping you going, but that probably means you'll take longer to heal.'

Anya gently stopped him reaching across to check the dressing. 'No healing right now. I need to sleep.'

Vedic nodded. He took the rope from around his waist and looped it around the branch. 'In case you fall off.'

Anya shook her head. 'Unlikely.'

THE WORLD WAS STILL DARK when Anya opened her eyes. She ached more than before she had fallen asleep, but her clothes had begun to dry. She could think in a straight line again. *I must have slept through the day*, she thought. Anya's memory returned. The sacking of her village ran through her mind, robbing her of the moment of calm. The wrenching guilt came sauntering after, wearing Fin's face.

Vedic was nowhere to be seen.

Anya lurched to her feet. She took a moment to find the woodsman – he was so well camouflaged he might have been one of the mythical Tream from her grandfather's tall tales. He was wrapped around the broken trunk, his legs gripped tight and holding him in place as much as his hands, which were clinging hard around the crystalline centre of the tree. There was a dull glow from the crystal that made it easier to see how one might mistake the core for diamond.

'Hey,' she whispered.

The forestal's eyes snapped to her. She watched the man pull himself up onto the top of the break, his feet balancing with a skill she had never seen in a man of that size. He leapt from the trunk and landed on the branch with a grace that any Shaanti swordsman or woman would have sacrificed much for.

'How are you feeling?'

Anya laughed. 'How do I look?'

Vedic shrugged. 'A little rested, banged up ...'

'It wasn't a genuine question,' said Anya, sitting back down with a sigh. 'How long was I out?'

'Most of the day. You missed the end of the storm and the sunset,' said Vedic.

'The wolves?'

'The odd one in the distance,' said Vedic. 'Bet they have not thought that we could travel this far with you in your condition. You are a tough little one.'

Anya frowned. 'I'm not that little. Old man.'

Vedic shook his head. 'I'll call you what I like, woman. I'm not a nice man.'

Anya felt her cheeks burn. She would have knocked anyone else on their arse for speaking to her like that, but she couldn't be choosy. Her companion was as he was.

'What were you doing?'

Vedic looked shamed. 'I was trying to see what the poor thing had learned.'

Anya blinked.

'What?'

Vedic tilted his head in curiosity. 'You must know the trees in the forest are aware.'

Anya felt the world lurch. She felt as if she'd run straight into one of the legends her grandfather had seemed to love so much. *Why not my mother?* thought Anya, not for the first time. She had never told her any stories that Anya could recall.

Your grandfather loved the sound of his own voice, but legends cannot defend against the blade of your enemy.

Anya forced herself back to the present.

'That's ridiculous,' she said. 'You will be telling me next that the Tream walk through the forest.'

Vedic stared at her. 'You are Shaanti, no?'

Anya nodded.

'Then speak with care,' said the woodsman. 'Before you dismiss those the gods protect. You may only be standing here because of one or more of them.'

Anya felt the hairs on the back of her neck rise.

'What did the tree say?'

Vedic sighed. 'I am not as skilled as the gods or the Tream at this, and the tree has been driven mad by its wounds. The banshee was seeking us.'

The Tream are real as well. 'The creature was after us?'

Vedic scratched his beard. 'Yes, but not for the wolves. The banshee was reacting to a faint message.'

'What?'

He shook his head. 'The message was garbled. More a picture of me and of you and a sense of need.'

Anya felt cold. The breeze that was wafting through the trees offered little in the way of drying her clothes any more than they were already. The thought that someone else was hunting them did nothing for her mood.

'Why fight?' Fin stared at her from his perch on a tree a few feet away. His skin was pale and mottled, and his head an ugly mess where the axe had taken him from the world.

Anya forced herself to close and open her eyes until he disappeared.

'You warm enough?' asked Vedic, gesturing at her shaking right hand. It wasn't the cold.

'I'll be fine,' said Anya.

Vedic held her in his gaze a little too long to convince her that he believed she was fine.

'Where will we go?' asked Anya.

Vedic gestured to the west. 'To the glade, and the only person who can protect us against whatever has come for you.'

Anya looked at him. 'That's where Danu is supposed to live.'

'Who else do you think I am talking about?' asked Vedic, smiling. 'The goddess rules this place, and she can protect us.'

Anya caught herself. *The gods are real.* The fear returned.

'I am not supposed to be here. It's forbidden.'

Vedic nodded. 'Yes, but I imagine if an old bastard like myself can come to an arrangement with the goddess, then a little one like you will be fine.'

Anya frowned. The gods in her grandfather's tales were not as even-handed as the woodsman was making out, and even Danu had her moments of capriciousness.

The wolf gave no warning. He scampered down the slope below, growling and sniffing the ground as if sensing a faint scent. He had a chunk of the banshee in his mouth, and his eyes glowed yellow in the dark.

Vedic and Anya pressed themselves flat along the branch. They did their best to meld into the wood as the creature paused, dropped the chunk of meat and howled at the sky. He picked up the meat and carried on.

'That was close,' said Anya, rolling onto her back. 'We need to move.'

Vedic got to his feet and began untying the rope that anchored Anya to the branch. A she-wolf leapt down from above.

How she had got there, they would never know, but she landed on Vedic and died as the forestal reacted faster than Anya could follow. He used the creature's weight and momentum to carry her over the edge of the branch, his hands finding her jaws. It was like the woodsman tore the animal in two, and she fell to the ground, gushing blood all over the mud. There were more howls as the woodsman dispensed with the knot and cut the rope free. They dropped to the ground and ran.

Anya found her thigh no longer ached with the fire of a fresh wound. Instead, it felt tight and itchy like a newly minted scar. She had no time to examine what magic the forestal had woven on her torn flesh. The animals behind her were not far away.

The woodsman moved as if he knew every inch of the forest, although surely the wood was far too vast for anyone to know the entirety in a single lifetime. He wove deep into the thickets of trees, passing willow, oak and pine and more that Anya had no names for. The wolves came on regardless.

They were heading uphill again. Anya had lost all bearings, and the suns were hidden. She could not tell if they were making for the north, east, south or west but knew only that if they were caught, they would be torn limb from limb. When Vedic disappeared in front of her, leaping from whatever ledge lay ahead, she didn't think, and she felt no fear as she followed.

Even death below was better than what lay behind.

The ledge gave way to the river at the heart of the forest, the Yiger, and she hoped the water was deep enough as the torrent came up to embrace her. She realised too late that she could not see Vedic. The forestal was gone.

CHAPTER SEVEN

THE HORSE WANTED TO RUN. Smoke billowed through the streets of the city like wraiths fleeing a burial site. Everything stank of a kaleidoscope of fear, pain and destruction. The sound of masonry crashing was like thunder. The general riding alongside the king glanced at Montu with concern. The creature moved beneath Montu, forcing him to pull the reins hard before trying to canter in the opposite direction. The king squeezed hard with his knees and ushered a command in Shaanti to stay. The clan had fought hard to defend the city of Anara, almost succeeding in getting away to the beacon and lighting the warning. There was always a chance that this would draw the thain out to the wrong battleground. He wasn't here to provoke the thain. Montu wanted control of when and how the thain learned of the invasion. It was important that she turned to fight rather than ran for the coast. Anara was about Cernubus.

Montu had lost his mount in the battle and was riding one of the enemy's steeds, having killed its owner in a vicious exchange. The king's armour was streaked with blood, but none of the gore was his own.

'Add the children to the prisoners,' said Montu. 'Kill everyone else.'

'What about the beacon?' asked the general.

Montu nodded. 'Dismantle it, carefully – no fire.'

'Aye,' replied the general. He kicked his own mount into a gallop and disappeared into the smoke.

Montu looked around. The city was hardly worthy of the title compared to the great stone edifices of the Kurah. Anara was a simple collection of wooden and stone buildings shoved up against the river and surrounded by a trivial wall, a basic stone keep at the centre – keeping the peace. The Kurah had taken a leaf from the Shaanti, travelling under darkness and only taking sufficient numbers of men to accomplish their task. They had given no warning, and now the last outpost between the Kurah and the plains that led to Vikrain were taken. They controlled the border of the forest and the main roads down from the more inhabited western reaches.

I'll not repeat my grandfather's mistakes, thought Montu. *Patience and planning win the day.*

The wooden buildings were all aflame. The stone ones were smouldering where they had wooden beams on display or, worse still, thatched roofs. Bodies lay strewn in the streets; crows and wild dogs were starting to venture in, lured by fresh meat. They scattered as Montu moved on his horse, down through the main street towards the dock.

The city of Anara sat on the banks of the Eukahn River, the waters providing a ready route to the sea and the trade that went beyond. The docks were the lifeblood of the city, and they were on fire along with everything else. Boats had been scuttled, their bows pointing to the heavens in a broken salute to the dying town. The warehouses were smouldering ruins, and the smell of burnt grain and meat permeated everything.

Montu had his sword drawn as he slipped from his horse and called out.

There was no answer.

Montu called out once more.

'Do not shout again, sire.'

Montu spun round to look at the guard who had spoken. The man's eyes were the only part of him that were on display. The rest of him was swathed in black from the boiled leather armour that protected his torso to the jerkin and leggings that kept him from freezing. Even the man's head was wrapped up.

Montu nodded. He moved to put his sword away.

'No,' said the man. 'Keep your weapon to hand. The docks are dangerous still. The Shaanti know they have nothing to lose now.'

'Careful,' said Montu. He disliked the man's tone. 'You work for me.'

The man shrugged. 'Suit yourself.'

An arrow thumped into the wall behind Montu. He dropped and cursed even as the guard spun and hurled a knife up into the smoke. There was a scream, followed by a thud.

'Damned archers,' hissed the man.

Montu gripped his sword tight. 'Which one are you?'

'I am Widen,' said the man. Montu thought he detected a smirk in the way the man said it. He let it go, for now.

'Have you found me my witch?'

The guard shook his head. 'No, sire. But she was here all right.'

The king felt the disappointment in his gut. It was vital he find this woman before they completed their alliance with Cernubus. He forced himself not to reveal his irritation on his face and instead gestured for the man to lead on.

'This way, sire,' said Widen. 'I believe you will want to see this in person.'

The king forced himself to focus on what they had found. 'What is it?'

The guard continued to scan the rooftops for a sign of the enemy. The docks had become a stop-and-start game of attrition with the two men running between buildings and seeking to avoid the archer's point.

'We searched the docks from top to bottom, and the city, but the woman is not here. But she was, some fifteen years ago, and she left a message for someone she envisaged would be coming after her.'

Montu frowned at the man as he led him into a warehouse that was intended for grain and had seen better days. Inside the warehouse, the stone structure was filled floor to ceiling with books, scrolls and other papers. There were desks in every corner, but

Montu was led to the one placed below the window overlooking the river.

The simple oak desk had been completed with a high degree of craftsmanship, though clearly built from driftwood. The table was covered in a thick layer of dust, a number of papers still on the desk. A small collection had been bundled together and tied with a piece of string. The king pulled the topmost note. It was written in Shaanti.

DEAREST,

I HAVE DETERMINED the secret of my nightmares, and it is worse than I could possibly have imagined. For all our sakes, I must see if there is another way out of this disaster that awaits all of us. I am sorry this means I have not been there for you, and I hope in time you can forgive me.

When I was young, I thought all I had to do was stand by what I believed in and everything would work out. Now I am older, scarred and scared. I have seen more things than I thought I could bear and gone on. My strength is failing, but I must press on while I can.

If I judge you right, you will eventually follow me, and so I know that I cannot reveal where I am going, for fear that others would follow. The answer lies beyond the sea. One day we will meet again. I do not speak of hope. I know it is true.

YOURS FOREVER AND ALWAYS,
M.

MONTU PLACED the note back in the bundle. He rifled his way across the desk, oblivious to the dust floating into the air, and looking for any other signs of his elusive quarry.

'We moved the more sensitive papers to the cache,' said Widen. 'The risk was too high with the fires. The warehouse is adjacent to a burning building right now.'

'Good,' said Montu.

'Sire?'

'No one can know we have been here and seen this,' said the king. 'If the god finds out, he may judge our agreement void. He is afraid of this witch-warrior, though she appears to have run for her life.'

'As you wish.'

'Did you gather when she left and in what ship?'

The guard nodded at the far wall. 'We are fortunate that the Shaanti who ran this port considered it a matter of pride to document everything about their visitors. The witch-warrior spent the harvest and winter of 9157 here at Anara before leaving in the spring on the vessel called *Perdition*. *Perdition* has never returned to these shores.'

The king sighed. 'Never heard of the vessel, and that was fifteen years ago?'

Widen nodded.

'She may be outside our grasp, then,' said the king, looking out of the window at the boats beyond. 'Let us not waste more time. Dispatch the guards that are here to the ports of the Shaanti.'

'We cannot hold all the ports and attack the capital,' said Widen.

Montu smiled. 'I know that, guardsman. You and your men are not to engage in open warfare but to ingratiate yourself until you find out if that ship has been seen in recent years.'

The guard tipped his head in acknowledgement.

Montu watched him leave. His eyes were unwavering points of light that bore down on the back of the guard, and he was considering killing the man. An execution always helped with loyalty. *No, I will learn the lessons and remember power is a rapier, not a machete.*

'Do you want me to take that to the camp?' asked the guard, looking back at the king and pointing at the documents.

Montu shook his head. 'No, Widen. And remember – anything you find comes straight to me. Our time is short.'

CHAPTER EIGHT

THE HORSE CARRIED the dying man across the eastern edge of the forest, never straying below its boughs. The animal's chestnut flanks were beaded with sweat, legs straining, eyes wild-tired – still the man spurred the beast on. He held his bleeding side together with his left arm, and the reins in his right, his head lolling round every few yards to check behind for signs of pursuit.

No one followed the rider as he stripped away the miles and passed to the exposed road, a dirt track that stretched out across the plains towards the distant city. He stopped only when the horse was about to drop with exhaustion, and even in those brief periods of rest, the rider did not sleep. Instead, he stood holding the gash in his trunk and looking back at the way he had just come, searching for an enemy that never appeared.

Whether he wanted to see the thing he looked for, or lived in fear of it looming over the horizon, was difficult to tell, as his face was warped in pain. He paced while his horse rested, as much to keep himself lucid as to stop himself falling into a stupor that would lead to a quicker death.

As the rider drew closer to the city, the road led to settlements, and the horse thundered through village after village. The dying man did not stop, even when some of the people recognised him and called to him by his name.

'Falkirk!' they cried out. But he did not acknowledge them.

'Where is Thrace?'

Thrace was dead and had been for three years. Falkirk tightened his grip on the reins and forced the horse on.

He ignored all his friends, men and women he had fought with, boys he had broken bread with and those he called kin. He barely recognised that they were talking to him – there was no time. He had a duty to complete, an obligation to an old friend, and every moment meant a step closer to the edge. He believed he would see Golgotha if he closed his eyes, and so he forced them to remain open. He wasn't afraid of the journey across the Acheron or the Fields of Asphodel. It was the thought of failure to reach Vikrain that haunted him.

Falkirk kicked the horse on. Amongst the villagers that saw him pass through their lands or heard of his journey, the retired warriors that lived with the villagers grimly began reviving the edges of their blades. As he rode on, his name began to go before him, riding faster than him.

'Falkirk came from the south, and behind him, the Kurah.'

When Falkirk saw the city rising up from the horizon on its hill, a giant made of wood and stone, perched on a seat of earth, a vital part of him loosened, and he began to slip in and out of consciousness. The horse began to weave as the rider's will started to leak away and fatigue took its toll. Still, the mount carried on.

The guards were not standing idle on the city walls – horns cried out from the gates as the rider approached. Warriors began pouring out of the mess onto the walls of the city. In particular, the sound of metal clashing on metal rang out as the men stationed at the gatehouse rushed to see who approached the city, their haste so desperate they knocked into each other.

Falkirk fell from his horse just shy of the gate. His horse continued a few yards before realising its rider was gone. Destroyed by his injury and the long ride, Falkirk did not have the strength to get up. He tried to push himself to his feet but fell back on his belly, barely able to hold his wound closed. He shut his eyes.

The mare turned and walked back to where he lay sprawled in the road. She nudged the rider with her nose, trying to elicit some attention, before wandering off to the grass by the side of the track. The sound of the gates opening didn't make Falkirk move.

Vikrain spewed its horsemen, armed and battle-ready, to where the man lay prone. The men broke from the orderly formation with which they had approached Falkirk, and placed their mounts round him to form a defensive circle. The oldest of them slid from her horse to the wounded man's side. She was older than Falkirk. Her hair was white and plaited in the warrior style. The woman felt for a pulse on Falkirk's neck, and when she found one – faint but steady – she rolled him over and cursed.

'It is Falkirk,' said the thain, rubbing her forehead. This was her only real tell of upset, and she brought the movement to a stop the moment she realised she was doing it. 'Are there any signs of pursuit?'

'No, milady,' said one of the other riders. 'Nor would I expect any. That wound is not fresh.'

'True,' conceded the thain. She looked at the ugly wound that had soaked dark blood into her friend's tunic. 'Well, we can't stay here all day or he will die. Get the bearers to take him into the city, and send one of the men to get the healers ready. I need to hear this man speak.'

Falkirk, hearing a familiar voice, stirred through the fog of his fever, his bloodshot eyes rolling round as he looked at the men, his arm twitching for a weapon that wasn't there before the thain found his hand.

'It's all right, Fal. You're safe now,' said the thain, her voice choked with emotion that made the other men look away.

'Thrace?' whispered Falkirk.

'No, laddie. It's your thain.'

'I'm sorry, Thrace. It's too much,' said Falkirk, his eyes rolling back in his skull. He passed out.

FALKIRK SCREAMED.

Yorg, the healer, stepped out of range of the gnarled warrior's reach and grabbed the man's flailing arms in his own. Falkirk flopped back down on the bench, his arms withdrawing to clutch at the torn mess that was his side as he whimpered like a child.

'He's dying,' said Yorg.

'I can see that, man,' said the thain. She felt her hand reaching for the blade she used on the field to dispatch men and women who were too far gone to save, too stubborn and fought all the way until the end. All the old warriors had helped a comrade on their way when hope was gone – but first you had to be sure.

'Can you do anything?'

The healer shook his head. 'Maybe if he'd arrived here a couple of days ago, but his wounds are infected. Can't you smell it?'

The thain nodded – of course she could smell the infection. She'd known as soon as she came within two feet of Falkirk that he was dying, but you always had to hope for a miracle, didn't you? A few of the other warriors were actually holding their cloaks over their faces, so putrescent was the odour. She'd be very surprised if Falkirk wasn't also aware that he was dying, and yet he'd still ridden as hard as he could for Vikrain. Why?

The thain suspected she knew the answer, but she needed proof. The council would only accept the truth from the man's own lips. She grabbed Yorg by the shoulder and took him to the far corner of the room.

'I need him conscious and coherent,' said the thain. 'I need to know who did this to him and ... what happened to Thrace. It's important.'

'He was probably just attacked on the road,' said Yorg. 'It was a poor harvest last year, and that always makes the roads dangerous.'

The thain looked the healer in the eye. 'Then why didn't he stop at one of the villages along the way?'

The healer blinked. 'I'll see what I can do.'

'You do that.'

The door cracked open, and Bene entered the room. The tall, pretty but deadly bodyguard entered the group with a scowl that could curdle milk. He eyed the other warriors with barely contained fury, and none of them met his face. The thain smiled as her bodyguard fought to force down the rebuke he had been about to lay on his men.

'Milady,' said Bene. 'How was your trip outside the gate?'

'Sad,' said the thain, gesturing. 'I found my friend wounded and dying. I need you to summon the council here.'

Bene glanced to the bench and stopped, his eyes widening. 'Is that Major ...?'

'Yes, it is,' said the thain. 'Falkirk. He never liked me going out without a full battalion either. And Thrace ... Thrace was far worse – nearly as bad as his wife.'

'Milady, your safety is my only concern.'

'Lad, if I thought for a moment it wasn't, then I'd be worried. The council need to see this first hand. Get them.'

'Milady,' said Bene, heading for the door.

The thain peered over Yorg's shoulder as he worked to draw out the infection from Falkirk's side. The fever did not look to be coming under control. The original wound had scabbed over badly, tearing again and again on the journey, and now heavy with rot. There was no way to tell what kind of blade had made contact. Still, it was an odd place to be cut, unless Falkirk had been pierced by a spear or he had been unarmed, in which case there would have been easier ways to kill him. The thain did not like where this train of thought was taking her.

The door opened and Golan entered the room.

'It is true, then,' said the merchant, looking down at the prone warrior. 'My uncle is returned.'

'Your uncle is dying,' said the thain, placing a hand on the man's shoulder, though it stuck in her craw to do so.

Golan looked at the healer, who nodded.

'Then it is good I have brought a shaman,' said Golan, waving the priest into the room.

The thain let her arm drop from the merchant's shoulder. She stepped back to Falkirk's side, becoming a blockade between the priest and the dying man.

'Milady,' said Crees, the shaman. 'Perhaps I can be of assistance or comfort to Major Falkirk?'

The thain wasn't sure. She disliked shamans, and Crees was

renowned for keeping his flock from treatment that would otherwise have saved them in favour of his 'medicine'. She looked to Yorg, who shrugged as if to say, *What difference does it make?* The ruler stepped to one side.

The shaman moved closer to Falkirk. His hand went to the wounded man's temple, and he started to chant in a low murmur. Yorg continued his treatment. The thain glanced at Golan, but the merchant was not looking at her; he just seemed to be staring at his uncle.

Bene returned. 'The rest of the council are beginning to arrive.'

The bodyguard's eyes were locked on the shaman, and his obvious contempt for the councillor's foolish belief in charms and prayer was written all over his face. *I'll need to pull him up on his body language again,* thought the thain. *I need him to be more discreet if we are to outplay Golan.*

'I have said for some time that the road to the Barrens is dangerous and requires patrols,' said Golan, folding his arms. 'Will you believe me now?'

The thain rubbed the bridge of her nose. 'So you are sure bandits did this?'

'Who else would it be?' asked Golan.

The thain shrugged. 'It is strange behaviour for bandits, and it would be a skilled man indeed who could disarm and wound your uncle so.'

'He is old. He may not have been armed.'

The thain pointed down. Golan looked and saw his own knife pointed at his belly. Smiling, the thain flipped the dagger round and handed the weapon back to Golan.

'You see,' said the thain, 'age brings compensations. Falkirk is ... was ... still in much better condition than many his age, including myself. He's a lifer – warriors like that never cease their training and conditioning. Why, when I was in his village last, he and Thrace were drilling the young warriors as if we were on the eve of war. Much as we are now.'

'War?' mocked Golan, shaking his head. 'Let the Kurah come. The gods stand with us. We are the descendants of the first men and women that appeared from the desert. This is the first city where humans settled, and all of the other gods came from the same forest where ours rule to this day. They will not forsake us.'

The thain looked at him. 'You speak so because you think the gods will always be there. You should know as well as I do that they only offer aid to those who help themselves.'

'I think the Kurah king has his hands full with Delgasia, even if the Del has fallen,' said Golan. He turned from the thain to look at his uncle once more. 'I make no apologies for this view. He will not attack us with only a few weeks of good weather left, and if he does, he will suffer the same fate as his grandfather. No army has ever managed to invade us, let alone before the rains.'

'Ah, the certainty of youth ...'

'He is awake,' said Yorg.

Falkirk clutched at his side. He moaned at the pain of his wound. His eyes popped open as if he remembered suddenly that he was alive. He searched the room and stopped when he saw the thain. He tried to sit up but was forced down gently by Golan.

'Please lie down, Major,' said Yorg. 'The thain is aware of your pain.'

'Indeed, I am,' said the thain, sitting on the edge of the bench.

'Milady,' said Falkirk. The cords in his neck were writhing snakes. The thain could almost feel the pain in her bones. 'I respectfully request permission to report.'

'Granted,' said the thain, smiling at her old friend's adherence to protocol. Typical Fal.

The room fell quiet.

'Kurah ...' said Falkirk. The man's breathing was laboured, the pauses between the breaths a little too long.

'I knew it. Order the gates closed,' said Bene.

'Wait,' said the thain, without looking at her guard. 'There will be refugees. We need to listen to the man.'

'Anaheim has fallen to the Kurah,' said Falkirk. He moaned again.

'Were there any more survivors?' asked the thain, ignoring the reaction of the other warriors in the room. 'Where is Thrace?'

Fal looked confused now. 'General Thrace is dead. The drink ... He died three winters ago – we sent word ...'

The thain's eyes narrowed. *Thrace. My old friend, gone? I am alone.*

Who stopped the message? How long has someone been betraying us?

'More ...' whispered Falkirk. The old warrior was fading. They all sensed it as if the Morrigan herself had come into the room to escort him down to Golgotha.

'What is that, Major?'

'There are too many,' said Falkirk, struggling. 'You must run.'

No one spoke. Major Falkirk never ran. What nonsense was this? He looked close to death.

'Fal, Fal, I need more than that. How many?' asked the thain, squeezing her friend's hand.

'Over ... over a hundred thousand warriors ...'

A few warriors swore. Bene sat down. Others left.

'This is madness,' said Golan. 'The Kurah have just fought a ten-year war. Where would the king find that many men? My uncle is driven mad by his wounds.'

'Hold your tongue, Golan, or I will have Bene silence you,' said the thain. Her chest was tight and painful again. She could feel the sickness between her shoulder blades. 'Where were they headed next?'

'Across the Barrens,' said Falkirk, coughing up blood. 'Taking the border villages. They mentioned Anara.'

'That will stop us flanking them,' said Bene. 'And they can take the end of the harvest if they have a long campaign. Clever.'

Falkirk coughed and blood appeared on his chin.

'Prisoners ...' said the major. 'They've taken prisoners ...'

The thain grew still. She felt sick.

'See – he's deluded. Even I know the Kurah do not take prisoners,' said Golan. He sat down next to the thain and put his hand on her shoulder. 'It is the pain talking.'

'Clear the room,' said the thain, her voice cold and hard. 'Now.'

'But, milady—' protested Golan.

'You heard the thain,' said Bene.

Bene ushered them all out of the room before returning to the thain's side. She was gentler with him.

'You too, Bene,' said the thain, without looking away from Falkirk.

'But, milady, you asked for the council, and now you are blocking everyone from the room. What is it?'

'Now, please. I will explain, but I must hear what else Fal has to say on my own. Golan heard of the attack. He cannot deny the truth in front of the council now.'

'As you wish.' Bene left the room.

'Fal,' said the thain as the door closed. 'Fal, what do you mean?'

Falkirk moaned.

'Falkirk, you said they've taken prisoners. That's not possible.'

'Prisoners.' Falkirk opened his eyes. 'The Kurah have prisoners and ...'

'Why?'

'Wrong ... question ... There is a ... g ... god with them, but wrong question ...' said Falkirk, his eyes bright as he looked at the thain.

'What?'

'Wrong question, not important why but ... wh—' said Falkirk. He was struggling to breathe.

'Who?' asked the thain. 'Who do they have?'

Silence.

'Fal?'

Silence.

The thain reached over and closed her friend's eyes. She sat there for a moment, gathering her thoughts before rising, her ascent slowed by age and grief. She paused to look back at the corpse of her friend, who she had known for half her life. The years felt like they were pulling her body over, bowing her spine as they gradually pressed her into the ground. She clasped the door handle. The thain heard the voice of her own mother whisper in her ear from across the years. *Appearances matter.* She straightened. The thain opened the door and let the men back in.

'Golan, please accept my condolences,' said the thain, composed. 'Your uncle has passed on to Golgotha. Bene, please ask the council members to gather in my chamber when they eventually get here. Please signal the gatemen to be ready for refugees.'

'What do I tell them?' asked Bene. He gestured at the city beyond. 'There will be a panic.'

'We are Shaanti. We do not panic,' said the thain. 'Tell them the truth – the Kurah have returned. Tell them we are at war.'

CHAPTER NINE

THE WOLVES WERE EVERYWHERE.

Anya watched them stream down the hillside, pouring round the trees like a flash flood, trying to find the scent trail again that would take them to their quarry. The torrent of water that blocked her from their view also made her own vantage point difficult, and it was hard for her to see whether the wolves had picked up their path. The caves behind the waterfall seemed vast, like a hidden road through the mountains.

The stag changed everything. The wolves scattered as if a lion had come amongst them. The stag was as tall at the head as a grown man, his antlers arching skyward like an elaborate set of trees that could have borne the weight of the world. His hide was a mixture of white across the chest and belly, blurring into darker brown flecked with strange black markings that seemed to move and dance across it. As Anya watched, the stag unfolded into a man at least seven feet tall. Bare at the chest and covered in tattoos from hairline to waistline, the man took in the forest air as he allowed the wolves to show submission by nosing his hands.

'What in Golgotha?'

Vedic moved next to her and stared without speaking. The giant-man seemed to be half listening to the whimpers of the wolves and half smelling the air. Anya held her breath as if he could hear them through the water of the falls. The giant-man glanced directly at them, held the water in his gaze for a moment and then passed on. He bent down and, a stag once more, followed the wolves down the riverbank and away from them. Anya heard Vedic exhale as he walked back into the cave.

The woodsman dropped his bow on the wet stone floor behind Anya. He had not said a word since he had pulled her up the river to the shallows.

'Who are you?' He sounded distant, tired.

Anya turned to look at her bedraggled companion. The cave smelt faintly familiar ... a sickly-sweet smell she couldn't place.

'I am Anya of Anaheim,' she said.

Vedic shook his head. He strode forward and shoved her towards the wall, bracing her with his left forearm against the rock while he held the machete to her throat with his right hand. Anya was so shocked she just stared at him wide-eyed, ignorant of the pain in the back of her head where she had bounced off the wall.

'You said you were the daughter of warriors, but that doesn't warrant all this. No one manages to get tracked so consistently when they are with me ...'

The magic that kept the woodsman tied to her was now making his left arm and legs tremble. The cords in his neck stood out like rigging on a ship, and sweat was beading down his forehead. This was costing him. Anya didn't care.

'I am what I have said.'

'Who were your parents?'

'Go to Golgotha,' she hissed.

'Who!'

Anya thought of her mother. She didn't need to hear the voice. She saw the opportunity in how the woodsman moved, and felt herself go limp. She twisted at the moment his breath gasped at her action – he thought he had gone too far. She swung around him with speed that would put her grandmother to shame, wrapping her legs around his neck before flipping back. Her weight threw the woodsman to the ground and drilled his head into the stone. The blow was hard enough to give him a headache, but she had avoided using her entire weight. She needed her guide alive.

Vedic did not attempt to pick up the machete. He sat up, rubbing a small spot of blood off the back of his head and chuckling.

Anya sighed. She sat down on a rock with her back to the falls.

'My father was a warrior by the name of Storn, and my mother was Dochas.'

Vedic shook his head. They meant nothing to him.

'My father died during his trials for the ink. My grandfather raised me – his name was Thrace. General Thrace, husband of Gobaith. Gobaith was my grandmother.'

Vedic stared at her. She was used to the reaction. Her grandfather always got people listening, but it was her grandmother that always made them speechless.

'You're the witch-warrior's granddaughter?'

Anya nodded. 'But don't ask me what she's like. I wouldn't know.'

'Dead?'

Anya nodded. 'When my mother was little.'

'Where's your mother?'

Anya shrugged. 'Who knows? Motherhood wasn't for her, and so she ran away when I was three, under some pretext from the thain.'

'Who was training you for the ink? Your grandmother?'

Anya looked at Vedic. He wasn't looking at her; he was staring out into the water.

'What makes you think Thrace didn't?'

'Thrace was a big man, nearly my height, and that move would have been beyond him.'

'You knew my grandfather? How?'

Vedic shook his head. 'No, little one. I knew of him. I saw him once, from a distance. I wasn't always a forestal.'

'But you know he is dead.'

'Like I said, you talk in your sleep.'

Anya felt dizzy. The smell in the cave was really affecting her – it was musky and oppressive.

'What of my grandmother?'

Vedic did not reply for a moment. 'Your grandmother's reputation preceded her; everyone has heard of her.'

'She left. Before my mother,' she said. *That's what women in my family do. That's what I was going to do.*

Anya frowned. The atmosphere in here was stopping her from thinking in a straight line. 'What is that smell?'

Vedic stood up. 'Yes, bad, isn't it? Place smells a little like rotting meat, but these caves are not occupied ...'

Anya picked up the machete. Vedic held out his hand for the weapon.

'Why would I give this back to you after that performance?'

Vedic raised an eyebrow. 'Because you can't bring yourself to strike any more. Look – your hand is shaking just holding it.'

Anya looked down. He was right.

'I could throw it out there.' She gestured at the crashing water that masked their hideaway.

'And risk discovery? Or have so little that I can defend us with?'

Anya sighed and handed him the weapon.

'Stick close,' he said. He turned towards the back of the cave.

The pair moved deeper into the dark, where the cave became a tunnel and then opened up into a second chamber that was drier than the first. The smell there was overwhelming, like a fetid hand that covered their mouths and noses. Anya gagged. As her eyes adjusted, she realised the light in this second cave was coming from the faint glow of golden liquid pooled around a prone body. The corpse – a male – had been mauled badly by wolves, though that may not have killed him. The dead man had no head.

Vedic swore.

Anya looked round for the rest of him but could not see any sign of the head. Vedic squatted down next to the body and rolled it over onto its back. The man's chest was a ruin as well: a fist-sized hole over his heart made it look as if someone had just pulled the organ out.

'Who is he?'

Vedic did not look at her. 'He is Eridanus.'

'How can a god be killed?'

Vedic shook his head. 'I don't know what could do this to a god. It shouldn't be possible.' He looked pale, even with the golden glow of the blood. Was she seeing Vedic afraid for the first time?

Anya felt her stomach lurch. 'Do the wolves know about the caves, then?'

Vedic looked around for tracks. The moment of fear had passed now, and he appeared to be focusing on what he knew of how to understand the cave. 'No, you are focusing on the body. Look properly. Show me what you can do, granddaughter of Gobaith.'

Anya flushed. She scanned the room. The blood had splattered onto the ground and into a small pool around the body. Above, in the shadows of the roof, there was a small set of bloodstains where the spurt from his neck had hit the ... *No*, thought Anya, *that's not right. Not enough blood, no head: he wasn't killed or left here.*

'There's a break in the rock above. He fell down, dropped by whoever killed him?'

Vedic stood. 'Very good.'

Anya sighed. 'But that means the wolves may find us if they come back, if they can get in through there as well.'

'Yes, but we have to leave regardless,' said Vedic, folding the god's arms across his chest. 'We have barely enough food for the next day, and so we must hunt or die.'

'But are they tracking us?'

Vedic led her back to their original chamber. 'Hopefully, on a fool's errand down the river while we go round through the forbidden lands.'

'Forbidden? The whole forest is forbidden.'

'Tream lands, Anya, we're going to go through the Tream lands.'

Anya shook her head. 'I can't believe they are real. But even if they are, do you know nothing? They hate us.'

Vedic shrugged. 'It's our only option. Do you want to run into whatever did that? Or the stag?'

She shook her head once more. She looked at him.

'What were you before you became a forestal?'

Vedic did not meet her look. 'Not a nice man.'

'You haven't changed.'

'Good. You're learning. Look – they are gone.'

Beyond the waterfall, there was nothing to see staring up the hill or beyond. The wolves had passed them by. But for how long?

Vedic sat down. 'Rest. We need to make sure they have really gone, and I can't hunt until dusk.'

Anya sat down with her back against the opposite wall and with stones near to hand. She didn't trust the woodsman. His manner was entirely too volatile for her liking. He reminded her of a dog she had adopted when she was much younger, before her grandfather's drinking had got out of hand. The dog would wait until she had just about forgotten the last time he had bitten her, or pissed on her, or sent her sprawling before striking again. He was just mean.

'I don't think I can sleep,' said Anya.

'Suit yourself,' said Vedic, closing his eyes. 'Real warriors can sleep on a washing line.'

'My grandfather used to say that.'

'Bet he'd be asleep by now.'

'You're not wrong,' said Anya, looking over at the ghost of her grandfather sitting near the entrance to the second chamber, Fin under one arm. He kept trying to speak to her, but she couldn't hear it. *He was probably slurring*, she reasoned, blinking him back to oblivion and hating herself for it.

She never saw her mother. Did that mean she was alive? Anya wasn't sure she would recognise her if she walked past her – all she had growing up was a sketch Thrace had done. There were more paintings of her grandmother. She was highly thought of, and Anya had never had to buy a drink for herself or pay for a place to stay.

VEDIC WOKE HER.

He shook her gently, and when she opened her eyes, he pointed to the low-slung suns beyond the water. The smell had dissipated a little.

'Stay here,' said Vedic. 'I'll be back before the moon hits the top of the sky.'

Anya was too tired to argue. She nodded.

Vedic left.

THE SUNS GOT LOWER, and lower, and lower, until the dark came. Hunting really was a long, tedious exercise that required you to spend vast amounts of time waiting. It was also the case that the woods, however you chose to view them, were dangerous. There were plenty of ravines to fall into, wild animals to fall foul of and an actual pack on the lookout.

'He's probably dead,' said Fin. The ghost was by the waterfall. He was looking not at her but out at the forest.

He's not really here, Anya told herself.

'Did you tell him you knew what you were doing?' Fin's ghost turned to her. 'Will you lead him into the void like me?'

Anya blinked but the ghost remained. Swearing, she got to her feet.

'I'd best go looking for him,' she said. 'You can get out of my head.' Anya picked up a piece of discarded wood as a makeshift club and left the cave.

The ice water of the falls brought her heart up into her mouth and painted the night forest in vibrant shades of navy, blue and black. Anya remembered her tracking, and although the woodsman had tried very hard to obscure his way lest the wolves returned, she could see his path. Vedic had stuck to the river. The strategy made sense: remaining close enough that the wolves would be less likely to follow, and if they did find Vedic, the water was fast-flowing enough to carry him away. This would leave him free to double back later on. Equally, animals would come to the river for water and thus make themselves targets.

Anya followed the woodsman's path for half a mile before the trail went cold. She scrambled around in the undergrowth, looking for any sign at all, but he had vanished. She looked over at the river. He could have jumped in, but the tracks didn't show that – they just stopped. Anya was about to give up and head back to the cave when she heard a faint voice carrying on the breeze. She ducked down.

As Anya's ears adjusted, she realised the voice was a woman singing in a language that sounded familiar but wasn't quite that of the clans. She was slightly out of tune, a trembling falsetto meant for no one's ears but the singer. Anya moved carefully through the bushes and long grass of the riverbank. The river curved round to the left – she followed its path and stopped.

The singer was immersed in the river, dressed in a flimsy white robe that had become more or less translucent in the water. The bather was working on a small collection of flowers that had been gathered near the base of a tree on the far bank. She was singing as she worked at her arrangement.

Anya exhaled a breath she had not been aware of holding. The woman wasn't Kurah. She could have cried with relief.

It was all Anya could do to avoid running down to the stranger. Caution held her back. This was the gods' territory. Though she couldn't recall any goddess behaving in this manner, that didn't mean that the woman was safe to approach with no caution at all or, indeed, that Anya was allowed to. Still, nothing ventured, nothing gained ...

'Hello,' Anya called out as she made her way down the bank.

The woman stiffened. Anya slipped on the bank, sliding into the water, which was freezing and made her gasp. The woman turned to look at this person who had intruded on her solitude. From the water, Anya could see the woman wasn't pale at all, she was see-through – made entirely of water, as if she had been sculpted from ice. The woman's eyes were whirling pools of fury in the ocean of her face. She wasn't a woman ... She was nyad: a water spirit. Anya felt her belly flip at seeing another creature from her grandfather's tales not more than ten feet from her.

'I can go if I'm bothering you,' said Anya, unsure what to do under this creature's gaze that revealed little. 'I just haven't seen another person in ... a long while.'

'You should not be here,' said the nyad.

'I didn't know,' said Anya, raising her hands. 'Are you a goddess?'

The nyad moved quickly. She strode forward, bringing herself to within inches of Anya.

'You have violated me,' said the water spirit. She brought her arm round in a thunderous wet strike that stung Anya like an unexpected wave.

Anya fell back, sitting down flat on her behind in the middle of the river, water pouring round her chest, her heart like a small ball of rock in her throat. Nyads weren't supposed to be dangerous. That wasn't how the stories went. *However,* she realised, *if they chose to, they could kill you in silent fury before even the most attentive companion realised you had gone.* Vedic didn't even notice she was there most of the time. The nyad approached her again, leant back on her haunches and looked Anya over as if deciding whether to squash her. She traced an icy-cold finger down Anya's face where her hand had struck. It sent shivers down Anya, her fear rising as the wet fingers made their way over her neck and down.

'Now you will pay tribute to me,' said the nyad.

The woman's hand stopped its descent, crawling back up to her neck, and as the nyad's hand passed over her, Anya felt like winter was taking her in its grasp. The fingers closed on Anya's neck. She was lifted bodily into the air and slammed down into the river with enough impact to push the remaining air from her lungs.

Anya was going to die. She struggled as hard as she could, but she didn't have the strength to move that ice-like arm. Her hands just slid off, and she couldn't get a purchase on any of the rocks on the streambed.

Anya struggled as fireworks exploded behind her eyelids. She was running out of energy with a speed that would alarm the coolest head: her legs struggled to respond to her command to kick, and her grip on the creature was falling looser.

In the distance, she heard the sound of splashing water as someone else entered the stream, and the nyad's hand was pulled from her without warning as if snatched away.

Anya broke the surface, gasping for air. She gave silent thanks to the woodsman as she sought to recover her senses. The cool air struck Anya as she pulled herself from the river, her soaking clothes welded to her skin. She turned to look at the water where the nyad had been, but it wasn't the water spirit or Vedic she saw.

The person who'd saved her was a good deal shorter – barely taller than Anya – and he looked as dangerous as the nyad from whom she had been saved. The man stood in the river in goatskin leggings, anger etched on his face and power glowing from his hands as the water-woman sat at his feet, shaking her head in an effort to understand who had managed to best her.

He hit her, thought Anya.

'You go too far, lady,' said the man. His tone was aristocratic, like her grandfather's.

'She is mine,' said the nyad, her voice like fingernails on slate.

'Where do your allegiances lie? With him or with your own flesh?' asked the man.

'My allegiances lie with me,' replied the water spirit, making for Anya.

The man went to draw the short blade at his side.

Anya would never forget what happened next, as long as she lived. The nyad hissed at him, then fractured – it was the only word for what happened – disintegrating into millions of water droplets, collapsing in a gush into the river.

'I'd close your jaw before a bird flies in,' said the man, turning.

Anya looked at him in shock. 'Did you see ...? She just... that is to say... is she dead?'

'She just ran away. You cannot kill water. What about you, Lady Anya? You are far from where you should be.'

Anya was too surprised at hearing her name to notice that the title *Lady* had been added. The man was strange: he was present in a way that no one she had seen had been – like he was bending reality around him. He was familiar. He was not tall; he had a young face crowned with an unruly set of dark brown curls; his bare torso was bronzed from too much sun; and a light covering of chest hair, curly like that on his head, sat well on him. He carried one short sword at his waist and a small leather bag, with a set of pipes lashed to it, hung from his shoulders.

'Who are you?' said Anya, regretting the words at once.

'Such a long pause for such a silly question,' said the man, smiling.

'I don't believe it ...' Anya replied as her inner voice mouthed his name.

'Ah, you wound me. Why do you not believe when you have seen the nyad and been given succour by my lady? Was I not always your favourite as a child?'

'But you can't be,' said Anya, shaking her head. 'I thought you were ... We were told ...'

'That I was dead,' sighed the god, folding his arms. 'It takes a lot to kill me, and even then, I rarely stay where I am left. Death is overrated.'

'You're really him?' said Anya.

'Pan, in the flesh and at your service,' said the god, bowing.

Anya smiled. She had been told stories of the gods and what they were like since she was old enough to listen. This creature could have stepped from one of the legends. It was true that the trickster tales had been her favourite and her grandfather had called her a little goat as a way of teasing her over her choice. The memory of the village came back to her, and the invasion. Her smile faltered. Pan didn't notice.

'Now, lady, would you mind telling me why you are in the eastern reaches of the forest when you should be on your way north?'

Anya's anger bubbled up. 'What are you talking about? We were chased from Vedic's cabin to here. We barely escaped with our lives.'

Pan looked startled, concerned. 'That was not the plan. My message got lost. Where is the woodsman? Quick now – time is against us.'

'He's not going to show up as well, is he?' asked Anya.

'I hope not,' said Pan, with a laugh that sounded forced. 'He's an insufferable bore.'

'I'm here, Pan,' said Vedic, rising from the long grass like a phantasm, bow drawn and tracking Pan's heart.

'Anya, step away from the god.'

Anya froze. Her mind had gone blank the moment the bow had been pointed in her direction. Vedic had ceased to be the woodsman: she was back in the clearing with a Kurah pointing an arrow at her. She was going to die. There had been no escape. She was still in the forest, running, and death had come to take her down to Golgotha. She felt her jaw clench so tight that she feared her teeth would crack.

'Good to see you too, Vedic,' said Pan, his tone flat but real enough to bring Anya back.

'Quiet, trickster,' said Vedic, his eyes refusing to move from the deity. 'I do not need your honeyed tongue playing tricks on me.'

Pan laughed. 'Ah, you wound me, sir! Tell me what you hope to do with a bow against a god?'

Vedic's aim wavered. 'Slow you down.'

Pan raised an eyebrow. 'Yet your bow is on fire?'

Anya watched the woodsman look in horror at his bow, his eyes registering a fire that she could not see. The forestal dropped the bow as if stung, the arrow flying into the ground at an angle. Vedic cursed and fumbled for his machete. He never made it to the blade – his left arm stopped him. The woodsman clutched the limb, cursing in a range of languages, sweat beading on his forehead and his muscles straining like cables. He fell onto his back.

Pan stepped over Vedic with his own sword drawn.

'Your health is not what it once was. Now,' said Pan, placing his blade point on Vedic's chest, 'why are you not on the northern path?'

Vedic looked up at the god with the closest thing to fury Anya had ever seen on his face. 'I have no idea what you are talking about … Is this curse your doing?'

Pan frowned. 'A messenger should have come before I got here. You should have been asked to go north, but … I can normally tell if you are lying …'

Vedic pushed the blade away and tried to sit up. 'There was no message. Just this curse that I assume is from you.'

Pan looked startled.

The woodsman frowned. 'No?'

'I sent the message in a hurry – the magic I used was not … ideal.' Pan sheathed his blade. 'But the messenger I sent should have reached you. Instead, you have been bound to the girl using crude magic by who knows what.'

Vedic shook his head. 'No messenger. Why has Danu not come?'

Vedic favoured his bad arm as he tried to sit upright in a more comfortable position, confusion writ on his face for both of them to see.

'Where is she?'

Vedic's arm was hanging at a more natural angle now, Anya thought.

Perhaps the pain had subsided? This silent thought was lost with the realisation that the god had not answered Vedic's simple question. Pan was staring back at the river with an expression that could only be described as fear. Anya looked down at her own arm and realised she had come out in goose bumps. They weren't from the cold of the stream.

'What's happened?' asked Vedic, his voice cracking. 'Where's Danu?'

Pan looked back at the woodsman, his normally bronzed skin pale. He shook his head.

'She's not dead,' said Pan, lost in his own thoughts. 'Not yet. But she is no longer the master of this forest.'

Anya felt dizzy. She sat down before she fell down. In the distance, she thought she heard a wolf howl, but it didn't really register in the quiet moment of shock. Who or what could defeat Danu? She looked over at Vedic to see the woodsman rising to shake Pan by the shoulders.

'What happened?'

Pan looked at Vedic as if seeing him for the first time. 'The gods are dead. Only Danu, the Morrigan and I remain.'

'Where is Danu?' asked Vedic. He looked as if he might still try to kill Pan – for all the good that would do.

'Danu is a prisoner. I was sent to bring you to help free her.'

'Who could do this?' asked Vedic, incredulous. His questions echoed Anya's thoughts.

Pan looked up at Vedic. 'You know there are more gods than just those who walk in the forest. Many once strode out across the world from this place, and amongst them was the hunter, a god of the forest for a time until he was exiled, and nearly as old as Danu.'

'The stag ...' whispered Anya.

Pan looked at her. 'You have seen him?'

Vedic nodded. 'He is with the wolves.'

'He has grown strong to move across the woods with such ease,' said Pan.

'I have not heard of this hunter,' said Vedic.

'He is from the oldest Shaanti legends,' said Anya, trying to recall the tale her grandfather had told her. 'From the time of sacrifice. I can't remember his name ... Cern ...'

'Cernubus,' said Pan. 'The hunter. My cousin was banished millennia ago.'

'Why?' asked Vedic.

Pan smiled sadly. 'The old ways were bloody but powerful, and nothing drives belief like seeing your gods and killing for them. The hunter was not willing to give up the blood when the rest of us decided the price was too high. Danu sent him far from the forest and the trees, where his power would be weak.'

'How has he managed to find his way back?'

'Ah, he is no longer a god – oh, he'd describe himself as such, but he has corrupted himself with other magic. That's what the tattoos are – dark magic,' said Pan. 'Anyone can reinvent themselves, isn't that right, *Vedic?*'

Anya ignored the jibe at her companion. 'If this god is so powerful, I don't understand what you expect Vedic to do.'

Pan eyed the woodsman. 'I confess I wasn't sure ...'

Vedic frowned. 'I find your confidence inspiring. Thank you, both.'

Pan continued. 'I imagine Danu's plan involves belief. My sister asked for you both, but I do not understand to what end.'

'Nothing straightforward about killing gods,' said Anya. 'You're immortal.'

Pan sighed. 'You already saw my dead cousin beneath the falls, did you not? We are immortal only while our hearts beat. If you take our heart and sever our heads, we disappear just as effectively as if you trod the paths of Asphodel in Golgotha to the Soundless Sea.'

'Then he can be defeated,' said Vedic.

Pan looked at him. 'I said gods can be defeated. Demons such as he has become, I have no idea.'

This time, the sound of the wolf was unmistakable.

'There is no time,' said Vedic, gathering his bow and snares together. 'We must leave at once. Can you help us reach the glade?'

Pan shrugged. 'I cannot be certain. The power he has is unlike anything I have ever encountered. But the alternative is death, and so what choice do any of us really have?'

'You always have a choice,' replied Vedic. 'Sometimes they're just all shit.'

'Follow me,' said Pan, heading up the hill away from the falls and their hiding place.

Anya watched Vedic head after the god. She wasn't sure about Pan: in her grandfather's tales, he was the trickster. This creature was more imp-like than she had imagined, and more serious. She didn't want to be dependent on him. The alternative was to try to find her way on alone and forgo any chance of Danu's aid falling on her. She increased her pace after them.

CHAPTER TEN

'I WON'T LET you kill us!'

The woodsman was holding the god by the shoulders, shaking him like a rag doll and shouting to be heard over the driving rain. They were all soaked. The raging storm made it next to impossible to hear anything. From time to time, the sound of the wolves howling carried on the wind, drawing ever closer. Anya thought of the stag and the once-god that the beast had transformed into.

'This is the only way,' Pan yelled back.

Why is he taking this assault? Perhaps he is afraid his magic will bring them down on us quicker?

They were on the slope of one of the mountains that rose up in the centre of the forest as if a giant were buried beneath, clawing at the sky to escape. The trees had gone from oak to pine, and if the suns had been visible, all would have been light and airy – but the storm had put paid to that. Pan wanted to go further up towards the top of the mountain, which was called Ragged Top, but Vedic had other ideas.

'We can take the Tream lands!' Vedic shouted. 'At least some have returned from there.'

'Hogarth will never let us leave!' Pan countered, pushing the woodsman away. It had been intended as a gentle shove, but Vedic was standing on slick mud and he fell, rolling, covered in the wet dirt, down the slope to the next tree. He looked up at the god, and Anya was sure that if Pan had been a man, the woodsman would have killed him with his bare hands.

Anya stepped between them.

'The wolves will be here any minute if you carry on,' she shouted. 'What is on the other side of Ragged Top Mountain?'

'No one knows,' replied Vedic.

Pan shook his head. 'We do not know for sure, but we call this the Cordon because there are ancient statues that guard the eastern and western edges. The wolves will not go into the boundary they mark.'

'There's no way we can do this,' said Vedic.

Anya silenced him with a look. 'Why can we not take the Tream lands?'

Vedic looked at Pan with accusatory eyes. 'Yes, why not, goat?'

Pan flushed. 'The gods have long fought with the Tream. They dislike our presence in their lands.'

'Surely you have shared the forest since the start of the world?' Anya asked, confused.

Pan shot Vedic a look before replying. 'It's not as simple as that, Anya. We must move. The wolves will not respect Hogarth's border, and Hogarth, the king of the Tream, may be hostile to us or even in league with Cernubus.'

'Anya, no one has ever returned from the Cordon,' countered Vedic.

Anya hesitated. 'That is why this will work.'

Vedic cursed in Kurah.

'Don't use that tongue again,' she hissed. 'Or I'll remove yours.'

Vedic blinked. 'You wouldn't get near me. Your hand shakes at the thought of killing.'

Anya smiled. 'I didn't say I'd kill you, now did I? I'm not a nice girl either ...'

Vedic laughed.

'I am Shaanti,' said Anya. 'I remember how we won the last war. Our warriors used this forest when they had been taught no one ever returned, and won the day.'

Vedic smiled. 'Well played. After you, little one. If we're going to die, let's get on with it.'

The way was steep and hard. At points, Anya had to almost crawl up the mountainside as the trees became sparse and the incline harsher. All the time the rain poured down. They slipped and slid their way up to the rock-strewn plateau from which the mountain got its name.

'We're exposed!' shouted Vedic.

Pan shook his head, lifting his hand. His fingers appeared grey and slick in the light. Anya could see that Vedic also looked greyer and darker than he normally appeared, and looking down at her own hands, she nearly missed them in the storm-light. Pan was straining with the effort of the spell. Vedic looked back across the valley, and Anya followed his gaze. At this elevation, the Kurah force were visible beyond the forest: a vast array of warriors swarming out across the plains everyone called the Barrens.

'More than last time,' said Vedic. His face was a rain-worn mask.

Pan did not reply. Anya could not look away. The wind howled around them like a trapped banshee. Vedic dragged her across the top of the mountain after Pan until they were looking down at the Cordon. The valley opened into a chasm that was so dark at its base, no light escaped. However, the rock that had been split apart millennia ago gave way to a different material before the shadows took it. The substance was like opaque crystal. The surface gleamed in the right light but was dull, translucent and glassy the rest of the time. It would not be climbable.

The rock either side had been carved into two figures that were neither god nor human – they were older than both. The statues were three times the height of a man, humanoid, but with elongated skulls and oversized eyes. Not many of their fingers remained, but they were longer, proportionately, than they would have been for man or god. The one on the west side had what looked like a weapon or stick in its right hand.

'Tream?' asked Anya.

Pan shook his head. 'The gods do not know what they were. We do not remember them, and the Tream have never told us what they believe.'

'But Danu birthed the world. How can you not know?' asked Anya, her stomach churning as it did when she saw the ghosts of her grandfather and Fin.

Pan looked haunted himself. 'Not now. We must get down from here.'

'I thought you said they would not follow,' said Vedic, his fists clenching.

'They will not,' said Pan. 'But who knows what Cernubus will do?'

Lightning flashed across the sky, lighting them up as if daytime had arrived. Thunder rumbled a few moments later.

'We need to move,' agreed Anya.

'This way,' said Pan, gesturing to a small waterway that the rainwater was pouring down. The gully looked almost like the start of an aqueduct that had been worn nearly entirely away by time. 'We'll make for the western statue and scale along its side until we get to the other side of the valley.'

'We'll need to stop soon for rest,' said Vedic. Anya did not like the way he looked at her when he said this, but she didn't see how she could argue. She had been drilled that a warrior needed to take rest when they could, and she had been operating on no sleep for far too long. Her still-healing wounds, although much improved by the woodsman's poultices, were aching, and she could have slept right there. The rain was slowing as the storm moved higher up the mountain range.

'Where are you going, little goat?'

The voice was low and deep, vibrating the base of their spines as if the words might actually be coming from inside each of them. None of them could be certain the voice wasn't. They looked up at the top of Ragged Top Mountain, but no one was there.

'You've disappeared from my view,' said the voice. 'Where are you hiding, little goat?'

Pan winced. He did not reply.

'You should be with me, little cousin,' said Cernubus. 'Are you not an echo of me?'

Pan clung tight to the rock. The rain had stopped entirely now. All was quiet save for the voice of the once-god.

'I will find you,' said Cernubus. 'You cannot hide in the forbidden places forever. Soon you will not be able to hide at all.'

Vedic tilted his head at Pan. Pan put his head to the rock briefly before nodding them on. They walked for another hour or so before they found a series of caves that looked like they had once been used by travellers before this part of the world had been abandoned.

'We should rest here,' said Vedic.

Pan looked reluctant but he nodded. Anya caught Vedic staring at her shivering.

'Can we risk a fire?' asked the forestal.

Pan looked at the woodsman. 'Where would we find dry-enough wood? If I use too much magic, we will be found.'

Vedic nodded. He pointed. 'Dead wood, piled up by one of the caves, no owner and kept dry by the rock.'

Pan shrugged. 'I don't think a fire will do any harm this far down.'

Anya was relieved. She did not like the cold. It seemed like an age since she had lain in Vedic's bed, wrapped up against the first of the storms, and woken unsure as to where she was. In reality, only a few days had passed. Only a little longer since the Kurah had thundered into her village. *No. Don't think of that.* Too late. Fin stared at her from across the cairn in which they had made their camp. She looked at her shaking hands and clenched them. *This is ridiculous,* she berated herself. *I am the granddaughter of Gobaith and Thrace. I am stronger than this.* She looked over at Pan, who was watching Vedic's efforts, lost in his own thoughts.

'Did you know my grandmother?'

The air smelt faintly of sulphur, as if Ragged Top's brother, Dragon Mountain, was active once more.

'I did,' said Pan, absent-mindedly. 'Your grandfather too.'

'What was she like?'

Pan seemed to notice Anya was there again. To truly see her. She wiped her forehead. She was still drenched from the storm. Pan moved over to sit next to her, embracing her and allowing her to rest her head on his shoulder. The closeness did not feel strange. She felt like she was resting on her grandfather.

'I see her in you. They were both part of the thain's forces when she led her army into the forest.'

'That was when they were young, before my mother was born,' said Anya. 'The war was fifty-odd years ago.'

Pan nodded. 'Do you remember your mother at all?'

Anya thought of the voice in her head that she knew was both her mother and not her mother.

'I hear her from time to time,' said Anya, shifting. 'But I cannot picture her face.'

'It is often the case when you are so young. I myself cannot remember anything from the first few hundred years of my life. My memories start up here, near the Cordon, during the first war with the Tream.'

Anya blinked. 'Why did you fight the Tream?'

Pan shrugged. 'We needed room to survive, and they did not want to move ...'

Anya did not understand. 'You said this before, but you are gods. Weren't you here first?'

Pan glanced at her. He looked worried again, as if he feared his words might bring the wolves down on them at any moment.

'You can see we exist. You can see that we are real beings, but we aren't your creators. You were already here when our memories started, as were the Tream. We came here from another place, but none of us remember when or where. It is too long ago. Just as your kind were once somewhere else, somewhere where you evolved like the trees did here or the animals Vedic was hunting the day we met.'

Anya felt light-headed. *Who created us if not the gods?* 'What is "evolved"?'

Pan smiled. 'Every time the living reproduces, they never quite manage it properly. The process introduces minor mistakes – you have a glint of gold in your left eye that none of your line had, for example – and some of those tiny changes allow some of your kind to live long enough to reproduce in greater numbers than others, which offers an advantage. Those changes then get passed on.'

'How do you know such things?' asked Anya. 'I never heard or read anything like this.'

'I have been trying to understand where we came from for a very long time. Some of the gods remembered fragments, although they are not ... they were not sure where from. Some of the trees have memories of the early times, the older ones, the ones who saw the creatures that came before us ...'

'The mad ones,' said Vedic. He was bashing two pieces of rock together to try to get a spark to kindle the unlit fire.

'Sounds like nonsense. Are you sure Danu didn't breathe life into the world and you're just attributing bad luck to her absence? What would we have evolved from?'

Vedic looked up from the smouldering fire, a grin on his face. 'He means monkeys. He's convinced that we once swung through the trees.'

Anya looked at Pan.

The god smiled. 'It's just a theory.'

'How can you be sure you didn't create the world if you don't remember?'

Pan shrugged. 'Because we are of it, just like you. We cannot leave this place or view ourselves from outside it. If we were truly creators, we would be able to, wouldn't we? And because of how we die.'

Anya had no answer.

Vedic tilted his head. 'Well, that information would seem to be important.'

Pan looked sad. 'It will not help with Cernubus. He has become chimera, a demon, and all I am referring to is our equivalent of old age. When belief dies, we become mortal and age and pass on to Golgotha, just like you.'

Anya thought of the god in the cave. He had not lost his belief. What had been done to him was violent and rage-induced.

'What of the gods Cernubus killed?'

Pan winced. 'Our belief has been waning for a while, but it is true that dismemberment, particularly removal of the heart and head, can kill us. The older, better-established gods may return. But that is an age away.'

'What of the Morrigan?' said Vedic. 'Has she not claimed them?'

Pan ignored him. 'But you asked about your grandmother ...'

Anya leant forward. 'Yes.'

Pan looked at the now-burning fire. 'She was like the flame: people were drawn to her, but those who flew too close were scorched.'

'Like my grandfather,' whispered Anya.

Pan nodded. 'She did not mean to. She could not help it. Hope is like that. I suspect that is why she left in the end. Who knows where she is now?'

Anya flushed and shook her head. 'No. My grandmother died. She was killed by a Kurah assassin. She did not get further than the mountains.'

Pan blinked. 'Yes, sorry. I get mixed up with your mother. It's so hard to keep things straight.' He tapped his head. 'My mind is a maelstrom of yesterday, today and tomorrow. You miss your mother?'

'Every day,' she replied, bitter bile in the back of her throat. 'My grandfather always said she would return when she found what she was looking for, but I suspect she never did, or she would have returned by now. No?'

Pan shrugged. 'If we lose hope, what does that leave us?'

'Rage,' said Vedic.

Pan frowned.

'Your grandmother was the finest blade I ever saw. On any field.'

Anya looked at Vedic. 'You met her?'

Vedic shook his head. 'I saw her. Not the same thing.'

'You were a warrior, then?'

Vedic raised an eyebrow. 'Or a nosy forestal?'

Pan laughed. 'Our woodsman doesn't want to give up his secrets, and who is to blame him? What is life without somewhere we can hide? Now, we should all rest.'

DARKNESS.

There is no colour. No light. No detail. Nothing. At first it feels as if I am in a void – a total loss of awareness, of up and down, of left and right. I want to try to move my arms, but I can't.

Perhaps I am dead.

Perhaps this is an in-between place.

No. I can feel the ground through my feet. I seem to be shifting from one foot to the other, but it is not me controlling my actions. Another dream? I can smell incense. Can you smell in a dream? The incense is made of pine oil – I recognise the scent from the forest. Someone has taken my arm. I am not in a void, and yet I cannot see. There is nothing covering my eyes, I am sure of that, but I cannot open them. There is a sound that makes my ears ring. I am unsure what. I shift my weight – I did not decide to do this. My body has just moved of its own accord and feels different ... like someone else's ... I have broken free of my guide, and I am running in the darkness. Somehow my feet pick a perfect path and do not falter. I feel the texture of the ground change before I realise I've entered a large room where the floor is made of stone. The thought, that this is a temple, comes unbidden as if there is another mind in here with me.

I still cannot see. Someone has started speaking. I can't understand what is being said as the speaker draws closer to me. I flinch when someone touches my face, pawing at me with hot, dry hands. I cannot tell if I moved my body or if someone else did. The contact is so unwelcome; I imagine both of us want to escape. This is worse than anything I have ever experienced. I'm not able to move, or see, or understand the purpose of the touching. Only that a paste is now being smeared over my eyes, wet and cold.

The person applying the mixture pulls me about like I am an errant child refusing to scrub my face and hands. The examination stops just as suddenly as it began, and I feel the calloused hand slide round to rest on the back of my neck. Someone new is shouting at me as I am propelled forward to another part of the temple, somewhere equally black and devoid of detail in my veil of blindness. Standing still, I can start to orientate myself, and by the smell of one of them, I know this is the person who brought me into this place. I cannot tell who has the staff that is clicking down on the stone flags as they pace. The clicking draws close until the owner stops in front of me, and I am able to conclude they are not my guide.

The tone of the question the man asks is hard to ascertain because he speaks so fast. The person who I am a passenger in responds. I, Anya, scream inside their head, but my host speaks with a brash enthusiasm. They cannot hear me. The words my host speaks are not in a language I understand.

The man with the staff begins to sing. A croaked, ancient singing voice that is soporific. He places his hand on my forehead. His palm is hot on my skin as he continues in a half chant, and the chanting is starting to hurt my ears as he rises in volume. My skull feels like someone is levering it up with an axe-head and pushing their fingers down behind my nose. A curious sensation that seems to grow with each passing line until only the people who have moved either side behind me keep me standing, their hands digging into my arms. The singer's left hand is wrapped around the top front of my skull, and his other is round my back as he reaches a crescendo. I can smell his breath, acrid and stale. I feel the world shift as whatever the man has done drops me to the ground like a puppet whose strings have been cut. I narrowly avoid splitting my skull on the stone floor.

For a moment, I am as disorientated as when I realised I was blind. A flicker. There, on the periphery of my vision: a small bead of light smears across the black, but when I try to look straight at it, all is dark. I try to stand. Pain drives me to my knees. A slamming, stabbing sensation in my skull has me calling out, and I do not need to understand myself to know I am asking for mercy.

Moments later I realise that my vision is altering from the endless void. Light bleeds into my eyes and explodes in fractal reflections as my vision returns. The light, the colour, is painful to eyes shut up in the dark for so long and makes me blink and squint as I take in my surroundings.

I see the temple. A vast chamber made of stone carved into bizarre curves and bends, rather like a collection of tree roots. There is nothing else like this temple in my memory. The two men with me do not look particularly large, certainly not as big as I thought when I could not see them. One is as old as sin, and the other is barely a man, his eyes uncertain as they flick from his companion to me and back again. Both are clad in white robes.

I whisper.

The older man asks a question, and I reply with the same two words, but louder. The younger man asks a different question, and I move my gaze right to him before replying and sending his face crimson.

I'm not listening to them. My attention has fallen on a large statue that sits on one corner of the dais and reaches to the ceiling of the chamber. My eyes shift to the construction of a raised platform. There are channels criss-crossing the surface in a seemingly pointless pattern. I step closer to the statue, close enough to put my hand on the smooth stone of the leg.

I am moving again now, striding down the chamber back towards the door. My host pauses occasionally to touch surfaces that, until now, we only had texture memories for. The afternoon sun is painfully bright as I emerge into the light of day, and I cover my eyes from the glare. My eyesight takes a good few minutes to adjust, and then, from my vantage point on the hill, I can see the lower districts of the stone city spread out below me. I gasp. I wave the other men closer and speak so quickly they struggle to keep up with my outburst.

Hooves strike the ground like rain; a group of riders comes at speed up the hill. There are eight bodyguards in the group, and one king. The king is gnarled with age, swathed in purple. He slides from his horse and approaches the old man at my side. The conversation is quick and harsh but ends with the king slapping the old man on the back with what looks like relief. Only then does the ruler notice me and ask a question that has to mean 'Who is this?'

I reply before either of my companions gets a word out. The man's eyebrows go up at my host's words, and his eyes flick to the elder man by my side. The king turns back to my host, taking in my appearance in more detail this time, feeling my arms and legs for muscle. Satisfied with what he finds, the king steps back with a smile before turning to the others and remounting his horse. He issues what sound like instructions before turning his horse down the hill. I find myself led back into the church towards the dais. I do not resist.

They place me on the dais, in the small, shallow dip in the centre. I grow worried as the older man returns with a knife that gleams in the afternoon sun, and the younger man rips open the front of my tunic.

I am different. The world is outside of me. I cannot understand why. The older man speaks softly as he traces the point of the blade down my flat chest. He booms out words I can't translate as he draws back the knife and swings as if he intends to impale me upon it. He stops. Just short of stabbing me through the chest, close enough to draw blood but not deep enough to slice bone or sinew.

My host lets out a breath I was not aware was being held. The older man places the knife back in his belt and claps. The younger man seems to express disbelief as he leads me out the back of the dais into cooler chambers beyond, my torn tunic flapping in the draught.

This part of the building is darker than the rest, and I enter a room filled with beds. The younger man leads me to a bed near the room's only window. His *words are short but not unkind as he points to a neatly folded, fresh white tunic that sits on the bed. I say nothing but nod when expected, waiting for the man to take his leave, and soon he does. I lie down on the bed. My eyes close.*

THE PRESENCE WOKE ANYA FIRST.

The creature was underneath her. She could feel the beast on the edge of her dream. It darted round, tumbled this way and that, flicking from one side of her to the other, like an eel formed of magic. As she became fully aware of the creature, the thing darted away to somewhere near Pan, and as the god stirred, she felt the energy leap further to Vedic.

'What is it?' she hissed at Pan.

The god shook his head. He did not know.

Vedic nipped up from his prone position with his axe in hand.

'What in Golgotha?'

The figure stood on the edge of the shadows just outside the cave, where the firelight faded. They were hooded in a grey cowl, neither their hands nor face were visible. The person was somewhere between Vedic's and Cernubus's height.

The figure spoke in a sibilant tone of indeterminate gender. 'This place is forbidden.'

'Morrigan,' hissed Vedic.

'No,' said Pan, raising his hand to stay the woodsman. He stood and moved out of the cave as close as he dared to the figure. 'I would know if it were her.'

'You cannot harm me,' said the creature to Vedic. 'I died when your kind were still in the trees.'

The figure turned to Pan.

'But you should know. There are protocols.'

Pan frowned. 'I know that our need was dire, and no other option had a chance.'

'You have erred. Things are breaking down as the alignment approaches. You must leave or all is lost.'

'The scarred one of my kind, the scarred god, he is coming for us.'

'That is why you must go.'

Pan turned to respond.

'Leave!' commanded the figure, and lightning broke from the ground and connected with Pan.

The god fell, skin smoking, and did not move. Vedic jumped for the stranger, but his axe swung through thin air. Anya went to Pan. The trickster had rolled onto his back and was drawing in deep lungfuls of air, staring at the blank black sky.

'Why are you always right?' asked the god.

'Because I pay attention,' said Vedic. 'You take your mind for granted.'

Anya could feel the presence below them. It darted and flicked around as if it were – worm-like – swimming through the earth.

'We are in trouble,' said Pan, pulling himself to his feet.

'I told you this was a bad idea,' hissed Vedic.

'Yes,' said Anya, her irritation showing. 'We're both very impressed with your prescient insight. Can we get across the valley before—?'

The ground shook, dropping Anya and Vedic to their knees. Pan tilted his head as if listening. The dark made it hard to see, but there was a noise like the grinding of rock on rock, and the shadows appeared to be unfolding from the sides of the hill, growing taller and taller.

'What in the goddess …?' breathed Vedic.

'The statues,' said Anya, her throat feeling dry and craggy like the mountain. 'The statues are coming alive.'

Pan gestured straight up the mountainside they were on.

'We must get back over the ridge.'

The first boulder struck the ground very close to the god and with enough force to throw him several yards. He lay there for a second before rolling to his feet. Vedic was already dragging Anya, without the few supplies and weapons they had, up the mountainside.

'Our packs!'

Vedic hissed in her ear. 'Rule one: survive …'

Pan turned from them, his hands glowing as he faced the emerging statues. The sky rained stone and wood as the things lurched and grabbed at whatever they could. The western statue, clutching its baton, was in striking distance and swung down to hit Pan. The god let loose his power by bringing his hands together, and a red beam of light flew from them, striking the statue in its back. The impact shook the whole valley.

Anya looked back at Pan, but the god was on his knees. 'He's going to get killed.'

Vedic shook his head. 'A little gnawed on, perhaps, but they can't kill him.'

'What good would he be to us then?'

Vedic frowned. He clearly didn't want to concede the point, but behind everything was the realisation that he would have to face Cernubus eventually. Anya wondered what hold Danu had on him that he would even think of it. Unbidden, the image of children's hands reaching for her from the dark rose up. *Wait,* she told herself, *I am coming for you.*

'Wait here,' he said.

The other statue jumped across the fissure at the foot of the valley, fist raised. The creature brought the hand down so fast there was a sound like a screaming wraith as it drilled into the ground where Pan knelt. The force of the impact sent Anya onto her back. She rolled in the mud and looked up.

The relief of seeing Pan and Vedic sprawled in the dirt a few feet from the statue's fist was short-lived. As the creature turned to seek Pan, the god shoved the woodsman away as the foot of the statue came down towards them.

The foot stopped about two feet above Pan, cracking against a shield that the god had hastily pulled up but driving him to his knees once more. They stayed like that for a moment, locked against each other. Then Pan began, sweat pouring down him, to stand once more. He shoved up with his hands, and the statue flew up into the air as if hit with an uppercut. The figure landed across the other side of the fissure. A leg draped over the edge.

Pan collapsed.

Vedic grabbed Pan and hoisted him up over his shoulders. Clutching the god's wrist against his leg with one hand and his axe with the other, he ran past Anya.

'Follow me,' he said. 'They will be back.'

Anya hesitated for a moment, looking back at her makeshift weapon and the blankets that had been discarded. In the distance, she could see the prone statues twitching, and the presence that had woken her was not far away. There was no time. She ran after the forestal as he raced to make the top of the valley.

Near the top, the ground shook once more, and they were spilled onto the rock.

'What now?' asked Pan, wearily.

Anya peered through the grey light of dawn. The fissure in the valley's floor was like a black, malevolent mouth, a smear of shadow darker than everything else. The blackness was moving and extending out onto the solid ground all around. A third statue unfurled with a metallic grinding noise until a hand was clasping onto the rock hard enough to hear the sound of crushing stone.

'There are more of them,' she whispered.

Vedic was already on his feet, dragging Pan further up the mountain with him. Anya did not need his encouragement to move again as rocks started landing all around them, thrown by the three statues as they moved up the slope after them. The top of the valley was still being battered by high winds, and they were almost crawling as they reached the peak. The weather was clearer than earlier: there was no rain, and the coming sunrise was painted on the horizon. The forest stretched out before them, seeming so much bigger than it did on maps that Anya had seen her grandfather pore over in the time before his drinking really got out of hand. Anya let herself hope for a moment that they would get to Danu easily.

'There you are, little cousin.'

Anya felt her heart stop. She looked across the ridge, three peaks over, at the unmistakable human form of Cernubus standing in shadow, looking over at them, surrounded by the full pack of wolves. Vedic moved between Anya, Pan and the enemy. He did not flinch or show any sign of fear as he raised his axe.

'No, forestal,' said Pan, pushing himself to his feet and limping forward. 'You cannot win this fight. I must face him.'

Vedic looked at him. 'But you cannot win. You already told me that. At least Danu thought I had a chance.'

'Not like this,' said Pan. 'You will fall if you try, and then what will become of Anya?'

Vedic looked over at her. She wasn't convinced he cared either way, and she was damned sure she didn't like feeling that she needed rescuing.

'I ...'

'Danu said both of you,' said Pan, softly.

'What about the Tream?'

Pan smiled sadly. 'You said it yourself, they may not even notice you're there. If you do see the Tream and he is amongst them ...'

Vedic held the god's gaze for a moment. 'I will tell Akyar.'

Pan nodded.

Cernubus and his hunting party had swept to the second peak now. The tattoos on his upper body were visible in the sunrise, writhing like snakes across his skin.

Pan flicked his wrists, and power surged into his hands, purple in the right and red in the left.

'Do you intend to show me some fireworks, little cousin?' asked Cernubus, laughing.

Anya shook her head as Vedic approached her. 'We can't just leave him.'

Vedic grabbed her arm. 'We have no choice – let his sacrifice have meaning. If we are still here when the wolves hit this side, we will die.'

Anya's last glimpse of Pan was as the god was beginning to weave a bigger shield than last time, the side of the hill still shaking as the statues climbed up the inside of the valley. Was he going to ...?

Vedic pushed her down into the treeline. They were running for their lives when the top of the mountain exploded and the world became light.

CHAPTER ELEVEN

'How long have we known each other?'

Jeb did not answer. He lifted his right eyebrow in a gesture as familiar to the thain as her own face. She remembered being given that look during her very first lesson on tactics from the only-five-years-older-than-her Jeb. Her mother had been adamant that he was the best mind in the clans to teach her to use her head before she learned to use her blade. She had been only twelve at the time. That felt like a hundred years ago. She heard her mother's voice, wry amusement in every word, pointing out it actually was nearly a century ago.

'I'll remind you,' she forced herself to continue. 'A very long time. I hope in that time you have built up trust in me.'

They were in her chambers. Bene was outside the door for security and for the sake of propriety, given Golan's propensity to use any little infraction of protocol to his own advantage. The thain was standing by her burning fire, warming her bones and sipping wine, while Jeb was sitting on the spare chair she kept for the odd audience she granted to her subjects.

'Milady knows I am ever her servant,' said Jeb.

Did she imagine the tone in his voice? A contradiction unspoken ...

'What is on your mind, old friend?' she asked.

Jeb sighed. 'I have never been able to hide anything from you.'

'Why would you?' she asked, her voice hurt. If she could not trust Jeb, her oldest confidant, she was alone.

Jeb looked round, as if seeking an escape tunnel. There was no way to avoid his old friend. He had been asked a direct question by his thain, and he must answer.

'One of my people saw a shadow leave your room,' he said.

It was an old fight. Jeb had kept the secret for so long they rarely spoke of the shadow any more, but he had broken that unspoken détente.

'That is not your concern,' she whispered. 'My people must bring me the information I seek when the council doesn't operate for the defence of our realm.'

Jeb nodded. 'This shadow stayed a long time. Was there much intelligence?'

The thain glared at him.

He raised his arms in surrender. *You asked* ...

'I must send you on one last mission,' she said.

Jeb blinked.

'What is that?'

The thain looked away from him. She was ashamed. She was going to send this man who was so near the end of his life he barely left the city walls at all on a journey that might kill him, even if he did succeed.

'I need you to go to the forest.'

Jeb stared at her like she had gone mad. 'Even if I got there, what do you hope to achieve?'

'You have your people in the city,' said the thain. 'Mine roam far and wide, bringing me intelligence of what they have seen, and our borders are collapsing. In order to survive, we need the forest and at the very least the safe passage that only the gods can bestow. Of those of us granted leave to enter, you and I are the only surviving members now Falkirk has died. I cannot leave. I must send you.'

Jeb poked at the fire with his stick. He looked as if he were stoking the flames against the journey to come.

'Of course,' he said. 'I will go, but I am unsure if I will return, even if she agrees.'

'I know,' said the thain. She felt as though she were three hundred years old.

'What do you think will happen? Will they help us?'

The thain shrugged. 'Who knows where the gods are concerned? I never fathomed Danu's reasons when we used to see her every day. That was a long time ago.'

'Golan will never accept the assistance of the gods,' said Jeb. 'He thinks we made them up to secure our power base.'

'Thankfully, Golan does not actually head the council, contrary to what he seems to think – that is still my task. This is our best option.'

The thain's eyes settled on the small likeness of her son that she had hanging from the wall above her bed. The firelight flickered an orange beast in the reflection of the mirrors in the room.

'You should never have formed the council,' said Jeb. 'It is misplaced guilt that led us here.'

The thain found herself unable to look away from her son's dark eyes.

'He was such a beautiful child,' she said, her voice soft. 'So gentle.'

Jeb lit his pipe. 'Too gentle for this world. I am sorry, Robin. I have not stopped being sorry since the day they brought him back.'

'You haven't called me that in ten years,' she said. His old nickname for her dated back to her first lessons with him. She had been a defiant talker when all he wanted was silence.

'Well, you haven't needed it in a while,' he said, a ghost of a smile on his lips.

'Maybe I did force us down this road too soon,' said the thain. 'But not out of guilt. My son saw what we would not. Who power resides with is the toss of the dice, but at least with a council, there is some say, some chance to correct a misthrow.'

'But only if the person tells the truth. Golan does not.'

'Yes,' said the thain. 'We have arrived at the problem. Not everyone thinks the same, or with the wisdom we have obtained ...'

Jeb laughed. 'You jest with me.'

The thain smiled. 'Only a little.'

'Perhaps we should have drawn council members at random.'

The thain frowned. 'Perhaps. Too late now. We must press on as we are or risk everything. Will you take the mission?'

Jeb rose from the chair, sucked on his pipe and exhaled.

'On one condition.'

The thain tilted her head, waiting for the constraint.

'How sick are you?'

The question drove the air out of her as if he had struck her in the stomach, and she placed one hand out on the mantel to steady herself.

'How?'

'The good doctor did not betray you,' said Jeb. 'No one knows but me and the person who observed the doctor visiting this wing. I am not sure even they will have drawn the connection. I worked it out myself.'

The thain walked to her chair and sat down. She placed her head in her hands. She could not bring herself to tell him.

Jeb swore. 'How long do you have?'

'Stop it.'

'Stop what?'

'Reading me like I'm one of your bloody books.'

Jeb shuffled over to her. His walking stick clacked on the stone like a giant insect approaching. He placed a hot, dry hand on her shoulder.

'I am sorry you felt you had to carry this alone,' he said. 'I would ... I will keep your secret. But you must not let the council take your place. You must appoint an heir.'

The old man was not telling her anything she did not know. The council were not ready. She had too little time to prepare, and yet she'd had so many years since she made that promise. She looked back up at her son's image. So long since she had held his head, the life leaving him, even as she had cradled him on the steps of the city like he was still a little boy.

'We all have the same time,' she whispered.

Jeb said nothing. He had heard her mother say that when he, too, was young. She knew that much. They had debated the truth of the saying when trekking round the Shaanti with the then thain, dealing with all the petty rivalries that had seemed so important before the Kurah came the first time.

The knock broke the silence.

'Yes, Bene, what is it?'

The general stepped into the room. 'Milady, Golan is down by the city wall, questioning the deployment of troops and food reserves.' The thain could feel Jeb's temper bubbling without turning.

'To be expected, I am afraid,' she replied. 'I will be along shortly, once I have seen our emissary off. Go to the wall and give Golan fair warning. If he causes trouble, I will have him arrested.'

THEY TOOK the ancient secret passage known as the hidden road from her quarters.

The network of corridors and paths had been lain down centuries ago to allow the thain to move from one part of the city to the other without being seen or being put at risk. She did not want Jeb's departure noted by her opposition on the council or the panic of the flightier, realising she was invoking the gods. They might realise how dire their situation was. How had she let it come to this? She coughed against the thought and tried to ignore the coppery aftertaste.

'You should not be out this late,' observed Jeb. 'I can saddle my own horse.'

They were at the gate. A chestnut gelding was waiting, saddled and provisioned, and held at the reins by one of the thain's shadows.

'You would not have provisioned enough food,' said the shadow, 'and would have starved before you got there.'

Jeb stopped.

'You said you were sending me alone,' he said, voice creaking. 'Why have you sent her to see me off?'

Here it comes, thought the thain. 'She is to go with you, old friend. I wish you to arrive alive and return in the same state. Indulge an old warrior.'

'I promise not to pick a fight,' said the shadow, her voice sad.

'Sister,' said Jeb. 'Our fight has gone on for thirty years. I do not see that it shall end this night simply because a robin has sat on our path and refused to budge.'

The thain smiled.

'I am not seeking to interfere,' she said. 'I need the two people I trust more than anyone else for this mission. I do not wish to send either of you away.'

'You know exactly what you are doing!' hissed Jeb.

'You promised,' she replied, softly. Then, louder, 'Let us part as friends, Lord Jeb.'

The thain pulled him into a hard embrace. She was certain that, successful or not, she would not see him again. Her moments of foresight were short and partial, but she had learned not to ignore them.

'She does not know. See my secret is kept,' she whispered in his ear.

Jeb did not reply, but the thain saw by his eyes that he had understood. The shadow's horse, the colour of night, made no noise but shifted on his hooves as Jeb made his way over to his own mount. He slid the stick he used to help him walk between the saddlebags and pulled himself into the saddle with the practised skill of a younger rider. He did not take the hand the shadow offered him.

'I am not completely without skill,' he said.

The shadow's face was unreadable as she went from looking at her brother to looking at her thain.

'Do not feel awkward on my behalf,' said Jeb. His voice was hoarse. 'I lost this battle a long time ago.'

The thain smiled. Yet she could not show how she felt in such an exposed location. Though she had taken every care, the risk was too great. As had been their custom between each other for decades, the thain touched her fingertips to her lips and watched her shadow do the same.

'Until tomorrow,' she heard the shadow whisper.

The thain climbed the city wall to watch them ride into the night. Somewhere, Golan was causing trouble again, and she should have gone straight there before he made foolish errors that would cost a great deal to undo. But she did not. She stood there watching them go, wondering about the feeling she had when she hugged Jeb, and trying to take comfort that her shadow had not given her the same thought. The guilt that followed made her feel sicker than she had in weeks.

'YOU WILL TAKE this grain back to the stores,' said Golan. 'I command it.'

The battalion chief, in whose face Golan was shouting, did not respond to the councillor's order, nor did he need to look at the rest of his men, who were all stood at attention. General Bene stood to one side of Golan, red-faced and angry but silent following a very public argument with Golan.

'Do not ignore me!' yelled the councillor like a petulant toddler. 'Order your men to return this grain.'

'I am not ignoring you, sir,' said the commander. 'I am following the direct orders of the thain.'

'And I am a member of her council.'

'And contradicting her orders.'

'The outer guard obeyed my orders to withdraw from the city road and make good the perimeter.'

'You mean that guard?' said Bene, pointing out over the wall at the very visibly-not-moving outer guardsmen, who were erecting camp just outside the city. By morning the refugees from the sacked villages would start arriving, a chaotic settlement that would weaken their defence and make spotting infiltrators from the Kurah almost impossible.

Golan looked out at the men and women moving in defiance of his orders. The man's cheeks flushed. He clenched his fists. The thain watched all of this from the shadows where she had come to a stop. Her custom was to occasionally use the hidden roads to arrive at sections of the city and listen to her people without them knowing she was there. This small abuse of privacy helped her stay grounded. When she felt her faith in the council dip, as it had currently, she reminded herself of the damage an individual could do with this access to people's places of work and homes.

'This is a *coup d'état*,' said Golan. 'The council will hear of this. It will be civil war.'

'We are already at war,' hissed Bene. 'That's the reason for the orders.'

'The thain no longer commands by sole decree,' said Golan, gathering up his robes like a peacock preparing to show its feathers.

'What is going on here?' asked the thain. She enjoyed the way the fat councillor jumped more than he should. Bene's relief was palpable, and for one moment, she thought he might embrace her.

'The outer guardsmen have lied to me and ignored my orders,' said Golan. 'These men are also refusing my orders but at least have the decency to do it to my face.'

The thain moved forward. 'I see. At ease, warriors,' she said, putting her hand on the commander's shoulder. The warriors relaxed a little. 'What are your orders, Lord Golan?'

'That they move the grain back into the city and the outer guardsmen maintain the perimeter. We cannot be defending and feeding a bunch of refugees at times like this – what if they are Kurah in disguise? What if we run out of food?'

The thain eyed his belly. 'I'm sure we can sustain ourselves on a little less than normal, if we need to.'

The councillor flushed as the warriors did little to hide their smirks. The thain thought this might have been an error on her part, but she no longer cared too much about Golan. He would need to be removed. She saw that now.

'My Lord Golan, if we did not help our own subjects, who have lost their homes and their livelihoods to the Kurah, what do you think will happen to the survivors?'

'They will find new places to live and new jobs to do.'

'Do you think they will be well disposed towards us?'

'I, er ...'

'Do you think they will come to the aid of the clans when we need to defend ourselves?'

'We don't have enough ...'

'I will tell you what will happen,' said the thain. 'They will tell themselves we do not care about their lives, and they will decide they do not care about the clans. At best they will not accept our rule; at worst they will join our enemy. Any ruler, even in a monarchy, can only really govern with the consent of the subjects. Real power just ebbs away otherwise. You see I am explaining this in terms that you will understand. And there is another reason.'

'What's that?'

'It is the right thing to do,' she replied, softly.

'Control of the grain stores are the purview of the council and my ministry,' insisted Golan. 'These orders are lunacy.'

The thain stared at him. 'Are you challenging my authority?' Her hand drifted to her sword.

Golan was not armed. She doubted he had fought since his childhood. She almost felt sorry for him off the back of his startled look. He had not meant to go so far.

'No,' he said. 'I merely ...'

'A hostile nation's army has invaded our lands – we are at war,' said the thain. 'Decisions pertaining to the defence of the clan lands – not just the city – reside with me. That includes supplies and managing the outer guard.'

Golan just stood there, his mouth opening and shutting.

'Commander, you are relieved,' said the thain.

Golan smiled. The commander looked shocked.

'Commander, please escort Lord Golan back to his house,' the thain continued. Golan's smile had gone. The commander was suppressing a laugh. 'Ensure he stays there until morning, when I can make time to explain things to the council.'

'Yes, milady,' said the commander. He turned to the merchant. 'This way, sir.'

Golan stared at the thain. There was a vein near the surface of the skin on his right temple that was pulsing as if he had run a marathon, and he was sweating despite the cold.

'I suggest you follow him,' said the thain. 'I will have you arrested otherwise.'

'You wouldn't dare,' said Golan.

'Wouldn't I?' said the thain, stepping close to him. 'These men have sworn to live and die by my orders, Golan. They don't much like you, anyway. How much consent do you think I need to get from them to do what I want?'

Golan eyed the warriors. He turned and stormed off, followed by the commander, who could not contain his sarcasm as he called after him.

'No, sir, wait. You might get hurt without an escort.'

'Commander,' she warned, softly.

'Sorry, milady,' said the commander. She knew he wasn't. 'As you were, warriors.'

The warriors dispersed back to their posts, leaving the thain with Bene, looking out from the wall into the night.

'How many refugees so far?' she asked.

Bene placed his hands on the wall. 'Around sixty. They'll still be taking refugees into the city for a day or so, I imagine, but if the force got further than Anaheim, we can expect that to quadruple from the places Falkirk rode through.'

'How long can we last with a siege?'

'A year on rations, assuming there are no illnesses,' said Bene. 'Which there will be, because there always are. We must not get trapped in here.'

The thain nodded. 'I am already taking steps to ensure this does not happen.'

'What steps?'

'I cannot say yet,' said the thain. 'But in the meantime, we must face facts. If we cannot stay and survive, we will need to move, and that means our supplies need to travel with us. Start looking into how we might manage this. Be discreet. I don't want a panic.'

Bene nodded. 'How has he managed it?'

'Who? Golan?'

Bene shook his head. 'No, Montu. How has he managed to march on us so soon after Delgasia fell? Surely, his lines would be stretched to breaking point.'

The thain nodded. 'The boy is wily. Who can say? But there is a chance in that. He may repeat the mistakes of his ancestors.'

'As satisfying as that was to watch,' said Bene, 'you humiliated Golan.'

The thain shrugged. 'I may have gone too far. But Lord Golan could do with some humiliation. Perhaps he will reflect on his less helpful qualities between now and dawn.'

The two of them stood watching the night.

Time. I need more time. That idea echoed through the thain's mind as she tried to think of new ways to approach the problem, new ways to see her people safe before she was pulled away from this world to Golgotha. The doctor's words were always just a little way behind each idea, circling back to remind her that time was short.

CHAPTER TWELVE

THE WOLVES WERE ALMOST on them.

Daylight had arrived but the storm had returned. Rain battered every exposed part of the forest, and everything was wet and slick. They were covered in mud from numerous falls. Vedic had the only weapon, and to fight would mean defeat at best. Beyond the mountains still visible in the distance, Anya had little idea where in the forest they were or what chance of hiding they had, but she had to follow Vedic or she might as well surrender. The woodsman led them down the slope as if he ran up and down Ragged Top all the time. His feet rarely missed their place. His head hardly turned around to check she was there or look back up at the duel raging behind them on the mountain. Only the scream stopped him.

It was Pan. They both knew it, and the pain behind the scream made them feel as though they, too, were being hurt, deep down in their bones. Anya gasped: she felt as if her heart had exploded. Vedic turned round, his face a mask as he looked back. He did not move.

'We have to go back,' Anya said.

Vedic shook his head. 'He would not thank us. The battle is over; he has lost. The entire pack will be coming for us.'

There was a sound like even heavier rain coming down the mountain.

'Here they come,' said Vedic. He grabbed her hand, and before she could object, he was half dragging and half pulling her down and across the slope towards who knows what.

They burst through another collection of trees. A wolf glared up at them with yellow eyes and a dripping jaw. The thing would have reached the height of Vedic on its hind legs. The woodsman let go of her hand and hurled his axe before the wolf had time to leap. The weapon cleaved the animal's skull in two, and the beast collapsed on its belly. He pulled the axe free and was about to speak when Anya saw another wolf leap and tackle him.

The woodsman swore in what sounded like Kurah, muffled by the fight. He made an untidy defence. He let the creature bite down on his left wrist guard while he knocked at the wolf's head with the blunt side of the axe until it split open and the creature retreated a few feet away, whimpering. Vedic leapt up and beheaded the wolf in one swift swing.

Anya rushed down to him. 'We need to get out of here.'

Vedic nodded. 'The gully is there.' He gestured at a few feet further down, where the hillside seemed to fall away. 'River. Another jump, I am afraid.'

Anya nodded. 'It'll mask our scent.'

'Yep, as much as we can, and the speed of the current will carry us away from here faster than we can run.'

'What's the but?'

Anya never got an answer. There was a growling from all around, and glowing yellow eyes appeared amongst the trees. There were too many wolves to make fighting a suitable plan. Vedic grabbed her again and part carried, part threw her off the gully edge before jumping himself. She hit the water with a force like she had hit solid ground from horseback. The air left her lungs, but she fought down the panic and kicked herself back to the surface. She had no pack to weigh her down, just the clothes and light boots she was wearing. She thought about kicking the boots off – they were pulling at her feet – but she would need them later.

The first rule is survive ... came her mother's voice in her mind. She kicked off the boots.

Vedic swam to her. Above she could hear wolves howling in confusion.

'Are you hurt?'

Anya shook her head.

'Boots off?'

Anya nodded.

'Good job,' said Vedic, unusually nice. Anya thought, *He's afraid.*

'We have to swim, but we need to avoid being seen. Try to stay under and hold your breath as long as possible. Do you understand?'

Anya nodded again. She took several progressively deeper breaths, as her grandfather had taught her when she was young. He'd taught her to swim almost as soon as she could walk. Sometimes she thought he had used teaching her as a distraction after her mother left. Eventually, he had run out of things he wanted to teach her, leaving only the knowledge he didn't want to discuss, and his trips to the tavern got longer and longer.

'THE KNACK *of staying under for long periods of time is to stay relaxed,' she heard him say. They were at the small lake near Harmony on a summer's day over a decade ago. 'You do this by remaining very calm.'*

Anya frowned. 'What if I don't feel very calm?'

Thrace smiled. 'You focus on seeing your rage from the outside, like it's a storm. You can imagine the clouds and the lightning and the thunder. If you have ever watched a storm from a distance, they can be very calming, like you're watching the gods dance from a safe vantage point.'

ANYA PUSHED ALL her thoughts of Pan, of Fin, of her grandfather and the Kurah into a storm for the ages and retreated to a safe distance to watch as she dived under the surface. She glimpsed a blurry Vedic swimming away ahead before she closed her eyes and kicked after him.

THEY WERE bone-weary when they pulled themselves from the river.

Anya could see a faint blue tinge to her fingers. The woodsman looked to have aged around thirty years in the dying embers of the day. They had been swimming and hiding for a long time. She started to gather firewood.

'No,' said Vedic. 'It's not safe to light a fire here.'

Anya stiffened. 'We'll freeze to death.' She was already shivering.

Vedic was also shaking. This was a loss of control that she would not have expected from him under any circumstances. 'We will need to keep moving to avoid getting too cold and to avoid getting caught. This part of the forest is not friendly.'

Anya raised her eyebrows. 'Tream?'

Vedic nodded.

'We have no boots,' she said, looking at the ground, littered with stones, twigs and sharp pieces of broken bark.

'We're not going to walk down here,' said Vedic. 'Too risky with the wolves. We're going up there.' He slapped one of the tree trunks.

'But first,' he said, 'some camouflage.'

Vedic knelt down and started smearing wet mud all over his exposed skin and his clothes. As he did so, he gradually started to blend into the forest. Anya knelt and started to do the same thing. As the mud started to cover more and more of her body, she started to feel less and less cold.

'It is warm,' she said.

Vedic nodded. 'The forest offers most of what we need. You just need to be mindful of where.'

Vedic went easy on her with the climb. They carefully walked a little distance until they found a tree gently tapering upwards. The wood felt a little rough underfoot, but the mud helped soften the scratching of the bark. The tree itself was warm to the touch, a low heat that was very welcome after the cold of the river, and she would have hugged the trunk left to her own devices.

The trees here were larger than most of the ones they had come across, with the possible exception of the evergreens on the edge of the Corden. You could walk comfortably across most of the branches, and the leaves were the size of plates, big enough to catch and hold the rainwater, and of a luscious waxy texture. The scent of them hung in the air. At first the smell was pleasant, but after a few hours, Anya just felt light-headed.

Vedic made them carry on until Anya started to miss her footing. The second time she did, she tripped, sitting down on the branch in shock, and he knelt beside her.

'You need rest,' he said. 'If one of us falls from up here, it will hurt.'

Anya looked around: there was no platform from which they would not roll while asleep and do as much damage.

Vedic smiled. 'I didn't lose everything.'

The woodsman unwrapped a roll of rope from around his torso and looped it around the trunk once and round his waist before he tied it off. He repeated the exercise with Anya.

'If you lie with your back against the tree,' he said, 'you're much less likely to roll off.'

Anya drifted off the moment she lay down. Her last observation as she did so was that she could have sworn she saw eyes blinking at her from the dark of the canopy above. What a strange dream ...

———

THE SUN IS *a burning fire of molten gold in the azure sky.*

Yet the stone under my hands feels cool. The glare reflecting from the stone walls and marble floor makes me squint in the midday sun. I have never felt heat like this. It is oppressive, stifling, and I long for soft grass beneath my feet, to feel cool spring water slide down my throat. The ground seems too far away. There are no trees that I can see, nothing green within sight at all. This feels wrong. I realise I am not alone: all around the stone and the dirt-streaked marble are people, more people than I've ever seen before in my life. I am Anya and not Anya. Where am I?

I appear to be on a podium. A sick feeling spreads through my stomach as the noise of the crowd fills my ears. It is disorientating, a tornado of sound that bounces off every surface. I'm standing in a town square. I am the focus of every-one's attention. I feel like I am cooking in the sun, or perhaps under the gaze of the crowd. The world is as hot as the forge. I lean heavily on the podium, but I did not will the movement. Perhaps I am about to faint. Will they bring me water if I do?

This isn't right. I feel heavier, my chest feels ... different – as if I am carved from the stone. Smooth curves of thick muscle move under my robe; my arms flex against my skin, threatening to split it with the movement beneath. Fresh scars catch on my rough clothing. I push back into an upright position, but again I did not perform the action. I feel more aware of the world as a thing outside of myself.

My host begins to speak, and I cannot understand the words spilling from our face. I only know that they are not Shaanti. The crowd falls to silence as my voice grows louder. I can feel their eyes on me – I can see the light in their faces as they hang on my words like a rope that is holding them safe above a terrible chasm. I believe I could say anything to them and they would follow me. An exultant feeling. I feel their attention flow through me. This is delicious, like warm spiced wine, and my head spins with it as if I have had too much. My host continues, expounding on their theme, hands rising and falling on the podium. No one has escaped the net of words my host has cast with the skill of a master fisherman. Once again I have no control. Who is speaking?

The crowd has filled the square and is made up of every type of person: small children, old men, wives, smiths, merchants, peddlers, whores and warriors. They all stand shoulder to shoulder, cheek by jowl, all looking at me, all listening to me. I have them utterly in my power, and it is good. There is no revulsion here, no bloodshed and death but only adoration, an energy flowing in translucent pulses to me. The mob hangs on my every word – not that they are my words. This must be how gods feel.

The crowd parts.

The king makes his way through the gathering to the podium. He is dressed in a simple robe of white overlaid with purple, and the mob bow low to him as he passes. The man conjures images of bright burning buildings against a night sky in my mind's eye. The man smiles at me on my podium, but the smile does not reach his eyes. The king's gaze roams around the crowd, noticing everything and seemingly troubled by it. As he steps up, I find myself leaning forward to help him. He embraces me, kissing me on one cheek then the other. His voice is low as he mutters a message to me that I don't comprehend, before turning to wave to the crowd. My host answers in an equally low tone before shouting one last sentence to the mob. The entire crowd erupts in a thunderous roar of approval that vibrates through the square and makes the king flinch.

The king embraces me once more for the crowd. Then he gestures towards the interior of the building behind us as the crowd cheers. I feel myself face the crowd with a brief wave before following the man into the coolness of a stone palace.

My eyes struggle with the darkness, but I can see that the chamber into which I have walked is a large hall. The air is cooler here, the marble cold, and I am grateful, though the sudden change makes my head spin. The king throws his purple cloak over the seat that lies at one end of the room and pours me wine from a silver jug. The guards who accompanied him to the podium appear to have been dismissed. I am trusted. The king is speaking. I hold the wine goblet awkwardly as if unsure what to do with the drink.

My host replies in words I do not understand.

The king laughs but waves his finger as if to remind me of a memory shared with my host that I, a passenger, have no recollection of. The man leads me towards the centre of the room. The chamber is not empty, as I first thought, but where I assumed lay nothing but bare stone, there is a large parchment map. The chart has been spread out across the chamber and appears to have been well thumbed. The purpose of the map is clear even without the notes that have been written onto it in runic script to mark where the invasion will begin. I move slowly round the map. I nod as I walk until my host spots a marker near the forest and I stop. I look at the man but point at the map, indicating the spot.

The king shrugs and answers in a matter-of-fact tone that suggests he does not disagree with me. My host answers with more force this time, spilling wine onto the map in the process. The king does not smile this time. His answer is curt. I do not reply but look away. I can feel my host's jaw working as if they want to speak but know it would be unwise. I feel a hand on my shoulder once more, and the king is standing next to me, talking in conciliatory tones. I nod once more as he leads me towards the door and out into the corridor beyond.

I am to make my own way out. I pause. My host is troubled, and I am looking back at the king receding into the shadows before I make my way out into the street and all is lost in the light.

THE WOLVES WERE in the wall.

Anya opened her eyes, certain that was the case. She saw no walls, only the trees and her memories stampeding through her conscious- ness. Vedic was kneeling a few feet away, looking down. He glanced up at her and placed his finger against his lips. Anya looked down and saw an undulating tide of fur as the pack ran through the forest beneath them. She pressed herself back against the tree trunk. Anya could barely see Vedic against the wood. Only his eyes revealed him, two points of marble in the shadows and leaves. What did that remind her of? She wasn't sure. Behind Vedic she could see Fin's ghost, head drip- ping and rotten from the axe wound that had killed him, staring at her. Thrace, her grandfather's ghost, was on the branch above, bottle in hand. The pack seemed to stretch on forever. She daren't move, and so she closed her eyes, but she could still feel them looking at her.

Vedic sat back. 'They have passed.'

Anya did not look at him – her eyes were still on the ghosts. 'They might return,' she replied.

'All the more reason to get moving,' said Vedic. 'Untie the rope and pass it here.'

Anya forced her gaze away and down to the rope that kept her from falling. She did not feel properly awake as she moved to where the rope was secured.

'What were you looking at?'

Anya was startled. 'What?'

'You were looking behind me the entire time they were passing below and even just now. What?'

Anya glanced back at the ghosts. They were still there.

'Nothing. I was just thinking about Fin.'

The woodsman stared at her. 'Your brother?'

Anya shook her head. 'No, but he was like a brother. He was the grandson of my grandfather's friend Falkirk. A year younger than me.'

'He's dead?'

Anya could feel the tears balling at the edges of her eyes. She hated herself for it. She just nodded.

'When the village was ransacked?'

Anya nodded again. In her mind she was back in the village, on the common, feeling the faint vibration of the ground as if a storm was breaking in the distance. She could see Fin lying down to put his ear to the ground to see if he could hear more clearly.

'First time you saw someone you know killed?'

Anya whispered, 'Yes. It was my fault.'

FIN STOOD. 'It's horses, lots of them.'

He sounded awed even before you could see the Kurah streaming down the slope of the valley. He pointed in the direction of the noise. There was a shadow on the horizon where the Kurah force were lining up, ready for the charge. Anya felt her eyes straining – she had better farsight than Fin, but even she needed a moment before she could make out the glint of spears. The flag made her heart stop in her chest.

'No,' she said.

'Who is it?' asked Fin. He sounded like a child.

'Kurah,' she said, running for the alert bell.

The bell sat in the centre of the village and was a leftover from the last war. It was to warn the villagers to take cover because enemy warriors were passing through on their way from one battle to another. The bell had moss growing on it now, and when Anya grabbed the ringer, it came away in her hands.

'Damn the gods,' she hissed, hastily trying to hook the ringer back on the inside with the hammer still functional.

'There's so many of them,' said Fin. 'We need to get out of here.'

Anya glared at him. 'We are Shaanti; we do not run. We must warn everyone and arm ourselves.'

Fin looked unsure.

Anya turned back to the bell and rang it with all her might. At first nothing happened. Then people started to emerge from shops and homes to see what the fuss was about. The arrow rain came shortly after, sending those too slow to seek cover to their end with shafts protruding from their heads, necks and cheeks.

'Weapons!' yelled Anya at Fin, who was taking cover.

The boy scrambled to the outside of the blacksmith's and grabbed two swords from a rack. He tossed one to Anya and lifted his own. Kurah appeared on horses throughout the village.

Anya turned to defend herself from one and sent him crashing from his horse as another nailed her in the face with his fist. She crumpled onto her back and saw the man's sword swing down. Fin blocked the strike and saved her life, but the warrior was so much bigger and faster. As his blade tumbled away, he swung down with an axe and embedded it in the boy's skull. Fin's last look was one of shock and confusion, and then he was gone from his eyes as his body collapsed.

'YES, THAT WAS YOUR FAULT,' said Vedic.

Anya felt like she had been punched. 'What?'

Vedic softened his tone, but he did not back down. 'You must have known that you had little chance with just two swords. The smarter thing to do would have been to withdraw and find other fighters to resist afterwards. You should have evacuated while you could.'

Anya shoved the rope at him. 'He did not have to stand and fight.'

Vedic shook his head. 'But he did. You may have been the better fighter, but he was the smarter warrior. I am sorry you lost your friend, but no one can take that guilt from you. You must take that feeling, turn it and try to use the pain for a cause bigger than yourself.'

Anya blinked. He might have a point.

'But remember to choose wisely. The righteous warrior is a terrible thing.'

Anya looked over at where the ghosts had been, but all she saw now was bare bark. 'We'd better move.'

There was a hoot in the distance, like an owl but not quite, as if a creature was mimicking the bird. Vedic froze. An answering hoot came a way off, from their left.

'Damn,' said Vedic. 'Move!'

The woodsman grabbed her hand, and they were running across the trees as if the woods behind them were on fire. All care was gone. The forestal led them due north at the fastest speed he could. If he could have gone at a flat-out sprint, Anya suspected he would. When he stopped, Anya nearly died.

There was no warning, and so she collided straight into his unyielding back, bouncing and landing hard on the branch. The surprise saved her. She made no attempt to stop her fall, and so she fell back onto the branch and landed in a perfectly seated position. The impact was hard, but on such a wide branch, she did not fall to the ground below. The forest floor seemed very far away.

Anya looked up.

Vedic stood on the edge of the branch, where a large gap in the canopy opened up in front of him and shafts of sunlight cast patterns on the wood and forest around and beneath him. Vedic was looking not at the liquid light but at the figure on the branch opposite him. The person was almost as tall as Vedic, lithe, with eyes that glowed a faint yellow in the shadows. The man – if he was human – had skin that made Anya and Vedic's improvised mud camouflage look like they had just rolled in the dirt. In what appeared to be his natural tones, his skin went from green to brown to yellow in a mottled effect that meant every time he blinked, he almost disappeared. Anya was confident this was a he, because the man was almost naked, his broad shoulders, narrow hips and his genitalia all on display. A sleeveless robe, which fell to his ankles, was open to the world and seemed to indicate a ceremonial role for the garment rather than serving any function against the elements. The man's hair, shoulder-length, actually seemed to change colour depending on where he stood. He moved into the light, sending his locks blonde.

'Vedic,' spoke the creature. 'You are a long way from home.' He swept his hair off his shoulders as his serene yellow eyes stared intently at the woodsman.

'We mean no offence,' replied Vedic. 'We are on an urgent journey for the lady. Wolves are hunting us, and this was the best way to avoid them.'

'You admit to knowingly walking through our lands without permission.'

Vedic sighed, heavily. 'You know I do. Why ask?'

'A courtesy,' said the creature. 'I am not unsympathetic to your cause, or I would have killed you while you slept.'

'You'd have tried,' said Vedic, shrugging.

'Indeed,' replied the creature. 'Yet empathy stayed my hand.'

'I sense a but approaching,' said Anya, almost whispering.

'Yes,' said the creature.

As Anya looked around, she thought she saw others like him, some male, some female, circling them from the surrounding trees. 'Your companion is correct. You have knowingly broken our laws by taking this path, and so, at the very least, I must bring you in front of the king for judgement.'

'Those rules were not meant for people cutting through your territory to render aid,' protested Vedic.

'No exceptions. You know Hogarth better than that. Especially now. If we did that, where would we be?'

'Why won't you help us?' asked Anya.

'We are Tream,' replied the captor. 'The original indigenous people of the forest, which your kind tried to eradicate. What do we care of your so-called gods' petty squabbles?'

Anya flushed. She'd always thought of the Tream as made-up creatures her grandfather or another enterprising storyteller had created to give extra spice to the gods.

'You hairless apes are more trouble than you are worth,' said the creature.

Anya shook her head. 'You sound like ...'

Vedic silenced her with a look. Anya wondered why mentioning Pan was a bad idea. The god did not have a good history with the Tream in legend, but that must have been a very long time ago, and it did not seem like they crossed each other's paths very often by choice.

The creature snapped his fingers. More Tream, dressed like their confronter – that is to say, naked save for a strange sleeveless, floor-length, open-fronted coat – broke apart from the trees where they had been hiding and descended on slender ropes, landing alongside Anya and Vedic. Vedic did not try to get away. He seemed resigned to their fate as Anya stared at him, willing him to speak, to do anything at all, but he just stood there as the creatures roped the travellers' hands together. Anya and Vedic were prodded into motion without words as their captors led them away south and west, away from the glade and away from Danu.

Periodically they stopped, and one or more of the Tream placed their hands on the surrounding trees, eyes closed as if in prayer. Vedic paid them no attention, taking the opportunity to squat down, stretching his hamstrings out and watching, amused, as Anya followed the break-off group of Tream out to where they stood by the trees, trying to work out what the interaction was achieving. She couldn't stop staring at these strange creatures who looked like the characters from her legends and yet unlike them. They were darker than the pictures in her grandfather's books, and when they got further away from her, they were invisible against the treeline. Likewise, when they placed their hands on the trees in silent prayer, they almost blended into the trunk altogether. The effect was utterly disconcerting.

Anya's guard, a male Tream of indeterminate age, let her move closer to his kin as they communicated with the trees but followed close by.

'What are they saying?' asked Anya, recalling just before she tried to raise her hands that they were tied.

The guard smiled. 'They are asking the trees what they have seen and heard.'

Anya frowned. 'You're either as mad as the woodsman or teasing me. Tream humour is not much spoken of in my people's history.'

'Nor human wisdom in mine,' retorted the guard, his smile growing wider.

'The trees listen and see,' said Vedic, rising. 'I don't fully understand how, but as I said before, it's similar to how the gods use them.'

'It is amongst the oldest of our secrets,' said the guard. 'I doubt the gods know it.'

Vedic smiled this time. 'Ah, lad, I'm sorry to break it to you, but the gods have known this for a while. Sometimes the trees even talk to an old bastard like me. Perhaps the wood is not as trustworthy as you believe.'

The guard blinked. He considered arguing the point with the woodsman, but Anya could see the moment the Tream dismissed the words as the bluster of a prisoner. He moved on to the task at hand. The Tream in communion with the trees stepped clear and nodded to the one who had first spoken to them. Their guard prodded them on after the now-advancing group.

'What is the name of your king?' asked Anya.

'Hogarth,' said the Tream that had spoken to Vedic.

'And what is your name?'

'You're full of questions for someone tied up and under armed guard,' said the Tream.

'His name is Akyar,' said Vedic, listlessly.

Anya did not answer. She had heard Pan mention Hogarth. She was trying to remember any clues as to why. She did not speak when they returned to the ground. Not a word left her lips as a female Tream roped her waist and carried her down like a child. And no sound was made when they were led into the darkness within one of the larger, more gnarled, time-worn trees that looked as old as the world.

CHAPTER THIRTEEN

VEDIC DID NOT CRY out when the fist smashed into his stomach.

He made a sound that was almost a word as the air rushed out of his lungs and his giant frame folded to his knees. The Tream with the circlet, the king, continued his attack on Vedic. A kick caught the woodsman on the side of his head and dropped the forestal to the throne room floor.

Anya strained at her bindings. She hadn't felt this helpless since the camp. Vedic lay prone, panting in pain as even their captor, Akyar, looked shocked at the level of violence.

'Your nerve in showing your face here,' said the king, stepping back to his throne, 'is breathtaking.'

Vedic spat blood out onto the wooden floor. 'It's not like I had a choice. We tried to avoid your territory.'

'So you say,' replied the king. 'How would I know whether you ...' His voice broke. 'You had better not be involved in this.'

'Involved in what?' hissed Vedic, the pain clear on his face.

The king sat on his throne. Anya tried to move closer to Vedic, but he glared at her and so she stopped.

They were inside a tree. A giant oak, bigger than any Anya had ever seen before in her life – the tree might have been as old as the world to grow so large. The inside had been hollowed out; there was no crystal left, and she could only assume the tree was dead. The small hall that had been carved from its carcass was covered in intricate carvings of Tream in various scenes from what was either their mythology or their history, or both. The place was lit with phosphor lamps that gave everything a strange glow as the light bounced off the polished wood. The area behind Anya and Vedic was filled with Tream who stared at them as if they were wraiths come to walk amongst them.

Akyar was near Anya, looking towards the king.

The Tream king, Hogarth, sat at the other end of the hall, facing them, on a throne that was in turn set on a dais. The queen was sat on a smaller throne next to Hogarth and was conspicuous in a large cloak and hood that hid her face. She was the most clothed of any of these creatures.

'Vedic is telling the truth,' said Anya. 'We attempted to take the path through the Corden, and it was a disaster. We lost our packs, our boots and our guide.'

Akyar looked at her with unblinking eyes.

'Who was your guide?' asked Hogarth, his eyes never leaving Vedic.

'Pan,' blurted Anya. Vedic's warning stare came too late, and he just shook his head.

Akyar seemed to flinch, and he put his hand out to steady himself against the wall. His reaction was a micro-movement the rest of the Tream might have missed, but Anya saw it. A moment later he straightened, and his face was a mask that was unreadable.

'The forest is at risk,' said Anya.

Hogarth turned to look at her. His skin was an ever-shifting miasma of green, brown and yellow. Unlike Akyar's, his eyes were a split of colour – one green and one yellow. He did not wear a robe; he was fully naked save for the small circlet of wood sitting on his brow that kept his silver hair off his shoulders. Hogarth shook his head and pushed himself out of his chair.

'The forest is at risk if your kind continues to breed like the sickness it is,' said Hogarth, walking round Anya.

Anya heard Hogarth draw his blade. Her heart was a piece of ice in her chest, and she could feel the cold steel on her skin. Anya felt the metal should be warm. She almost laughed at such a ridiculous thought.

'Perhaps I should kill this one,' said Hogarth. 'One less breeder.'

'Sire,' said Akyar, his voice giving only the slightest hint that he was concerned the king would go too far. 'They do not know the boy was taken.'

The king moved the blade away slowly as if weighing up Akyar's words versus actually decapitating her.

'What boy?' asked Anya. She felt dizzy. Her memory of the Shaanti children she had left behind as prisoners was like a festering wound. Why would a Tream child have been taken? What would Cernubus want with it?

'Your goddess Danu,' said Hogarth, 'she has taken my son.'

Anya forced herself to look at Hogarth. 'Why do you believe it was Danu?'

Hogarth paced, his fury simmering and palpable as, catlike, he circled them. His fists balled and unfurled repeatedly. The grief was heavy, slowing everything down, like a blanket across the whole court. When Hogarth stopped and looked at them, it seemed as if a decision had been made in his head. The king strode back to the throne.

'You have not met my wife, Jiana, have you?' he asked Vedic.

The woodsman shook his head. He spat more blood onto the wood.

Jiana, the queen, rose from her throne with the care of the recently injured, frail as if she were afraid she was made of glass. The king embraced his wife with a kiss to her forehead, his eyes glassy with emotions that Anya could not even begin to name. Anya's sense of wrongness increased as she noted Jiana's eyes looked different, devoid of emotion, dead.

Anya couldn't look away as the queen pushed back her hood to reveal a swathe of silken bandages. The Tream queen unwound her dressing, refusing to make eye contact with Anya as she revealed her face.

Anya gasped. Jiana was about the same age as Akyar, younger than Hogarth, and she had been beautiful. The smooth skin of her cheeks now bore knotted and gnarled scars that ran to her jaw. Her ears had notches where none should be, and part of her nose had been cut away.

'This is how I know Danu broke the truce,' said Hogarth, holding his wife to him. 'She took my boy and tortured my wife.'

'Why does the queen not speak?' asked Vedic, his voice hoarse.

'Show them,' said Hogarth.

Jiana opened her mouth to show a dark void where her tongue had been.

It was Anya's turn to put her hand out to steady herself. The violence that had been done to the queen left her feeling sick. What could possibly be the reason for doing that? What hate would someone have to feel?

Hogarth's eyes flashed with fury.

Anya stepped back, afraid of Hogarth, a creature that could pass for a shadow or a demon, and spoke one minute with the fine tongue of a king, and the next with a rage that threatened to spill into violence. He paced across the dais like a caged panther.

'It could not have been Danu,' said Vedic, calm. 'She is being held captive by the god you know as the hunter.'

Hogarth clenched his hands. 'Do you call the queen a liar?'

'I know enough of the queen from Lord Akyar,' said Vedic, 'not to call her a liar, but she may be mistaken. The gods' forms are such that it's hard sometimes to be sure who you are seeing. I think I know who did this.'

Anya thought she could see one of Vedic's hands working at his bindings.

'Who?' asked Hogarth, his eyebrow arched.

'The Morrigan.'

Anya's head snapped round at Vedic. She remembered the sound in Vedic's voice when he thought the wraith they had seen in the Corden was the Morrigan. Terror had sounded strange on him. But she looked nothing like Danu.

Vedic smiled at her. It was not a nice look. 'Yes, Anya, she is as real as Pan and Danu, and twice as dangerous.'

Anya felt her jaw clench to hold back her retort.

'What is the Morrigan?' asked Akyar, stepping forward. 'I have never heard of this god.'

'There are three sisters amongst the oldest gods,' said Anya, reciting her grandfather's words. 'First came the earth and life: this is Danu. Then came the death that gives life meaning: this is Anu – the Morrigan – goddess of the darkness, and of the last sister, we do not speak, for she is gone from the world.'

'Anu I have heard of,' said Akyar, confused. 'But she is the ancient hag that haunts forbidden paths. Jiana saw a young woman, as fair of body as she was as foul of mind. How can this be?'

Vedic closed his eyes briefly as if what he said pained him. 'The Morrigan appears most often as young. The hag is an Shaanti name, because they view seeing her as bad luck. Did the woman you saw have a crescent-moon-shaped birthmark on her neck here?' Vedic pointed to the right side of the nape of his neck.

Akyar flinched again at this. Hogarth put a hand on his vizier's shoulder to reassure him. About what, Anya could not tell.

Jiana nodded.

Anya turned to the king. 'It is the Morrigan. Danu carries the birthmark for the sun, and Anu – the Morrigan – that for the moon.'

Vedic's hands broke free.

The woodsman rolled onto his back and nipped up.

Anya was pushed back by Akyar as the king and Jiana were forced back onto the dais by their guards. The Tream circled the bloodied and grinning Vedic. The forestal looked like a demon himself as he gestured for the Tream to try and get him. Anya saw Hogarth draw his sword again.

The woodsman dodged a strike and pulled the blade from the unfortunate Tream, who was sent crunching into the other wall, shattering a display cabinet. Anya saw a glint behind the broken wood. Vedic's blade parried another strike from one of the guards, and he took the poor man's sword-arm in a swift strike that sent green blood arcing into the roof of the hall. Akyar stepped forward with his own sword drawn and shattered Vedic's blade with one violent strike.

The woodsman looked down at his broken weapon and up at the vizier.

'Do you really want to do this?' asked the woodsman.

Akyar was pointing his blade at the forestal.

'Stop now.'

Vedic shook his head and dived for the broken cabinet. He pulled the wooden doors apart to reach for whatever was in there. Anya couldn't see past his bulk. He stopped, closing what was left of the doors as if stung. He stepped back, ignoring the Tream who immediately twisted his arms behind his back and forced him to the floor.

'Where did you get that?' hissed Vedic, oblivious to his restraint.

Akyar was staunching the wounded arm of his fallen comrade. 'That's not important.'

'Why keep it?' replied the woodsman, his voice sounding hollow as if the broken cabinet had stolen his soul.

'As a reminder,' said Hogarth, stepping forward from his guards, 'of what monsters lie outside the forest.'

Vedic did not answer.

'You see how dangerous he is,' said Hogarth to Akyar. He swung his blade round and lined the weapon up with Vedic's neck.

Akyar shook his head in disgust.

Jiana placed her hand on her husband's arm, stopping Hogarth from drawing back and striking. The king looked at her. Anya could see some kind of communication passing between them in spite of the queen's injury.

'But look at what he has done,' Anya heard the king reply.

The queen shook her head once more and this time physically removed the sword from Hogarth's hand. She took him away by his arm and called Akyar over with a nod. Anya could make little else out of their conference save that the exchange was brief and spirited, ending only when Jiana put a hand on each of their arms and held them in her gaze in turn. Whatever she was communicating, she'd bound the other two with its power.

Hogarth nodded at Anya's guard. She was cut free.

'Thank you,' said Anya, rubbing her wrists.

'Do not thank me,' said Hogarth, looking at his wife. 'You are not free. I have merely decided to make use of your companion's singular talents.'

'You need wood chopping?' asked Anya. She was too weary to watch her tongue.

'That would be the human notion of humour?' asked Hogarth, unimpressed. He bent down over the restrained and broken Vedic. 'What would you do to save your Danu?'

Vedic did not answer, though his knotting and unknotting jaw spoke for him.

'I will let you leave here,' said Hogarth, standing. 'If you both agree to free my son first. This one,' he continued, kicking Vedic, 'is the only person here with any idea how to kill a god.'

'There's no need for threats,' said Anya. 'We'd help you anyway.'

Vedic stared at her from the floor as if she had lost her mind. Anya enjoyed it.

'It is not you I am concerned about,' said Hogarth, almost sympathetic. 'Forgive me, Lady Anya, but Vedic is not to be trusted – he is not a nice man; you should remember that. This is the only language he understands.'

'Please continue,' said Vedic, still prone, spitting once more. 'Pretend I'm not here.'

'What do you say, woodsman?' asked Hogarth, bending over him again. 'Will you help me?'

Vedic replied, 'I have a choice? Always true to your law, eh, Hogarth? Even if it is a token gesture.'

Hogarth kicked him again. 'Your answer?'

'Yes, I will rescue your son, but I make no promises on killing the Morrigan. I doubt that's possible.'

'Bring Meyr back alive and we'll talk,' conceded Hogarth, standing. He nodded for the guards to release the woodsman. 'Akyar goes with you.'

Vedic rolled to his back and sat up with obvious pain.

'No,' said the forestal, pointing at Anya. She flushed. 'I already have one person slowing me down.'

Anya stared at him, her hands reaching for a sword that wasn't there as she struggled to contain her retort.

'It was not a request, Vedic,' said Hogarth, his fingers tapping on his thigh like he had a tune he couldn't get out of his head.

Akyar whispered in Hogarth's ear once more.

'You may take our wall ornament,' said Hogarth, gesturing at the cabinet that had taken the fight from Vedic. 'Your own weapons are hardly adequate to take on a god.'

All colour drained from the woodsman, and he bent one knee as if contemplating running again. Beads of sweat had appeared on his forehead. Anya had never seen him look like this, not even when the wolves were so close they could smell them. He was terrified to his core. *What is in there?* thought Anya.

'I cannot accept,' said Vedic, his voice broken.

It cost him to say those words, thought Anya, bemused.

'But you cannot mean to go against the Morrigan with a bow and a hatchet?' said Hogarth.

'Perhaps not,' said Vedic, looking away. 'But this I will not, *cannot*, accept, nor, I fear, would this bring me luck. Take it, destroy it; the weapon is an abomination.'

'Vedic,' said Akyar, stepping forward. 'Listen to reason. You are to all practical purposes unarmed.'

'I cannot take that. You do not want me to take that – believe me,' said Vedic, getting to his feet.

Anya turned her eyes from the woodsman to Hogarth. 'I'll take a weapon. I lost my last blade.'

'No,' said Vedic, his eyes flicking to Anya. 'She's lost her nerve as well as her steel; she'd be an even bigger liability. If you are willing, I will take a Tream sword.'

Hogarth unbuckled his own weapon and handed it to Vedic. This drew murmurs from the court. Vedic drew the steel in a swift arc that moved into a couple of sweeps to test the weight. He returned the blade to its scabbard.

'It'll do.'

'You're welcome.'

Jiana made a noise in her throat as she stepped down to Anya, withdrawing a smaller sword from the folds of her robes. She handed her blade in its lacquered sheath to Anya, who took it with a smile.

'Thank you,' said Anya, bowing.

Jiana nodded but did not return the smile.

'Foolish,' said Vedic, frowning.

'My wife's gifts are her own to give, Vedic,' said Hogarth. 'She is wise beyond your understanding. I have found it best to trust her judgement. You will do the same.'

Jiana pointed from Akyar to Anya to the sword and back again.

'It would be my honour,' said Akyar.

'Fine,' said Vedic. 'We need to rest before we go anywhere. We've been travelling for days.'

'One night,' said Hogarth. 'You leave at sunrise.'

CHAPTER FOURTEEN

THE GOD RETURNED with wolves at his side.

Montu was asleep in his tent when the god re-entered the camp. The noise of the god's arrival was like a clap of thunder overhead, and there were shouts from the guards. Montu started out of bed with his sword drawn. The woman next to him stirred briefly, but she was so full of wine that all she could manage was to pull the blanket back down over her. His heart pounding, it took him a moment to realise he wasn't actually under attack. He pulled his soft leather trousers on and walked to the tent entrance. He pushed his head out into the cold.

'What is it?'

'Lord Cernubus,' replied the guard.

Montu felt his fear return. The god was impossible to control; he came and went as he pleased, and that made him wonder about how far Cernubus would go to hold up his end of the bargain. He wished his men had returned from the coast with any kind of insight into how to kill this creature. A simple assassination after he had the clan lands would be easier than this tightrope he was now forced to walk.

'I'll be out now,' he said. 'My wife?'

The guard did not show any emotion at this question – he knew full well there was another woman in the king's tent. 'She is a day's ride away, according to the last scout to come in.'

The king nodded. 'After I have left, please get rid of the woman in here.'

'Sire?'

The king waved him away as he turned to go back into the tent. 'Kill her if you have to. I just don't want her in the camp or running away to her Shaanti brethren and giving away our position,' he replied. 'I want no Shaanti bastards running around, mounting insurrection in the decades to come. Besides, my wife already wants me dead.'

Back inside the tent, he pulled on his tunic and his boots before strapping his sword to his belt. He cast one admiring look at the soft curves of the pale redhead in his bed and threw the thought that she was a waste over to one side. He stepped back out into the camp, feeling ready to march all the way across the continent. He would bring the god to heel with the force of his will and the mages that were even now working on a binding spell. He forced the thought from his mind lest the god fish it out and discover his betrayal. It was Cernubus's own fault. He was too dangerous.

'Hello, Montu,' said Cernubus.

The god stood facing the tent with a wolf either side of him and a surround of guards training their weapons on him. A few Kurah lay dead or unconscious at his feet. The wolves were well trained, with neither trying to take a bite of the fallen. They were huge, yellow-eyed creatures with jaws that dripped onto the grass below.

'Why have you brought overgrown dogs into my camp?'

Cernubus raised the side of his mouth in a sardonic grin, but his eyes never moved from tracking the king. *He's angry*, thought Montu, *but why would he be angry at me?* The wolves both growled.

'Do they understand our tongue?'

Cernubus touched their heads and they settled.

'They are not the kind of wolves you find in Kurah, Montu,' he said, stepping towards the king. The wolves stayed where they were.

Montu frowned. 'Safer, I hope.'

Cernubus laughed. It was not a nice sound. 'You hope? I told you that hope left a long time ago. You could search every town from here to the coast, and hope would not appear. I will replace hope, of course, but only once our little joint venture has been completed. Speaking of which, walk with me.'

He knows about the mages, thought Montu, following the god. *No, he can't. I am breathing.* They were staring at the construction of the gantries and the pyre on the western side of the camp, looking out towards the edge of the forest, the plains that lay beyond, and Vikrain.

'You appear to be dallying on the construction of our bonfire.'

Montu didn't mind the barb at the fires, as long as that was all Cernubus was referring to. 'You'll have your sacrifice, Cernubus. We'll be ready for the alignment of the sentinels. Of course, if you don't keep your side of the bargain and get me the thain and her army ... well, you won't have your witnesses ... your future believers.'

'You will have your war,' replied Cernubus. 'As long as I have my sacrifice. All will worship me, and I shall keep this world safe in the long, dark winter of the universe. Only my will can keep the light.'

He's mad, thought Montu. 'What about that light show last night?'

Cernubus shook his head as if coming out of a dream.

Montu clarified. 'In the forest?'

Cernubus folded his arms behind his back. The ink etched onto his skin seemed to flow and change into a series of hieroglyphs showing a mighty battle between two figures, one of whom was the god.

'You saw some of it? That's good. A little extra belief is like a fine wine after a long march. That was nothing but me keeping my promise to keep the forest free of your enemies.'

'And is the wood free?'

Cernubus hesitated but only for a second. 'Of course. Nothing within can harm you.'

'What about you?'

Cernubus clutched his chest with one hand. 'Ah, Montu, you wound me,' he said. He placed a giant arm around the king. 'You know me better than that. I never forget a friend – or an enemy. Why, there is one of my foes in my captivity now that I have hunted for a thousand years. Imagine what I would do to enemies easily within my reach?'

They were back at Montu's tent now. The god had led him round in a wide, looping circle, through the maze of tents and back to where they had started. He could see the tent's entrance being shoved and distorted as he approached. The guard who had stood outside his tent for the last three weeks fell backwards out of the entrance, a sword in his chest, and stopped moving. The woman from his bed stood in the torn tent's entrance, her clothes soaked with the man's blood and her lip broken. She saw the king and the god, and her eyes widened. She leapt for the sword in the guard and pulled the blade free. She adopted a position that suggested she had at least seen her own kind's warriors train if not been trained herself.

Montu drew his sword. 'Shaanti women are so much trouble. Always trying to escape. There's a reason we don't take prisoners.'

Cernubus put his hand on Montu's shoulder.

'I will deal with this,' he said.

Montu watched as the god stepped forward, waving away the wolves, which were looking at the woman with hungry eyes.

'Do you know me, child?'

As he walked forward, the god was letting his antlers show. They were so large up close, as if he had part of the forest growing from his head. The woman's steel waivered in her grip.

She nodded. 'Hunter ... god.' She spoke in the Shaanti tongue.

Cernubus smiled. 'That was my title, but what is my name?'

The woman took a step back. 'I ... I don't remember ...'

Cernubus was face to face with her – he could reach out and touch her or be stabbed by her. His smile had faded.

'Drop the sword,' he commanded.

The woman dropped the weapon. She looked, wide-eyed, at what she had done.

'Look at me,' said the god. The woman's head snapped back to him. 'I know your name, Seren. Just as I know we have no stars any more, just sentinels.'

The woman whimpered. Montu was surprised to see a line of wetness appear down the woman's skirt as she lost control of her bladder. The god approached Seren like a python approaching a petrified rabbit. The almost-warrior who had killed his guard had gone.

'You are impure,' said the god, stepping around the woman,

speaking into her ears. 'Not because you lie with the Kurah but because you have forgotten the lore of your own people. You have forgotten your one true god who kept you warm in the long nights when we first came here. You must be punished. Cleansed.'

The god lifted his right hand, and the woman lifted into the air. The woman's whimpers had become a sound close to low-level choking.

'First, you must be laid bare,' Cernubus continued, closing his right hand.

The woman's clothes and skin disappeared. Montu flinched. A few of the men around him started vomiting.

'Now cleansed by fire,' said Cernubus, opening his hand to reveal a flame. He blew at his palm. The woman caught fire and was burned to ash in two blinks of an eye.

The god stood for a moment, looking at the pile of ash. He closed his eyes. The glowing embers of the woman's ashes cast the god in a strange ur-light. Montu thought the hunter looked slightly taller for an instant. A slightly younger Cernubus looked at him.

'Your secret will be safe from the little woman for a while longer,' he said, leaning over so only Montu could hear. Louder, to his audience, he spoke: 'Do not attempt any more magic to bind me. If you drag me back again to put an end to your childlike attempts at betrayal, you will wish you were that pretty little thing.'

This was a clever ploy. Montu could almost admire him for it. Cernubus had framed the execution in terms the Kurah would understand and respect. She had been armed. She had been trying to fight. He had given her a warrior's death of sorts and close enough to what he had planned for the others. He showed mercy to Montu but had warned him in front of his men not to try to bind him as the king had tried with the mages a few hours before. He demonstrated his power over Montu.

The mages are dead, thought Montu. It was an instinctive feeling.

Is this my first mistake? thought Montu. He knew that they would begin to happen. He had known ever since he had taken that knife from his father and slipped it into the old man's ribs, watching the life go out of his eyes. Necessity had caused him to bring the man's end sooner than nature intended. He had loved his father in his own way, but the man was destroying the empire his grandfather had built. He had been weak. The nations across the water were paying attention and eyeing up their lands like vultures on a battlefield. Absolute power corrupts completely. You have to strive to be objective. He knew his art of war well.

'You could thank me,' said Cernubus, leading the king back into his tent.

'I think that was more about helping you,' said Montu, too tired to be diplomatic. 'Did your fight in the forest deplete you?'

A flash of anger crossed Cernubus's face and was gone in an instant. *Ah*, thought Montu, *I touched close to home with that barb*. Already men were stitching up the torn entrance. He waved them away for the time being.

Montu sat on the chair that passed for his throne when he was on campaign, his sword placed on his lap and his irritation showing on his face. Cernubus looked at him as a parent might an errant child.

'When will the clan forces make their way to fight us?'

Cernubus shook his head. 'We should be laying siege to their castle. I could break the walls in a day.'

Montu shook his head. 'I understand how belief fuels you, hunter. My power base is not dissimilar. This must be my victory, where my grandfather failed, and not yours.'

'I do believe you don't trust me, Montu, king of the Kurah. And yet it is you who has tried to alter the terms of our agreement.'

Montu did not look away from the god. 'Would you do anything different in my place?'

'*Touché*,' he replied. 'The thain will make her way to fight you. Falkirk has already upped the ante and was unaware your prisoner had escaped. Meanwhile, I am sure your agents are doing everything they can to provoke the thain into action. It is a matter of timing. If they arrive too soon, what will we do?'

'Who did you kill in the forest? The girl?'

The god looked surprised. 'I killed no one.'

Montu pointed his sword at the god. 'You and I have a deal – no surprises from the forest.'

The god laughed. 'Your pointy stick does not impress me, young prince, any more than your pathetic attempts to uncover any lore that can control me.'

Montu felt fear slide over him like a wraith.

The god stepped close to him, pushing the blade to one side with two fingers, and whispered in his ear. 'I was a god, but now I am my own creation. My ears are still everywhere, and my eyes are not tied to this form. You should remember that. I can see your camp. I can see my prisoners in the forest. I can see my allies, and I can see our escaped prisoner in the trees with the natives. And I can see your wife outside this tent.'

'What is going on?'

The queen stood in the entrance to the tent. She was not yet six months pregnant, but the swell of her belly was visible beneath her riding gown. She was wrapped up with a scarf and gloves against the cold. Montu moved away from the god and embraced his wife, spinning her round so that she could not see the state of his bedding.

'You are here!'

'I am here,' she said, her voice cold. 'Why is the god here?'

Cernubus looked at the bedding. There was a flash, and the bed was made, the sheets clean and crisp. Montu lost his trail of thought. *What had his wife said?*

'Why is he here instead of keeping the gods busy in the forest?'

'Well,' said Cernubus. 'I was in the process of telling your husband a tiny white lie that I hadn't killed anyone, to make my control of the forest more impressive.'

Montu let go of his wife now and stared at the god. 'How many?'

Cernubus folded his arms. 'All but three gods are gone. The forest is mine.'

'Where are they?'

'Somewhere I want them to be,' said Cernubus.

'What of the Tream?'

'Taken care of.'

'You should finish it,' said the queen. 'All the gods. All the Tream.'

Cernubus did not even acknowledge that she had spoken. He walked up to the king and patted him on the cheek. 'I'll be leaving my wolves as a warning. No more attempts to control me, or our deal will be modified.'

The god left.

A guard ran into the tent, his face panicked and his clothes covered in blood. 'Sire!'

Montu looked at his queen. 'The mages?'

'D-dead, sire ...' replied the guard.

'Show us.'

The guard led the king and his queen to where the tent that housed the mages had stood. All that was left now was torn sections of fabric, soaked in blood and flapping in the wind. There was the faint odour of sulphur from whatever cant the god had used, and the limbs and torsos of the mages littered the ground. Only one mage still stood, shaking, covered in blood, in the middle of the carnage.

'Why did he live?'

The guard shook his head. 'We do not know. The god was here and with you. We don't know how.'

'Why did you make a pact with that demon?' asked his queen, looking at the remains of the Delgasian mages. They had only switched sides after the invasion. The king imagined some of the mages might have been the queen's friends.

Montu stared at the remains. 'It seems I may not have learned all the lessons my grandfather had to teach me.'

CHAPTER FIFTEEN

THE VIZIER AKYAR rolled the stem of his wine glass between finger and thumb.

'So, I made my counsel known to the king, who ignored it.'

He took a long sup of wine.

Anya and Vedic were in the Tream's house, high amongst the Tream city. The room and the house were formed from a tree, hollowed out from sections that were no longer of use, while the living wood continued to grow up around it. The furniture, the table and chairs, were also part of the tree, seeming to flow up from the rest of the wood. The remains of their meal lay scattered around them as they talked.

Vedic took his pipe from where he had left it drying near the fire and packed the bowl with leaf from Akyar's table. He found that the smoke helped him think more clearly, and he was in need of time in his own head. The woodsman did not entirely trust this feeling; he had spent many decades trying to spend as little time in his head as possible. The thought of Danu, caged, floated in the centre, like the suns, orbited by idea after idea how to get them to the glade as fast as possible. He dismissed each thought in turn as too dangerous to succeed. He glanced over at Anya.

The girl leant back in her seat. She seemed so very young as she played with her hair absent-mindedly, listening to Akyar talking. The Tream never seemed to shut up. Vedic wondered how Pan put up with it. After all, the god liked the sound of his own voice as well. He mused, *Perhaps they just talk over each other. Can you imagine?* He almost laughed at this. Akyar was looking at him. He'd missed what the vizier had said. Vedic grunted.

'Do you think we can do it?' Akyar repeated. 'Do you think we can find Meyr?'

The woodsman shrugged, an ambiguous gesture that was meant to hide the fact he had been thinking about how to get himself and Anya free of their obligation to find Meyr. He had no idea how to rescue the boy.

Akyar's smile faded. He looked old in the flickering light.

'You did not tell me about Pan,' said Akyar.

Vedic flushed. He did not like the fact Anya had let their meeting with Pan slip, and in front of the king at that. Pan's fate had been their only piece of leverage over Akyar, and it had been spent cheaply in Hogarth's throne room.

'You know Pan well?' asked Anya.

Vedic grinned in spite of himself. 'They do.'

The girl was wearing that confused look again. He wondered how on earth she had survived as long as she had, and caught himself before his thoughts went further. Of course she had survived: she was a clan warrior, granddaughter of *the* clan warrior. The resemblance to her was quite strong now he knew who her grandmother was. She had Thrace's eyes, but the rest was all Gobaith.

'Pan and I are old friends,' said Akyar. 'He is very dear to me.'

'I am sorry,' said Vedic, surprising himself, 'that you found out that way.'

Anya's eyes widened a little as the penny dropped. Vedic enjoyed the small moment of personal horror as she realised the emotions the vizier had been suppressing during their audience with the king.

'You must remember he is a god,' she said. 'Almost certainly still alive.'

Akyar smiled sadly, his hand moving to cover Anya's. 'You are as sweet as you are fierce, Lady Anya,' he said. 'Yet I am forced to recall that all of the gods you saw up until Pan were dead and killed at the hands of Cernubus.'

'They were weak compared to Pan or Danu,' Vedic replied.

Akyar nodded. 'I understand. But as he would remind me, hope left these lands a long time ago.'

Vedic had no answer to this. He looked away and blew smoke rings across the ceiling, taking great delight in sending smaller rings through the larger ones. His mind continued to shuffle escape scenarios. There was little point in trying anything while they were still in Tream land, and that would cost them in time lost. Still, to be resupplied could be the difference between survival and death.

'You two also know each other well,' said Anya, her voice sounding faintly accusing.

Akyar laughed. 'Tell me what you see that has led you to this conclusion.'

The woodsman raised an eyebrow.

'Vedic doesn't play well with others,' she said. 'In fact, he's never polite or pleasant to anyone, and yet with you he is. As for you ... you seem to be the first person who's met him and not wanted to kill him.'

'Then he obviously doesn't know me,' said Vedic, a rare smirk on his lips. 'To know me is to want to kill me.'

Both Akyar and Anya laughed.

Vedic stood, walked over to the window and looked out across the canopy. He took a draught of smoke from his pipe, the bowl a glowing amber light against the night sky. They were in the uppermost levels – being vizier had some advantages – and it was possible to look across the roof of the forest to the lands beyond. The distant home of the thain, Vikrain, the largest city in the clan territory, was a simple prick of light at the western edge of a sea of leaves. Vedic did not look at the stretching canopy. He'd had enough of forests for a lifetime. Instead, he focused on the sentinels' slow plod through the skies. They would align soon. The Shaanti used to worship that. He closed his eyes to enjoy the draught from the window as he smoked.

'Are you telling me fibs?' asked Akyar.

Anya sipped her wine before replying. 'Truthfully? Yes. I knew he was acquainted with you, because when you appeared out of the canopy like a kind of flying wizard, he let you live.'

'You don't miss much,' said Vedic, 'do you?'

'Ah,' said Akyar, standing to clear the table. 'So sure are you of the forestal's martial prowess?'

'Forestal, my arse!' said Anya, pausing to take a larger sup of wine.

This is not strictly wise, thought Vedic. *She thinks the drink will help with her nerves, but wine will only make the shakes worse.* Vedic tried to remember if there was ever a time when the kills had made him shake. He found he could not.

She continued. 'Vedic is a warrior, or I'm a—'

'Charming lady who perhaps should slow down,' said Akyar, attempting to take the glass from her.

'I'm fine,' she said, turning to the woodsman. 'It's true though, isn't it, Vedic? You're a warrior.'

The woodsman turned towards her. He rested one arm on the window. He exchanged an amused look with Akyar. The bottle of wine on the table looked to be almost empty, and Anya swayed gently like grass in the wind.

'It's true, I know Akyar,' said Vedic.

'Stop teasing me. You're a warrior.'

'We have an early start,' replied Vedic. He no longer felt like smiling. 'You should get some sleep.'

'I'm not tired.'

'I am,' said Vedic. He needed time to think, away from the others. He emptied his pipe into the fire and pulled himself up the ladder out of the living area in search of a bed.

Vedic could hear Anya's voice lose the pretence of drunkenness as she continued talking to Akyar. He paused.

'I was sure he'd let something about himself slip if we were drunk,' said Anya, 'if he thought I wouldn't remember.'

'Ah, I see you can hold your liquor after all.'

'I could drink most of the men in my village under the table. Not that I'm proud of that.'

'You humans do like addling what little intelligence you have.'

'My grandfather certainly did.'

'I think there are lots of things you're better at than your male brethren. Hence, you are here and they are not.'

'Vedic manages not to see it,' said Anya, saluting Akyar with the glass. 'So, how do you know our charming woodsman?'

Akyar laughed. 'Oh, I'm not sure *charming* is a word I would use to describe him.'

'How would you?'

'Ah, Anya, you seek to draw me on secrets that are not mine to bandy about. You must ask Vedic these questions.'

Anya's disappointment was again obvious, prompting Akyar to add, 'I have from time to time passed messages from the gods to Vedic, but unlike Pan, I have no quarrel with the woodsman.'

'I thought the Tream hated the gods?'

'Some do. Some simply distrust them, having studied them for decades. I am of neither opinion. They fascinate me.'

'I can't tell if Vedic was made a forestal as a reward or a punishment,' said Anya. 'He seems to think he did something awful in the past.'

'Ah, to Pan it was,' said Akyar, sighing. 'Indeed, to you it might be as well, but to myself, a Tream, I've seen humans do worse, and I probably will see them do the like again. It is not your fault, it's in your blood: you're violent creatures. The monkeys that we see in the eastern reaches will tear apart interlopers if they get the better of them. Humans are no different.'

'Aside from not being monkeys ... I don't know what he did,' said Anya.

Vedic thought she sounded frustrated, but he did not want her prying. He felt bad enough that he was lumbered with another when he needed to get to Danu.

She continued. 'No one will tell me. But it seems to me the crime couldn't be that bad, not compared to what I have seen men do, or he would have found a way to leave me to die. No one truly evil could risk themselves again and again.'

Akyar did not reply loud enough for him to hear. Vedic thought for a moment the vizier was laying out his story. Perhaps this might be better. *What about your arm?* he thought. *If she behaves stupidly when she knows, and Pan is gone, how will you ever get free of this magic?* He had a vague vision of himself following Anya like a poor man's shadow until the end of time while Danu rotted in a cage. He shook his head. He did need to sleep.

AKYAR WATCHED the weary and drunk Anya – whatever she claimed about her tolerance – stumble from the main living quarter of his home into the bedchamber. He had given the bed up willingly – he did not want to be scraping his new ally off the forest floor. He suspected she was the only reason Vedic had not attempted to fight his way free. Cursed woodsman.

In the quiet of the empty living quarter, only the faint odour of stale smoke and fine wine to keep him company, Akyar pondered his failure. He had been so sure. Jiana's description, her mental picture, had been as clear as any in the archive, as sharp as his own. He'd been talking to her ever since they were little; she was like an extension of his own mind.

Why would the records not show the Morrigan as she was?

You know why. It was his own mind's voice answering. The truth was that neither god nor Tream really controlled the trees that kept both races' archives. They only revealed what they wanted. Many were insane after so much abuse from the world of men. Others had grown bored, and a small few enjoyed playing games a bit too much. His head spun a little. He stood and opened the door.

The night sky outside was clear enough to see the sentinels marching across – a slow-motion dance of light, like fireflies in a cosmological mating dance. Akyar stepped outside into the crisp night air.

The vizier had always loved the sentinels, the three watchers in the night sky, who had kept him company when he could not sleep. In the older archives, and amongst the older gods, he had found tales of them bizarre enough to put him at risk of execution even with Hogarth on the throne. Once upon a time, he would have risked death to bring the knowledge back to his people. Pan had changed that.

It hurt to think of the god as dead.

'Why did you lie to me?'

Hogarth stood a little way away on the same branch. He was cloaked. Akyar imagined he looked a lot like the wraith Vedic and Anya had described seeing in the Corden. Akyar acknowledged his old friend with a nod. Neither of them had much time for the pretensions of royalty in private. Hogarth had taken to seeking out his company and counsel more and more for this very reason.

'I did not lie to you,' said Akyar. 'I thought the woman was Danu. I have told you how I saw her.'

'I'm not talking about the goddess,' said Hogarth, not lowering his hood. 'I am talking about Pan.'

There it was. Akyar felt his stomach lurch and his cheeks burn. He felt as if he had been spotted wearing human clothes and reading their absurd paper scrolls.

'What?' he replied.

'I already suspected,' said Hogarth. 'The amount of time you were away. I thought the goddess had caught your eye, perhaps. You were so against confrontation, but the minute they mentioned Pan's death ...'

'He is not dead,' said Akyar, his voice quiet.

Hogarth drew back his hood now. The king looked tired. He had aged a decade in a few days.

'You're keeping secrets from me, Akyar, and I do not understand why. What is this god that has come between us?'

'You do not know everything just because you have a crown on your head,' said Akyar, his temper rising. 'You would not go into the deep archives; you would not listen to the lost boughs. You expect me to sift the truth from their broken lies, and you no longer listen when I warn you.'

'You can make mistakes, Akyar,' said Hogarth, his voice gentle. 'It is not your fault that Meyr was taken.'

'I was supposed to be with them.'

'And if you had been, I might be mourning my fallen friend as well, might never have heard of the woodsman's infraction and have no hope at all of anything but war with this scarred god.'

Akyar did not answer. The truth was he blamed not himself but the king for the boy's predicament. The king's boyhood prejudices against the gods had likely provoked them into taking a hostage against the prospect of yet another war with the Tream. Even without this incident, the king's attitude towards their neighbours was getting worse every year, driven by his anger at his brother's fate so many years ago. Akyar had made a great deal of effort to secure the lives of Vedic and Anya to help in recovering the boy.

'What is it?' asked Hogarth, an edge coming to his voice.

Akyar did not look away from his stare. 'You, milord,' he replied. 'You do not listen to me any more. I think on my return this will be my last time as your vizier. I am no longer useful.'

Hogarth folded his arms. 'I am still king. I will take my own counsel on when my ministers resign.'

Akyar shook his head. 'No, not in this. I cannot guide you on the road to war, which is where you are headed, consciously or unconsciously. I will find the prince and bring him home, and then I will leave.'

Hogarth stepped forward and placed his hands on Akyar's shoulders. 'Old friend, this is an overreaction ...'

'Is it? I told you not to send our forces through the Wound. Do you know whose land that is?'

Hogarth shook his head.

'The Morrigan's,' replied Akyar. 'I checked after my mistake became apparent. You never listened. The Wound is a dark place in both our and the humans' histories.'

Hogarth looked like Akyar had struck him.

'All those years ago,' said Akyar, pushing the lesson home. 'Did you forget what your father was trying to teach you when he sent me to negotiate for you?'

'My father was too soft with them,' said Hogarth. 'The humans are violent and petty in whatever form they choose to take, god or mortal. You cannot be weak.'

'Is it weakness that drives that girl to help you?'

'Self-interest. She wants to save her people,' said Hogarth.

'No,' said Akyar, slapping his fist into his palm. 'She would help you even if you had not made it part of your bargain. She is the only reason Vedic is helping you – because she has shamed him.'

Hogarth pulled his hood back up.

'I will accept your resignation when Meyr is returned,' he replied, his voice hoarse. 'You may leave my lands thereafter and join the gods you have so come to cherish.'

'Banishment?'

Hogarth hesitated. 'A gift.'

'Jiana will not understand.'

'Jiana is not as she was.'

Hogarth slipped away into shadows. Akyar watched him go, hoping that there was still time to fix this terrible error that had led to the child being taken. Perhaps, if he were lucky, he could find a way to make the king see that only Cernubus was the enemy and not all the gods. The Kurah invasion put them all at risk. Hogarth could not see the danger.

Akyar looked back up at the sentinels, hoping to see their soothing light once more, but was disappointed to see that the racing clouds had obscured them and brought about the full dark.

CHAPTER SIXTEEN

THEY LEFT AT DAWN.

The clouds still covered the sky above the trees, and everything appeared to be covered in a strange silver light, as if the world had been spun anew from cobwebs. Anya pulled the cloak the Tream had given her tight around her worn clothes. They had not been able to do much else for her, given they did not wear any clothing themselves. However, the sword Jiana had given her was strapped to her back, and there was a knapsack containing food, and full waterskins on her shoulder. Vedic had his pack thrown across both shoulders, his Tream sword wedged in on the right shoulder and his axe strapped to his hip. He had not bothered to replace his bow. There was no need, because Akyar was carrying one, along with his own sword and pack. Vedic led the way, followed by Akyar and Anya, who walked side by side.

To Anya, it felt as if they were sneaking out.

Jiana did not come to see them off, but Hogarth did. He stared at them from the Tream palace's gates on the forest floor, and as they travelled out of the Tream lands into the gods', Anya spotted the odd Tream face up in the trees, watching them with the intensity of a panther watching its prey.

The companions did not talk. Their evening of drinking had left them comfortable enough in their company not to. *Or are we all travelling with our own ghosts?* thought Anya. Fin and her grandfather were back walking by her side, but she had not heard her mother's voice in an age.

'Where are we going?' asked Akyar of Vedic. 'The boy was taken due east of here.'

Vedic did not look at the vizier, but he replied, 'Where he was taken is irrelevant. We know the Morrigan took the boy, and so she is likely to have bound him at her palace. In the Wound.'

Anya tilted her head at this. She had never heard of the Wound. 'What's that?'

Vedic didn't turn around to look at her either. 'We're making for the Raized, Anya, but in the Tream language, it is called the Wound.'

Anya felt cold. She knew what the Raized was. Every Shaanti did, and she had little desire to go there. The thought of the frightened Tream prince carried her on.

'I don't think a frontal assault is a very good idea,' said Akyar. 'She'll be expecting us. Is there not another, more hidden way to this creature's lair?'

Vedic did look at the Tream now. 'What aren't you telling me?'

Akyar shook his head. 'Nothing. I just think we should be wary. She'll be expecting a response of one nature or another from Hogarth.'

'I think Akyar is right,' said Anya. She wanted no part of the Morrigan's lands, and she knew enough of them to be very afraid.

'What we want to do is irrelevant,' said Vedic. 'What we have chosen is the issue. If we must free the boy, then we must go into Golgotha.'

'And I suppose it is just coincidence that none of our guards that are trailing us will follow us in there?'

Vedic grinned at Akyar. 'You're getting the idea now.'

The vizier looked at Anya with pleading eyes.

Anya frowned. 'No, the woodsman is right. In the legends of the Morrigan, you can only gain entry via a tunnel in the Raized.'

'What if she hasn't taken him there?'

'The rest of the forest is under the control of Cernubus,' said Vedic. 'And before that, Danu. I don't know about Cernubus, but Danu would never tolerate this kind of action. Who do you think has kept the peace on their side for the last thousand years?'

'What if Cernubus ordered the kidnap?'

Vedic stopped. The vizier had landed a point, and Anya certainly didn't know the answer to the question. Vedic thought before he spoke.

'We have to accept that possibility. We cannot know, but I would be surprised if the Morrigan has gone over to Cernubus – even for her that would be a step further than she has ever gone. Cernubus has Pan. I have a hard time imagining she would allow anyone to do harm to Pan, for example, who was always one of her favourites, and Cernubus has done him harm.'

Akyar didn't move. 'But you can't be sure.'

'It doesn't matter,' said Anya, stepping forward. 'If the Morrigan is doing it for Cernubus, then it is a deliberate trap for the Tream, to distract you while the Kurah do their work. She will have gone to Golgotha. You can't hide the boy in the open forest – you would find him too easily.'

Vedic nodded and resumed the march. Akyar hesitated for a moment before following Anya at a slow pace, his eyes darting back in the distance to where he knew the Tream scouts were following. For now.

THE COMPANIONS WALKED all through the morning, passing trees that seemed younger than those they had walked amongst in the Tream area, and were increasingly so the further they travelled. The forest was once again becoming sparse as it had done on the edge of the Corden. Anya tried hard not to think about why that was, but she could almost hear her grandfather telling her the legend as a little girl. *Stay focused*, her mother's voice echoed round her head, prompting her to draw her cloak tighter despite the suns above.

The woodsman and Akyar did not talk. In point of fact, Vedic didn't seem to want to talk to her either. Periodically he would stop and bend down to look at the tracks and marks on the ground, pick up the dirt and rub it between his fingers, even place his hand on the odd tree. Anya did not know why he was so cautious: they had heard no wolves for some time, and she doubted they would see much life at all this close to the Morrigan's lands.

'We understood the Wound to be a wasteland where the Morrigan lived,' said Akyar. 'You seem to think there's something else in there. Are you trying to trick me?'

'And yet you are following,' said Vedic.

Akyar shook his head, but the woodsman did not look round.

Anya put her hand on the Tream's arm. 'He's following the legend.' In the distance, her grandfather's ghost looked at her, but she could not see the expression on his face.

Akyar smiled back. It was a sad smile. She reminded herself that he was worried for his friend's son, and he was also grieving for Pan. She pressed on – as much to settle her own nerves as to explain to the Tream.

'When I was a child, my grandfather told me tales of the Morrigan. I think it was meant to be an allegory, though I never managed to determine what for. In all of those tales, there was only ever one way into the Morrigan's actual realm, Golgotha, and that was through a tunnel in the Raized. Well, two ways – but dying would be counterproductive.'

'I thought Golgotha was your underworld, a metaphor. How can we get there?'

'I thought our gods were metaphors until a few days ago,' said Anya, laughing.

'But surely your grandfather ...'

Anya's laughter faltered. 'My grandfather was ... unreliable as I grew up. Falkirk never talked about the war. None of them did.'

'War's only ever interesting to those who haven't been in one,' said Vedic. 'The rest of us just want to forget.'

Anya ignored him.

'The Morrigan was not always mad. Once she was merely the guardian of Golgotha. We had more gods then; many have been forgotten.'

Anya paused. *Perhaps they had not been forgotten? Perhaps Cernubus had been quietly killing them, stealthily hunting them down through the ages.*

'Please continue,' said Akyar. 'I am the keeper of the records for the Tream, and I have only fragments regarding the Morrigan.'

Anya smiled. 'So, the story tells, a young god by the name of Bres, who was a cousin of Pan and one of his lesser-known acolytes, became fascinated by the Morrigan.

'This was in the early times, as man spread across the lands, our beliefs forcing us apart until the first war with the forest. The Morrigan moved to a distant part of the woods in order to enjoy her time with Bres without threat or misadventure. She wanted him all to herself. Few gods love death. She is as old as Danu, and powerful.'

'To the Wound ... sorry ... the Raized?'

Anya nodded. 'It was not called that then. Nor was that part of the forest in the gods' territory. It was Tream land, and all across the forest, humans were taking land and clearing trees. We did not yet worship this place in the way we do today. Your people were alarmed at all of this, particularly the rate of destruction of the forest that had once swept all across this continent like a cloak. They demanded the gods stop the humans. The gods created us and so should have been able to rein us in, but the gods refused the Tream.'

'Our records say the humans appeared from the desert and the gods came shortly afterwards,' said Akyar.

Anya paused. There was that statement again, about gods coming after the humans. The idea buzzed around her like a flea, making her skin itch and her head spin. She swatted away the thought.

'The Tream left their parley with the gods in anger. They sent an emissary to the thain of the day, asking that he stop people encroaching on the forest. We did not always have leaders as wise as the woman who leads us now. The thain then was an arrogant man who sought to see the gods with his own eyes, which even then was forbidden, and so he demanded that the Tream send the messenger back with the words "If I am to desist, let Danu herself come forth and command me from her own lips."

'The Tream king flew into his own rage when he heard this, and declared war on the gods and the humans. They marched on all the places the gods used on the western side of the forest, and when they came to the Morrigan's land, they found only Bres.

'Kept away from humanity, and from the other gods, Bres was too weak to resist. What few followers he had were with him that day and slain – somehow the Tream were able to slay the immortal, cutting him to pieces with their swords. He took the final journey across Golgotha as all of us will do.

'When the Morrigan felt his soul pass into Golgotha, she flew into her own rage, and it was like the giant spring storms in the south. She burst through the ground beneath the Raized, where the Tream still were, and destroyed the trees for miles around, killing every living thing in the area – Tream, wildlife, insects, everything. She salted the earth with her tears, preventing anything from growing there for centuries to come.'

'If everyone died, how did anyone know?'

'A Tream was found dying by a boy who had been close enough to see but far enough away to survive. He passed on the knowledge and himself passed into legend when as a man he went into Golgotha to find his true love.'

'The entrance?'

Anya nodded. 'Vedic's looking for the entrance because this is the only way to find the Morrigan and the prince.'

Akyar tilted his head as if weighing up this statement. 'Perhaps. He's acting as if he were up to something.'

Anya watched the woodsman move. He was quicker than Thrace and nimbler than Falkirk. The man did not move like a woodsman, he moved like a warrior – no wasted motion, no unnecessary noise and an almost-preternatural sense of where he was. He was at least five metres ahead, and she was certain he heard every word they were saying.

'That war pulled the gods in,' said Akyar, 'didn't it?'

Anya nodded. 'So legend goes. Danu had to intervene.'

'It sounds a lot like the first war. That started with the humans as well – no offence.'

Anya shrugged. 'The past is a whisper. It distorts and warps with distance. Who can really tell who did what and when? It does not matter.'

'And the Morrigan left the entrance open?'

Vedic stopped again. He called back as he examined a bent section of branch. 'She couldn't close it – she did try. The way she burst the rock apart, the emotion she vented into the land, meant it would not close. Even Danu failed.'

'It seems unlikely that such a big chasm like that would remain hidden,' said Akyar.

'You tell me,' said Vedic. 'The Wound starts on this slope, the wasteland proper over that hill, but then you already know that, Akyar.'

Akyar stopped. Anya turned to him. The Tream looked worried now as he eyed Vedic's hands. The woodsman did not move or make to draw his weapon; he was standing over what looked like faint tracks that had almost been worn away by the weather. They couldn't have been more than a few days old.

'Tream went into the Wound,' said Vedic. 'Before or after the kidnap?'

Akyar did not look away from the woodsman's gaze. 'Before.'

Vedic stared at the tracks he had found, biting his lower lip and then laughing. It was not a nice sound. Anya turned to look at the Tream in surprise and felt herself flush with hurt. Entering the Raized was something the Morrigan had forbidden the Tream and the other gods to do. It was a provocation. They had lied.

No, came the voice in her head. *They omitted. They acted like warriors and not children. Learn from them.*

Vedic pointed up the shallow rise. 'The Wound continues down into the next valley, and somewhere in there is the entrance you are looking for. We will see you after all this is over.'

The woodsman turned to go. Akyar drew his sword.

'Do not make me do this, Vedic.'

The woodsman stopped. He turned round to look at the tip of Akyar's sword. The Tream had pointed the weapon at the man's nose.

'Vedic,' she said. 'We gave our word.'

Vedic shrugged. 'Under duress. I led us here so Akyar could continue alone and we could go for Danu. If we free her first, she can save the boy easily using her power and leave us free to mop up the rest of the Kurah.'

He continued, his hand half drawing his sword from his shoulder. 'Now you are where you need to be, armed with what little we know about the Morrigan and as fair a chance as I can afford to give. Come on, Anya.'

'No,' said Anya. 'I promised to help.'

Vedic shook his head. 'Very well. Stay. I'm going to free Danu.' And the woodsman started to head away from them.

Akyar bellowed and charged, picking up the woodsman's legs and dumping him on the ground. Vedic rolled back to his feet and blocked the vizier's sword.

'You can't win,' said Vedic. He sounded weary. 'Don't do this. You will get hurt.'

'You're every bit the scum they all thought you were.'

'I'm a little long in the tooth for insults, Akyar.'

The Tream drove the woodsman up the rise and over the crest. Anya realised Akyar wasn't trying to hurt him, not really, he was trying to force him deeper into the Raized. Anya ran after them, trying not to fixate on the sick feeling in her stomach over what they might find there. Anya stumbled to a halt at the top of the rise, looking across the Raized.

The blistered landscape was a silent scream to an ancient war. There were no trees. They had left the wall of green behind them, and the next section of forest was too far in the distance to be anything more than a green band on the horizon. All around lay the broken epitaphs of a vast region of woodland. Blackened, crumbling, reaching upwards like decaying digits, the fallen boughs littered the ground.

The woodsman and vizier duelled across the landscape, knocking ancient echoes of the forest to dust as they went. Vedic didn't seem particularly stretched to Anya: he continued to block the Tream with ease as Akyar grew more and more frustrated. Vedic could easily have killed the creature. Anya could see that now in the way he moved, but the woodsman was showing uncharacteristic restraint.

'Hey! Stop it!' she called down as she set off towards them.

Vedic struck the moment she spoke. He swept the Tream's legs out from under him as Akyar tried to lunge towards him. The vizier landed hard on his back with a thud. Vedic held his blade to the Tream's chest. The Tream waited for the killing blow, but the forestal did not strike.

'You're the one who wanted to kill me,' said Vedic, raising an eyebrow, 'not the other way round.'

Akyar knocked the blade to one side, rolling as he did so and picking up his own weapon. He swung again.

'Stop it!' yelled Anya. The pair froze as she stepped between them with her own blade drawn. 'Just stop it. What the hell is wrong with you both?'

The pair stood silent.

'Akyar, if he wants to go, let him. I'm still here and Meyr still needs rescuing,' Anya said. 'We should be looking for the tunnel into Golgotha, not trying to beat this husk of a man. As for you, Vedic ...' She turned to look him in the face. 'You're pathetic. I said "husk", and I meant it. You might have been someone once, but now all you are is a wraith, a shadow of someone who the world long since forgot. You wouldn't go into Golgotha for anyone, would you?'

Vedic didn't reply. He didn't meet her gaze either.

'I never thought I'd see fear from you,' she continued. 'You reek of it though. Why are you so determined to run away?'

Vedic stepped back, his grip tightening on his sword.

'Yeah, go on, run away. But don't pretend you know the Shaanti legends better than I do – turn up to Danu having left a child to die or worse, and see what she does with you. Go in front of the mother goddess with Tream blood on your hands. She may let you live, not that you'll enjoy it.'

'Careful, little one,' said Vedic, his sword lifting once more. 'My patience has its limits.'

'Or what? You'll fight me?' she said, laughing. 'Run if you must. I'm going to look for this boy.'

Anya stepped away from them in search of the tunnel. She could see them in the periphery of her vision. Had she reached them? Akyar looked winded from his numerous falls. He watched Vedic warily as the woodsman moved further away.

'Will you help?' asked Akyar.

'No,' said Vedic, shaking his head. 'I'll not go to Golgotha. Danu has asked for me – I'm oath-bound to respond.'

Akyar looked up at the sky. 'You are an oath-breaker. And old. And slow.'

Akyar leapt. It was a sudden motion that a human being would not have been able to mimic. Vedic could not get his sword up to block, and it was all he could do to get under Akyar and turn the Tream's blade away from his body.

Anya dropped her sword, running to try to stop them, yelling at them as she did so – but it was too late. Vedic used Akyar's momentum against him, and the Tream was thrown over, hitting the ground first, sliding through the dirt with the force of the impact. Anya saw a moment of sudden realisation on the woodsman's face, but it was too late to stop himself falling through the fissure, after the Tream.

They'd found the entrance.

Anya felt her old ankle injury, which had seemingly been healed so well by the mud, now aching like she was a hundred years old. She could feel the heat dissipating from her as if an ice snake were winding round her legs.

Anya did not have to speak their languages to understand from the tone that both were berating the other for getting them into this. She moved closer to the opening. The fissure was barely bigger than a man, camouflaged perfectly against the blood-dark mud. Anya looked down into the black, weighing the danger of following them before they had clearly got to the bottom versus the risk of being left behind.

'Looks like Vedic has a role after all,' said Anya to herself.

In the distance, a crow cawed, and Anya was reminded of the task at hand. She took one last look at the sky, just in case, and hoped she was doing the right thing.

Anya jumped.

It was a long slide. She fell down a tube of rock and dirt made slick by an indeterminate fluid that Anya had no urge to classify. A faint smell, the sweet putrescence of the tunnel, pawed at her throat and nose, and made her eyes water as she tried to slow herself with her arms, bruising them. Below, she could hear the grunts and curses of the other two as they struck the tunnel edges in their descent. As she slid further, the speed increased.

And without warning the journey became a free fall.

The tunnel dropped away beneath her. Darkness was broken by a dull, sick-tinged orange light that blinded like a migraine, and she felt the sensation of having left one's stomach ten metres above as she shot straight down, like an arrow, for what looked like a fatal landing. She cursed her own stupidity. Her last thought before the ground punched her was a prayer for her life not to end like this.

The landing was so hard it felt like a blow, driving the wind from her as her feet drove into the ground. Except the impact wasn't met by the fatal crush of hard soil. It was a slow pool of liquid mud, made painful by the speed of her fall but allowing her to live by virtue of her angle of descent. Her gratitude for the serendipity was lessened by the realisation that – embedded up to her chest already – the slow pool was going to swallow her.

Anya shouted, loud, long and with anger. To come so far and to be stopped, to be killed in this manner – swallowed by mud – it infuriated her.

The slow pool pulled her under. Instinct made her hold her breath, and intellect told her hanging on was foolish, but she couldn't bring herself to end her life by opening her mouth. She hung suspended in the muck for an eternity. Anya's chest seemed to grow, her lungs pressed up against her ribs, and bright points of light burst under her eyelids, showering the shutters of her eyes with streaks of colour as the pressure to open her mouth grew. An insidious voice inside her head begged her to take a breath: it wouldn't take a moment. This voice wasn't her mother's. It didn't sound like anyone she knew or had known. Maybe it was her air-starved brain, but she thought it sounded how she imagined the Morrigan might. Her head exploded with fire.

CHAPTER SEVENTEEN

THE GROUND TILTS. *Smoke fills the air and grips the throat.*

It isn't the thick belching of burning wood but the insidious, cloying sweet-ness of incense smouldering in effusive abandonment throughout the dim stone chamber. Tendrils of smoke stretch into the high ceiling, and the audience seated in front of me on row upon row of benches are obviously uncomfortable. I can see the restlessness etched on their faces, in the shuffling of hands over mouths and the way they shift in their seats in an undulating wave of uneasiness. I wonder why they are prepared to stay. I dislike the hungry look on their faces.

I am gripping a long stone knife with a force that is not under my control. As I look behind me, following the audience's gaze, someone – a young man, an Shaanti – is pushed through the ragged curtain at the back of the dais. The man is maybe twenty, confused and frightened, and he stumbles forward in front of me with a moan. I speak, loud and clear. The crowd agrees with me. The pris-oner smells acrid. He is terrified.

'W-w-why am I here?' stammers the man.

I reply in words I do not understand. My tone is unsympathetic. The knife does not leave my hand.

'I don't ... I ... Please ... let me go ... I will say nothing ... go far away ... do anything ... Just let me go ...'

I step forward, raising my free hand and talking to him in a calm, slow voice. The man cannot understand. I cannot understand. He steps back. He is pushed forward again by someone behind the curtain. A few of the crowd laugh, but I do not. I grip the blade tighter. I try to hold back my own arm, but I am familiar with this dance by now and know I cannot stop the beat.

The man notices the knife. His pupils grow as wide as blossoming flowers as he tries to draw back from the weapon. I move forward swiftly, draping my free hand down the man's face, my words coming quiet under my breath. The man's eyes glass over at the incantation, and there is a cheer from the crowd. The noise prompts me to raise my hand in a gesture for them to be silent.

I look carefully at the man: a beautiful creature with the ivory skin of the nomads who live on the ice, with jet-black hair and large, unblinking brown eyes. I feel my hand close round the back of the man's neck. He struggles briefly. I stare deep into his eyes, and his attempts at freedom stumble into a horrified daze. I lead him to the stone depression in the centre of the dais. He is left mesmerised and standing in the concave curve of the stone. I can feel power ebbing up from the room.

At first I don't know what the sound is. Only when I turn do I realise the audience is chanting softly, that at the front of them stands the man with the purple cloak. I begin to dance in time to the chant, as if drawing energy from the words. This is a strange movement. My limbs move in time to the beat of the chant as I slide, spin, drop and weave, representing the soft words of the crowd as movement. I have never done the like; this feels unnatural, wrong, as if someone else is operating my body, and yet it is oddly right, like I was born to conduct this power.

A bad act is about to happen.

I cut the throat of the Shaanti with a sudden strike. The man's blood sprays, his head lolling briefly back before his whole body crumples into the dip in the dais as if I had also cut whatever strings held him upright. His blood pours into the carved channels, leading from where he fell to the absent hollow that seems to denote a sacred place by its shadowy void. The crowd looks on in silence as their sacrifice bleeds out, but they are not in shock – it is rapture that holds their voices.

The room feels like it is spinning as would a toy I played with as a child, wobbling as it reaches the end of its turn, and yet I'm as steady as a rock as I *bend to the crimson river running down the channels by my feet. When I rise once more, my hands are coated in blood, and as I lift them, the congregation answers as one with two words that even I understand: 'Praise be.'*

CHAPTER EIGHTEEN

ANYA CURSED.

She sat up with a lurch. This made her head feel like it had been beaten with the flat of her sword. She was on the bank of the slow pool, and Vedic stood a few feet away, also covered in mud and dirt. His pack was laid out on the rock next to him. Anya spat the mud in her mouth out. Disorientated and frightened, she lifted her sword, blade pointing at Vedic. In that briefest of moments, she was uncertain if she were dead or alive – she could feel herself breathing, and yet the sun was wrong; the landscape looked like it had been drawn from one of her grandfather's books, and from there memories seeped back as if with the air filling her lungs.

'Are you hurt?' asked Vedic.

Anya looked down. She was still pointing her sword at the woodsman, and after recent events, she wasn't sure lowering the weapon was wise. She glanced around for Akyar. There was no sign of the Tream anywhere she looked, nor was there any sign of him in the slow pool. Nor would there be if he'd drowned.

'I don't know where he is,' said Vedic. 'He wasn't in there. You were the only other person I could find.'

'You pulled me out of the pool?'

Vedic nodded.

'What happened?'

'You were drowning,' replied Vedic, pointing. 'I pulled you out.'

The woodsman was covered in the same lumpy liquid mud as Anya. It dripped from his matted beard, and his eyes were the only thing that stood out from his face, their pale blue looking like marble in the ur-light. He looked hurt, weary and on edge. He was the picture of a mad prophet.

'What about the slow pool? I thought we were dead.'

'There's a technique to moving through them. This wasn't my first time in one of those accursed things.' The forestal scratched at the mud on what remaining hair he had.

'I think I passed out ...' she said, confused. 'I never pass out.'

'You were under a long time,' he said, not unkindly. 'It's a miracle you're alive at all.'

Anya moved quickly, jumping up a rocky outcrop. She bounced up and flipped over the woodsman, landing behind him with her blade at his throat. 'Where is he? Where is Akyar?'

'What?' asked Vedic. His irritation was palpable.

Anya whispered in his ear once more. 'Where is he?'

'Akyar?'

She nodded. He seemed calmer again. She was ready for whatever trick he had planned next.

'We both know you're not going to use that now, little one. You're not going to watch the life drain out of me like that guard – you don't want my death following you round.'

Anya smirked. She pushed the blade hard enough against his throat to hurt but not enough to do anything other than make it bleed a little. 'Try me.'

'Anya.' The woodsman raised his hands. 'I don't know where Akyar is. I lost him in the tunnel and only saw you falling behind me. Now put the sword down before one of us gets hurt.'

'That isn't going to be me.' She maintained the pressure on the blade. 'Even you aren't quicker than this.'

There was a yell.

Anya glanced up at the sound, and it was enough time for the woodsman to twist around the blade, pulling her sword-arm and throwing her onto the ground. He rolled for his sword, coming to his feet even as Akyar fell from the roof of Golgotha, a stream of Tream curses trailing after him. Anya couldn't understand how he had managed to hang there as long as he must have done. Tream were legendary climbers, but everyone had their limits. The crushing impact silenced Akyar and folded the Tream over like a broken doll.

Anya and Vedic stared at each other, swords drawn. Anya touched a bleeding lip, courtesy of the blow that had flung her away from Vedic. She noted Vedic favoured his scarred arm as he wiped away the blood that had beaded on his chest from his grazed throat.

'See,' said Vedic, gesturing at where Akyar had landed.

Anya looked over at the fallen Tream. A cloud of dust hung suspended in the air around where he'd struck, and it was hard to imagine anything surviving that kind of fall, let alone a slight Tream.

Vedic shrugged and sheathed his sword. 'I have no interest in harming Akyar. I just have an obligation to Danu. The Tream are not my problem.'

Anya ignored him and ran to where the Tream lay unmoving, neck bent at an awful angle. Anya was about to close Akyar's open eyes when he sat up swearing. The Tream's spine gave an almighty crack as he pulled his body straight. This was followed by yet more Tream curses as he twisted his head, crunching round to the right angle, and Anya felt her gorge rising. *What magic was this?*

'But you ...' she said, confused. 'And your neck ... Are you immortal?'

Akyar smiled, tiredly. 'If only.'

'Tream are a bit tougher than humans, particularly with regard to falls,' said Vedic, amused. 'If they died from every little drop, they'd never make adulthood. You can kill them though, if you're good enough, and eventually, they do grow old. Although this one won't if he tries to attack me like he did on the surface again.'

'I won't need to,' said Akyar, rising. 'You're here.'

'He does have a point,' said Anya, turning to look at the woodsman. 'You're here now. You might as well help us.'

Vedic did not answer. Anya watched him look back at the rocks surrounding the slow pool before returning his gaze to the roof of the cavern in which Golgotha sat. The rock, ceiling and all, was dull grey with ribbed veins of amber, which gave off a lot of the orange-tinged ur-light that Anya had noticed in the slow pool. There was no way to reach the aperture through which they had fallen: the roof was too far away. Vedic would need to find another way out of the underworld, and Anya knew as well as he did that the only option was to go through the heart of the Morrigan's domain, where the boy was most likely being held.

'Our paths lie together again,' said Vedic. 'We all have to return to the surface eventually, and as long as our trails converge, I see no reason not to travel together. Do you?'

Anya shook her head, but Akyar pressed home the point. 'But if they diverge?'

'Then I am gone,' said Vedic, shrugging. 'I must return to Danu. I swore an oath, and I will live up to this one.'

'You pick your moments to find your honour,' said Akyar, his face knotted with anger. 'Careful, old man. Yours is a trinket that is tarnished.'

'And you are on thin ice,' said Vedic, hand on his sword hilt. To Anya: 'Don't you want Danu's help? Are you really going to help the Tream over her?'

Anya sighed. Vedic seemed determined to antagonise the Tream into killing him. 'I told you, Danu would want me to help a child. I'll not go in front of her having condemned one to death, human or otherwise.'

'You're guessing. You've never met her. What if you're wrong? What if your own kind die because of this?' asked Vedic.

Anya shrugged. It was not like she hadn't considered that possibility. She had not started this war. The invasion wasn't her fault. She was just trying to save some of the captured, to give the deaths of those who had already fallen meaning. The woodsman was a strange one, a forestal, appointed by Danu herself, a former Shaanti warrior, and yet he did not seem to understand what the goddess stood for. This was all academic to him. She was a figurehead.

'This is the right thing to do. I do not need a god to tell me that.'

'See,' said Akyar, turning back to the woodsman. 'A girl of seventeen knows more than you.'

Vedic drew his sword.

'Stop bickering, you two,' said Anya, striding past them. 'We will all be safer if we stay together.'

Akyar nodded.

Vedic interjected. 'More importantly, where are we?'

The area in which they had landed was pockmarked with slow pools, but most of the wider landscape was a dry and dusty desert. There was not much of anything around them save for a ribbon of water some way in the distance, a river that brought the dunes to an end. The far side of the cavern ate light in a line of void where the rock became a volcanic jet-black that above ground would have looked like the sky had not quite been finished. It smelt of overheated, stale air and overcooked meat.

'Golgotha,' said Anya, her voice somewhere between awe and fear.

'Thanks,' said Vedic, folding his arms. 'I thought we'd landed in Kurah.'

Anya rubbed her arms against the cold and gusting wind that buffeted them. Here, imagination may have been playing tricks on her, but she was sure the sickly orange glow from above was beginning to fade as she tried to orientate herself. She pulled at the memories of what she had read in her grandfather's books, at the lilting poetry she had been made to memorise as a girl. There would be little time if this place kept a form of night. She did not want to be out in the open, with the dead, when darkness fell.

'Seven rivers ...' she said. 'Seven, and the first of these is ...?'

'What are you blathering on about?' asked Vedic.

'There are seven rivers in Golgotha,' she said, pointing at the distant river. 'And that's one over there. That must be Acheron, because I think we're in the Fields of Asphodel.'

'There's no grass here, just sand,' said Akyar, picking up a handful of dust. There was a flash of white below the surface of the sand.

'It's not that kind of field,' said Anya, aware of the smell coming from the ground. 'And it's you that made me think we were there ...

When you landed, you broke the ground. There's an easy way to find out.'

Anya bent down, pawing sand away from the small indentation Akyar had made in the ground. The thing she sought stared back at her with empty eyes. Carefully she lifted a skull from the ground. She placed the bone to one side and continued shifting the sand to reveal yet more skulls, densely packed. The bones appeared to run under the surface in all directions.

'What's this?' asked Vedic. He was as pale as Anya had ever seen him look.

'A field of skulls,' she replied, placing her hand on Vedic's shoulder. 'In Shaanti legend, the souls of the dead gather here before making the onward journey to the land beyond. This is a place of preparation, of acceptance of your fate. Some wander for several lifetimes before crossing the Acheron. Time is relative here.'

'Then where are they?' asked Akyar, holding one of the skulls up against the dull light.

'Here,' said Anya, reaching for the skull. 'I fancy the light is fading.'

'Yes,' said Vedic, his pupils gleaming black and wide.

Anya shifted. 'I think we should keep moving. We need to find shelter – some of the legends say that souls walk Asphodel at night.'

'Yes,' said Vedic, too quickly. 'If we are engulfed with ghosts, then the Morrigan will realise and come after us.'

The last of the light disappeared.

'Damn,' said Anya. 'How are we supposed to see?'

'I can see,' answered Akyar.

'Lead on, then,' said Vedic, his voice cracked like the bones beneath them.

Anya frowned. This was beyond normal fear of the unknown, and Vedic was no coward.

'Happy to,' said Akyar, stepping forward. 'Where are we going?'

'Towards the river. Into Golgotha,' said Anya, confident. 'We must cross the Acheron and find the Trivium if we are to have any hope of returning to the surface or finding the boy. It's the only way I know.'

'I was afraid you were going to say that was the path ahead,' said Vedic, sighing as he drew his blade.

There was a cry that sounded like neither wolf nor human. They didn't want to meet the thing that had spewed such noise into the rank air. They gathered their tattered cloaks, along with what remained of their packs, and strode off towards the river. Akyar led their night-time hike. Anya came next and Vedic went last. In this way, arm-in-arm, they marched all the way to the river without stopping. They saw no ghosts, but as the wind grew, they all fancied they could hear voices in its screams.

'PERHAPS WE CAN GO ANOTHER WAY,' said Akyar, looking round.

They stood on the edge of a riverbank. They were all exhausted from their long night-time march as the dull ur-light of the false dawn began to lift the black. In that strange rusty light, they could see the river, crimson dark with the blood that flowed through it, slapping rocks and skulls with its fury as it rushed to whatever delta marked its end. The river flowed far too fast, was much too wide for anyone to cross on foot or to swim.

'There is no other way,' said Vedic, kicking the ground in frustration. 'Unless you want to kill yourself and travel the spirit road.'

'That's right,' said Anya, too tired to move. 'I don't know any other way but the Trivium, and that itself is based on a very old myth that I was told as a child. We may be stuck here after all – there's supposed to be a ferry.'

'We are lost, then,' said Akyar, poking the ground with his sword. 'What of Meyr?'

Vedic grunted. It was unclear if he was sympathetic.

'There's no one been here in some time,' said Anya, looking along the bank for any sign of a boat or other people. 'If there ever has been.'

Someone had to have been here before, because the river was just where it should have been in legend, and so someone had to have made their way out to tell of it. Unless ... Could the Morrigan have planted the legend? How much did gods seek the belief that seemed to fuel them?

Anya turned her back to the water, rubbing the back of her neck to try to assuage the tension she felt she had been carrying since she'd been pulled out of the slow pool. There was a growing sense of foreboding in her. She had missed some vital aspect of the events in which she had been caught up, but she could not put her finger on what. Her stomach churned, but whether it was with worry or hunger, she could not tell, and she forced the sensation from the front of her mind.

Focus. She couldn't remember the exact wording of the legends of Golgotha, but she'd been certain she wasn't wrong about this river.

'What is the legend?' asked Akyar, tired.

'There should be a ferryman,' said Anya, waving her hand at the river like it was a person who had betrayed her. 'He takes the dead across the river, and he can be bribed. According to the legend. It's the only way to the other side – you can't cross the Acheron by fording or swimming. Arawn used him.'

'Perhaps whoever the ferryman is only comes for the dead,' suggested Akyar, his eyes flicking around as if he expected to see a ghost slipping from the murk. 'We haven't seen any yet.'

Vedic's eyes caught Anya's: *Shall you tell him, or shall I?*

'That doesn't mean they're not here,' said the woodsman, softly.

Anya thought she saw Fin on the other side of the river, playing hopscotch in the dust. She forced herself back to the matter at hand.

'Perhaps the ferryman was killed or removed after Arawn,' she speculated.

Vedic sat down. 'No. The ferryman remained. More likely he has wandered off somewhere.'

Son of a whore, thought Anya. 'He remained? Have you been here before?'

Vedic didn't answer.

'You have! Why aren't you leading the way?' She couldn't keep her anger back.

'That I have visited Golgotha before does not mean I know my way through,' replied Vedic, his skin still pale in the rising light.

Anya thought she could see sweat on his brow, which would make little sense in the cold.

'But how?' asked Akyar, kneeling next to the woodsman. 'How did you get in and out? You're not dead.'

'Obviously, I had help.'

'Danu?' asked Anya.

Vedic coughed. He seemed embarrassed. 'Actually, no. It was the Morrigan.'

Anya watched Akyar look away from the woodsman. The Tream seemed unsure how to react to this latest piece of intelligence but was at least not going for his sword. When no further elaboration was offered, he sighed in disgust and turned to the river.

'Did you die?' Anya asked.

Vedic looked at her, startled. 'What?'

'Did you die? Did she allow you to return? Was that why you became a forestal?'

Vedic looked sick, but he shook his head. 'No. It wasn't that. I'm as alive as you are. Though a fair bit older.'

Anya frowned.

Vedic rubbed his arms against the cold. 'I promise you, if I knew the way out of here, I would share it with you.'

Anya waved his platitudes away. She sat down on her own and drank a little water from the skin in her pack. They had very limited water now until they found a fresh source instead of blood rivers, and so she just took the minimum to moisten her throat.

'Well, how are we going to get across?' she asked, breaking the silence.

'I don't know,' said Vedic, unpacking his pipe from his belt. 'I'm thinking.'

'You keep on doing that,' said Akyar, walking along the riverbank, away from them. 'I'm going to ask this fellow.'

Anya and Vedic's eyes followed Akyar's path before they skipped ahead to the spot along the river where he was pointing. Upstream, a low mist billowed down the river, travelling at the vapour's edge. A long boat appeared, moving as if the fog were pushing the vessel. The craft was similar to the skiffs Anya's uncle used to fish with on the lake at Larvon. In the rear of the boat, standing and powering the craft along with a few steady thrusts of a long wooden pole, was a tall, hooded figure. The ferryman had arrived.

THE BOAT WAS A DIRTY WHITE.

At first, Anya thought the hull was made of ash, stained by the blood of the Acheron, but as the boat drew closer, plasma glooping against the hull, it became evident the vessel was made of a single piece of carved bone. Anya tried not to think what would have had bones of sufficient size to produce a boat of that length. What would be the limits of what the Morrigan could do with her power here, in her own realm? If she made an attack on them now, in the open, where there was no possibility of shelter or escape, there would be little chance of survival.

The narrow craft slid partially onto the bank with the low grinding noise of shingle on bone. The ferryman placed the craft's pole down inside the hull before stepping, carefully, onto the bank. His hood remained down, and only the pale flesh of his hands, made sickly by the light of the cavern, let slip that there was anything under the robe but shadow.

'Do you seek transport?' asked the ferryman.

There was an unpleasant smell coming from the boat – or perhaps from the ferryman. Anya found it hard to tell.

'We do,' said Vedic.

Anya noted he had shifted his weight to the balls of his feet. *Do you feel the danger too?*

'Are you willing to take us?'

'You live,' the ferryman replied, tilting his head.

'I see,' said Vedic. His voice was calm, but he looked like a mountain lion ready to pounce on his prey. Anya was reminded of his words – he was not a nice man.

'And what might we do for you to … overlook that?'

'You live, but so do many who come here,' said the ferryman, continuing as if he had not heard. His head moved beneath the hood, taking in all three of them. 'I will take you to the other side of the river, but I cannot take you back. Think carefully before deciding.'

'Well,' said Akyar, turning to Anya with a smile. 'That's progress.'

'I don't like this,' replied Anya, frowning.

The ferryman moved. Anya fell silent. He stepped up to Vedic, ignored him and moved on to Anya. At her, he paused. There was a sniffing sound, loud and filled with fluid. His hand rose up, hovered around her face, clenched one, two, three times before falling back to his side, and she caught a definite smell of putrefaction. He walked on to Akyar, where he stopped and sniffed again.

'You,' said the ferryman, his voice cracked as if he smelt a rank odour. 'You, I am not permitted to take.'

'Why?' asked Akyar, fists clenching. 'Because I am Tream?'

The ferryman shook his head. 'Your kind do not come here, but that is not why. You have the gods' mark upon you. You must wait here or leave by another route.'

Vedic turned to Akyar. 'That bloody goat god isn't even here and he's causing trouble.'

'How much?' asked Akyar, ignoring Vedic.

'There is no price,' the ferryman continued. 'You are marked.'

Vedic stepped closer to the him. 'That is not possible. You take all of us or none of us.'

Anya was surprised. She had been about to say the same thing before Vedic could accept the ferryman's proposal to take just the two of them. She had not thought Vedic would show any loyalty.

'Then I will leave,' said the ferryman, turning his back on them.

Anya watched him walk down to the boat, her eyes flicking between him and the woodsman. Vedic did not move. He was going to let the ferryman go. Amidst the panic that their only means of escape was leaving, she pushed away the voice at the back of her mind that said he must have a reason and that Vedic did nothing through altruism. She had to act.

'Wait!' said Anya, jumping onto the shingle. 'Surely there's something you want, an act that you would be willing to accept for transportation of all of us.'

The ferryman stopped. 'The living have nothing that I desire, and everything I need. You do not understand what you say. Your offer is meaningless. You would refuse me.'

'Sir,' said Akyar, stepping forward. 'I realise I am not human, that my presence here is foolish, but I seek a small boy lost from his parents, and nothing more. Will you not help me?'

'Many lost children come here,' said the ferryman with a shrug. 'It is nothing to me – they make the final journey as do we all.'

'Even a Tream child?' asked Akyar.

'Perhaps,' said the ferryman. 'Usually I do not pay that close attention to my passengers.'

'Please,' said Anya, her hand on the ferryman's robed and bony arm. 'We will do anything.'

The ferryman paused. 'Anything?'

Anya nodded, her heart thumping hard in her chest.

The ferryman turned.

'I accept your terms.' He extended a pallid hand towards Anya.

Anya accepted the handshake. It was icy to the touch, and there was more movement beneath the skin than there should have been. She did not linger over holding his hand.

'So warm,' said the ferryman, before climbing into the boat.

'That was an unwise bargain,' said Vedic, holding his left arm as if it were aching. 'We know nothing of his intentions.'

'Are you sure?' asked Anya, irritated. 'You're the only one of us who has been here before.'

The ferryman gestured to the seats. The trio hung back, unsure. 'Well, are you joining me?'

SILENCE HUNG between them as the mist hung on the water.

The only sound was the slap of blood on the hull as the boat glided through the river, punctuated by the ferryman's staff being occasionally extracted from the river, ready for another push. The river seemed far wider now they were actually on the blood and travelling. Anya sat in one corner of the bow, watching her companions. The woodsman was in turn watching the ferryman and looked like he was struggling with some dilemma. Akyar sat in the middle of the boat, staring at the bottom of the vessel and not looking at the blood. Tream did not like boats.

'You're not taking us to the other side,' said Anya as the boat reached the midpoint and swung round so the hull was parallel to the bank. Vedic looked tense. He still rubbed his left arm periodically.

'Have no fear,' said the ferryman, continuing his steady pushes into the water. 'I'm taking you where you need to go.'

'And where is that?' asked Vedic, his axe in his lap under his hands.

'The road. You need to get to the road, do you not?'

'What road?' asked Akyar.

'The road to the Trivium,' said the ferryman, gesturing in a down-river direction. 'You're seeking the Cave of Shadows and the route to the Fortress of the Nine Towers.'

Anya nodded. That was her plan, to find the road, although she had been banking on the ancient path being near where they struck the river. She knew the road led to the Trivium – in legend, Arawn had taken that path. The road had led him past the Morrigan's fortress, and this was her hope now. If the Morrigan had the boy, that was where he would be.

Akyar opened his eyes. 'And how does a ferryman, who appears from nowhere, happen to know that?'

'I did not appear from nowhere. I came from upstream when I saw your vapour on the air,' said the ferryman, continuing to push the boat forward. 'The Trivium is the only way to the cave, the cave the only way to the surface. Anyone living tries to leave here as fast as possible – it was hardly a deductive leap.'

'But we must rescue the boy first,' said Akyar, leaning forward.

The ferryman made a strange noise, like someone gargling, and they took a moment to realise he was laughing: slow, low and wet.

'The mistress of this place has the boy. Have no fear, you will find the hag at the Trivium.'

Akyar frowned. 'She guards the way out?'

'She is the goddess of death,' said Vedic, shifting in his seat. 'People do not come back from the dead.'

'No,' said the ferryman, turning to look at the woodsman. 'She is not the god of the dead. Death is absence. She is the goddess of dying itself. The Morrigan, Anu, is the goddess of Golgotha, of the final journey, not the destination. No one has ever seen the god of darkness, and no one is certain that such a thing exists. That final door into the void is one-way, and no one – man, god, Tream or otherwise – returns to tell tales.'

You don't know as much as you pretend to, do you, woodsman? thought Anya. *Why is that?*

'I thought this was your afterlife,' said Akyar, waving at the landscape.

'No,' said Anya. 'This is the final journey. We have no legend for what lies on the other side of the doorway, just superstition. In this way, we are different from the likes of the Tinaric.'

'Golgotha, place of the skull, because in the final moment there's just you, alone, in your own head,' said the ferryman, tapping his hood.

'Ferryman,' said Anya, wondering if she could get the ferryman to reveal more. 'Why did she take the boy?'

'I cannot answer this,' said the ferryman. 'Perhaps she seeks to break Danu's hold on her so that she can attack the humans. Gods are bound not to interfere with human affairs.'

Anya sat forward, the memory of her village burning in her mind's eye. 'Cernubus has.'

'The hunter is no longer just a god. He has done terrible things to himself in order to take the forest.'

Akyar looked at the ferryman with narrowed eyes. Anya felt concern ice along her arms.

'Why can't you tell us what the Morrigan wants?'

The ferryman turned to the Tream.

'Anu ordered me not to.'

Vedic's axe was up in an instant, the edge of the weapon at the ferryman's throat, and their would-be ally's hood drawn back, revealing his face.

Akyar hissed in shock, and Anya felt herself muffle a cry in spite of all the wounds she had seen. The ferryman's face was only partially there: from the upper right-hand quadrant of his head in a diagonal sweep to the left side of his jaw, the flesh was normal, if pallid. Where the rest of his face should have been was a mass of purple and red meat, blood occasionally dripping down onto his robe, staining his teeth where his lips would once have been. The creature laughed.

'You're working for her,' said Vedic, visibly choking back bile. 'Where are you taking us?'

'Of course I work for her. This is her domain, and I have been bound here to serve this purpose. Did you think the Morrigan was unaware of your presence?'

Anya drew her own blade.

The ferryman pushed the axe from his throat. 'Now put the weapon down. You can't hurt a dead man.'

Vedic's fingers slipped to the ferryman's throat, checking for a pulse that wasn't there, before complying with the boatman's request. He stepped back.

'How can we trust you? Why shouldn't we jump from the boat?'

'You must trust me,' said the ferryman, pulling his hood back over his head. 'You have no choice. If you jump, the river will drown you, and the boat will not respond to anyone other than me. I do not plan to put into the bank until we reach the road.'

'We are your prisoners,' said Anya. 'You're acting on orders.'

The ferryman shook his head. 'No. You are the people I am helping in spite of my orders.'

'But you said—' replied Akyar.

'I said I could not tell you her plans because she bound me not to,' said the ferryman. 'I have no such orders about taking you to the road. Gods are capricious and do not always think about what they are doing. Look at your curse, forestal.'

'What other orders did she give you?'

The ferryman shook his head. He couldn't or wouldn't answer.

'Great,' said Anya, slapping Vedic's shoulder. 'Now what do we do?'

'This was your idea, Anya,' said Vedic, folding his arms. 'Maybe you can get us out of it.'

'So where is this road?' asked Anya, irritated again that the woodsman was right.

The ferryman looked at her before replying. 'Downriver, where the Acheron meets the Cocytus. You should get your rest – the road is long, and the Cave of Shadows not a trial for the weak-hearted. The Morrigan will not make it easy.'

As if in answer, rain began to fall – rain the colour of liquid coal, hot like ash and gritty as it struck them. Within moments they were soaked. The rain fell in syncopated rhythm on the river and boat, and they could make out shapes in the murk, some human, some not, all staring at the boat's progress.

'We're not going to be a secret after tonight,' said Akyar, huddling down in the boat.

'No,' said Vedic. 'But there was no guarantee we'd make it out of here, anyway.'

CHAPTER NINETEEN

Anya felt like they had been on the boat for days. It had only been a few hours, but the storm and the ferryman's presence had left all of them subdued, even the woodsman. The rain had stopped, although everything was still wet, including the ferryman's robes, which hung in thick, wet billows from his wiry frame and smelt of wet sack.

Anya had grown tired of waiting for the companions to strike up conversation, and she had little desire to talk to their ferryman. Instead, she had wedged herself in next to the hull of the boat and was watching the flow of the blood-water as the ferry moved. She had always wondered about the Acheron – what creatures would live in such a river? Would there be fish? Why wouldn't the blood clot? She had been watching the rain, dark as coal, hit the water, thinking it would change the colour. It didn't. The precipitation dissipated into the blood. She saw no clots either, and so perhaps the rainwater served as a kind of clot prevention.

There was no life that she could see in the murk, no fish to speak of, and she was a little relieved to see that, because, after all, what kind of fish would you find in Golgotha? Would you really want to encounter them? Staring at the blood was an oddly hypnotic exercise, and she found her hand reaching out, in spite of her common sense, to touch it. That was when she saw them.

At first she just saw a single flash of jet black – the creature streamed up to the visible surface and dived again so fast that she wasn't sure if she'd imagined it. Another occurred a few moments later. And another. Suddenly the water around the boat was full of black, writhing coils of eels.

'We may have a problem,' she said, sitting back.

Akyar did not move from the centre of the boat, but Vedic stuck his head over the side for a look. 'What the hell are they?'

'Kresh,' said the ferryman.

'Kresh are birds,' replied Vedic, frowning.

'Kresh are anything that serve under the Morrigan's pleasure,' said the ferryman. 'Technically, I am also Kresh.'

An eel chose that moment to leap from the water at Vedic. Anya thought the creature was going to land right on him. The woodsman, distracted though he appeared, drew his sword without looking and sliced the thing in two.

'How far are we from the road?' he asked.

'We are not far away now,' said the ferryman. 'Assuming you survive this.'

Akyar looked up. 'Survive what?'

The boat lurched as the eels struck the starboard side en masse and flooded into the hull. The boat protested for a moment, trying to right itself, before pitching over and capsizing, tumbling all the occupants of the vessel into the blood and the writhing eels. Anya caught a brief glimpse of the ferryman flopping into the blood like he was already a corpse. There was no more time for thought as she was engulfed.

The blood of the Acheron River was warm, like Anya had fallen into the artery of a giant. She barely had time to gasp in air before the eels, swarming over her like vines run amok, pulled her under. Their slick skin slid over her, coating her in mucus. She could feel the thick, knotted muscles of the creatures trying to squeeze the life out of her but struggling to find purchase in the bloody murk.

She tried to move herself. As she struggled, it became apparent that there were so many of them that in spite of their frenzy, the eels could not strike. Their real threat lay in the crushing power of the weight of their bodies as they came together in the melee like logs rolling down a river, and the prolonged periods under the blood, unable to breathe. The odd nip hurt Anya, but the constant fight to get back to the surface to draw a breath was what was wearing her down. Unable to get to her sword, she drew a short dagger from her belt and did her best to stab at any eel that came close enough.

Anya was able to get her head free of the blood long enough to draw in another lungful of air. She glimpsed Vedic managing to get to his feet a few yards further towards the bank, standing either on the riverbed or on the eels and hacking off any heads that tried to go for him. There was hope, then, that she could at least get to her feet, if she moved further towards the bank. This was swept away as she was pulled under once more. The last thing she saw before she disappeared under was Akyar emerging from the river, swinging his bow to bat away the eels that tried to strike at him.

All was churning blood. She was going to die.

Your grandfather was right. You should not have sought the ink.

Anya fought with all her wit. She sliced with her dagger and shoved with her free hand. Where her blade struck, the eels slammed back with their jaws in an attempt to hit their attacker but more often bit themselves. Where she shoved, they attacked one another. This allowed her to surface, briefly orientate and form a plan. She dived under the eels. Below them she could swim through the blood even if she couldn't see. She made for the bottom, where the riverbed was littered with bones but solid enough to cling to, and using the current as her guide, she made her way to the bank over the uneven surface of the bottom. Her body protested at the dwindling air from her lungs.

As the riverbed began to climb, the prospect of breathing and getting out of the waterway made Anya push for the surface. She took the first eel with her dagger, ripping its belly out, but as the creature sank below, it pulled the tiny steel from her hand, nipping at her legs in its death roll. Unable to reach her sword, bitten on the thigh already and her warm blood attracting more attention, she beat the eels around her with her fists.

Desperate, she tried to reach the bank. She could see land, could almost touch it. She felt a tentacle-like creature slide up her leg, in a winding, spiralling creep, as an eel wrapped itself round and pulled. She yelled in frustration, throwing herself for a handhold that she couldn't see and wasn't sure was there. Someone caught her outstretched arm.

The ferryman's hand was pallid, cold and dead to the touch, but also strong, and he pulled on her limb with all his strength, or so it seemed to Anya. The dead man's strength gradually won out, and the ferryman pulled her back towards the bank, stretching her between river and land, eel and hand.

She shouted in pain. 'You're tearing me in two!'

The ferryman tilted his head as if shaking his brain into alignment in order to translate the words. He did not let go, but without moving or pulling any further, he drew Anya's sword from the sheath on her back. The dead man moved in a sudden twist that would have been impossible for a living person, sweeping the blade round at the eel, slicing the creature in two and letting the spin of his strike whip his other hand round, flinging Anya onto the bank. The two of them collapsed in the mud in a tumble of limbs.

'STILL ALIVE?'

Anya looked up at the woodsman. He looked like he had just come from a battlefield from one of her grandfather's nightmares. He was covered in the blood from the Acheron, and like Anya he had a few nasty-looking love bites from the eels, as if he had pulled arrows from his own flesh. There was gore dripping from what was left of his hair. Somehow he had managed to pull his pack from the river, and it dangled from his left arm. Akyar limped along behind him.

'I'm hard to kill,' she said, in her best impersonation of Vedic. The Tream laughed.

'Where's the ferryman?' asked Vedic, kneeling by her leg and checking the bite wound that had gone through her leggings and the remains of his original dressing.

'He said he would try to find the boat.'

Akyar shook his head. 'In this current? I don't think so.'

'Perhaps he ran away, then,' said Vedic, pulling a small hip flask from his waistline. 'Fortunately, your original wound was pretty much healed, but I won't be able to do much until we reach the forest again.'

Anya eyed the flask; she couldn't believe he'd brought drink with him. 'I'm not sure a drink—'

Vedic poured the wysgi onto her wound without warning. Her leg erupted with pain, and she cursed with language she'd never had the courage to use before.

'Sorry,' said Vedic, in a tone that suggested he was anything but. 'Got to make the bite clean. I did mine just now. Hurts like a banshee on heat.'

'A little warning,' said Anya, through clenched teeth, 'next time.'

Vedic shrugged. 'You argue everything. You'd have been infected by the time I convinced you I didn't want to drink it. You lost this.' He dropped her dagger at her feet.

Anya flushed.

Vedic sniggered. 'Don't worry, little one. I'm going to drink this as well.'

Anya returned her gaze to the horizon. She really couldn't work out where they were, and that wasn't even the worst thing. Looking around each of her companions, there was precious little left in the way of supplies that hadn't been contaminated by the Acheron. They needed to get out of this place as soon as they could, or risk dehydration or starvation. Anya knew what happened to people cut off from food. Her grandfather liked to tell stories when he was drunk as well as when he was sober, and he wasn't the most temperate censor of the content. Anya had nightmares about the ones in which battalions were cut off from their supply lines. They needed the ferryman to return. She cursed herself for letting him go in the first place.

'We should rest,' said Akyar, sitting down next to Anya. 'We're exhausted.'

The woodsman looked like he was about to argue the point. He seemed to share the same worry that Anya did regarding their supplies, but the fact was Anya couldn't have moved right then, even if she had wanted to – the river had taken too much out of her. She was grateful for the Tream's intervention as Vedic acquiesced and flopped down next to them.

'You were brave on the river,' said Anya, lying back to look at the mottled orange sky. 'I saw you fighting the eels. No fear.'

Vedic picked his pipe from his belt. Finding it broken, he threw it away in disgust. 'I was just trying to get away from them. Self-preservation is a great general. I'm not sure I thought about it much.'

'No,' she said. 'It was brave to fight those things. You're better than you give yourself credit for. They were evil; they just sought to bite and tear and destroy.'

Vedic looked at Anya. 'As do most living things. You don't know whether they had eaten, what the Morrigan had done to them or why they attacked, beyond a few spurious words from someone who now appears to have deserted us.' He looked away at the river. 'I am many things. Brave is not one of them.'

Anya blinked in surprise. This was one of the longest things she had ever heard the woodsman say in a single sitting. 'You don't think they were evil?'

Vedic paused, nudging the ground with his boot. 'I don't know what evil is. I just know the description you gave could apply to any creature that was desperate. My actions had little to do with bravery. Most people stand and fight if they have to.'

Anya looked at Vedic with sharp, unwavering eyes. 'No, they don't. Nearly everyone in Anaheim ran. Even the few warriors we had.'

The woodsman looked away at this. Unpleasantness hung over them. She wasn't sure what dark precipitation the cloud was carrying, and she would have said more if she hadn't seen a glint on the distant river. She leant forward.

'I see it too,' said Akyar.

Anya smiled. 'Our runaway has come back.'

The ferryman, on his boat, slid up the river, clearing eels with a makeshift plough carved from wood and attached to the bone hull with leather thongs. The vessel came to a rest at the edge of the bank, where Akyar helped him lash the vessel to a secure stump of bone that protruded from the sandy bank.

'I never doubted you'd return,' said Akyar, offering his hand to the ferryman. Anya wondered at where he'd learned to do that and that he wasn't offended when the ferryman ignored it. *What does the ferryman have against Akyar? What could anyone have against him?*

'Time to go, little one,' said Vedic.

'I wish you'd stop calling me that,' said Anya. 'I have a name.'

The woodsman looked startled, as if she'd slapped him.

'I'm sorry,' she said. 'I'm just tired.'

'No,' said Vedic. 'You're right.'

The woodsman left her standing on the bank as he got into the boat. He settled in the stern with what was left of his pack, and Anya reflected again that he looked pale as his eyes darted around the landscape. He looked as if he feared another attack, and while that was a real danger, she conceded, he had not reacted to the eels or the wolves in this way. *What happened to Vedic when he was here before?* Pushing that thought to the back of her mind, she gathered her things and limped into the boat.

'WE ARE NEARING THE ROAD,' said the ferryman.

The road was actually nothing more than an empty, dusty track that led up from the river into the hills of Golgotha. In the distance, the ribbon of dark that lined the far horizon-like cavern wall seemed wider and closer. They could see the trail they would take from the river, and a huge range of cliffs marked a finger of red against the black. Anya rubbed her arms. She felt cold as the prospect of another artificial night in Golgotha loomed. She'd realised that whatever else Vedic knew, and whatever had led him down here with the Morrigan, he wasn't very familiar with the Arawn legend. She was the only one who had any idea what they would have to go through to escape this underground prison. She expected the Cave of Shadows to focus on her over the others as a full human clanswoman and because she had run away. Ghosts already haunted her, and so she was terrified by what she would see in the final climb to the surface.

Of course, that was assuming they could rescue the boy from the Morrigan.

Vedic nodded at the ferryman. The woodsman had lost weight on their travels. This had left him rangy, his skin loose in places where his well-developed muscles had retreated from lack of sustenance. This made him look much older, the dust of Golgotha settling in the crevices and crags of his face and almost casting him in stone, like the figures you might find in the ruins up near the desert. Perhaps it was the dust that gave him such a grey look as they drew ever closer to the road. Anya wasn't sure. At times, she thought she saw his hands shake, and his eyes continued to wander around the landscape. Perhaps he was seeing his own ghosts.

'I don't understand this place,' said Akyar.

Anya cast her gaze from the woodsman, who was studiously ignoring her, to the Tream, who was not. Akyar was different: generally ready with a smile or a bit of encouragement, but like Vedic she was sure that the Tream was withholding information.

'What's that?' she asked, turning in her seat. She really was uncomfortable.

'Well, Golgotha is your underworld, your afterlife, right?'

'Yes,' she answered. She was unsure where he was going with this.

'So where are the dead people?' asked Akyar, raising his hands to indicate the empty banks.

'What?' asked Vedic.

'Well, we heard a creature on the wind last night, but we've actually seen no one the whole time we've been here – not one corpse, just bones,' Akyar continued, folding his arms.

'Maybe it's just the Shaanti that come here,' suggested Anya, uncertain. She'd seen her own ghosts, but they seemed to be in her head, as no one else had reacted to them. The ferryman didn't show any sign of seeing them either.

'No,' said Akyar. 'That still wouldn't make sense – do you really think no one has died in the time we've been here? With the Kurah invading?'

'The living cannot see the dead,' said the ferryman. He did not look from where he was gazing, guiding the boat. 'Even in Golgotha. Only in one place can that happen.'

'The void?' asked Vedic, softly.

'No,' said the ferryman, turning to look at him. 'No one knows what lies there. I speak of the Cave of Shadows.'

'You're saying we can't see the dead?' said Akyar. 'Then they could be all around us.'

The ferryman looked directly at Akyar. 'They are all around you. As far as the eye can see, an endless sea of the dead, streaming from the shores of the Acheron to the Styx and the crossroads and the void beyond. They cannot see you, and you cannot see them. This land is full of the dead.'

Akyar raised his eyebrows in surprise. He shifted in his seat, worried by what he couldn't see, and wrapped his robe around himself in an attempt to ward off the cold.

Anya let her gaze wander from him back to the bottom of the boat; she didn't want to think about all those souls, about what that meant, what was going on above them and whether or not the dead souls could see her. Whether they could or would judge her for what she had done in running away.

Vedic leant over to her. 'Keep your weapon handy,' he whispered, his face pallid and his brow sweating despite the cold. He looked feverish.

Anya drew her weapon and placed the sword on her lap. She wanted to ask the forestal questions about his time in Golgotha and what he meant by her keeping her blade to hand. Vedic did not look in a question-answering mood. He sat where he'd placed himself when they got back in the boat, in the rear, against the edge of the stern with a storm on his face.

'The Kurah must have taken the Shaanti lands,' said Anya, putting her head in her hands. 'And many people are dead. For they must all be dead to fill this land.'

'So sure are you?' said the ferryman, with a low, wet chuckle. 'Your people still live, Anya. To the Kurah this is Purgatory; to the Delgasian this is Limbo; and to others this land has names for which you have no equivalent. This is just one aspect. The truth is far stranger than you can comprehend. Be wary before you seek it.'

There was a growing feeling in the pit of Anya's stomach that she did not much care for, a pressure on her chest that felt like her soul was being pulled out of her. This was probably her imagination, but she wouldn't have been surprised if the Morrigan had sent ghosts to attack them. When the wind rose up, she could see Fin and, occasionally, her grandfather running along the bank alongside them. This, too, must have been her imagination – she was almost positive, as again the ferryman showed no signs of seeing them. She wished she could see them for real, just once, just to say sorry.

'There is a dangerous magic around you humans,' said Akyar, annoyance painted on his face. 'It seems to me that my ancestors made a sound argument – humanity is too dangerous for its own good. You just imagine these creatures and places, and they appear, up out of nowhere.'

'Be quiet, Akyar,' said Vedic, picking at the hull with his knife.

The sound of stone shingle on the hull and a sudden stop told them they had arrived.

Anya stepped off the boat, following the other two. Behind her the ferryman cast off his cloak, stepping uncovered from the vessel. Ahead the two men looked back at Anya, their faces frozen by what they saw. Akyar's hand dropped to his sword. Anya turned. Walking towards her, hands outstretched and broiled with festering sores, came the ferryman. The good side of his face was flushed with heat. The bad side of his face glistened purple and green with rot, and his teeth were yellow and cracked, visible through his ruined cheek.

'Payment,' he said, reaching for Anya.

She fumbled for her sword, unable to get her hands to obey her mind. On the wind, she thought she heard the sound of Kurah jeering and the voice of the boy-warrior she had killed.

'No,' said Akyar, stepping in front of her, his blade drawn.

'Promised,' said the ferryman. He stank of rot. 'She promised: anything.'

'Anything, sir,' said Akyar, circling the ferryman. 'Not everything.'

You would let the Tream fight for you? The mocking tone of her mother did nothing to help. Anya felt sick as she watched the dead man draw his own sword from where it hung on his back, a curved scimitar that gleamed like the moon. The ferryman's motion was mournful, as if the act caused him intense pain. The ferryman swung the sword in lazy arcs before slicing at Akyar. The Tream flipped over him, running the ferryman through with one smooth motion before withdrawing. The ferryman turned and tried to strike again.

Alarmed and confused, Akyar danced out of range.

Anya wanted to run in with her own weapon but found she couldn't bring herself to raise her sword, because her grip felt loose and trembling. *Weak.* She pushed her mother's voice away. The fight was mesmerising, such an intense ballet of violence. She feared they would have to make an end to the ferryman – more blood on her hands and another ghost to carry.

'He's not alive,' called Vedic, not moving to help. 'And you don't know what he wants yet.'

'Shut up, woodsman,' said Akyar, blocking another blow and trying to strike the ferryman with the broad edge of his sword. The blow made contact with the ferryman's neck but bounced off in a shower of sparks.

The ferryman's foot connected with Akyar's jaw in a smooth roundhouse and sent the Tream sprawling onto his back. Winded, the Tream spat blood onto the shingle and struggled to rise. *He is going to be killed*, thought Anya. She placed a hand on the Tream's shoulder as he tried to rise once more. Stepping past him, Anya walked up to the ferryman with her own sword gripped tight in one hand until she stopped, whereupon she drove the blade into the ground.

'How did your face wind up like that?' asked Anya, looking directly at the ferryman. The scimitar in his hand was very familiar: Shaanti design, Escanti blade.

The ferryman replied, 'I was killed, but the Morrigan would not let me pass over, could not bear to let me go. She cannot hold off death forever, but she can keep souls here until near the end, when she, too, must take the journey.'

His sword hung from his hand with no power, just despair. He pointed at the Tream.

'This one's kind did this to me. In life I was a god, and now I'm less than nothing.'

Anya closed her eyes. She had known he looked familiar to her. 'What's your name?'

'You know my name, Anya,' said the ferryman, weary. 'I heard you speak it in the forest. That is why I came to help you.'

'Say your name!'

'In life I was Bres. Now I am simply the ferryman.'

'And what would you have of me, Bres?' asked Anya.

The use of the ferryman's name seemed to rock the dead man. He dropped his sword.

'I thought ... I wanted to feel alive ... but ...'

'You can't ask for such a thing,' coughed Akyar, spitting bright green blood onto the shingle. 'Life is not a feeling. Life is there or life is not.'

The ferryman stopped. The wind whipped across the land, leaving his eyes glistening in the faux sunset.

'You're wrong.'

The former god turned, sank to the shingle and placed his head in his hands.

Akyar looked away, his face unreadable, but Anya stepped forward, at first hesitant and then with purpose. She stopped at the ferryman's side. He smelt faintly of rotting flesh.

'Bres,' she said. The ferryman turned the ruined side of his face from her.

'Please, just leave me alone,' said Bres, seeing the look on her face. 'I don't want your pity.'

Anya cupped the ruined side of his head gently with her hand and turned his face to hers. 'It's not life you want, now is it? You want rest.'

The ferryman looked at her with tears streaming. He nodded.

The kiss was soft and gentle – Anya was afraid of hurting him. At first he tried to pull away, but after a moment he returned the kiss. When their lips parted, Anya rested her forehead on Bres's for a moment and spoke words that only the ferryman could hear. She kissed his forehead and turned away from him.

Akyar tried to talk to her, but the wind screamed out from all directions, knocking the three travellers to their knees and casting a maelstrom around the ferryman.

'What did you do?' yelled Vedic.

Anya did not answer. This wasn't the wisest thing she had ever done, nor the kindest, but it was the right thing to do, and though she wasn't sure how this would end, there was no shame. The woodsman wouldn't understand.

The ferryman smiled at her through the dust storm. He lifted his hands to his chest in a gesture of thanks, stiffened, closed his eyes and fell apart into the violence of the dust and ash. The storm streamed across the cavern in the direction of the road, marking their way, and then all was silent.

'That let the Morrigan know exactly where we are,' said Vedic, glaring at Anya. He stomped past her in the direction of the dust cloud.

Anya stared at the path the god had taken. *What had she done?*

Akyar paused by her. 'What cant did you use? Will that work on the Morrigan?'

Anya laughed. It was bitter. 'I'm sorry. I am no mage, and I have no idea what just happened.'

'Then what did you say?'

'I told him the Shaanti had forgotten him,' she said, 'but that I remembered and that he should go to rest now because he had done his work. Bres just wanted a connection with someone.'

Akyar put his hand on her shoulder. 'That was well done, Lady Anya. Now, let us move on and see our own work through.'

CHAPTER TWENTY

THEY WALKED FOR HOURS.

The hills reached out to encircle them, hiding the rivers, the Acheron and the Styx. The trio had walked on in silence, conscious that time and water were in short supply. They all wanted to find the boy as quickly as possible and get out of this place. This had less to do with freeing Danu or returning Meyr and more to do with the inherent wrongness of Golgotha. As the faux night settled once more, the strange noises, the clicks and screams and howls, resumed. The Golgothan chorus had stopped making any of them jump. They were resigned to their march.

'Thank you,' said Anya to Akyar.

'For what?' asked Akyar, falling into step alongside her.

'For trying to help,' replied Anya, looking down to ensure she didn't trip over the bones that littered the ground. Anya wasn't sure what had happened when they made land, but she was seeing her grandfather and Fin less now.

'I did little,' said Akyar, his eyes on the woodsman ahead. 'I thought he was going to take you away.'

'So did I,' replied Anya. She didn't want to think about what the ferryman – she couldn't think of him as Bres – could have demanded.

'What made you talk to him?'

'Desperation. I thought he was going to kill you.'

The Tream chuckled. 'As did I for a moment or two. How did you recognise him?'

Anya thought back. Had she recognised him? Was it just a sense that he had not revealed his full story? She saw the large curved blade in her mind's eye. 'It was the scimitar. There is a ... there was a picture in my grandfather's house, a scene from his fall, and he carried that sword.'

They walked on.

'I'd have spoken to him anyway. I'd have given him a boon because I did promise and so a debt was owed.'

'You'd have ...?'

'No,' said Anya. 'He wasn't asking for what you think. Creatures down here, according to legend, can take life from those who still live.'

'How?'

Anya shook her head. 'The myths are full of different versions – blood, breath, touch ... I would not have agreed.'

'You'd have fought?'

She nodded.

If your hands could have stopped shaking, her mother's voice hissed in her head. Anya ignored the words as best she could.

'I think, perhaps,' said Akyar, 'I should be thanking you.'

Anya smiled. 'Not a bad team, are we?'

Akyar nodded. 'Although one member seems to wish he was on his own.'

Anya watched the woodsman march. It was hardly surprising that he wanted to get out of Golgotha as fast as possible – they all did. For Vedic, this was a drive that was forcing him to ignore everything else.

'You worried?' she asked Akyar.

'Yes, I'm worried for Meyr – he's young and he's been gone a long time now.'

Anya smiled. 'You care for the child a lot.'

'He is the son of my two best friends,' said Akyar pulling his cloak closer around him.

'But you think of him as your own,' said Anya, placing a hand on his arm. 'I can tell. When my mother went away, my grandfather's friend Falkirk looked after me as much as my grandfather. I often saw the same look on his face as you have now.'

'What happened to your mother?' asked Akyar, smiling at her. Anya thought there was a hint of sadness in that smile, but she did not press.

'I don't really know,' Anya shrugged. 'She left. My grandfather and Falkirk were parents for me. I was lucky. The Shaanti clans in the border towns can be quite judgemental over broken families, but my grandparents' reputation protected me from all that.'

Grandfather's drinking – not so much, she thought, hating herself for it.

'Didn't you ever want to seek her out?'

'Not really,' said Anya. This was the first time she had ever lied to Akyar. The falsehood sat uncomfortably with her. She pressed on. 'She left because she said something was missing and she needed to find it. I'm not sure I want a person who can abandon a child in my life. What about you?'

'I've never met your mother,' said Akyar, trying to lift the mood.

Anya smiled a little. 'What's your story? How did you wind up vizier?' *How did you fall in love with Pan?*

Akyar looked ahead. The Tream seemed tired and older than he had when she had first met him in what felt like another life.

'I was appointed by Hogarth's father,' said Akyar. 'Hogarth kept his promise to keep me in the position – this was the only condition of his father. Hogarth is a Tream of his word. And a good friend.'

'You sound more like you're trying to convince yourself than the girl,' said Vedic, calling back. 'What's wrong? Is your friend giving you pause for thought?'

Anya could have cheerfully knifed her forestal for that barb, nerves or not, but the woodsman seemed oblivious. He marched on.

'Vedic is right. Hogarth is on a path to war that I wish to stop him going down, because the butcher's bill from wars past has been far too high. He sees the Morrigan's actions as evidence we should have finished what we started millennia ago, that the forest will not be safe while human gods are allowed to live in it.'

'Why?' asked Anya.

'Lots of reasons,' said Akyar. 'We aren't that different from you. We suffer from pride, fear and an overwhelming urge to leave our mark on the world. The provocation from the Morrigan is extreme – his only son. But ultimately his belief, which he has had as long as I have known him, is that the forest was vast before the humans came, and since then it's become smaller and smaller. Humans destroy. Gods are the fuel.'

They walked on. *Yet you think so much of Pan that his death ... possible death ... caused you physical pain.* Anya did not understand this inherent contradiction, and this made her feel younger than she would care to admit.

'You've known him a long time?'

'Hogarth?'

She nodded.

'Oh aye,' he said. 'I've known Hogarth nearly as long as I've known Jiana.'

'How long is that?'

'Jiana? Since birth,' replied Akyar, nodding. 'I think her parents thought we'd marry one day, but neither of us found that an appealing idea.'

'I'm surprised myself,' said Anya. 'You seem to care for each other.'

Akyar laughed. 'Be like marrying my sister.'

The sunset, or whatever passed for the equivalent in Golgotha, was beginning to happen, sickly hues of orange began to increase, offering a vision of what lay beyond the iron-tinged darkness. The soil underfoot was becoming thinner, and the ground beneath them crunched more and more with the sound of collapsing bone. At first those sounds were sickening and irregular. Then they grew more frequent, and the group became almost used to the rhythmic crunch of their march across Golgotha. Anya could not decide which was worse – the sound or the fact they barely noticed any more.

'Why did Hogarth believe that Danu had taken the boy?' asked Anya, as much to break the silence as anything else.

He is keeping a secret, came her mother's voice in her head.

'It was my fault,' said Akyar.

'How so?' Anya could feel the woodsman slowing in the distance to hear. For someone who could sneak up on you as if he were a wraith blown from smoke, he could be remarkably unsubtle on occasion.

You like him, came the disapproving voice of her mother.

Not like that, she hissed back.

'I first went to court when I was a boy to apprentice under the old vizier, Omar,' said Akyar. 'I remember being astounded at the freedom that was given Hogarth. It's true he was not the heir to the throne then – his older brother had that distinction – but even so, Hogarth was indulged by his father and his brother alike.

'I remember the day I first arrived at the palace. The vizier Omar came out to greet me, but I don't think I heard a word he said – I just couldn't get over the size and age of the palace. He was so amused by my reaction he had me talk to the palace that day, and that turned out to be one of the smartest things he ever did for me. I was hooked. That tree has stood for three thousand years. The things it has witnessed ...'

He shook his head and continued. 'I met Hogarth in the small amounts of free time I was given, often out in the forest, where he liked to roam, and occasionally when he was in the palace, spending time with Utah, his older brother. Utah was a quiet but wise Tream; he would have been a good king.'

'Why didn't he become king?' asked Anya.

Akyar's expression became serious. 'We are coming to that. Anyway, Hogarth roamed the woods far and wide, with no regard for the gods' territory. I still think he knows the woods better than any Tream alive. He lived for hunting. I went with him on occasion and was shocked by how far he would follow game, tracking them right up to the gods' lake and the glade. Even then I think he cared little for the gods and humanity. Certainly, he didn't adhere to the peace treaty.

'One day,' he said, kicking the ground, 'Hogarth went off on his own. I was supposed to go with him, but he was insistent on hunting a doe he had seen that had eluded him. I find hunting dull. Instead, I went to the archive, to the oldest sections, which are forbidden because the trees are mad, and began looking at the Jeylin archives. No one knew I was still in Tream territory until after nightfall, when Hogarth had not returned.'

'Did the gods capture him?' asked Anya.

Akyar appeared not to hear. He was lost in thought. The wind had picked up a little, and Anya had to raise her jerkin to cover her mouth against it. Vedic was only a step or two in front now, hanging on the Tream's words.

'I was brought before the king,' said Akyar. 'He was angrier than I had ever seen him, demanding to know how long Hogarth had been flouting the treaties for and where he had gone hunting. I kept nothing back, because I feared for his life as much as the king and Utah. I did stress that I thought he was independently minded and had most likely found the trail of the doe and was determined to have his quarry. I did that much. But it wasn't enough.

'Utah ignored his father's wishes.' Akyar sighed. 'He had that much in common with his brother. He went out looking for Hogarth – children are precious to the Tream because we are long-lived but reproduce slowly, if at all, and brothers and sisters are rare. Utah was not the woodsman that his brother was.'

'The quest went ill for Utah?' asked Vedic.

Akyar nodded. 'As I predicted, Hogarth wandered back into the city at sunrise the next day, doe over his shoulders and a look of surprise at all the fuss. His emotion turned to alarm when he realised Utah was gone, and rage when his father stopped him from going to look for him. I understand why he stopped Hogarth, but it was the wrong decision, because if anyone could have found him, it was the young prince.'

'They thought the gods took him?' asked Anya.

Akyar nodded again. 'And they sent me to negotiate with them.'

'You must have been quite young,' said Vedic.

'I was,' said Akyar, with a wry smile. 'And fair too, believe it or not. This mission was Omar's idea. I think he thought I would fail and the gods would abuse me for my temerity in approaching them. I had undermined him by going into the forbidden archives and not going insane. I had begun to learn things that he himself could not manage to get from the archives. I think the king had an idea in mind, though, that Omar was blind to, and I think even then he thought I would be a good vizier. Even kings make mistakes.

'The wood was falling on autumn when I left for the glade. No one but Hogarth, Omar and the king knew I was going. I was forbidden from discussing it with anyone, including Jiana, who had only recently come to court herself.

'When I arrived, there were no beauties to greet me, no sun-soaked picture of paradise to seduce me. Indeed, the rains had come; the lake was overflowing; and everything was covered in fresh mud, including me. Pan met me on the far side, suspicious bordering on hostile, and denying any knowledge of Utah.

'I was brought into Danu's presence only once, just after I had arrived, Pan hurriedly drying me with his magic. I did not see her face. She wanted to communicate with me directly that they had not been involved in the disappearance of Utah. She gave Pan to me to help find him as a sign of her good faith.'

'Where did you find him?' asked Vedic.

Akyar looked older than the earth at this. Anya thought the Tream was not going to continue, but after a few steps, he did. It was as if a knot were loosening within him and he had to tell someone, anyone, what he knew.

'He was dead when we found him,' said Akyar. 'No one other than Pan knows it. We found him two weeks later, wedged in a gully near the northern border of the forest. It appeared he had been gored by a giant stag or a creature with similar-sized horns. Pan swore that no god could have done this; there were none in the forest. I thought I could trust his word on this. But we had a dangerous situation for both sides – the heir had been found in the gods' territory, dead and as the result of an attack.'

'That would have meant war,' said Anya. 'Even with a measured king like Hogarth's father, it still might.'

Akyar nodded. 'I persuaded Pan to bury him where he could never be found, deep, deep down where the soil meets the crystalline rock beneath the forest. I left a mark that only he or I would know, should we need to ever find the place again. And I returned home a week later and told the king we had been aided by the gods but found nothing.

'He was grateful, and a month later he made Hogarth heir. They mourned. They moved on. They are Tream. Hogarth was the only one who didn't really believe that his brother had just gone missing, that it was not possible to find him still. He would sneak out looking in the early days but could only roam so far without his father noticing that he was gone. Utah was the only thing we fought about. Hogarth wanted to go to war, and I wouldn't support him. I believe that is why, when Omar died a year later, I was made vizier younger than any other Tream. The king thought my ability to stand up to Hogarth would keep his impetuous son safe.'

'That must have been awful,' said Anya, 'to carry that secret all these years.'

'It is a lie,' said Vedic, turning from the Tream, 'not a secret. Lies always beget horror.'

Akyar frowned at the woodsman. 'It is a slight omission. No one doubted the boy was dead. The knowledge of where would have brought the whole nation to war.'

'I did not say the lie was badly intended,' conceded Vedic, his voice gentler. 'Hogarth blamed Danu, yes?'

Akyar shook his head, stopped. 'Well, kind of. He blamed her, cursed her with every fibre of his being, but it was himself he was angry with. He knew that he should have come home that night. He wears a small band of the doe's hide on his wrist to remind him not to be so rash.'

'And Pan?' asked Vedic.

The Tream flushed a deep green that Anya found quite endearing. 'Hogarth's father used me to negotiate a more friendly set of terms with the gods, improving the treaty we had agreed. This meant I had to go back and forth to the lake regularly. Pan was the gods' envoy. When Hogarth took over, he continued to use me for any negotiations or contact with the gods, and I ... I was able to persuade them to let me use their archives to help build our knowledge as well.'

Vedic laughed. 'Were you behind Pan's theory about the desert?'

Akyar frowned. 'It's a sound theory.'

'Feel free to let me in on the joke,' said Anya, irritated.

'Pan thinks we, humans, came from somewhere else,' said Vedic. 'You heard part of this when we were in the Cordoenenn. He wants to go to the heart of the desert and see what he can find.'

'He actually went,' said Akyar. 'Or he was supposed to. That's why I can't understand what he was doing back in the forest.'

Anya flinched. *Stag.* Her mind's voice spoke, but this time the words were her own and not her mother's. 'Why did you think it was a stag that had killed Utah?'

Akyar stopped. 'Because of the shape and depth of the goring and the marks the creature had made in the ground around the body.'

'Coincidence,' said Vedic. 'That was too long ago for it to have been Cernubus.'

Anya frowned. She didn't believe in coincidences any more than Falkirk did.

'Cernubus's form was that of a giant stag,' she explained. Akyar's eyes widened at this.

'Keep moving,' said Vedic. 'We're almost at the lakes.'

Anya forced herself back to the matter at hand. They were deep in the hills now. Rising high above them and closer than they would have thought possible were the great jet-black cliffs. The winding nature of the road blocked the view ahead. Thus, it was a surprise to them when they traversed another rocky edifice and found themselves looking out over the steep rock to a valley stretched out below. In the strange light, the valley looked like there might be caves or windows cut into the far cliff face. The valley was not large, but two almost-overlapping lakes blocked their path, gleaming like glass in the ur-light. The shore of the closest was only a few yards away. They would have to traverse round at least one to reach the dark opening in the base of the cliffs that sat on the far side of the valley.

'I have been here before,' said Vedic, his voice raw and cracked with dust from the road. He stared at the lakes like a man watching an army marching towards him.

'The Trivium is through there.'

'Yes,' said Anya. 'Her fortress is in there somewhere. The building shouldn't be that far, but there's only one route in, according to legend. Let's hope she isn't expecting us.'

'We have to expect an attack,' said Akyar, his voice soft. 'I think she probably knows exactly where we are.'

'Agreed,' said the woodsman.

'It'll be fine,' said Anya, stepping towards the Tream's back, her hand reaching out for him before she thought better of it. 'We'll work it out.'

Vedic laughed. 'No, little one. We won't. If she's in there at the moment, then we're dead already and just haven't realised the truth yet.'

Anya flushed. *You should kill him*, came her mother's voice. *He has no respect.*

'If that is true, then we are beyond worry, and seeing as we are all still worried, I think we should get on with our plan,' said Akyar, stepping between them. 'I'm going to refill my waterskin. We've a long climb ahead of us.'

The woodsman put his hand on the Tream's shoulder before Akyar could dunk the skin in the water. He shook his head. 'Bad water, trust me. The lake will take more than it gives.'

'What?' asked Akyar.

Anya noticed the woodsman's other hand was trembling. He replied, 'This is the pool of Lethe.'

Still Akyar looked confused. The woodsman sighed and answered the unspoken question. 'This is where the dead come to forget, and for those that seek this path, beyond lies the Mnemosyne, the well from which truth can be taken. If you drink from the Lethe, you will lose all memory. You will cease to exist even though there will be breath in your lungs.'

'And the other?' asked the Tream.

'No one can know everything,' said Vedic, shaking his head. 'This amounts to the same thing. Although you remain breathing for rather less time.'

Akyar shoved his nearly empty skin back in his pack. 'Then I guess we'd best—'

'What in Danu's name is that?' asked Anya. She pointed to the sky where the dark band of night that seemed to ring the whole of Golgotha had detached from the horizon and was moving closer towards them with cogent purpose. Sulphur wafted on the breeze, carried from the same direction. Akyar, the keenest eye, stepped forward.

'Winged Kresh,' he said. 'The Morrigan knows we are here.' As if in answer, they heard a faint cawing on the wind.

'We need to get into that cave,' said Anya, gesturing to the dark opening at the base of the cliffs. 'Quickly.'

You are going to die because you are weak. Anya pushed her mother's voice away. There was no time for any of her mother's second-hand lessons delivered by bad memory. She needed to focus on what was at hand. Vedic's behaviour was worrying her. If she didn't know better, she would have thought he was on the edge of terror.

The three of them looked at the strip of rock that circled the lakes. The stone formed a narrow, crumbling wall that they would have to traverse. The path ahead looked treacherous and impassable, as if a sneeze would send the rock into the lakes. The cawing grew louder.

'Best get on with it, then,' said Vedic, his face pale as he took one look around at the horizon, as if searching for a lost horror. Anya shoved him. On the wind, they could hear the caw of birds drawing near. They had no time, and the path over and around the lakes was narrow and slow. They were in trouble.

The ledge across the first lake was less than a shoulder's width apart. They couldn't walk along it, and so they needed to shuffle out one by one. In order to make it easier, they split out the weight from the remaining packs so they were evenly distributed between the three of them, as Vedic had suggested.

They were making progress around the Lethe, but Vedic, who was up front, was beginning to slow as they drew closer to the second lake. Anya's sympathy was starting to wane as the Kresh drew closer – the cawing was continuous now, and she was tired of the stale wind in Golgotha. She wanted the warm red of her own two suns.

The sound of the Kresh grew louder again; the birds' wings could be heard now, moving en masse as a dreadful thump in the air, like a giant's heart. There was no more time for contemplation. The crumbling, narrow wall of rock that arced around the Mnemosyne stretched out before them, barely deeper than a foot's length, and in some places rather narrower. Far away, or so it seemed, they could see the dark mouth of the cave that would offer them a sanctuary of sorts, if they could only reach their new home.

The woodsman went first, followed by Akyar, and Anya shuffled out last. Vedic moved with the nimble grace that Anya had been so surprised by when she first met him, but he was also gripping the ledge so tightly his knuckles turned white. His focus was never on the surface of the water or his feet. Instead, he concentrated on the rock in front of him as if his life depended on it.

Anya glanced down out of curiosity. Up close the pool was the colour of molten silver. There was no breeze, but there was a stirring in the water: the lake moved in gentle and differing shades of silver that met and parted with the ebb and flow. The occasional bubble burst, and once or twice Anya thought she saw faces in the tarnished silver of the meeting currents, shimmering images that didn't always look entirely human: too much hair, or simian creases that were familiar but demonic.

Traversing the lake was hard work. On the road, the problem had been dust that clung to the throat and forced them to deplete further their meagre water reserves. Here, it was the sharpness of the red rock as they clambered across the edges of the lakes. Anya's hands were raw by the time they were halfway round the Mnemosyne, and even Vedic had to tear strips from his pack to cover his hands.

The cries of the Kresh were all-encompassing now, like the rush of blood in their ears when they occasionally slipped on the path. Vedic cursed in a language Anya didn't understand.

'Keep moving,' hissed Anya.

Only Akyar was silent, his face a dust-covered gargoyle as he tried to keep pace with Vedic. They gradually, inch by inch, made their way with quiet determination towards the Trivium and what they all thought would be a reckoning. As with the coming of the river Kresh, their avian cousins arrived in a downpour of black rain, icy and cold, which struck them like needles, prying at their fingers and turning the dust to slick, treacherous mire.

'We have to go faster!' yelled Anya.

'We'll die if we do,' shouted back Vedic, his beard matted with ash-laden rain.

Anya didn't answer back. She was too busy keeping her grip in the downpour, and she could see Akyar struggling with the same. Out of the corner of her eye, she saw him shake his head, as if to clear it. The Kresh were almost on them now. She could see them sweeping down in waves. The cave was still an agonising distance away. They weren't going to make it.

Anya nearly collided with the Tream. He had stopped. He was looking down at the lake as if mesmerised.

'What's wrong?'

'There are people in the water!' yelled Akyar.

Anya felt her heart quicken. She wouldn't have thought this possible, given how frightened she was. She put her head close to Akyar's left ear.

'No, there aren't,' she said. 'But we will be if we don't move!'

Akyar looked confused. He hesitated. Anya thought she was going to have to actually shout again, but a moment later he resumed his movement. In the distance, Vedic had already built up a lead. *He doesn't even know we're having a problem.*

Anya glanced back to Akyar and frowned as she saw him move his right hand to a hold that looked like a muddy face. Akyar was looking not at where he put his hand but at the water. For Anya, however, she saw the wet mud slide away with Akyar's hand to reveal the skull sat behind. Akyar swung out with one arm, a gasp of panic escaping his lips. Time seemed to slow. She saw him swing back and try to grab the skull, but the thing had been loosened by the rain, and the bone just came away in his hand, spinning to the water below. The Tream hung precariously from one hand.

The Kresh attacked.

One of their number struck Akyar's hand. Its sharp yellow beak – hooked and razor-edged – hacked at his still-clinging digits, sending him windmilling into the Mnemosyne. The resulting splash sent vapour over Anya and Vedic, drenching them and leaving them staring at the shock wave dissipating across the pool. The Kresh circled for another wave of attacks. They waited for him to come to the surface. He did not.

'He's gone! We have to go on!' shouted Vedic, gesturing to the cave. Anya couldn't believe he was going to leave the Tream.

'We have to help him!'

'It's too late,' replied Vedic. 'Nothing can survive the lake.'

The Kresh struck again. All they could do was cling on while they tried to claw and peck at them until they rose once more to dive on them again.

Anya stared hard at the woodsman. He was bleeding from his head again. 'First my clan, then Pan – I'm not leaving anyone else behind. We have to help him.'

Vedic shook his head, his mind made up.

Damn him to the Morrigan, thought Anya. She dropped her pack on the ledge and dived into the water before he could get to her. She thought she heard him cry out in pain. She knifed under the waters of the lake and kicked for the bottom, where the light fell away, seemingly as reluctant to follow as Vedic.

THE WATER WAS COLD. Anya was a good swimmer, having been taught by her grandfather as a young child. He had only learned how to swim as an adult, when the thain had realised her warriors' lack of this skill would prevent them raiding the Kurah as they moved across the rivers near the border. Like the thain, her grandfather didn't want Anya to need the skill but wanted her to have the ability, and so they'd spent many hours practising down by the river. These were amongst her last memories of him truly sober and truly relaxed.

When she was a little older, it became her turn to teach Fin how to swim. The boy had been more at home in the water than on the battlefield. He was a gentle child; she wasn't sure Falkirk had ever realised. She pushed thoughts of her ghosts from her mind. There was no time.

With graceful sweeps of her arms, Anya pulled herself deeper into the murk, looking for Akyar. She could barely see the creature ahead, a dark shadow, shifting in the bottom of the lake. The motion was faint at first, but as she drew closer, the violent movement became clearer. She drew her dagger without thinking. As it emerged from the darkness, the skin of the creature luminescent, Anya could see Akyar fighting for his life. He was clamped within the thing's tentacles, being rolled over and over. This was all happening so fast.

Anya could feel her lungs starting to burn. There was no obvious shape to the creature, and so it was impossible to see where to strike. When the thing touched her leg, she nearly lost what was left of her air. She spun away, her knife blade whipping round, cutting the tentacle into the water. She grabbed at the detached piece. The tentacle looked like glowing seaweed, but instead of floating like a passive plant, the thing flipped and twisted in her hand, a lone sucker puckering towards her.

You're afraid. The voice of her mother didn't sound mocking, just disappointed, only now the tone was starting to merge into a version of Vedic's voice. She felt her anger rising. She cast the piece aside. Brandishing her blade, she dived into the churn of Akyar's fight with the weed. Her chest scorched with a molten heat that made her trunk feel as if it was slowly being crushed, and her limbs felt like the suspended silver had solidified around them and was dragging her further down. She knew she didn't have long before she had to surface or drown. Sweeping in below Akyar's struggle, she sliced her knife through the base of the tendrils before twisting round Akyar's body.

Anya grabbed the first thing she found, his hair, and swam for the surface with desperate kicks. Anya felt as if they were clawing at the edge of a great void and Akyar, hands now locked on her wrist, was a dead weight that threatened to pull her into the darkness below. The temptation to kick him free was like a coiled snake in her belly: trapped and frightened, it twisted and spun, eager to strike and only barely within her control.

She pulled towards the air as the dim light of the world above seemed to pull ever further away from her. She noted blotches of light exploding in her eyes as individual streams of silver described a dance around her. She was drowning. She knew this as an abstract fact but was unworried. The knowledge felt strangely elating: a cessation of worry and an absolution of blame. She saw her death and wanted to embrace it. Akyar's hand shifted in hers, the loosening of the grip bringing her back to herself and reminding her of other hands reaching for her from the dark shadows cast by firelight.

ANYA BURST FROM THE SURFACE, dragging air into her lungs in great heaves until she had enough presence of mind left to pull Akyar onto his back so he could draw breath. He wasn't moving. Pain flared in her skull as she was struck on the back of her head, drawing blood and forcing her to swim away. She looped Akyar under one arm and began swimming for the side.

'This way!' yelled Vedic.

Anya corrected her course in the direction of the woodsman, who had dragged himself to the side of the lake nearest the cave to the Trivium. He stood like a demon that had crawled from the earth, soaked in mud and dust, bleeding from a number of wounds and holding her pack as protection against more. His other hand was outstretched for them. *Why isn't he in the cave yet?*

Anya pushed the Tream on ahead of her as she neared the bank. He was too heavy for her to lift up, and so the woodsman had to grab him by his cloak and hoist him up. Still the Tream did not move. Anya found herself dive-bombed by the Kresh again, but this time she managed to draw her knife and bury the blade in one of the creatures' chest a couple of times before the bird fell into the water, cawing. *That's my girl*, she heard her mother's voice say, and hated her for it. Whether she was angry at her mother or herself, she could no longer tell. She grabbed Vedic's arm and allowed herself to be pulled up.

The Kresh shrieked in outrage.

'The cave,' hissed Vedic, throwing the Tream over his shoulders and rising.

Anya nodded, fishing her pack up from where the woodsman had discarded it and raising the bag now as her own shield. 'Do it!'

They ran. The packs helped to shield them, but really, it was swinging their swords like bats that cut their path to the cave. Inside, the woodsman dumped the Tream like a sack of potatoes and hacked the Kresh inside to pieces. Anya was already throwing rocks into the mouth of the cave to deter the others.

'Good thinking,' said Vedic, throwing his shoulder to a nearby boulder and shoving it straight across the entrance. Anya got the idea and started filling in the gaps even as Vedic chucked more boulders on.

THE SCARRED GOD

She looked round for Akyar and saw him still prostrate on the floor of the cave.

'Shit.' She scrambled over to him, placed her cheek over his mouth and realised he wasn't breathing.

Anya had no idea how Tream kept themselves alive. She gambled Tream bodies weren't that different from her own kind, and tilted the creature's head back so his airway was clear, and tried to find a heartbeat before starting to breathe for him. She had just pinched his nose when he vomited up lake water in big silver gouts. She tilted him onto his side so he could clear the water.

'A narrow escape, Master Vizier,' said Vedic, his own relief palpable. 'I do believe she was about to kiss you.'

Akyar's coughing turned to laughter. 'It is I who have saved her, then,' he replied, although he clutched her hand tightly. 'My thanks, Lady Anya.'

'You need not thank me,' she said, a smile ghosting her lips. 'I need company to put up with that gnarled bastard.'

'I heard that,' said Vedic.

'You survived, then,' she said, looking at the ugly welts all over the Tream's body. The squid creature had been serious about trying some of his flesh out.

'I am not overfond of water,' said Akyar, 'but it cannot hurt me, even a foul pool such as this. You're hurt?'

Anya smiled. This was a defiant gesture that belied the weariness that she felt permeating her body. The swim had left her muscles burnt, but it was the blood leaking out of her scalp that was attracting attention as it seeped down her forehead, mingling with the water on her face. Anya tried to wipe away as much as she could. Blood was streaming down her face, and keeping it out of her mouth was proving an ordeal she wasn't winning.

'It's just because they're on the scalp. They're not deep ...'

The taste of copper in her mouth mingled with a different flavour that was utterly alien to her. The light drained from the room as if a demon were leaching all the colour. Anya felt the world lurch away ...

THERE WAS no sense to the vision.

It was not knowledge Anya received but a torrent of images, of scenes flowing with a speed that she could never hope to follow and that washed away her sense of self in the thundering river of information. She could not have screamed or cried out or even acknowledged there was an entity known as Anya to be swept away. It crushed her; it melted her, turned her inside out and spread her being across the entirety of existence. Her brain was aflame, and her heart with it. It made no sense.

FOREST, hot and humid, far away from anything she has seen in Golgotha or her own lands, and screeching with noise from a menagerie of animal life. A single sun burns liquid gold in an azure sky. Creatures, not Tream or man, covered in patchy hair, both like the monkeys found in the south but at the same time different, creatures lost in myth, which swing through the trees above and look out from the undergrowth on the forest surface. One of them lets out a surprisingly human cry of pain and drops to the ground. The creature's confused eyes fix on Anya's point of view.

THE RIVER SWEEPS her away again.

THE DESERT, far to the north ... the smell of smoke coming from over the horizon ... footprints, hundreds ... no thousands of footprints ... streaming across the sand towards the craggy edge of a canyon ... Lights flash across the sky despite the suns sweeping across the vista ... The ground shifts uncomfortably below her feet as if broken.

THE TIDE SWEEPS her away from the heat.

THE TATTOOED COUPLE writhe in the lamplight of a skinned hut ... The woman is both unfamiliar and familiar as she moves on top of the Shaanti ...

The woman's long hair covers the man's face, hiding his features ... She rolls him over so he's atop her ... Anya's wounds, long healed, ache, and tears fall, leaving the bitter taste of salt on her tongue ... There is no fear in this cabin, no violence and nothing of the darkness outside, yet Anya can feel bile in her throat ... The sense that this has been ripped from her is overwhelming ... She comes closest to understanding in that moment, but it is lost from her.

THE TSUNAMI of the torrent strikes once more.

THE DOCKS ARE *bright with light from the sun, erasing the scene from her mind and crystallising into a small boat pulling in, a series of wooden boxes being unloaded with care. Men move to carry them down the jetty, where a woman checks them and, looking round for observers, waves them into a small building. This woman is swathed in robes that make her impossible to identify. There is a sense of panic throughout the city, and many of the people are fleeing. The sailors are keen to discharge their duty and be away. The woman seems sad, a downward turn of her shoulders, but she is not overly afraid.*

THE PAIN of the information churning through Anya is excruciating. It knots her up before it unravels her like rope fraying under tension.

NEWBORN GODS STREAM *from the lake at the heart of the forest ... Tream look on, confused, weapons raised while the men they have been fighting fall to their knees, forgetting the deadlock with the Tream ... Their deities are real and have revealed themselves in their hour of need ... Truly, they are blessed.*

THE VISIONS ARE A FLOOD NOW.

A GOD STANDING *on the edge of the forest, his hair wild as antlers, his body torn and bleeding as the pantheon stare at him with open hatred.*

. . .

A BURNING CITY full of dead Delgasians, a stone temple where someone of impossible height moves out from the shadows.

A GODDESS – she could be Danu or the Morrigan – points to the Barrens, where human army clashes with human army.

A SOLE FIGURE treading across the desert towards a small tree, his leather bag bouncing against his hip.

A CRYING man she should know waves a tattooed woman off as she heads eastward. Anya never sees her face.

THE GOD with the wild hair defies his kin, and one of the gods, hidden by the others, raises her hand in power. The wild-haired god is hurled far away, his departure a streak of light that arcs across the sky.

ALL IS FIRE. All is water. Anya cannot breathe. She needs to start breathing again, or she will die. The knowledge is certain. Yet the information is starting to make sense: she thinks she knows what she is seeing, but she can't quite join the picture together.

MEN, woman and children streaming into the mountains to the south, buildings are carved from the rock even as more people cross the ocean to other lands.

THE WILD-HAIRED GOD lifts a stone knife to his own chest and begins to carve in the runes from the tablet in front of him.

. . .

TREAM FIGHT THE GODS. *Anu splits the forest and drives a spike deep into Golgotha as the trees she has destroyed smoke into the air. Anya can actually feel the echoes of their screams through the soil, and the truth destroys her even as it hovers on the edge of her grasp.*

THE HAIRY, *leathery creature in the forest screams as a being emerges from between its legs. The baby is dark, like the creature, but has far less hair and cries almost the moment she emerges into the light.*

BREATHE.

THE WILD-HAIRED GOD *stands atop a stone creature that moans in pain as he rips its head from its shoulders, and the men surrounding him drop to their knees in supplication.*

THE LAND IS BROKEN, *fused with rock. All around, smoke stains a nightmare landscape of stone and twisted metal. The air is hot with gas.*

BREATHE.

ANYA CAN BARELY MAKE *out anything save a city on the coast, burning with fire, and ships that remind her of the other dreams.*

THE THOUGHT DISSOLVES.

BREATHE.

.   .   .

AND ALL IS LIGHT.

THERE IS HER MOTHER. *She stands in the light. She is not human here but made of glass, as if she stepped from the stained window of her town hall, where she was venerated as a hero of the clan. Anya can see the sword that everyone remembers in her left hand, even as she, the daughter no one knows about, looks on. Her mother is speaking, but Anya cannot hear her. The voice sounds different from the one in her head, and the words are all coming out in nonsense. Her mother reaches out for her with the hand that is empty. She thinks she can make sense of two words that are repeated at intervals: 'No fear.'*

BREATHE.

ANYA'S LUNGS FILL. Colours bleed into vision as the air, cool and fresh, streams back into her. The light fades to the darkness of the cave.

'BREATHE.'

Someone she knew was speaking. The voice wasn't her mother's. The slow sinking of the images in Anya's head into the duller tones of half-recalled paintings obscured the name of the speaker. It was a bittersweet victory when the woodsman's name slipped into her mind, along with the memories of the attack on the village and his failure to help by the lake. She lay still a moment longer, enjoying the silence. One of them had bandaged her head; she could smell wysgi on the garment, and she was grateful for it. She didn't relish the thought of infection, and she doubted the dirt here had the healing properties of the forest.

Outside, the Kresh beat themselves across the rocks, searching for an opening.

'She might die yet,' said Vedic. She guessed the woodsman was rubbing his arm. The limb must have been very painful given how close to death she had come.

'Do something!' insisted Akyar.

'I can't,' snapped back Vedic. 'I did warn her.'

Akyar's blade sounded like a serpent hissing as he drew it. Anya pushed herself to her elbows.

'He's not being a bastard,' she said, nodding at Vedic and enjoying their surprise. 'There wasn't anything he could do.'

Vedic let out a long breath and sat down. His cursed arm stretched a little less awkwardly across his lap. Anya noticed the scar on his arm looked angry. She gently pushed the Tream, who was trying to help her, away.

'Are you all right?' asked Anya of Vedic.

Akyar winced. 'Don't worry about Vedic. He's just worried about himself.'

'No,' said Anya, her eyes still on Vedic. She was trying to cling to the images she had seen and failing: they were receding like fine mist on a sunny winter's morning. 'There is more than the fear of the pain that the curse gives him when I am in danger. I don't think his worry for Danu is behind this feeling either. The woodsman has been terrified since we fell through the fissure into Golgotha.'

Vedic leant back on his stone, against the far wall of the cave, his eyes closed in meditation and his sword resting on his lap. He didn't answer but continued to focus on his breathing. There was no shaking of his hands or nervous movements of his legs, and he gave the appearance of being elsewhere. Anya knew this was a lie. He could hear her. She got to her feet and walked towards him.

'What happened with the Morrigan?' asked Anya. 'You felt fear, real fear, down here, perhaps for the first time ... That's the secret ... is it not?'

Vedic opened his eyes. 'You saw things in the water, did you? Why don't you tell me?'

Akyar looked from Vedic to Anya and back again.

'You saw strange visions with the semblance of sense but that you could not stitch together,' said Vedic, turning to look at her. 'You have drunk of the pool of Mnemosyne, albeit by accident. The water will have given you knowledge – in time, you may understand.'

Anya blinked, distracted by the implication that all she had seen was real. 'What if I had swallowed more?'

'You'd be dead. The human brain is only designed to take so much reality. The knowledge burns your mind out. Frankly, in its undiluted form, I'm surprised you could take any at all. It is ... potent.'

Anya batted aside the distraction of her other visions. 'This happened to you, didn't it? The first time you came here, you were already a forestal, and she diluted the water for you, but you drank of the lake. That's why you won't go near the water?'

Vedic blinked.

'I think you may be right,' said Akyar, watching the woodsman. 'I wonder if you saw a vision that we should know.'

There was no answer to this, but the woodsman looked tired and old in the faded light of the cave. He closed his eyes and returned to his breathing.

Anya kicked his feet. 'Well, can we expect any help from you in here? Because at the moment, it seems to turn on the head of a coin.'

Vedic's hand dropped to his sword.

'Anya, let him alone,' said Akyar. 'Whatever it is that's gnawing him, he doesn't want to share.'

'My death.'

Anya found herself staring at the woodsman, the hairs on her arms standing on end and a similar expression of fascination and revulsion on her Tream companion's face.

'I saw my death,' said the woodsman, refusing to look at either of them. 'The Morrigan brought me here to show me her realm.'

'Why?' Anya couldn't help herself.

Vedic looked at her. 'She wanted me to serve her, not Danu ... thought I was better suited to the land of the dead, and she showed me what was waiting if I did not.'

'What did you see?' asked Akyar. 'Exactly.'

'It made no sense. Like for Anya, the vision was overwhelming. I saw many things.'

'You clearly remember the dying part,' said Anya, folding her arms.

'I do,' replied Vedic, closing his eyes again. 'I'm in a burning wasteland. I think the fire is close, but I can't be sure. I am surrounded by the bloodied ghosts of the enemy, waiting to take me when I fall ...' Vedic bowed his head. 'It doesn't matter. The vision was a lie, a twisting of the lake's power. We are safe in the caves and still breathing.'

'You thought the wasteland was Golgotha,' said Akyar, his voice tinged with pity.

'Don't you?' asked Vedic. 'The dead are all around us here.'

Anya nodded. She had him now. 'Perhaps. We need to find the boy. Can we count on your help? The Morrigan wants to get under your skin – she succeeded. Now it's time for revenge.'

Vedic opened his eyes and looked at her. 'Yes.'

There was a howl from deep inside the tunnels and caves behind them. The cry was deafeningly loud and went on for what felt like an eternity. The howl contained so much anguish and longing, though it was clearly animal, that even in their fright, they felt for whatever had made the noise. Vedic stood and looked at the other two.

'Well, are you coming?'

CHAPTER TWENTY-ONE

THEY RODE IN SILENCE.

Jeb had not spoken to his sister in so long that he suspected he had forgotten how to, and the forest in the distance was something to focus on, a hypnotic smudge on the horizon that grew darker as they drew closer. He shifted in his saddle, which was becoming increasingly uncomfortable as the journey went on and a distraction from imagining what was going on in Vikrain.

'Are you all right?'

Jeb looked across at his sister.

Sevlen barely seemed there. Her shadow's attire was a seamless sea of black that, in the moonless night, faded and merged her form into that of the horse. If he had not known she was there, it would have been easy for his old eyes to skip over her entirely. She sat more upright than him. She was a lot younger, the offspring of his father's second wife, and more like a daughter to him than a sister because of the age difference.

'I will survive,' he said.

She laughed. 'No doubt.'

'Why are you here?'

Sevlen did not answer. They rode on in silence. Jeb found himself thinking about the moment when his father had brought baby Sevlen round to the barracks to show her off. He had been a young man already and living with the rest of the warriors at the palace, around a year from being asked to tutor the young thain-to-be. She had been the strangest baby. She did not cry. Not once. She looked up at him with those big brown eyes that seemed to see everything, and it was as if she had known him forever: an old soul. She was probably looking at him like that now, not that he could see her eyes.

'How can you ask that?'

He shifted. 'We have not spoken for ten years or more.'

'Twenty.'

He shrugged. 'What is a decade at our age? You make my point for me: what is it to you if I never come back from here?'

'There are no chances to play again in this life,' said Sevlen, the shadow. 'I have travelled far and wide for our mistress and seen things you people wouldn't believe. Humans have a capacity for harm and self-delusion that is unparalleled in the world, and amongst the worst is the belief there is still time. Even I, who have seen all our sins and used them to my advantage, nearly forgot. You are my brother. I would make amends.'

Jeb flushed. 'You cannot change what you did.'

'Could you change the course of your heart?'

He thought of his wife, Sola, who had been dead for thirty years. They had met when he came back from the first skirmish with the Kurah, back when the previous thain had been nearing the end of her reign, and Sola had dismissed him as another knucklehead. It took him three years to persuade her he wasn't another soldier in search of glory, trying to live up to the witch-warrior or determined to die trying. He missed her so much. In the night, he would still wake and roll to her empty side of the bed, struggling to regain the scent of her, long gone from the house, and would occasionally smoke her old pipe just to fill the building with the tobacco smoke she favoured.

'No,' he said. 'I suppose not.'

She grunted. 'You think everything is so black and white, man and woman—'

'That wasn't why,' he said, exasperated that the old argument was starting again. 'My objection had nothing to do with who you or she fell for,' he said. 'She was ... she is my oldest friend. This was about the Shaanti clans. There was still time for her to have another heir, and we needed one because, whatever she says, we are not ready for the council. Human nature is too fickle.'

'That's foolishness,' replied Sevlen. 'She could have adopted an heir at any time, still could for that matter, and you know it.'

Jeb flushed. The horse shifted under him, trying to pull a little to the left and pulling the reins in his right hand enough for it to hurt. He squeezed as best he could with his knees and pulled gently on the reins. The horse obeyed, but the beast was getting twitchier the closer they got to the forest.

'Have you been in the forest before?' he asked.

Sevlen shifted in her own saddle. 'No. That is the one place we are not allowed to go, even as shadows. She handled any communication with the gods through other messengers, usually a short dark-haired man that would occasionally come to the city gates and be ushered through the thain's path to her chambers.'

Jeb nodded. He knew who the short man was. Not that he was a man.

'I didn't want this life for you,' he said. He was tired of leaving this unsaid.

'Pardon?'

'I didn't want this life for you,' he said. 'This life of shadows and of stolen moments between long periods away from all of us, away from her, and I could not see any way out for you after you gave away your heart.'

'Oh, Jeb,' she said. 'You silly old fool. It was my choice. I have had a good life, and we have ... we have few regrets. I was always heading for the shadows whether we had caught each other's eye or not. It's the only thing I've ever been really good at. Your idea of a romance is fantasy. No one has it.'

Jeb thought again of his wife. 'Oh, they do. If they are lucky.'

His sister rode up alongside him and put her hand across his. 'I was sorry when Sola passed. She was a wonderful person, and I know how much it hurt you to lose her.'

Jeb let her keep her hand there. The contact felt good. He would have liked to have frozen time there, to have potentially lived a little longer in that moment. He had only one sister, and he was conscious of how lucky he was that neither of them had died before this ride and that things were being said that needed to be said. The forest was only a league away now. He could smell the trees.

'The land is too quiet,' she said, withdrawing her hand.

'You worry too much,' he said. 'The gods do not permit harm within the forest.'

Sevlen pulled her horse to a halt. Jeb carried on. He would not fail his mistress on this final mission that she had been good enough to give him when most would have sent him to the yard to amuse the children.

'Jeb,' she hissed.

'I would have your company, sister,' he said. 'But I will not stop on my course.'

'Where are the birds?'

Jeb looked at the trees, only yards away, and searched for any sign of life. There was nothing that he could hear, nothing that he could see, not even an owl in the trees, searching the dusk for any prey they could pick up. The last time he had entered the forest, not far from here, the trees had been full of birds, and the edge of the forest had been teeming. Now there was nothing but those yellow, gleaming eyes.

The wolves attacked before he had time to think. They took his horse down, two of them, bearing down on the creature with a ferocity that spoke of actual intelligence even before the wolves spoke. Jeb managed to roll away from the beast as she went down, and pulled his sword with a pace approaching his old speed. The first wolf went down with his belly split, and the second lost her head.

'Jeb!' cried his sister, goading her horse on.

There were more wolves. Jeb killed another. And another. A stag emerged from the shadows, and he seemed as big as the moon. Jeb saw in another blink that it was not a stag but a giant man rising, naked, with a spear that gleamed and his skin covered in tattoos. The god's name came into his head. He couldn't remember where he had left his slippers most of the time, but here was the name he had been taught as a boy nearly a hundred years ago, popping into his head like it was yesterday. Cernubus.

Jeb turned to his sister. She was attacking the wolves from horse-back, slicing at them with her sword, killing a fair few. One bit Jeb. He howled and killed it.

He turned back to his sister. 'Run!'

She hesitated even as he turned to block Cernubus's spear.

'Run!' he yelled. 'He's a god!'

Jeb knew she would understand, that the shock would bring out her duty, sending her away on the horse, giving him that one last victory before the death that he knew was coming. He'd be damned if he would make this easy.

'Why make it so hard?' asked the god. He seemed to be speaking from everywhere all at once.

'Why have you turned on us?' asked Jeb, staggering. His right leg gave way, and it allowed Cernubus to drive the spear into Jeb's side.

Cernubus stepped in close to the old man. Jeb was gritting his teeth against the pain in his side. He felt like he had been cut in half as he grabbed the spear with his left hand. He could feel his own blood leaking over the shaft.

'Your people abandoned me,' hissed the god, 'sided with that woman, Danu.'

Jeb held the spear tight. 'Always,' he replied, driving the sword into the god's chest up to the hilt.

Cernubus laughed.

'The old man has teeth,' the god shouted, wrapping his left hand around Jeb's and extracting the blade from his torso without leaving any tears or blood.

In one sudden movement, he pulled the spear from Jeb and spun and struck the old man in his neck. Everything splintered. Jeb was on the floor. He couldn't feel his body.

'Should we follow her?' asked a wolf.

'No,' said Cernubus, looking out across the plains after her. 'It is better this way.'

Jeb had time to consider what this meant before everything faded to a sickly orange. He was in another place, where the light did not seem quite right. He felt an irresistible pull towards the river and beyond. He had been on a mission. Going somewhere. He couldn't remember what it was. He was sure he'd remember if he just kept on walking, and so he did. He didn't notice that nothing hurt any more.

CHAPTER TWENTY-TWO

THE WORLD WAS DARKER than the inside of her head.

The ribbons of phosphor that had lit the walls of the cave they started in had tapered out long enough ago that Anya felt she had been walking down the throat of the mountain for an age. None of them mentioned that the route was taking them slowly lower and therefore further from the surface and their route back to the real world. Vedic went first, his courage recovered for the time being, no doubt because he had not seen a vision of tunnels in his dream of death. Anya thought it was strange that he set such faith by a vision that could have just been a hallucination.

You're one to talk. Her mother's voice was in her head more and more the deeper they went. Occasionally she thought she saw Fin and her grandfather disappearing ahead of them, their forms glowing lightly in the dark. She knew they were in her head. She didn't know why she did, but the certainty was there like the knowledge that the suns would rise in the morning, unfailingly. This didn't stop her hands shaking when she thought about having to fight real people again, to end their stories with her sword.

The Tream went next after Vedic, his left hand clasped to the woodsman's right wrist, and Anya came last, her left hand linked to

Akyar's right wrist. On the occasions Vedic stopped, they tended to collide into each other and mutter apologies in the dark.

The breeze stopped them. Air rattled down the passageway, and with it was the faint smell of the Tream throne room.

'Meyr,' whispered Akyar.

Vedic drew his sword. The blade was invisible in the dark, but the noise was unmistakable as the metal left the sheath.

'Trivium,' he replied.

Anya could smell another scent on the air. It was dirty, wet and foul, and faintly familiar, as if the scent had a cousin on the surface. Then Anya placed the odour – wet dog that had not been washed for an age, if at all. There was a growling up ahead.

'Kerberos,' she replied.

'Is meant to be dead,' said Vedic, his irritation showing.

'We're in the land of the dead,' replied Anya.

'Who is Kerberos?' asked Akyar.

Anya let go of his wrist and drew her own weapon. 'Kerberos is the guardian of the three roads that split from this at the Trivium. Three roads: one leads to the void, one to the Cave of Shadows, and one leads to the Morrigan's home – or so we say. No one has ever come back from that road.'

Akyar laughed. 'You humans have some very strange ideas. I think death is a great deal less complicated than this.'

'Yes, but we're not the ones who talk to trees,' said Anya.

'He does,' said Akyar. She imagined he was pointing at Vedic. This made her laugh.

'Shh,' said Vedic, as if he were straining to hear.

The howl, when it came, was almost on top of them. They all had their weapons out, but there was little room to actually fight in the tunnel – it was a poor place to try to defend. Vedic cursed. There was the sound of tearing and of fabric being pulled tight, and then there was light.

Vedic was holding a human thigh bone wrapped in part of his tunic, which he had torn off and managed to light with the flints he used for his pipe. He placed the torch in a section of wall where it would hold while still burning, and picked up his sword.

'Right, are we doing this?'

'Are you?' asked Akyar.

Anya steadied herself. She nodded at the Tream's question.

'I've had enough of this,' said the woodsman, shifting round to face them. 'I'll be damned if I'm going to fall in some godforsaken tunnel.'

Vedic's eyes flashed angrily, almost as if he were a demon himself. Anya wasn't sure for a moment if that meant Vedic was going to fight them or whatever was coming up the tunnel. There was a glimpse of someone else there for a moment, another Vedic, and a sense that the growls weren't the most dangerous thing in the caves.

'One last charge, is it, Vedic?' asked Akyar, finishing the last of the water.

'What choice do we have?' asked Vedic, nodding in the direction of the growls. 'Fight and likely die, or lie down and definitely die.'

'I'm not making the journey across Golgotha again, not for a long time,' said Anya, gripping her blade, forcing her hand not to shake. Fin stared at her across the tunnel, but when she blinked, he was gone.

The woodsman smiled. 'I wish I could be so confident.'

'This isn't what you saw,' said Akyar, putting his hand on Vedic's shoulder. 'In the water, you saw your death, and it wasn't here.'

'Small mercies,' said Vedic, shaking his head.

A howl went up again from wherever the tunnel ended. They turned as one to look at the darkness ahead, willing themselves to move on. Claws scratched on stone, and Kerberos sniffed, trying to scent them.

'Well, we don't have that comfort, but I'm not sure I like how my story is going,' said Anya, checking her blade. 'I don't plan on the tale ending here.'

'We're all just shadows,' said Akyar. 'All light fades in the end and passes into darkness. All we can do is hope to burn bright enough that our afterglow lasts as long as possible.'

'Balls to that,' said Vedic.

The woodsman couldn't run – there wasn't enough clearance – but he managed a swift shuffle down the tunnel, his sword in one hand, and his axe in the other. A rolling growl came, deep and loud.

'Now he decides to be courageous,' said Akyar, padding after the woodsman.

Anya hesitated for a moment, her heartbeat a swift staccato in her chest, and the black seemed too close to that sweet darkness when she had lain bleeding in the forest, as close to Golgotha as she was right now. She looked at her shaking hands. It would be so easy to just go back, to dwell in Golgotha until the darkness forced itself on her. Who would blame her? She forced the shake away, and the grip on her sword tightened.

'*Balls to that*,' she whispered. And then, louder: 'Balls to that!'

KERBEROS, the three-headed dog, guarded the Trivium from souls trying to do exactly what they were attempting to do: return to the world of the living.

Kerberos, the Morrigan's hunting companion, had supposedly been slain by the hero Arawn. The Shaanti recalled the hero who dared to return his love to the living as one of their treasured myths. The dog had lived on as a way to scare children into obedience, and perhaps that, Anya thought, was what had sustained it: childhood terror.

Anya had always baulked at the story, the only tale from the *Pantheon* that she had never really had any patience for. Her grandfather had spent each night reading from the *Pantheon*, from the time she lay in the cradle to the last night she saw him alive. To Anya, a three-headed dog and someone riding into hell for love just seemed foolish. This didn't seem as fanciful as they burst into the Trivium and saw what was waiting for them.

The chamber was high, a granite dome, which, had it been painted, would have done the Kurah proud as a chamber for their stone god. Behind Kerberos, at the far end of the room, lay three openings arranged in a semicircle. They had no time to appraise them or form a strategy, because in the middle of the chamber was the beast. Kerberos, his fur as black as the passages behind him, his muzzles flecked with silver, his eyes as amber as honey and his maws as red as torn flesh. He smelt of earth and decay.

Kerberos leapt for the woodsman. Vedic and the animal went down in a mass of jaws and axe swings. The wrestling pair took out Akyar as he tried to intervene with his sword, launching him from his feet in a sweep of tail and legs that sent the Tream across the ground, crunching into a wall. Akyar's blade scattered one way, while the torch landed somewhere near the central opening.

Anya circled the fight with her blade up, ready to strike if she got a chance. In her periphery, she saw Akyar nip up, unarmed and scrambling for his sword, before she was forced to duck as Vedic was thrown by Kerberos across the chamber. He struck the wall and lay still.

Kerberos panted. His fur was blood-tinged, and not all of it from Vedic. All three of the heads glared at Anya, though one was hanging limp and wounded from the creature's right shoulder. Anya raised her sword, letting her voice bellow with the war cry of the Shaanti, projecting her fear out of her as she ran for the creature. She had no problem killing this monster. She was in control.

The dog leapt but not for Anya. The Tream tried to roll out of the way, but the creature merely bounced onto his rolling form and raised his heads up, one set of jaws holding Akyar, fists flailing at the maw. Kerberos shook the head that contained Akyar, trying to finish off the Tream.

Anya gave Kerberos no time, adjusting her attack. Lighter than Akyar, she dodged the first head and rolled, coming up from the ground with her sword in an arcing swing that took off the dog's central head with one sweep.

Blood gushed briefly from the stump. Kerberos's left head howled in pain. He leapt on Anya with leopard-like speed. She landed on her back with her sword-arm caught underneath her. Her shoulder burned with a pain unlike any she'd ever felt, and she thought she heard something pop. It took nearly everything she had to get her free hand up under the jaw of the creature's left head, holding the blade mere inches from her throat.

The animal grunted and howled from its wounds. All was muscle, blood and teeth. Anya was cast free of the fetid fur, rolling out of the way as the animal howled again.

Someone stood, blade extended into the side of the creature:

Vedic. Bloody, scowling and cursing in a language she didn't understand, the woodsman twisted the blade, the ghost of another man just hovering on the edge of his expression. *He's enjoying this*, she thought, catching the look on his face.

The dog howled again.

'Die!' grunted Vedic, slamming the blade in up to the hilt.

The creature yelped, dropping Akyar. The Tream rolled away, clutching his pierced sides but not getting up.

Kerberos crouched between Anya and Vedic, one head staring at each of them. A stalemate. Kerberos's left head swung round so quickly it caught both the woodsman and Anya by surprise. The hound was faster than either of them. The jaws clamped round Vedic's waist and tossed the woodsman like an errant puppy. Vedic sailed through the air, his eyes widening as he arced towards one of the openings – a tunnel that led down into the black.

He hit the ground just in front of the drop, his hands scrabbling for a hold as his body slid towards the yawning darkness. There was nothing to hold on to. He issued a grunt of surprised dismay and disappeared from view altogether, falling into silence. The woodsman was gone.

Kerberos turned to face Anya. Her heart pounded at what she had seen. Her chest hurt and her belly churned. Kerberos's jaws dripped blood and saliva. The dog limped from the bite of one of their blades; gashes lined its flanks; but still the beast came on with the feral tenacity of a killer gone mad. A growl rolled from deep within its body. The dog tensed its haunches to jump. Anya held her blade two-handed and ready to fight. She would not give Kerberos the satisfaction or spur of showing fear.

Kerberos yelped in surprise, his right head nipping at his side. Anya glanced and saw that Akyar, unable to find a weapon, unable to really move much at all, had resorted to the only thing left to him and sunk his own teeth into the dog's tail. Anya didn't wait. She flipped over the snapping right set of jaws, slicing the head from the neck, and rolled under Kerberos. She drove her blade up beneath the creature's breastbone with every bit of upthrust she could muster. Anya felt Kerberos's heart resist her sword momentarily before splitting like an overripe fruit as she twisted with all her might, the creature's belly pressed down on her shoulder. It grunted, pressing the air from Anya's lungs as the beast collapsed on her and expired.

———

'Anya?'

Akyar could not see the girl. The Tream stood slowly, his body cracking and protesting from its swift healing. The healing was not as fast as it had been in his youth, and his wounds gave him the occasional twinge – just to remind him they weren't entirely gone. The dog was prostrate in front of him, blood congealing on the floor around the animal, and there was no sign of either Vedic or Anya. He did not think he could be the only survivor.

'Vedic?'

There was a muffled sound from Kerberos, and the dog's ribcage moved. The Tream leapt back, grabbing his sword from where the blade had fallen, and he pointed the weapon at the creature's corpse. Kerberos could be feigning death to deal with his last opponent – cautiously he moved round the body. There was another muffled sound despite the creature being clearly dead. Placing his sword on the rock next to him, the Tream lifted one leg of the beast, and a familiar mat of hair was just visible.

'If you could actually help instead of just gaping,' said Anya. The girl sounded irritated. 'Didn't you hear me calling?'

'I couldn't hear anything for a while,' said Akyar. He felt guilty that he had not heard her. 'Healing that quickly takes a lot out of a Tream.'

Akyar set his back to the creature's body, rolling it off his companion with a meaty slap as the corpse settled on the far side of the cave. The girl dusted herself off with care – she held her right arm awkwardly – trying to clear some of the dust and blood from her bruised body. She appeared upset – the Tream could feel a thought hovering in his memory just before he had lost consciousness, something about Vedic. Akyar remembered and felt his stomach flip over.

'Vedic?' he asked.

Anya shook her head at him in response, pointing to the tunnel through which the woodsman had skidded and fallen. Akyar picked up the torch, moved to the opening and raised the flickering light to the darkness beyond. Rock – the same as in the Trivium – extended a few feet into the tunnel before falling away into the void. He made to step into the tunnel, reasoning that the light might cast further if he moved further in, but he felt a hand on his shoulder.

Anya shook her head. 'It's the void, one of the final doorways. You can't follow.'

'Where does it lead?' asked Akyar, his eyes not leaving the darkness.

'No one knows,' Anya replied. She, too, found it hard to not look at the void. 'It goes somewhere else ...'

'He's gone?'

'Yes, dead.'

Akyar let himself be led away from the opening.

The girl sat herself down well away from any of the tunnels, doing her best to clean her wounds through tears that the Tream felt certain she did not want him to see. Akyar watched her, letting his mind wander over the woodsman's death, the certainty that he now had to find Meyr without the one person who actually knew the Morrigan or had any notion how she might be bested.

'I can't really believe what I am seeing,' said Akyar, his right hand trailing in the dust of the cavern floor. 'This wasn't what was foretold for him, but even before I heard that ... I always assumed ... the gods ...'

'Neither can I,' said Anya, tying a piece of torn fabric around a gash on her leg. 'I'm trying not to think about it.'

'It'll be harder now,' said Akyar, holding his sword up to the torch. 'Neither of us knows enough about the gods to fight the Morrigan.'

'I never really knew him,' said the girl, staring back at the opening. 'He saved me, and I never even knew who ...'

'I could tell you,' said Akyar. He could feel the woodsman's history on him like a lead weight. The girl should know. It would ease the pain. 'He's gone now, anyway. It won't make any difference.'

'No,' she said, looking away from him. 'If he didn't want to tell me, then I don't want to know. I know what I need to: he saved me.'

The Tream nodded. 'Under duress, don't forget that. He wasn't a—'

'Yeah, I know.' Anya closed her eyes.

Akyar regretted his words. It wasn't for him to talk ill of the dead. There was a gasp.

There came the scrabbling of fingers searching for a purchase on rock. The two of them turned their disbelieving eyes towards the tunnel opening and a hand that loomed over the bottom of the entrance. A moment later a frost-covered head crept over the edge and was followed by the rest of the woodsman as he pulled himself, brow knotted in tension, back over the edge of the void. He paused on his hands and knees on the edge of the tunnel, staring wide-eyed at his companions. The Tream was on his feet first, and he pulled the woodsman in from the edge.

Vedic flopped onto his back in the centre of the cave and took in deep pulls of air, his beard flecked with ice, and his muscles twitching involuntarily from their climb. The woodsman lived.

'ARE YOU ALL RIGHT?' asked Anya.

Vedic hadn't said a word since he climbed back from the edge of the void. He'd lain on his back and taken in as much air as possible before he sat up. He'd lost his sword, but his axe still littered the floor of the cave, and he retrieved the weapon, moving slowly across the Trivium, his eyes not settling on either of his companions. When he was armed once more, he took a long draught of his waterskin, wiped his damp beard with his arm and stared at the dead dog.

'You do that?' Vedic asked Akyar, nodding at Kerberos.

The Tream shook his head and pointed to Anya.

The woodsman smiled. 'Good work, Anya.'

Akyar blinked.

'Vedic, are you well?' asked Akyar, stepping closer to Vedic.

'I'm alive,' said Vedic, hand to his head as if to confirm. 'I'd say that means I'm feeling pretty good.'

'What did you see?' asked Anya, touching his arm. 'You went

through and you came back. That's ... huge ... That's legendary ... People will write songs about it.'

'We have to make it back and tell someone in order for that to happen,' said Vedic, with a tired smile. 'Besides, having stories told about you isn't everything it's cracked up to be. As you'll find out, O Slayer of Kerberos.'

'You fool,' laughed Anya.

The sound was strange, an alien sound in that dark place, and yet it made both of the men – human and Tream – grin in the flickering shadows of the Trivium. Vedic even accepted a brief hug from Anya that made neither of them flinch.

'But what did you see?' asked Anya. 'You've been somewhere no one else has.'

'On the contrary, everyone gets to go there,' said Vedic, smile fading a little. His eyes wandered back to the tunnel. 'I saw nothing.'

Anya's heart lurched. *It couldn't be, not after all this.* She'd seen her grandfather, and Fin ... It couldn't be. She whispered, 'Nothing ...?'

Vedic's eyes stared into the void. After a moment, he tilted his head as if just registering the question.

'No, I didn't see anything. I was too busy trying not to fall. All I saw was the rock as I tried to grab on. I just about managed to grip an outcrop of granite as I went over. No time to look around. Sorry.'

Anya wasn't sure she believed him – she wasn't certain she wanted to know the answer any more. What would she do?

'I'm just glad you're back.' The words felt hollow.

'Me too,' said Vedic, looking away from the tunnel. 'Me too.'

'I thought you had gone,' said Akyar, handing him the torch. 'It was not a reassuring thought.'

'So did I.' The woodsman's face was unreadable in the low light of the cave, and his eyes were as black as the void.

Anya moved away from the woodsman – she still had to finish dressing her wounds. Besides, she wasn't sure she wanted to be around this stranger who had climbed out of the depths of the void.

'Blessed,' said Akyar, softly.

Vedic hugged himself against a cold Anya couldn't feel.

'I really did think that was it, that I was dead. I don't think any breath I've ever had ... I feel ... It's good to be here.'

'Blessed,' repeated Akyar, resting his hand on the woodsman's shoulder. 'Tream would say you are blessed. You've seen the dying of the bough and lived. You're reborn.'

Vedic looked at him in the dying light of the torch. 'One life is all you get. And no one really to judge you but the people you leave behind.'

Anya wasn't sure Vedic found his own words that comforting.

'One lifetime,' Akyar shrugged. 'But you can have many lives.'

The light died.

'We should get out of here,' said Anya from across the cave.

'Yes,' said Vedic, turning from the Tream. 'Just tell me which way.'

'Well, not the one on the left,' said Anya, standing.

'Very funny,' said Vedic. 'How about using that razor-sharp clan wit to find the correct tunnel?'

'Just keep talking until I find where you're standing.'

'I can't make out any difference,' said Akyar, feeling his way along the tunnel entrances. 'They both lead uphill.'

'Careful,' said Vedic.

'There you are,' said Anya, grabbing hold of Vedic's arm and releasing it immediately.

'Anya, is there any way of working out which tunnel it is?' asked Akyar.

'No,' she said. 'Unless you can make anything out? In the legend, Arawn used a ball of string in case he had to return, but he went up the correct tunnel first time. I never liked that part.'

Anya felt Vedic move over to her right, keen to avoid the edge of the one tunnel they were sure about. There was a sound of scuffling as he stood in the opening of each tunnel, trying to guess the right path.

'How far should the palace be?' asked Vedic.

'Not far,' said Anya. 'Supposedly, Arawn made it to the surface despite being chased by Kresh and the Morrigan.'

They considered what to do.

'I'll walk up each of these in turn until I find it,' said Vedic. 'If I walk for longer than I think fits, then I'll turn back.'

'What if the tunnel forks?' asked Akyar. 'You don't have string.'

'I don't like this,' said Anya, kicking the dust. 'We don't know where the other tunnel leads. What if it drops away suddenly?'

'I'll be careful.'

'I'm not sure,' said Anya. 'What if you get hurt?'

'Okay,' said Vedic, and there was the sound of his boots being removed. 'Take off your clothes.'

'What?'

'I'm going to use our clothes as a marker. If I go further than the end of the clothes tied together, I'll score the ground and direction I take with a stone. If you need to find me, you can.'

'I'm not sure about this,' said Anya, trying to ignore the sound of Vedic's clothes being tied together. She stepped back from him.

'How will we see your rock markings?' asked Akyar.

There was a crash of an axe-head striking rock, and sparks flared briefly, showing the three of them standing almost huddled in the cave before the darkness robbed their sight again.

'Fair enough,' said Akyar, removing his one garment and accepting the axe in return.

'I don't like this,' said Anya, still not undressing.

'I know,' said Vedic, keeping his distance. 'It's fine: we can't see anything.'

'Well, stay over there,' said Anya.

The air of the cave was cool on her skin, but Anya did not try to warm herself – she held her sword tightly in her hand and kept her distance. Vedic knotted the clothes together before handing one end to Akyar.

'If I tug on this once, it means trouble,' said Vedic. 'Twice means I'm heading back. If I pull the clothes continuously, I'm heading on further.'

Anya shivered in the cold dark of the cave. There was a breeze coming from somewhere, and she tried not to think about what would happen if the Kresh found a way in. She had no idea how to free the boy from the Morrigan. In the fighting, Anya had forgotten that she had been counting on finding a weapon in Golgotha to help them. Feeling vulnerable, she hugged herself.

The nakedness of the Tream had not really bothered her until now, in the dark, with her own clothes gone from her.

'You okay?' asked Akyar, shifting on his feet. The sound of dust and rock underfoot was loud in the relative silence of the cave. The dog stank more with each passing minute.

'Sure.' She rubbed her arms to stay warm. 'Just stay over there.'

'I'm not moving. Just try not to get too cold.'

'I'm fine,' said Anya, as edged as her sword.

'It's not that one,' said Vedic, his voice close to Anya. She jumped back.

'The right-hand tunnel leads to the Cave of Shadows and the way out,' Vedic continued, passing Anya her clothes. 'Put these on. This middle tunnel is the one that leads to her palace.'

Anya had just pulled on her boots when there was a flare and the cave was flooded with light. A torch flickered in Vedic's hands, a new blade – an Shaanti-made one – hung from his belt, and he chucked a bow to Akyar.

'Where did you find that?' asked the Tream.

'In the reason no one ever returned from this tunnel,' replied Vedic. 'Kerberos didn't attack us further up, because his job wasn't to guard the Trivium. It was to guard the palace. The dog obviously used the tunnel as a kind of den – there were bones all over the place and this kind of stuff.'

'So you robbed the grave?' asked Anya, shaking her head as she checked her own weapon was properly strapped on. 'Typical.'

'It's not a grave.' Vedic shrugged. 'It's a larder, and these things weren't helping their owners any more. They might well save our skins.'

'The woodsman is right,' said Akyar, testing the bow. 'I imagine the dead would want someone to benefit from what they've left behind.'

'I just don't think taking weapons from corpses when we're trapped in the underworld is the smartest idea,' said Anya, folding her arms.

'Let's get out of here,' said Vedic.

CHAPTER TWENTY-THREE

THE REFUGEES WERE RUNNING.

The thain had seen the mass exodus of the borderlands twice before: once when she was a girl, when the problem was her father's, and the second just before the last war with the Kurah, when she had earned her fearsome reputation. She had always been able to keep her people safe. Until now. Both times before, the people had plodded over the plains to Vikrain, broken and beaten but not defeated. Now, the people were completely terror-struck, running from destruction. There was no sense of safety in reaching Vikrain, just a brief pause, and many did not stay beyond the first night.

The thain placed her hands on the wall and watched the steady stream of arrivals as she waited for Golan to join her. She wasn't sure if seeing the camps first-hand would make a difference, but she preferred to think Golan was just being blockheaded than an all-out traitor. Late at night though, when she couldn't sleep, her gut made her think of betrayal. The air smelt of people in all their unwashed glory. From her childhood, she associated such a stench with fear, and she wondered if the other tribes, scattered across the world, continued to fight as the Kurah and Shaanti did.

'Milady,' said Golan. Bene stood by his side, having escorted the merchant from his quarters in the market. 'Let's get this over with. I don't see how spending time amongst the wretches helps. We're just going to have to move them on.'

The thain flinched. The man was bereft of compassion. She did not understand how someone like this could be related to someone like Falkirk, who had always thought so unfailingly of duty and the people around him. *Blood is so easily tainted.* She felt shamed by the thought. She knew better.

'Let's go and take a look at the camps,' she replied. 'It does the people good to see us and know that we care.'

Golan said nothing. He nodded and followed her down to the main gate and out into the camp. As they passed through the gate, Bene's men and women fell into step around them at a loose distance, as per her instructions. They could defend her if they had to, but they were far enough away for people to interact a little.

'Shouldn't they be closer?' said Golan, nervous.

The thain smiled. 'I'll defend you, Golan. These people don't want anything except safety.'

'Seems negligent to me,' sniffed the merchant. 'I've never been sure about General Bene.'

The thain turned to look directly at the merchant. 'They are keeping their distance on my instructions. I want to be seen close to these people who have lost everything. I don't want them whispering that the lords don't care, that we have lost touch and isn't it time the common folk look out for themselves. Clans fall when they forget to look after each other.'

'Did you read that in a book?'

The thain gave him a wan smile. 'No, in war. In a battle, you can live or die by how well the man or woman next to you protects you. The armies made up of free men and women sworn to protect each other do better than those armies made up of warriors that only try to protect themselves.'

Golan's eyes had gone wide.

The thain followed his gaze. She realised her hand had fallen, instinctively, to her sword, and the merchant had noticed. She let go, and the blade, partially drawn, fell back in its sheath.

'Bene,' she called over to her bodyguard. 'How many people here now?'

'Seven hundred,' he replied. 'Fifty or so are arriving each hour. There will be over a thousand by dusk.'

'You see,' she said. 'The Kurah tactics have changed. They are not giving chase as they did in previous campaigns. Last time, there were far fewer survivors.'

'What about the food?' asked Golan.

The thain shook her head. 'What about it?'

'We will not have enough to hold out.'

The thain sighed. Merchants were always the same – *what about me? I don't have enough. We're all in this together, but I'm more affected than you.* 'We will have plenty, if we stay here at all.'

'What do you mean?'

'We are at war,' said the thain. 'Whether you like it or not. We may decide this isn't the best place to remain.'

'This is the most defensible area we have. The mountains behind us mean they could only approach from the plains.'

The thain smiled. 'You did retain something during your brief time in the army, then,' she said. 'You'll also recall that if we wait for that, we will lose our ability to leave. Siege would be dangerous.'

'Only if he has managed to reinforce his supply lines,' replied Golan. 'None of his predecessors managed to do that, and the winter will cut him off.'

'We'll make a warrior out of you yet,' said the thain, airily.

They made their way through the tents and makeshift shelters, passing children playing in the dirt and the odd dog hanging round in the hope of scraps. At the edge of the emerging camp, there were survivors fresh from the road, dirt-encrusted, sweat-stenched and, in some cases, still bleeding. One of the men stood on their approach.

'Are you her?'

The thain stopped. The man was not dressed like an Shaanti: his clothes were darker and would have shone had they been clean. His skin was as pale as milk, and he was lean like he had been on the road far longer than the rest.

'Who wants to know?'

Bene drew his sword, but she waved him down.

The man bowed low. 'I am Gor-Iven of the Del, and I have come as a warning of what is approaching.'

Golan frowned. 'Delgasia fell. How are you here?'

The man nodded. 'Some of us escaped, but where my companions made for the ports and looked to our cousins in the cross, on the far side of the world, I have sought you out. This evil will follow us across the skin of the world if we do not stop it here.'

'I think world domination is a bit much even for the Kurah,' said Golan, his tone mocking.

The thain gave him a look that made him shut up.

'My companion is a touch unkind in his tone,' she said. 'But I am inclined to agree. The Kurah are not interested in world conquest, not yet.'

'I am referring not to the Kurah but their ally.'

The thain frowned. 'To whom are you referring?'

Gor-Iven looked round at the camp. 'You may wish for me to tell you somewhere other than here. It may spread panic.'

The thain looked around. The camp was staring at them, and anything they said here would travel like wildfire. Perhaps he had a point.

'Main hall, two hours,' she said. 'Dinner with the council – don't be late.'

'I apologise in advance for my state of dress,' said Gor-Iven, with a smile designed to open purse strings.

'Don't push it, Gor-Iven,' said the thain, keeping a smile from her own face. 'Your clothing is fine. Bring your information.'

They moved away. Golan's face told his story. She wondered if the merchant ever played cards or how he had managed to negotiate the sort of deals that had enabled him to amass almost as much wealth as herself. Perhaps this was an act. The man was in league with a traitor that was sending messages across the Shaanti lands to the Kurah. Someone who was quietly whittling down their supplies and sabotaging the city walls while the council argued amongst itself about what to do.

'My sources report that milady has sent Lord Jeb from the city,' said Golan.

The thain paused. Golan should not have been able to find this out, and yet here he was, asking the question. His network had grown too big while she had been worrying about dying. The pain in her lungs was sharp, but she pushed it away.

'Lord Jeb is on a private errand for me to an old friend,' replied the thain. 'Even rulers have personal lives.'

'No, milady,' said the merchant. 'With all due respect, they do not. That is the price for the seat on which you sit – your life is open to scrutiny. What business does Lord Jeb have in the forest? I am a councillor. I should know.'

The thain smiled. 'Lord Golan, you are also standing in the middle of a refugee camp. We will not discuss this matter further. Or are you challenging my authority as a war leader?'

'There has been no formal declaration,' said Golan.

The thain let her hand drift to her weapon again. 'Tread carefully.'

Golan flushed and turned. He marched off without taking his leave, and Bene stepped forward to stop him. The bodyguard's fury was honest but unhelpful. The thain waved him away.

'Let him go,' she said. 'And have my shadow's deputy look into how in Golgotha that fat merchant knew Lord Jeb had gone.'

'He presents a very grave threat,' said Bene, sheathing his blade. 'Do you propose to let this charade continue much longer?'

The cough came on her before the thain could reply. She was unable to speak: the cough just kept rolling and rolling, and her chest felt as if someone had lit a firework within it. The handkerchief she pressed to her mouth came away bloody, but she thought she got it inside her cloak before he saw it.

'Do you need a drink?' asked Bene, concerned.

She shook her head.

'We should return within the walls ourselves,' said Bene, looking around the camp. 'These poor people will be carrying their own share of sickness. You know how coughs travel through camps.'

'You are right,' she acknowledged. 'But let us not hurry like frightened rats.'

'You did not answer my question.'

The thain did not reply. She knew she had not answered his question, and truth be told, she was not sure how long she could let her deceit continue. She wasn't sure she understood the game that was being played. And she didn't like that. Not at all.

THE DINNER WAS A MOROSE AFFAIR.

The banquet hall was largely empty save for one long table at the end of the room nearest to the throne. Seated around it were the top five generals, the commanders of the thain's army, and the council. Seated to the thain's right hand was her invited guest, Gor-Iven of the Del. He wore a simple robe in black, as was the custom for an official in Delgasia, and had been cleaned up by someone – the robes were fresh, and he was tidy and shaven, his hair oiled back in a top knot. The thain wondered who had helped him. Her suspicion was that Golan had, and she was walking into a trap.

'You must forgive our fare,' she said, leaning conspiratorially towards him. 'We are all on rations, as the exodus from the borders will put us under strain. We may have to defend ourselves against a siege.'

Gor-Iven smiled. The grin did not reach his eyes. 'I understand, and please appreciate this is a feast to someone who has been on the run for over ninety days. I would have been shamed to see myself here if your bodyguard had not lent me these clothes and his quarters.'

The thain hid her surprise well. Bene was a private man, and kind, but she had never seen him take a stranger in like this. She glanced over at him, but he was lost in conversation with the speaker and only keeping her, the thain, in his periphery. She wasn't bothered by this – it was positively liberating to be trusted with one's own safety for longer than five minutes.

'We know each other,' continued the Delgasian. 'He is not one who is free with his resources, as you know, but we were at Pep together when he was just a swordsman and I was a bowman.'

'Remind me never to play cards with you, Gor-Iven,' she said, turning back to him with a smile. 'What was Bene like back then?'

Gor-Iven smiled. 'Pretty. Full of energy but not contained like it is now – he was like a flame that burned if you got too close. You no doubt remember, you sent him to Pep.'

The thain laughed. A long time had passed since a stranger had managed to elicit that from her, and she was thankful because the act of laughing felt like she had emerged into sunlight after a long storm. She hadn't been aware how dark her thoughts had become. Looking round, she took in the sight of people she had known all their lives, sitting around chatting and discussing, with such sombre faces. Despite the mood, this was peaceful. Soon all this would turn to hastily gobbled food in war tents and a constant fatigue punctuated only by relentless, freezing drops in temperature as night came.

The room fell silent when she stood.

'You have been good enough to share my company for dinner,' she said. 'And I would have you enjoy the meal, despite the circumstances, but we must hear what our guest has to say.'

'Does our guest have an explanation for how he escaped?'

The room was quiet enough that you could have heard a heartbeat if you concentrated. The guests were staring at Golan as if the merchant had lost his mind. The thain knew he had not. Golan had had time to think and now felt that whatever Gor-Iven had to say, he was a threat to Golan or whoever he was working with, and so he wanted to discredit him. The thain did not let her feelings show. Fortunately, she was not young any more, and she had more cards up her sleeve than he.

'I do not think ...'

The Delgasian rose. 'Milady, if I may,' he said. She nodded. He continued. 'My lord asks a fair question. I was not an escapee.'

Some of the warriors seemed uneasy now. Bene was looking like he was going to come over. She shook her head.

'I am on a mission from the last king of Delgasia.'

'Pah!' said Golan. 'How do we know this?'

Gor-Iven smiled. 'I'm glad you asked.' He produced a ring from within his robes and held it to the light. The piece was made of a metal brighter than silver, and the jewel in the centre had been formed into a cat's head that was so realistic and finely detailed it was hard to tell if an artisan had done the work or a mage. The last time the thain had seen the ring, it was on the hand of the king of the Delgasians.

'You could have taken that from his corpse,' said Golan.

'No,' said the thain. 'He could not. Once the ring is passed to each ruler, it cannot be removed unless the bearer decides to remove it, or someone related to them removes the ring in death. This man is no relative of the king, unless his skin has been bleached.'

Gor-Iven laughed.

'Then this was given by Jorn as a sign of good faith.'

Golan sat down, but his eyes never moved from the Delgasian.

'Please,' said the thain. 'Tell us everything.'

THE KURAH CAME *with the dawn.*

Gor-Iven heard the war bells before he saw them. He had been stretched out in his bed with his lover, the warrior-poet Ilya, next to him. Ilya moved faster than Gor-Iven, springing naked to the window. For a moment, Gor-Iven was too busy looking at the younger man's naked back – he had a notion to pull him back under the sheets – to notice his lover's expression. Ilya turned.

'Kurah,' he said.

Gor-Iven's ardour evaporated. The Kurah had not attacked in his lifetime, but his father had died when he was two, never having really recovered from the last war. He had been a one-legged cripple, unable to see past his experience to notice his family. Gor-Iven was a live-and-let-live kind of man – but not when it came to Kurah. Already screams were reaching them from below. There was a loud thump, like thunder, and the room shook.

'Trebuchet,' said Ilya, pulling on his leggings.

'Get away from the window,' said Gor-Iven, doing the same.

Ilya threw his tunic on as he replied. 'They aren't in here ye—'

The crossbow bolt caught him through the back, between his shoulder blades, and cast blood over the wall above the bed. Gor-Iven couldn't move as he watched the man crumple to his knees and slump over. Another bolt slammed into the wall. The strike broke Gor-Iven's hypnotic grief, and he dropped down out of sight, pulling his own tunic on and grabbing his dead lover's chain shirt almost as an afterthought. The warrior who had fired the bolt must be close, from the force of the projectiles. His own weapons were back in his quarters. He grabbed the dead man's sword and lousy excuse for a bow and crawled out of the room.

Once he was safely in the windowless corridor, he ran for the stairs. Gor-Iven took them two at a time until he reached the archers. The attack had come from nowhere. The floor was almost empty. Three archers lay slain. His eyes took a moment to adjust before he spotted the Kurah warrior bending over one of the corpses, his grey robes concealing him in shadow. Gor-Iven let loose an arrow without drawing properly. The strike took the man in the eye, and he went down screaming. Silently the Delgasian moved forward and ended the scream by thrusting a dagger up under the man's chin.

Gor-Iven looked out from the arrow slit next to a dead Delgasian bowman. He should have known his name, but he forgot them so quickly now. They all looked like children. Had he ever been so young? The image of Ilya, sinking to his knees and bleeding all over the floor, came back to him. He drew his bow and looked for the man that had fired the crossbow.

All across the city, Kurah poured through the streets, and there was little effective resistance. The king had abandoned the outer wall right away, from the look of it. There was a ragtag defence forming at the palace wall. The Kurah sniper was on the roof of the temple, firing occasional bolts down on the passing Delgasian warriors but, more often than not, looking to the high-rise windows of the palace and high-status buildings. The archer clearly had a strategy to decapitate the Delgasians by assassinating their leaders. He was not alone. Other snipers were in similar positions on half a dozen roofs across the capital.

Gor-Iven noted the Kurah crossbowman was no longer looking this way at all. He clearly thought the clearance had been done, and this was such a natural thing for a bowman to think. It was also fatal. Gor-Iven locked his bow on the man, adjusted for the wind and the narrow space of undefended torso, and let the arrow fly. It arced out wider and swooped back in on the wind, embedding itself in the assassin's neck and sending the man writhing for the wound, his crossbow forgotten, as he slid down the roof, coming to rest on the ledge. He did not move again.

The Delgasian got two more before the others realised they were being picked off. The bolts started flying, but it was only when the boulders from the *trebuchet started landing that he moved and made his way, running, to the palace walls. There was no fear now. He knew that he was going to die, and his sole purpose was to take as many Kurah with him as he could.*

Gor-Iven arrived at the palace walls just in time to see them fall. In a thousand years of the Del, the palace had never, ever been breached, and it was thought by most in the land to be impenetrable. Magic struck like lightning. Tendrils of light and the bright orange of fire warped and wrapped themselves round the ancient stone before blowing it asunder. The explosion took Gor-Iven and smashed him into the side of the palace, and scattered Del warriors like they were leaves blown by the wind. The Delgasian passed out.

GOR-IVEN WOKE UP, *aching all over but relieved to find he was alive.*

The majority of the men he had seen thrown from the wall as it was breached were dead. Those who'd survived were fighting Kurah. Gor-Iven wasn't sure if he had been hurt too badly to move. He lay as still as he could lest he be seen, checking himself as subtly as he could before risking a move. Around him, his comrades fought and bled. Gor-Iven hated himself for his caution. Satisfied that he was able to fight, he lashed out with a sword. He hacked the legs out from under the Kurah fighting a few feet away. Gor-Iven caught sight of another Delgasian, a tall man with a purple breastplate stained with mud and blood, becoming overrun by Kurah. He ran to help, ducking swipes from Kurah and killing all he could. Gor-Iven killed one of the men attacking the purple-armoured Delgasian. He killed the next Kurah by ducking under the warrior's wild swing and shoving a dagger through the man's eye. Before long Gor-Iven was fighting back to back with the Delgasian in purple armour, and he realised the tall man was actually his king, Jorn.

'What's your name?' shouted the king over his shoulder.

'Gor-Iven,' he shouted back.

'The city is lost,' yelled the king. 'You need to get out.'

'Not likely,' shouted Gor-Iven. 'They need to pay for this.'

'Courage is not dying for no reason,' yelled back the king. 'The Kurah have won today, but they will not stop here. The Shaanti must be warned.'

'Why?'

'*You're Brent's boy, aren't you?*' yelled the king, ducking a blow and taking another Kurah's head.

'*Aye,*' said Gor-Iven. *The man remembered his father. In that moment, he would have gone into hell for him.*

'*Then you know why,*' said the king. '*They saved us once. We must hope that she still has it in her.*'

'*Who?*'

'*The thain,*' said the king, turning and pressing the ring into Gor-Iven's hand.

What happened next still gave Gor-Iven nightmares. The fire-lightning snaked into the broken corridor and wrapped its tendrils around the king and lifted him into the air. Gor-Iven drew back in fear. This saved his life. The creature that came through the breached wall, lightning emanating from his right hand, was over seven feet tall and had hair that fell in crazy locks that could have been antlers. His skin was covered in tattoos that moved and merged and blended and shifted in the light. He was dressed in Shaanti leggings; his chest was bare; and in his left hand, he carried a spear that gleamed like the moon. Delgasians did not believe in the same gods as Shaanti, but they had spent enough time on this continent to know one of their gods when he appeared, however old he may be.

'You claim that an Shaanti god is with the Kurah?' asked Bene, rising.

'I wish that it were not so,' said Gor-Iven, his face a picture of grief. 'I truly do, but I cannot tell my story other than I saw it.'

The thain felt cold. Her mouth was dry despite the wine she had been sipping, and the silence of the room was feeling more like a collective scream.

'Please continue,' she said. 'You saw more. You have not told us of your escape.'

Gor-Iven *fell in his shock.*

Clutching the ring tight, he saw the god step close to the dying king. Gor-

Iven lay down and pretended to be slain. The god stepped up to the king, the fire-lightning turning his skin red raw where the god made contact, and looked at the ruler as a boy might look at a tadpole – as a creature that was other, weak and strange. A man, the Kurah king, stepped through the breach next and made his way to the god's side, his sword dripping with blood and his bodyguards spilling into the corridor after him.

'There you are, Jorn,' said Montu, the Kurah king. 'I didn't expect you to still be fighting, but here you are, like a true king, ready to die with your men. That's not how this went with my grandfather, is it?'

Jorn did not reply. He was straining at the magic that bound him in mid-air. Tears were streaming from his eyes and evaporating as they hit the energy. Gor-Iven watched as his ruler's hair turned from greying brown to bright white.

'Where is his ring?' asked Montu, bending down to look at the other king's hand.

'I did not pay attention to his jewellery,' said the god, and his voice was like the dark had come alive.

Gor-Iven began to slowly push himself back along the corridor while they were distracted, but it was slow-going. He could only move when all of them were looking elsewhere.

'Where is the ring?' asked Montu, staring at the king.

Jorn did not answer.

Montu sighed. 'You don't need this one for your sacrifice?'

'No,' said Cernubus. 'The only reason to keep him is if you want him.'

'Not my type,' said Montu, moving away. 'You may do with him as you wish.'

Cernubus waited until the Kurah were out of sight before he spoke to the prone king.

'This may take some time,' he whispered.

Gor-Iven watched as the god slowly moved his spear above the king's head, and a tiny tear in the king's skin started to appear. Jorn screamed. After a few moments of the sound, Gor-Iven drew his bow unnoticed and put an arrow in his king's chest. Cernubus's head snapped round as the fire-lightning vanished, and the king fell dead at his feet.

'We have a new player,' hissed the god. 'So glad you could join.'

The Delgasian did not waste arrows on the god. He knew when he was beaten before he started. The bowman took off at a run. The god appeared to match his pace with ease. Gor-Iven was counting on Cernubus having limited knowledge of the layout. He took the god on a winding, circuitous route through the palace, often only just managing to outpace him by taking sudden turns and sweep-backs. The latrines for the banquet hall were not somewhere that would have appeared on any invader's map, and so when he passed them, he ducked in, pausing only to throw a stone or two down the corridor.

Gor-Iven pulled the plank of wood from the chute and jumped before either the smell or the thought of what he was doing stopped him. He slid down the shit-encrusted passage into the muddy slime of the base of the pit and was thankful the weather had been dry for the last few weeks. He could easily have drowned in there otherwise. Instead, he had a soft landing amongst the slowly rotting faecal matter of his fellow citizens. He did not wait to see if the god had heard him drop.

The bowman ran for the broken walls of the city and the old boat hatches for the river. He hoped the Kurah had just come across the land and not from downriver, near the coast. He had little choice. Gor-Iven took one last look at the city where he was born before he dived through the hatch into the icy water, glad for its cleansing kiss, even if it was colder than the desert night.

'THIS IS A LOVELY TALE,' said Golan. 'But I fail to see how a god who died millennia ago could be helping our enemy. Why would he?'

None of the generals looked at the councillor, but the thain was disappointed to see other members of the council nodding their heads in agreement. They still believed this was about power, about politics, and not survival.

'We are grateful for your candour,' she said to Gor-Iven. 'My learned friend is merely seeking to understand what we cannot comprehend.'

'The Kurah force is vast,' said Gor-Iven. 'In the thousands. Your council did not believe that the attack was real, according to my friend Lord Bene, but the truth is the Kurah have learned their lesson. They have backed up their supply lines, and it is almost as if they have resurrected all their dead warriors to aid them. Perhaps this god has.'

'It is a long time since I heard his stories, but I'm certain Cernubus did not have that power,' replied Bene. 'I don't think any god can do that. Nor was Cernubus covered in tattoos. On this continent, only Shaanti warriors carry the ink.'

Gor-Iven shrugged. 'I am not sure he is a god any longer. Perhaps something else. A demon?'

'It matters not,' said the thain. 'He is an enemy, and he is powerful beyond imagination. Only Danu has anything like his power.'

'You underestimate our capabilities,' replied Golan. 'We will defeat him.'

'How do you kill a god?' asked the thain.

The merchant couldn't answer. He went bright red and muttered under his breath as he took another draught of wine.

'I thought not,' said the thain, rising. 'We have always fought overwhelming odds. We will prevail once more – on that myself and Lord Golan can agree. The tattoos suggest the god is corrupted and may therefore have a weakness we can use to our advantage. Go now to the archives, and find me information on any of the cants he may have used on himself. I think there may be an entry in the *Book of the Northern Reaches*. We must stop him from getting to the forest.'

The door to the banquet hall popped open with a crack that echoed round the hall. The shadow leant on the door frame. She was bleeding from a wound to her leg and covered in dirt to the point that she looked like she had been dragged from the forest. She stared at the room and then at the thain.

'Cernubus has the forest.'

CHAPTER TWENTY-FOUR

THE MORRIGAN'S palace was made of glass.

It wasn't the translucent glass that you might drink wine from in some lord's castle but the smooth black glass that you find on the slopes of the fire mountains. The palace stretched up into the dark of a gargantuan cavern within the rock of Golgotha. The three companions stood in the flickering light of Vedic's dying torch. The chamber smelt sickly-sweet, like rotting meat.

'No guards,' said Akyar, his sword already drawn.

'No need,' said Vedic. 'Kerberos is enough. The living do not come here very often.'

'Are we still alive?' asked Anya. 'Feels like we've always been here.'

'That's your fear talking,' replied Vedic.

'You sound like my mother,' snapped Anya.

The woodsman did not reply. Whatever else he was, it seemed he held her mother in the same kind of awe as everyone else she had ever met. She found it hard to square with her mother's absence. *How could you be so brave and so cowardly all in one body?* She clutched her shaking hands to herself and ignored the questioning voice in her head that demanded, *Do you really not know?*

'How do we get in?' asked Akyar, approaching the large double door that had been carved into the obsidian wall of the palace. There was no handle.

Vedic tilted his head. 'It was open last time I was here.'

Anya forced herself forward.

'Weapon, little one,' said Vedic, nodding at the palace. 'Just in case.'

Anya flushed and drew her blade. She found it hard to believe she was the same person who had slain Kerberos only an hour or so ago, but of course, he was not a god. He wasn't a person either. The Morrigan was close at hand. She knew this in her bones and could not explain why. The goddess was the thing of nightmares. Only the Priest had terrified her more as a child.

Anya held her blade in her right hand and placed her left on the door. The obsidian felt warm to the touch, and she remembered the words of the legend of Arawn. She closed her eyes. In her mind, she saw the doorway sliding open. At first nothing happened. Then there was a grinding as if the world were splitting in two, and she felt the door move. A gust of air rushed out of the palace. It smelt of Tream.

'Well done, Anya,' said Vedic, gently moving her behind him. 'I'll take point. Just in case.'

Anya let herself be moved. The old Anya, the one who thought running away to take the ink was the sole reason for her to be in the world, would have liked to have thumped the woodsman, maybe even killed him, for that. However, the Anya who had killed that young Kurah warrior and found the act to be squalid and improvised, rather than glorious and right, felt almost grateful. What if the Morrigan had other living guards in the palace? She wasn't sure if she could kill another person again.

'Meyr is in here somewhere,' said Akyar, behind her.

That did it. The thought of that Tream child somewhere in this dark palace, on the edge of the void, and the row upon row of small hands reaching through the bars to her in the Kurah camp spurred her on. She tightened the grip on the sword. What kind of person would you be if you enjoyed killing, anyway? *My grandmother*, her own voice answered. *You'd be your grandmother*.

They made their way into the entrance corridor. It was domed like a worm had carved out the passageway as it made its way through the obsidian, and part of Anya racked her memory of the stories for any such creatures. She could not recall any. Still, they kept to the walls with their swords ready as they made their way deeper into the palace. The woodsman stopped at each doorway, listening carefully for signs of anyone, but on this level the place was empty.

'Who wants to keep company with death?' asked Akyar. 'No one is here.'

'She's not death,' said Anya, her voice soft. 'She guards the doorway, that is all.'

On the second level, they found a person. The main hall door was open, spilling light from a fire into the corridor, and the three companions approached with caution. Vedic killed his torch with the remains of his cloak. Anya was the smallest and found it easiest to hide, and so she placed herself at the crack of the door as she looked into the chamber.

The Morrigan stood with her back to Anya, looking at the fire that burned in a large black fireplace and seemingly warming her hands against the heat. Her hair fell in dark ringlets down her shoulders over the feathered crow-black fabric of her dress, its black surface moving like it was made up of a thousand connected pieces of cloth, reflecting copper light in different directions. The silver of her necklace gleamed around her neck like a metal snake. Anya had always imagined her to be pale like the Delgasians and the Tinaric across the sea, but the Morrigan's skin was the same shade as her own.

A wolf sat on its hind legs, staring at the Morrigan. Anya prayed the smell of wood smoke was enough to mask her scent, or this was going to be a very short rescue attempt. She pressed her ear to the crack.

'My lord grows impatient. He wonders why you have not sent the Tream to him already. That was the agreement.'

The voice was low and raw, as if the words cost the speaker a great deal of effort. Anya risked moving closer to see if someone else was in the room.

'Our agreement also included not hurting Pan,' replied the Morrigan.

Anya danced across the open doorway to the other side, where she could get a better view. Vedic glared at her as Akyar took over her old station.

'I cannot send the boy until I know the woodsman has been dealt with. The man is more dangerous than your lord does him credit for. Only moments ago my servants passed word that Kerberos is dead. They may already be in the Cave of Shadows. Do you know how few people have managed that during my stewardship?'

Anya felt her skin prick at that. For the Morrigan to know Kerberos was dead meant there must be some of her agents behind them in the tunnels, and they would still need to get to the Cave of Shadows to escape back to the living world.

'You promised the lord that would be taken care of already.'

'And I will. My point is simply that transportation is difficult while he is on the loose. Your lord has no right to question my word. If anything, I should worry about his oath.'

'I am aware of your history with the lord.'

Anya peered closer. She saw the wolf scratching its shoulder. The realisation that the wolf was speaking hit her like a blow to the stomach, and she only just managed to muffle her surprise. The wolf tilted his ear but did not turn to look at her.

'Is that what your people call it? History?' replied the Morrigan.

'I understand you gave a good accounting of yourself, that you had moved past this to embrace our lord's leadership,' said the wolf, stretching.

'I do not embrace your lord. He merely made me an offer that I liked, and so here we are.' She gestured at the hall.

'Here we are,' agreed the wolf. 'I have seen the boy, and that is enough for now. How long should I tell my master to wait?'

'I do not know,' said the Morrigan, yawning. 'As long as it takes.'

'Woman, the alignment approaches. He cannot wait as long as it takes,' said the wolf, growling. 'You have until the dawn after tomorrow, or I will return with the pack for him.'

'You are grown bold,' said the Morrigan, rising, 'since my sister is not here to control you.'

'Dawn after tomorrow,' repeated the wolf, walking towards the door. Anya gripped her sword tight.

The Morrigan moved swiftly. Her hand flashed as magic flew from it, catching the wolf on the chest and surrounding him in burning energy that flickered the colour of the moon. The wolf yelped like a kicked puppy and vanished. Anya watched the goddess stare at the empty space.

'Tell me what to do in my own house,' muttered the Morrigan.

Anya flattened herself behind the doorway as the Morrigan turned back towards the fire. Anya could see the Morrigan's brow furrowed as she looked deep into the flames.

'Where are you, Laos?' she whispered. 'What are you up to?'

The Morrigan had no answer from the flames. She turned, walked into the wall and vanished with a sudden swirl of her skirts. Anya was left staring at an empty room. She waved her companions over.

'The Morrigan has gone,' she said. 'She's looking for someone named Laos, and so we have some time to look for the boy. He's definitely here.'

Vedic looked pale. Anya hoped they weren't going to have another episode like out by the lake, as she had little patience left. She hadn't even got to the important part yet.

'Did you hear the last bit?' she asked Akyar.

The Tream shook his head. 'I dared not get too close. The wolf would have recognised my scent from the boy's cloak.'

'Vedic was right,' said Anya, downcast. 'The Morrigan is in league with Cernubus, and taking the Tream prince was a trap to catch us and this Laos person.'

Akyar's eyes flashed to Vedic and back to her. It did not escape her attention that the woodsman did not return the look.

'We have an advantage, then,' said Akyar. 'She did not expect us to get this far.'

'What about guards?' asked Anya, her voice low.

Akyar shook his head. 'I don't hear any. She knows we're trying to get out; they'll all be looking for us.'

'Where would she stash the boy?' asked Vedic.

'The dungeon?' suggested Anya, although she didn't want to go down there.

'We should just search from the top down,' said Akyar, shaking his head. 'What if we miss somewhere?'

Vedic nodded. 'It's risky, but we don't have much choice.'

They made their way up to the top floor of the palace. There were two rooms on that floor. Both doors were locked, and Vedic was forced to knock the handle off the first. The noise put them all on edge as they entered the room. The air was fetid with the stench of herbs and earth. The smell was deeply familiar to Anya, who had lain in a fever while Vedic treated her with a similar-smelling unction. The memory distorted her perception of the room. Anya felt as if someone had walked on her grave.

The god lay naked save for the tangled sheet barely covering him, unmoving save for the slow rise and fall of his hair-covered chest. His eyes were closed, and his hair was matted with sweat, and there was no mistaking the badly mauled body.

'Pan,' said Akyar, rushing to his side. 'What the hell has she done to him?'

'Not the Morrigan,' said Vedic, shaking his head. 'Wolves. They've tortured him.'

'He's in a mess,' said Anya.

'We can't leave him.' Akyar looked at Vedic. 'He'll die.'

'I doubt he'll die,' said Vedic, sheathing his sword, 'or he'd be dead already. But you're right, we can't leave him.'

The woodsman walked over to the Tream's side and wrapped the god in the sheet.

'This is going to be really hard. He's not light,' said the Tream.

'I'll carry him,' said Vedic. 'First things first though.'

The woodsman pulled a small pouch from the fold of his jerkin. He opened it, and his companions got a faint whiff of a pungent, salty smell that the woodsman placed beneath the god's nose. Pan's bloodshot eyes opened, his hand slapping the salt from Vedic's hands.

'Welcome back.' The woodsman gave the god a wry smile.

Pan coughed a couple of times before looking at the three faces staring back at him. 'What are you doing here?'

'Rescuing you,' said Anya, trying to lift him upright in the bed.

'You're not supposed to be here,' he groaned, trying to push Anya's hands away. 'You should be saving Danu. Only she can end this.'

'Lie still,' said Anya. She grabbed a sponge that lay near the bed, and pressed its cool surface to the god's forehead. The skin was hot enough to fry an egg.

'You must go,' said Pan, trying to push her away feebly. 'She wants you to come. Then she can lock you up and take the boy to him.'

'Why Meyr?' asked Akyar, putting his hand to the god's cheek.

The god looked at him, confused. 'Akyar ...?'

'Long story,' said Vedic. 'Hopefully, we'll tell it to you when we get out of here. Please just tell me where the boy is.'

Pan nodded as if some statement of great import had been imparted. 'Ah, good work ... You're buying time by disrupting the sacrifice. I understand. He's in the next chamber. Grab him and get out. You're risking everything.'

Akyar looked almost apologetic as he dropped his friend's hand and ran from the room.

'Akyar, wait!' Unable to stop the Tream, Vedic turned to Anya. 'Stay with Pan. Don't let him cry out.'

Anya looked at Pan.

The god smiled, faintly. 'So, Anya, what is the news with you?'

THE TREAM DID NOT LISTEN.

Akyar had already kicked the door in as Vedic left Pan's cell and followed him into the boy's. Meyr sat by the window, where he'd been looking out at the cavern beyond. His silver hair was matted and dirty, falling in metallic-looking dreads. His dirt-caked face was a picture of shock at the sudden intrusion, a look that changed to a smile as he recognised Akyar.

Vedic was surprised to find he was smiling at the reunion. He forced it away. He was getting soft. There was no time for feelings. They had only got him into trouble, and he no longer trusted his own emotions.

'I knew you'd come,' said Meyr, embracing his mentor.

'Of course, my prince,' said Akyar, with a soft smile.

'Your father would have come himself if the elders would've let him.'

Meyr nodded and his face fell.

'Mother ...?' he whispered.

'Safe now,' said Akyar, his own face no longer smiling.

'She hurt her,' said Meyr, hugging himself. 'I couldn't stop her. I tried.'

'I know,' said Akyar, hugging the boy. 'It wasn't your fault. She's safe now.'

'Akyar,' said Vedic, glancing out the window. This was wrong; he could feel it in his bones as sure as he had been able, once upon a time, to read the breaking point upon the battlefield. 'We have no time.'

The vizier nodded and picked up Meyr. The floor was vibrating and the bed rattling as they bundled themselves out of the room and into the corridor. Anya was already waiting there, Pan stood next to her, his arm over her shoulder. She had not bothered to draw her weapon.

Someone was coming.

'I know,' she hissed. 'Just move.'

There was a moaning coming from the walls of the palace now – it sounded like a banshee working up to a full scream. They moved as fast as they could to the stairs and down towards the door. At the foot of the steps, they saw the Morrigan standing in front of the entrance.

'Oh no,' said the woodsman.

Vedic drew his sword and stepped forward between his companions and the goddess. The Morrigan watched him as a child might watch an errant spider before crushing it underfoot.

'She really is quite plain,' said the Morrigan. 'Not at all like her mother. I'm surprised you kept her with you. She must be such a disappointment.'

'You do not need to do this,' said Vedic. 'Cernubus does not mean you well. He killed Bacchus.'

The Morrigan flinched. 'And he would have killed Pan. I stopped that.'

'And what of Danu?'

'What of her?'

'She is your sister,' said Vedic, swinging his sword in lazy arcs.

'She is the cause of all of this,' hissed the Morrigan.

Vedic moved forward, cautiously. If he could just move her away from the group ...

'You can't escape,' said the Morrigan, stepping forward. 'You're going to die. Then you'll be mine anyway. You'll beg and you'll plead, and eventually you'll do my bidding in order to stave off that final confrontation with all your ghosts. An eternity with those you wronged.'

'We both know that isn't true,' said Vedic, tracking the goddess with his weapon. 'I've looked into the void.'

'The Mnemosyne doesn't lie ... Perhaps your understanding has merely changed.'

The woodsman stepped back, extending his sword in a Tream defensive pose, daring the goddess to attack with the faint ghost of a smile on his lips. The Morrigan stared at him, her eyes narrowing. He felt very aware of everything in that moment – the stone underfoot, the faint smell of wood smoke and feathers mingled with other scents, the flecks of gold in the Morrigan's night eyes.

'I see you've left a path of destruction through my land to rival the ones you left in the land of the living,' said the Morrigan, stepping forward.

'Why change the habits of a lifetime?'

'You should not be here,' she said, the rage threatening to break loose. Vedic feared what would happen if she lost control. 'You were thrown through the portal. You no longer belong in this world.'

'I hung on,' he said.

She stared at him. She sniffed. It was like she was unpeeling him and looking inside with the interest of one of the mages of Delgasia.

'And now you're no longer afraid,' she said, stepping towards him. The goddess spat to one side. 'No longer evil. Just brave and honourable.'

'Oh, I wouldn't say that,' said Vedic, as she sprang at him.

Vedic dodged her and swung, but the magic struck him clean in the chest, and had he still been human, he would have died. The magic knocked him clean across the hall into the wall. The woodsman felt like he had been crushed by a tree. He bled from his mouth, and his head was throbbing in time with his heart. He pushed himself to his feet and picked up his blade, but Pan was already stepping forward.

'Enough, sister,' said Pan.

'You?' she whispered. 'I kept you safe when they abandoned you, and the hunter wanted your head and heart in his box.'

'To fight Cernubus would not have been that much more of a leap. You still could.' Pan held out his hand to the goddess.

The Morrigan let magic build in her hands. 'Are you strong enough to fight, little goat?'

Pan exploded into motion, his remaining power burning from him like an oil-soaked torch lit by a spark. The gods collided in a maelstrom of magic that shook the entire palace from ground to ceiling.

Run, said Pan's voice in Vedic's mind.

Anya had already seen the opportunity to get them away from the Morrigan, the woodsman was pleased to see as she took Meyr from Akyar and ran out of the palace. Akyar stared at the duel. The vizier's desire to get Meyr out and to help Pan were at odds with each other.

The woodsman grabbed the Tream by the shoulders and made him look him in the face. 'We must go.'

Akyar looked at him blankly. He turned to look back at the duel.

Vedic hit him, hard.

Akyar flushed angry, glaring at him.

'He would not want you here,' said Vedic, not unkindly. 'What about the boy?'

Akyar regained his calm and nodded. They ran out of the entrance together, leaving the gods bouncing off and through walls in their battle. Vedic wondered how Pan could hold on. He did not expect to see him again.

PAN AND ANU FOUGHT.

Anu tried to run after her prisoners, and Pan blocked her, flying at her with all the strength he could muster. He wrapped her in a bear hug and clung on as she carried him, tumbling end over end. They slammed into the walls of the palace, cracking them and eventually shattering the front wall entirely as they burst out into Golgotha.

Sprawling in the dust, they clambered to their feet, facing each other, like Shaanti warriors of old – although their weapons were not steel but the magic they were harnessing from all around them. Pan was not confident. Anu cast her incantation at him, the spell hotter than the suns, glowing brighter than the day, and it took a cold close to the temperature of the void to render the cant useless.

Pan followed up with an ancient spell of binding that he thought she might not know. Anu defended with ease. They fought as they had sparred in youth, knowing each other's tics and tendencies almost as well as their own. They resorted to physical fighting in an attempt to break the deadlock. Pan was forced to parry a series of sweeping roundhouses and side-kicks before he had the presence of mind to step into one of the Morrigan's kicks. Seizing her leg, he used one of Anya's tricks and caught the god by surprise, pulling her to the ground and into a leg lock. He added his own twist by sending a second binding spell into the hold. Anu strained against it.

'Do not deceive yourself,' she said, probing the spell. 'Danu deserves everything she gets.'

'She is trying to save all of us.'

'Not all of us.'

Pan could not reply. He missed Bres too. The trickster god did not have many true kin, but Bres was one of them.

'That was a long time ago,' he replied, struggling to hold her.

'Perhaps we have lived too long, then.'

Pan had no answer – his grip was slipping. He needed to hold on longer: the others would barely have made it into the caves by now. He looked around for a weapon to help.

'Everyone faces me sometime,' said Anu.

The Morrigan was free. All was fury.

THE TUNNELS still smelt of dead dog.

Anya stared at the carcass in the Trivium. He was healing. The wounds they had inflicted were almost gone, his severed heads regrowing from the stumps of his neck, and the creature would start breathing again soon.

'Leave it,' said Akyar, taking back Meyr. 'We must press on.'

'He will come after us again,' said Anya.

'But not today,' replied Vedic.

'We don't know that.'

Anya noted neither Vedic nor Akyar replied.

'Go on ahead. I will be along in a moment,' she said, and drew her sword.

Akyar hesitated, frowning at her. His duty to Meyr won out, and he ran towards the Cave of Shadows. Vedic did not look at her, but he squeezed her shoulder as he passed.

Anya ignored the triumphant voice of her mother in her head, knowing it was her own mind and not her mother's ghost haunting her. She cut each of Kerberos's new heads off in turn and threw the severed heads into the tunnel from which no one returns.

'Regrow those.'

Anya followed Vedic into the Cave of Shadows. The cave was an open stack of rock that led up to the surface of the forest and whose phosphor-layered walls looked almost organic in the damp murk. Akyar was hugging Meyr in the centre of the cave. A gust of wind came down, whispering like many voices were trapped in the walls. Vedic stumbled to a halt, his sword falling from his hand and clattering on the stone. Everything smelt faintly of pine and iron, as if blood and forest were at war with each other.

'What was that?' she asked.

There was an explosion in the distance that shook the whole cave hard enough to throw her into a wall, where the air was driven from her lungs. She swore.

Anya sat up and saw Vedic had been thrown on all fours. His eyes wore that desperate, mad expression he had had at the lakes, and Akyar was clutching Meyr safe under him.

'What was that?' asked the vizier.

'I don't know,' said Anya. She looked at Meyr, peeping out from Akyar's cloak. Looking up at Akyar: 'What is wrong with Vedic?'

Akyar looked wide-eyed at her. 'Ghosts?'

The gust rattled through the cavern before the Tream could say more. Anya had hoped the legend had been exaggerating, or perhaps the stories of ghosts were a metaphor, but like everything else in this gods-forsaken place, the myth seemed to be real.

'How long until they get here?' she asked Vedic.

'They are here already,' he replied.

The second gust rattled through, and it seemed as if the wind itself were speaking, though she couldn't make out the words.

She stood. 'We need to climb.'

Akyar nodded.

The third gust didn't end. The wind screamed around them, sending cold across their already-weary limbs, shaking at their backs and stopping them from climbing the rock. The voices started: a cacophony of cries, a multitude of mouths shrieking as one and making their ears burn with pain. The words were an incomprehensible storm of nonsense that threatened to drive them all as mad as Vedic.

'What?' screamed the woodsman.

'Don't talk to them,' snapped Anya. 'It's a trick.'

'What do you want?' asked Akyar.

Anya could have struck him in that moment for not listening to her. Even if they were the dead, they had been driven mad by tarrying so long in Golgotha and did not wish any of them well.

'Not you, tree-walker, or the witch-warrior's whelp,' said the ghost voices.

Vedic stood up. The effort cost him. Anya could see his hands clenching white at the knuckles.

He looked resigned to his fate. 'You seek me, then.'

'Is that it?' Anya asked. 'You seek the woodsman?'

'Is that what you're calling yourself these days, *Laos*?'

A single voice spoke this time, thick with an accent that seemed familiar and yet alien to Anya. The voice was of one she half remembered. Anya heard the intake of breath from Vedic over the wind.

'Laos is dead. I am Vedic. Now, what do you want?'

The chorus spoke this time. 'If Laos is dead, then he belongs with us.'

The wind drove back through the cave and whirled around Vedic, whipping up what was left of his hair and threatening to pick him up into the air.

'What do you want of me?'

'We want to know what you have learned. We want to know why we should let you go from this place, why you of all people should be allowed more chances.'

'Who are you to question me?' hissed Vedic.

'I demand an answer,' said a solitary voice. The voice sounded like it came from the space in front of Vedic, and the effect was immediate. Vedic's face fell; his eyes looked down; and for a long while, he did not speak, his head bowed as if someone had landed on him from a great height and he was trying to remain on his feet.

'Is that you, betrayer?' The woodsman spoke in quiet tones that barely contained his violence. Anya had never heard that level of fury in anyone.

'That's no way to talk to an old friend, Laos, or is it Vedic these days? I never thought I'd see you take a clan name. How can I have betrayed you? You claim to be Vedic, and I know no such person.'

'You betrayed me,' said Vedic, bending to pick up his sword.

'You betrayed yourself, Laos, when you began to think yourself more powerful than I.'

'I served you faithfully.'

'It wasn't me you served,' said the unseen accuser. 'That was always the problem.'

'No,' said Vedic, sheathing his weapon. 'It was always you, and you betrayed me.'

Why is Laos such a familiar name? asked Anya of herself. There was no answer, not even that snide version of her mother's voice.

'I knew you'd betray me in the end, and I was right. Here you are, consorting with the enemy.'

'We want to know what he has learned,' protested the chorus.

'All right,' answered the unseen attacker. 'Tell me, Vedic. What have you learned?'

'Go to hell,' said Vedic.

Anya closed her eyes and whispered, 'Wrong answer.'

The voices screamed again and again. Vedic was lifted into the air, shaken and pulled, but he would not scream out or beg. The noise was so intense Anya found herself on her knees, clutching at her ears. Akyar and Meyr were also prone, defeated by the sheer volume of the attack.

'Tell them!' she yelled at Vedic.

'I can't!' he responded, swinging in the grip of the ghosts. 'I have learned nothing. There is no reason to let me go save to defeat a god. Gods! I'd throw myself down into the void if I thought there was anything better waiting for me, but there isn't. There is no afterlife, no chance for me to earn anything, there is just this one life, and mine hangs on magic I do not understand.'

A sigh went up from the ghosts as the wind subsided. Vedic dropped to the floor with a thud.

'It's true, then,' said the singular voice – he sounded pleased. 'You are broken ... I shall enjoy watching you fall.'

'I fell a long time ago,' said Vedic. 'You remember, you pushed me.'

'You pushed yourself, Laos,' said the voice. 'I am remembered for all time in relation to the things you have done; why should you be any different? I'll be seeing you soon, but first ... a parting gift.'

There was an upgust of wind that left the unseen attacker whispering in Anya's ears.

'Anya, remember the monster under your bed? You're walking with him. The Kurah warriors have nothing on the beast that rides with you, or does he ride you? Is that why you put up with him?'

'Go to the void,' hissed Anya.

There was, on the last of the wind, a gust of laughter that echoed in the chamber, but it gave none of them anything to smile about. The ghosts were gone, leaving only the soft glow of the rock. Anya blinked and turned to look at Vedic. He would not meet her gaze.

'You're not a monster, Vedic, or Laos, or whatever in Golgotha is actually your name,' said Anya. 'Whatever you were once, you're not a monster now. You're the forestal who came back for me, and the man who saved Meyr.'

'No,' Vedic replied, looking at her now. 'He was right. Don't forget it.'

THE MORRIGAN SLAMMED Pan back through the wall to her palace.

The two gods lay, covered in dust, in the main hall. On the dais sat the Crow Throne, where Anu, the Morrigan, oversaw the long and never-ending journey through Golgotha. *She will kill me now*, thought Pan.

Anu did not.

The Morrigan got to her feet, dragging Pan by his arm to the foot of the throne and pulling out a rope that felt metallic as she began to try to bind him.

Anu could not kill him. Pan reflected that this had been so close to their arguments when they were both young that it hurt more than his wounds. Anu had never been able to bring herself to really hurt the tricksters: they were what she really cared about. If you spent so much time near the dark, you had to take the light from where you could. The god's sympathy was tempered by the fact that he knew if this continued much longer, the hunter, Cernubus, would appear, and he really would be in trouble. Pan needed a way out – he was almost trapped.

Pan nearly missed the opening.

The Morrigan sensed the woodsman enter the cave. Pan did too, but it made the goddess pause, her attention not on the rope. She tilted her head as if listening. Pan could see the broken palace swaying all around them. His mistake had been attacking her directly – all he really needed to do was trap her as she sought to do to him.

'Goodbye, sister,' he said.

The Morrigan looked at him, puzzled.

Pan erupted from the metal rope, shattering it, and up through the ceiling of the palace into the cavern, out into the ur-sky of Golgotha. The structure beneath him collapsed and folded in on itself, even as Pan bound the ruin with magic almost as old as they were. This wasn't gods' magic but the cants the forest had taught them long ago.

Pan waited a moment to see if the spell would hold. The rubble bubbled once and settled. He had succeeded. He had bound the Morrigan. His sad smile faltered as he realised he had also blocked his way back to the Cave of Shadows. The tunnels lay behind rock now. The ground shook a little as the Morrigan tried to free herself. Pan fancied he could hear his sister screaming through the rubble. The Mnemosyne glinted in the distance.

The god made for the lake with his remaining strength, dropping like a rag doll into the silver water. Pan pulled himself down for the bottom of the lake, sliding past the creature that lived in there, ignored, as he was nothing the creature could eat. In the murk, he could just about make out the water ahead, and he was pleased that the tunnel he remembered was still in use, as he swam across to the opening.

Pan emerged from the tunnel into a pool and kicked himself up to the surface, where he enjoyed a few brief draughts of air before he heard the howls. Cernubus might know what had happened already, and if he didn't, he would soon. They couldn't get in now. But if they did? He still did not have enough magic to fold space. He doubted he would ever have enough again if he didn't get out of Golgotha soon and back into the forest.

'Move,' he hissed at himself.

The god ran down the tunnels, thankful the crumbling palace had not blocked the path he had to take. It had been a long time since he had cause to visit his sister in her home, and it was a struggle to find his way through the network, back to the Trivium. He saw the corpse of Kerberos, struggling to regrow its heads. *At least,* he thought, *I know I am on the right track.* Pan ran up the corridor that led to the Cave of Shadows and in.

The ground shook once more. There was no time. Anya, Vedic, Akyar and Meyr were all only halfway up the wall and barely making progress. Pan wanted to ask why they weren't out yet, but he had no time and little power. The hunter was coming.

The god turned and let loose a cant at the tunnel behind him. The ceiling of the tunnel collapsed in a hiss of magic and sulphur that made his companions look down.

'Pan!' yelled Akyar, delighted.

Pan had no time to respond. The cave-in would not hold back his cousin long, and there was no alternative for him but to use what magic he had left. The trickster spoke a cant, which spiralled him into a whirlwind, lifting off the ground. Spinning up to Akyar and Meyr, the whirlwind pulled them into its midst and lifted off again, only to take Anya and Vedic. Pan screamed as he pulled all four up out of the tunnel into the light of the forest and dropped them in the grass before he collapsed face down. His hair had turned silver-white.

ANYA LOOKED up at the sky and felt air in her lungs and grass underfoot.

It was good to be alive. She couldn't believe they were, and she wasn't surprised to see Meyr's little face peering over her in concern.

'I'm all right,' she said, squeezing his hand.

'Pan?' asked Akyar.

Anya saw the Tream scrambling over to the god and turning him onto his back. The Tream gasped. Pan now looked old, his hair pale and his skin cracked like the desert mud. He smiled faintly at Akyar.

'I think I overdid it,' said Pan, with a rasping chuckle.

'How do we fix this?' asked Akyar.

Pan shook his head. 'You do not need to do anything: the forest will heal me. This just takes time, and Cernubus is slowing it down.'

'He's close?' asked Vedic, getting to his feet.

Pan coughed. There was blood on his chin, golden and gleaming brighter than the suns above. 'No, but he is coming. I would not like to be my sister when he gets to Golgotha.'

Meyr stepped closer to Akyar, wrapping his hand round the vizier's.

Anya slapped Pan's arm. 'It'll be fine. We're safe now.'

'Are we?' asked Akyar. 'Surely, he will return for us.'

Vedic did not say anything. He stared into the treeline, still breathing hard and looking like the only thing he could manage was a slow stumble.

'Yes,' said Pan. He looked round at the carnage wrought on the forest. The soil still looked reasonable, and he began rubbing mud over his wounds and skin.

'We should split up,' said Anya. She couldn't say why this was the right thing to do. It wasn't a voice in her head but an instinct.

'Why?' asked Akyar.

'Cernubus needs Danu more than Meyr,' said Anya. 'If we split up, he has to make a decision who to follow. He's more likely to come after Vedic and me, as we'll be trying to free Danu.'

'It's a long way back to Hogarth,' said Vedic, hoarse.

Anya nodded. She countered, 'This is about belief, right? He has taken the forest, and we have to believe the thain knows that by now. He wanted to execute the Tream heir. He has Shaanti children ready to kill as well ... Maybe he even wanted the daughter of the witch-warrior. He can do without most of these sacrifices, but he needs Danu to convince the Kurah he is all-powerful. He will come after us with everything he has.'

Pan stared at her. 'She is right.'

'The Shaanti will be wiped out if they meet the Kurah in open battle,' said Akyar, 'won't they?'

'Without help, they will be wiped out either way,' replied Pan.

Akyar looked at Pan. The god did not look away.

'I don't see how we could get back to the palace in time for Hogarth to make a difference. The battle will already be over, the Shaanti dead.'

'I can do that,' said Pan.

'You're not recovered yet,' said Akyar.

Pan put his arms around him. 'Do you think I am going to let you out of my sight again with that mad bastard roaming round here?'

Akyar smiled, resting his forehead against the god's. 'The feeling is mutual.'

Meyr smiled. 'We will go back together?'

Pan nodded and lifted up the boy. 'We will indeed.'

'What about Danu?' asked Vedic, glaring. 'We could do with your help as well, little goat.'

Pan turned to look at the woodsman. 'Well, I never thought I would hear you say that.'

Vedic shrugged. 'I was always able to assess the field.'

Pan nodded. 'I will return as fast as I can. But we need both you and the Tream in play if we are to win the day.'

'How long until he finds us?' asked Vedic, standing and checking he still had his sword.

'Hard to say, Vedic,' said Pan, weary. There was brown returning to his hair now. 'We should move into the treeline.'

The god passed Meyr back to Akyar and tried to move. The effort made the trickster dizzy, and he doubled over, coughing and gagging as if he had spent all night drinking and smoking. Akyar put his hand on the god's back.

'We have to let him regain more of his strength first.'

'It appears so,' said the woodsman, his eyes darting round the clearing.

'A small rest will do us all good,' said Anya.

Vedic sat down again, muttering in a language Anya couldn't understand. She was too tired to labour her thoughts on his strange tongue and instead sat down on a fallen tree trunk.

'It's a good thing,' said Akyar, putting the Tream child down. 'You couldn't fight your way out of a pile of washing right now. You nearly died in Golgotha, Vedic.'

'I've nearly died a few times recently,' said Vedic. 'In my youth, it was practically a full-time profession for me.'

Pan silenced him with a look.

Anya spoke up again. 'We haven't eaten properly in days; you're exhausted. Do you have a way of breaking that spell holding Danu?'

Vedic did not answer.

'Me neither. And we have to stay with these guys until Pan attempts his cant to take them back to Hogarth. What if the wolves came?'

'They're Tream,' said Vedic. 'Hard to kill. They will be fine.'

Anya was surprised at the woodsman's words. She had thought he had changed in Golgotha, but she could still see that uncompromising hardness on his face. Vedic was like the trees he tended: he could sway but not bend.

The woodsman hissed a little as he shifted, still favouring his left arm even though Anya was not in any danger. She thought he looked like he might actually die at any minute. Vedic was pale and clammy as he started to pull what little dead wood there was around them into the start of a fire. Pan got to his feet, sighing, and walked over to the woodsman, forcing the man to sit down. He placed his right hand on the woodsman's cut chest.

The space under Pan's fingertips, where he touched the woodsman, glowed the colour of fire. Anya thought she saw Vedic's chest respond in the same colour before the god stepped away. Vedic looked up. Many of the cuts on him were gone, as were a few of the lines around his eyes, and he looked sharper. His eyes glinted in shadow.

Pan's hair was grey again.

'How long will we be delayed?' asked Akyar, his voice even.

Pan shook his head. 'I'm regaining my power quicker than my appearance suggests. Eat with them, and we will try before the sunset.'

'What about Cernubus?'

'He is on his way to Golgotha,' said Pan, hiding his face. 'He cannot easily get from there to here now.'

'The Morrigan?'

'Alive,' he whispered.

Anya was concerned at the way he sounded upset. 'She kept you captive, tortured you. Why are you crying?'

'She wasn't always like this.'

Akyar chipped in. 'But she is today.'

Pan looked up at him with tear-streaked cheeks. 'And yet she is still my kin. Once, the Morrigan remembered how to laugh.'

CHAPTER TWENTY-FIVE

THE BATTLE RAGES.

It's nothing like the stories grandfather told me. Kurah clash with Shaanti men and women on the edge of the forest, in what looks like a chaotic brawl, and everywhere the Kurah are being driven back. I am not sure exactly where we are. This is further north and west than the Barrens, where the forest meets the edge of the plains. In the distance, if one could see so far, Vikrain sits shimmering on the horizon. This is Boulay. I have been told the tale of this battle since I was a child, but I've never imagined that the fight was like this.

I bark orders in the Kurah tongue. I am back in someone else's body, a passenger once more. We are carrying that giant sword again. I still can't remember its name. We bellow and point.

The thain is younger than I remember her being. The hair poking out from her helm is not white as it was when she visited the village to see my grandfather. She is fighting out at the centre of the battle, and she is vulnerable as we move towards her. The smell of the battlefield is overwhelming; why did no one tell me this? The field stinks of the foul concoctions of the engineers and mages, and the blood and piss and shit of the dead and dying. We are standing in the dead, fighting my own people, and I do not understand any of this.

The warrior comes from nowhere, it seems. The Kurah are moving to surround the thain, and suddenly the woman is there. She is dressed in armour that glints purple when the light falls one way and black when the light falls another – it is almost Shaanti but seems to have come from somewhere else. Grandmother. I think I once knew the story of where she got the armour, but I have forgotten the words. In her hand is the sword that sings, the sword she left to my mother. The weapon looks nothing like I imagined. The blade is closer to a Tream weapon: thin, slightly curved, and faster than you would think possible. The steel seems to be able to cut through Kurah armour, and my grandmother is leaving a swathe of dead in her path as she clears the area around the thain and puts the leader at her back so they form each other's guard.

I cannot see my grandmother's face. She is wearing a helmet that, again, no one has ever told me about, and her hair is pulled back in a tight plait that hangs down the back of her armour. If the armour didn't give her away, it would be easy to mistake Gobaith for a young and slight man.

They call her the witch-warrior when they think we aren't listening, but there is no sign of magic here, unless you count her skill on the field. Grandfather will be here somewhere as well. They both fought at this one. This was the battle that led the Kurah to run back to their own lands with their tails between their legs. My host turns us round to face the witch-warrior as the tide of battle brings us together.

'You again,' she says, bringing her blade round to block the giant nightmare that my host swings two-handed.

'Heathen,' my host replies in Shaanti that sounds awkward and accented.

'You're broken,' she replies, attempting a parry, but my host is surprisingly nimble for such a large person.

'The stone god is with us,' my host replies. 'If it is his will that we perish today, others will win the field tomorrow.'

'You do not understand the true nature of the gods,' she replies, flipping over us.

We're on the ground now. I realise she has kicked our legs out and I've lost my blade. The singing sword is pointed at our throat.

'They are not your betters,' she says. 'You are too dangerous. You could have been so much more.'

My grandmother swings back the blade over her head, and I know she means to take my host's head. This is the Shaanti way of dealing with murderers, and rarely a wise move on a battlefield.

She freezes.

The witch-warrior staggers back as if struck, and her arms drop. Her free hand grasps her stomach before pulling her helmet free, and she looks on me with her face. I have forgotten what she looks like in the paintings. She is younger here but so much calmer than she is when I dream of her. She almost looks like I imagine my mother once did. I see the moment the look turns to fear. I have never imagined her afraid.

'What are you?' she asks.

I, or the person I am riding in, do not answer.

'Do not fail her ...' she begins to say, and then a Kurah shoulder tackles her, and everything erupts in chaos as my host scrambles for his sword.

The retreat horns signal from the Kurah side, and we are fighting at the rear guard of their force, buying the rest of the army time to get away. I see the Kurah king riding away and the thain pressing home the advantage, but we do not see her again, or Thrace.

Falkirk is getting closer to me with his shock warriors, and I wonder if my host will fight him. The storm is breaking overhead, turning the ground to sludge, and all around, Kurah are dying. My host strides over to the body of one of his comrades and pulls the man's signal horn from his belt. We sound the retreat.

CHAPTER TWENTY-SIX

THE SKY above the distant forest was marbled with light and smoke.

The ground shook in pulses from whatever events were unfolding within the wood as the Shaanti made camp. The thain had marched them for days, driving a hard pace from sunup to sundown and only stopping when she absolutely had to. Such a pace had allowed them to move swiftly along the most dangerous part of the journey out of the mountains and across the central plains. The central road was the riskier route. The path brought them closer to the Barrens and the Kurah, but it also offered the only reasonable line of defence, having been cut into a series of trenches. Originally these measures had been taken to prevent bandits from seeing who was on the road. During the war, they were enhanced to help the army attack the invading Kurah. Now the road would serve one last purpose against that same enemy, allowing the people who built it to run away and survive.

'The gods do battle,' said the thain, folding her telescope.

She stood on the perimeter of the camp, Bene at her side and men milling further away – pretending to be busy but desperate to pick out some words, some sign of hope, from the ruler. The smell of wood smoke was beginning to waft across the camp as the Shaanti got their evening rations underway. The next camp they made would have less cover, and fire would be too dangerous. She had yet to break the news.

'It might just be Kurah,' said Bene, shaking his head. 'You can't be sure.'

The thain shrugged. She passed Bene the glass. 'Look for yourself.'

The warrior looked through the glass, one of only four they possessed, and his sharp intake of breath told the story. The thain led Bene away from the others. No good would come of discussing matters within earshot of the camp, and she was satisfied that the Kurah would not attack from the forest, or they would have arrived days ago.

'The guard are right,' said Bene, adjusting the reins on his horse. 'You're being foolish dismissing them this close to the perimeter.'

'Maybe,' said the thain. 'But I need to talk. We are at the cross-roads, or will be by tomorrow, and we have little time.'

'It bothers you to run?'

The thain's head snapped round at Bene's words. The warrior was not glowering though, or sneering with sarcasm, as many of her other people had done. His expression was open and devoid of accusation. The thain's shoulders dropped. She knew that Bene would not turn on her. This was an honest question from a man who would follow her into Golgotha if she asked, and so deserved an answer.

'No, I do not worry about trying to save my people,' said the thain. 'It is my role to play, and I do not resent it. I worry that I may fail.'

Bene shrugged. 'We may fail.'

'You agree with Golan, then? I am mistaken.'

Bene smiled. 'I didn't say that, milady.'

'No, you didn't. Tell me what you think.'

'We may fail to get our people out of this dreadful place; we may perish at sea; we may be ambushed. There are lots of possibilities. If we had remained in Vikrain or if we attempted dialogue with the Kurah, then I assure you we would all be dead.'

The thain nodded. 'You repeat the words I tell myself every few hours, but still I doubt. Is the chance of survival real or imagined? The gods have forsaken us. Golgotha! They appear to have forsaken each other.'

'A wise woman once told me that the gods help those who help themselves.'

'An old woman,' said the thain, kicking the surface soil before her. 'I doubt any would call her wise these days.'

Bene did not answer her. *I've pushed him too far*, thought the thain. She looked away from his earnest eyes because they just put her in mind of her own earnest boy, who she had held dying on the steps of the palace long ago. *Ridiculous, they look nothing alike.* Everything reminded her at the moment. She found old memories bubbling up like air trying to escape a swamp. She hated it.

'Oh, it's all right,' said the thain, turning to face the sprawling camp. 'I'm not entirely reliant on the gods, fat lot of good they do us most of the time, but faith is easy when you have seen your gods, when you know they will come to your aid. Knowing they are gone, that I do not have them to call on, has left a void, and I am not sure what to fill it with. Perhaps they have decided to take us all home to Golgotha and beyond. Perhaps we should let them.'

Bene's eyes narrowed. 'Let our people die?'

'Why not? All things end, and as some are saying, perhaps this is the will of the gods.'

'Then to Golgotha with our gods! I will not follow anyone who believes in death on such a scale. Believer or not, we only visit this world once, and what we have here is precious.'

Bene's words were not punctuated with any signs of deference to the thain, and his normally placid voice was raised in anger.

'Perhaps we should negotiate, then,' said the thain, folding her arms. 'As Golan would have me do ...'

'You cannot negotiate with the Kurah,' said Bene, shouting. 'They would kill you where you stood, as they did Jeb. You heard the shadow.'

'Feels good, doesn't it?' said the thain, smiling. 'The anger fills you up, gives you an alternative to faith to hang on to. We can use that. Forge the rage into a new weapon. Maybe the hope that long since left this world.'

Bene's expression froze before melting into a smile. 'You were testing me.'

The thain shook her head. 'I was testing myself. I know doubt, but I needed to hear someone else argue my views.'

'Glad to be of help,' said Bene, turning away.

'Don't be sore, old friend,' said the thain. 'I have an important task for you.'

Bene looked at the ancient ruler in surprise. 'You're sending me away?'

'Not just you,' said the thain. 'I want you to take a platoon of the guardsmen you trust the most.'

'To do what?'

'To free the prisoners,' said the thain, folding her arms. 'I'll not leave my kin to die in an archaic ceremony because the Kurah are deluded enough to think they can control a god.'

'I thought such a mission was suicide,' said Bene, smiling.

'To lead the army against the Kurah would be. To try a raid to free the prisoners is ... challenging ... but it does have a chance of success that a large battle would not.'

'Whatever you wish, milady, but I would like to know why.'

The thain closed her eyes. 'Falkirk.'

'The major?'

'He said that they had prisoners, but he wasn't trying to tell me about all of them, just one, and I think I know who he was referring to.'

'Thrace?'

The thain smiled. 'No, not Thrace. If it were just Thrace, I would not send you, because he would not thank me. Thrace passed away over a year ago. I think he meant Thrace's granddaughter.'

'General Thrace had a granddaughter?' asked Bene, incredulous.

'A daughter too.'

Bene stared at the thain.

'Yes, amusing, isn't it? Thankfully, the granddaughter takes after Gobaith,' said the thain with a smile. 'She doesn't need that gnarly bastard's looks.'

'You want me to free her?'

'I want you to free them all, but, yes, she is my motivation. I made a promise a long time ago to her grandmother, and I must keep my word, or I am a fraud.'

Bene did not meet her gaze.

'Will you go?'

Bene raised an eyebrow.

'Oh, you have a choice,' said the thain. 'I just know what you'll say.'

'I need not answer, then, milady. Instead, I shall see you, with Thrace's granddaughter, at the port in a month's time. Can I add your shadow to my warriors?'

The thain raised an eyebrow. She was surprised by his request, and she was so rarely surprised by anything these days. 'Why?'

Bene shrugged. 'She knows the Kurah better than any of us, and she can slip in anywhere.'

'Your counsel is wise as always, and I wish I could let you take her with you. She has another mission. She is there now, and I cannot spare her from it.'

Bene frowned. 'What else is underway?'

The thain did not smile this time. 'I cannot answer that.'

If she told him, she knew the warrior would not leave for his own mission, because he would want to tear the camp apart looking for the traitor. She knew Golan was part of the conspiracy. She just needed to find the other one.

Bene's steps crunched into the distance as the ancient ruler wrapped her cloak around herself. The thain stood watching the gods' light show above the forest for a long time, with only the sound of the wind for company. Her memories of the young family she had let leave the city all those years ago, against her better judgement, swirled round her head. Things were worse now. She prayed she wasn't making the same mistake.

CERNUBUS DID NOT FOLD the world to get to Golgotha.

The hunter took a different path into the underworld. Wearing his stag form, he led the wolves into the ur-light of that in-between place and felt the Morrigan's rage permeating every speck of dust. The god's anger made even him flinch. The wolves whimpered as he forced them on for the palace, sensing even as he ran that the palace was no longer standing.

The whole of the Trivium and the cliffs in which the complex had been carved were gone, leaving only a pile of rubble. Through the detritus, there was the occasional glimpse of darkness so black even his eyes could not permeate the murk. The gaping void of nothing was uncomfortable to look at.

Where are you? Cernubus asked, reaching out with his mind, his body unfolding into his human form. The wolves circled him like dogs. Scared, they fought for the feel of his fingers on their snouts. He ignored them. They had failed him just as the Morrigan had.

Free me, she replied in Cernubus's head.

Cernubus raised an eyebrow. *Where is the boy?*

There was no answer.

I thought you had this under control.

I did, but Pan …

The trickster did this?

Yes.

You stopped me killing him.

Free me.

Cernubus let his senses shift into the dust and bone of the under-world. He had not always had this gift, but there was so much he had added to himself with ink and needle and magic. The Morrigan was buried deep, so very deep, and the hunter could not imagine how close Pan had come to pushing her into the doorway to the next world. Cernubus could see how easily he could do this himself. Pressure here. Pull there. Yet no one knew what would happen if there was no guardian of the dead.

Free me.

No, he replied. *I must hunt them down now. If there is time.*

Pan must live.

Why?

The Morrigan's rage flared in the dark rock. *You made a deal.*

And you broke it. If Pan crosses me, he will die.

No! There must be laughter, there must be, or …

Cernubus could not listen to any more. The god broke the link even as he changed back into a stag and leapt out ahead of the wolves for the only other way back up into the real world. He would need to move faster now. All around, the ghosts of the dead stared at him with fear as he began his cant to fold the world.

THE CAMP WAS A MAKESHIFT AFFAIR.

There were swiftly erected tents and bivouacs that the clansmen could assemble and dismantle easily, and so with the coming dawn, it was swift work to make ready for another day's marching. The thain watched her people form up into the trail, a mile and a half of them stretching down the road just travelled. She moved the group out, leading from the front as always and followed by various members of the council. Bene took his group out to the eastern flank, preparing for when he would peel away.

It took a few hours to reach the crossroads, the eastward road – under cover and an aftermath of the last war – leading to the Barrens, and the westward road leading to the port but devoid of cover. Their path was clear, and the group turned onto the westward road. The thain did not wave Bene's men off as they made their way to the east as if on patrol. Instead, she led on, praying that no one would notice Bene's departure. She thought she had got away without being discovered, until she heard the heavy steps of Golan's overloaded horse.

'Milady,' said Golan, drawing near. 'May I talk with you?'

The thain glanced at Golan and grunted. The councillor could do what he liked as long as he didn't stir up the people, and so she allowed her horse to slow enough for Golan to move alongside.

'If this is about talking to the enemy again, I am in no mood.'

'Indeed not, milady. I can tell your mind is made up, and that is why I assume General Bene's absence, along with his guards, is because Bene has deserted.'

The thain fixed Golan with an icy stare that the councillor appeared to ignore, plunging on. 'One of my men saw him heading eastwards, and I thought it best to advise you lest we walk into an ambush. Perhaps we could seek cover or alter our route.'

'Lord Golan, you are mistaken,' said the thain, shifting her reins to one hand. 'They were proceeding under my confidential orders.'

Golan stared. 'Your orders?'

'Yes.'

'Milady, what were the orders?'

'Confidential, Lord Golan. Better you do not know.'

'You have sent those men to their deaths on some foolhardy mission,' said Golan, testily. 'As you sent Jeb.'

'The men were free to choose,' said the thain, eyes ahead. 'I did not force them.'

'Oh, that's all right, then,' said Golan, raising his voice. 'Never mind that we need every warrior.'

'Are you not up to defending us, then, Golan?' said the thain, dropping any pretence of civility. She had grown tired of this loathsome man. 'Perhaps you underestimate us.'

'You've lost your fucking mind, old woman,' said Golan, hissing to contain his rage. 'I will bring you down here and now.'

'You have forgotten your place, Councillor, or are you challenging me?' asked the thain, her free hand resting on her sword handle.

Golan halted his horse. 'Yes.'

The thain blinked. She had not expected the coward to accept that he had challenged the thain, and she was not afraid to fight him, but they were not yet far enough from the city or the forest. Golan's eyes followed her carefully and smirked. *The little bastard knew that I wouldn't want to fight here*, thought the thain. *Or does he know I am sick? Either way, I can't back down.*

She slid from her horse and drew her sword. Around them, the army and people drew to a halt. A handful of Bene's guards had stayed behind to protect the thain, and they formed up into a circle around her and Golan.

'Challenge accepted,' said the thain.

She would fight this oaf. She wondered if her other traitor had put the vile merchant up to this and if it were to actually discredit her or because the man had become a liability.

Golan went pale.

'What is the meaning of the stop?' asked General Vort.

'Lord Golan has challenged my authority in time of war,' said the thain. 'As is the law, we will now fight for the title of thain.'

'Perhaps this could wait until we were a little closer to safety,' said Vort.

'No, lass. I wish we could, but Golan here issued an open challenge in front of the men.'

Vort looked at Golan with contempt.

'Very well,' said Vort, sliding from her horse. 'Fifteen paces between you, and swords drawn. Well, come on, Golan, we don't have all day.'

Golan looked from Vort to the thain to the surrounding crowd. His face turned scarlet as he drew his sword and stepped back to where he would start. His blade shook in his hand. People pointed and laughed. Uncomfortable, unsure, he slipped his cloak from his neck.

The thain kept her wolf-like eyes on him as she stepped to her own start point. She saw her shadow, in the distant crowd of watching warriors, and she knew the woman would hate this foolhardy risk.

'You may begin,' said Vort.

Golan lifted his sword as if the weapon were heavier than the world. He made a half-hearted attempt to step forward to fight before he threw his sword down on the soil and fell to his knees. 'I withdraw.'

Vort spat. 'Pathetic.'

The thain strode forward, sword outstretched, and lifted the councillor's chin with the tip of her blade.

Golan stared, cross-eyed, down the end of the blade towards the thain, barely able to speak. 'I yield ... You wouldn't kill an unarmed man ...'

'I would kill a traitor,' said the thain, quiet enough for only Golan to hear her. She could smell piss from the man. His fear reeked. 'Who is working with you?'

Golan shuffled back from her. The thain smiled. Inside she cursed herself for the weakness she was showing by not killing the councillor, and swore because Golan was right: she would not slay an unarmed man. She turned from the councillor.

'Vort, get that scum out of here. He is stripped of office.'

'No, milady,' said Vort, drawing her blade across Golan's neck and opening his throat to the morning suns. The councillor fell forward, gasping for air that was no longer available, and expired on the soil in front of the shocked people.

'I did not order his execution, Vort,' said the thain, looking down on the mess. 'Am I grown so old that my warriors seek to protect me in such ways?'

'No, milady,' Vort argued. 'Nevertheless, the law is clear. The challenge was to the death, and yielding is not an option.'

The thain tilted her head. 'You are fortunate in your understanding of the rules and your importance as part of the army. Were you not a warrior in a time of war, I would lay you out beside him. You are stripped of your rank, General. Your major will lead your battalion, and you will serve as warrior unless she decides to promote you to a more senior post. Get out of my sight.'

Empty words. The thain had not acted when she should have, and she knew it. The woman she was chastising was as much her ally as Bene. *No*, she thought. *With Bene gone, until I know who the traitor is, I only have one ally left*. She looked for her shadow but could not find her.

'My apologies, milady.'

'It is over. Let us get this show on the road.'

The corpse was bundled onto the man's horse, and the army and the people moved on, avoiding the bloodstained grass as they went. No one else questioned where Bene had gone, and the council kept itself to itself as they made their way across the plains towards the port. The thain's slump in her saddle became more pronounced.

CHAPTER TWENTY-SEVEN

MONTU WATCHED the spy ride hard across the Barrens as if Cernubus himself was on his heels.

There is little chance of that, thought Montu. Days had passed since the god had been seen at the camp or sent any word with those cursed wolves that left the men so uneasy. The forest light show that the king assumed was Cernubus doing whatever he had left to do in the woods had come to an end with a ground-shaking thump that brought down one of his trebuchets. More importantly, there was no sign of the Shaanti. The alignment was three days away, and the god had yet to make good on his bargain.

The scout reached the edge of the camp. Montu did not wish to watch him weave his way to him: he would look too desperate for news, and that knowledge would travel through the men like wildfire. He turned, ignoring the fetid smell of a camp kept too long, and re-entered his tent. Incense was smouldering from a small table near the bed, and his pregnant wife lay sprawled on the bed, half-naked – she was too hot all the time. She looked up at him.

'You are still agitated?' she asked.

Montu did not answer. He thought his mood was evident enough, and he still did not understand his wife, who seemed to move from friend to foe dependent on which way the wind was blowing. He blamed her Delgasian heritage. She had not spoken to him for a month following the invasion of her homeland. Only the pregnancy had stopped her trying to kill him. *I will have to correct or kill her*, he thought. *Once the child is safe,* he added.

'Is it the god?' she pressed.

'No, a scout,' he said, throwing a blanket to her. 'Cover yourself. He will be here in a moment.'

'I'm too hot—'

'Do it,' he said.

Montu went to the wooden chair that acted as substitute for his throne, placed the small gold circlet that was sitting upon the cushion on his head, and sat down. The king's bodyguard poked his head through the flaps of the tent.

'Milord, the scout Kiln seeks an audience.'

Montu nodded.

Kiln came in looking as if he had not slept in a month.

'What news of Vikrain?'

Kiln bowed low. 'They are out of the city.'

Montu leant forward.

'They are heading for the coast,' continued the scout, his head still bent.

'She is running?' asked his wife from the bed. 'Surely not.'

Montu did not let his feelings show. 'Why would she run? She heard what happened to her elderly scout?'

'Yes, milord. The spy made it back to the city as you planned, but our people in the Shaanti say that someone escaped from the Del.'

'Who?' He was conscious his wife had gone quiet and was listening as if hearing of the mythical city of light for the first time.

'Gor-Iven, he was the commander of the king's archers.'

'Do you know him?' Montu asked his wife.

The queen looked lost in her own reverie at the name. Montu wasn't sure he liked the look. He knew she had opposed the match when her father had proposed the marriage as a way to stop Kurah aggression and prevent another war. However, she had done her duty as a good daughter of Delgasia, and Montu thought he had tamed her. The expression on her face suggested she wasn't quite as defeated as he had believed. *Did she just play a part for me?*

The queen caught Montu looking at her. She regained her composure.

'I know of him,' she said. 'A minor underling. I fail to see—'

'He had the ring,' said the scout.

Montu gripped the arms of the chair. 'He was there when the Del king was killed.'

Montu's mind went back to what had been said in the corridor and how much the man could have heard between himself and Cernubus. 'How much do they know?'

The scout sounded a little relieved as he responded. 'Not much, milord. It was the size of our force and the news of the god that sent the thain into the field. The Shaanti forces are smaller than they were. I believe she knows she would lose.'

'Do not discount the Shaanti. How many days until they reach the coast?'

'It depends on if they can maintain the pace they set out of the city,' answered Kiln. 'They could take a week, but I imagine people will die if they do that. Say two to be sure.'

There is still time, thought Montu. 'Send a runner to the tenth division to move up through the plains and take the hidden road. They are to move the Shaanti towards the forest, cutting them off from Vikrain and making the Barrens their only chance.'

'That may not be enough,' said Kiln. The man sounded weary enough that he was willing to risk death to avoid another ride that might end in the same.

Montu lifted the man to his feet by his shoulders. 'You have done well, Kiln. Do not spoil it now by making me kill you.'

Kiln nodded. Montu dismissed him.

'Beden,' called Montu to his bodyguard. The man appeared through the tent flaps.

'Yes, milord,' said Beden.

'Bring me the mage Zoren,' Montu ordered. 'I think he can help us.'

Beden nodded and vanished back through the flaps and into the camp beyond.

Montu moved out of his chair and to the table that was about five feet from the bed and that held a map of the terrain, laid out under rocks to stop the parchment from blowing away as people went in and out. He felt rather than saw his wife unfold from the bed.

'Remind me again why we did not simply take Vikrain as you crushed the Del?'

Montu sighed. 'The terrain in the Shaanti lands is different. If they wanted to, even under siege, the clans can harass and attack us from the hills with impunity. Meanwhile, we cannot, even with our resources, keep our supply lines intact all the way to Vikrain, and so a smart thain – and this one is – would attack there.'

'Why did we not wait until summer?'

'There is no good time,' replied Montu, irritated. 'There is no way to guarantee the weather. We must be ready for the attack that will come from across the sea.'

'Sire,' said Beden, rushing into the tent. 'The god is back.'

MONTU HAD his sword out as he entered the god's tent.

The king had only been in there a handful of times since they arrived. The god had left strict instructions for no one to enter and, even when absent from the camp, seemed to know when anyone had passed close to the tent. He would comment every time, marking the moment for emphasis. Cernubus had not used a tent at all until they'd arrived at the Barrens. Montu would have attempted to uncover what the god was hiding if the danger of being caught had not been so high. Inside was dark, with only a single lit candle to see by. Cernubus used no groundsheet, and Montu was walking on bare, uneven earth that was pockmarked with small, ragged holes.

Montu moved with care until he could see the god. Cernubus was closing a wooden chest covered in the same maelstrom of runes and letters that covered his body. The god looked dusty and weary, but there was no sign of any harm to him. The god threw back a drink from a flask within the chest.

'Tough day?' asked the king.

'You don't need that pig tickler,' said Cernubus. 'Sit down.'

Montu lowered his sword but did not sit. 'Was that fireworks show over the forest you?'

'I was cleaning up your mess,' said Cernubus, 'making sure the Shaanti get no aid from the forest.'

'I thought you had already controlled matters,' said Montu, his grip tightening again.

'Worry about your side of the deal,' Cernubus replied.

'You must have seen the pyres on the way in.'

The god nodded. 'But you have already killed one prisoner to see if your plan to control me would work, and other prisoners may try to escape. Especially if they work out they are only going to die if they stay.'

'You will have your sacrifice, demon,' he replied.

Cernubus laughed himself hoarse. 'There are no demons. Just me.'

'Why are you back?'

'Why did it take you so long to move your troops back in to launch the attack on the Shaanti?'

Montu sheathed his sword. 'We did not hear until an hour ago that the Shaanti were out of Vikrain.'

'What of the communication mirror I gave your man on the ground?'

'Too dangerous for him to use while they are on the move. One of my spies has already been lost.'

'Lost?'

'He was foolish,' said Montu. 'He provoked the thain into a challenge and was killed. My other spy is more cautious. She believes her an ally.'

'The fat one is the fool?'

Montu smiled. 'Yes, Master Golan was a little too well fed.'

'You'd make a good diplomat if you weren't so busy invading everyone,' said Cernubus.

'War is diplomacy on a deadline,' said Montu. 'I have men set to bring the Shaanti here – are you in control of the forest?'

Cernubus looked at him. 'Yes.'

'What's in the trunk?'

Montu moved forward a little, straining to see what the god was preoccupied with. Cernubus placed a cloth bag down by his right leg and closed the chest before the king could see what was within. He shook his head.

'My secrets are my own,' said Cernubus. 'Until they become your problem.'

Montu flushed at this. He recalled his words to the god when he had uncovered what the mages were up to, throwing his own words back at him. The god was reminding him more and more of the priest that had forced his grandfather into destroying the old religion.

'Will you stay and fight the Shaanti?'

Cernubus smiled. 'I will, but they will not be here for a while. I have unfinished business in the forest this evening, and I will be gone as soon as the magic I use has renewed me.'

Montu went cold. 'How many will you kill for your magic?'

Cernubus laughed. 'At least four.'

'Shaanti?'

Cernubus raised an eyebrow. 'Why not? It will be more effective in binding the men's belief to me.'

Montu left the tent.

———————

'YOU WILL TELL me if and when the god leaves his tent and to where he is headed,' whispered the king to the man guarding Cernubus's tent. 'Do not let him strike up a conversation with you, or answer any of his questions.'

'Sire!' called out Zoren, the only mage who had survived the encounter with Cernubus.

The poor man was looking all around to ensure no one was following him.

'Zoren,' said Montu. 'Thank you for coming.'

'How can I help, milord?'

'I have a mission for you,' said the king. 'It is a dangerous mission, I'm afraid, and may leave you worse for wear or dead.'

Zoren bent low. Montu was amused by the mage's grovelling nature, and thought, not for the first time, that it was good that this man had not led the mages. *You must never back down*, said Montu in his head.

'You are to use your magic to put more of my guard with the tenth division as they attack the Shaanti,' said Montu.

The mage looked frightened as he replied. 'I can create a spell called a join to bridge the distance between here and there. Would that suffice?'

Montu nodded. 'Keep the join open as long as possible, in case we need more.'

Zoren looked pale.

Montu enjoyed the man's discomfort. The mages were his best hope to contain the threat of the god. However, they had encouraged him to form the alliance, and they had failed him at the most crucial of times. The pact with Cernubus had been dangerous ... was danger- ous ... and so Montu had been forced to send a few of his best men away to scour the coast. Again, it was the mages who claimed the witch-warrior held the key, though the search was to no avail – and they had not even managed to keep their efforts from the god. None should have left the tent alive. Montu did not understand why the god had spared this one.

'Sire,' said Zoren, 'the magic involved is almost beyond a man's power and will certainly leave that individual very old if not dead.'

Montu put his hands on the man's shoulders. 'And should you perish, we will honour your sacrifice.'

Zoren looked down. He nodded.

'What do you need?'

'For what, sire?'

'The spell.'

'Oh,' said Zoren. 'It is already in hand. I do not require anything. Please assemble the reinforcements up on the hill in three hours.'

'Zoren,' said the king.

'Yes, sire?'

'The trunk in the god's room,' he said. 'Did you open it?'

Zoren nodded.

'What was in it?'

Zoren looked really pale now.

'Out with it, man.'

'Heads,' said Zoren in a rush. 'It was full of heads on a bed of earth and a shard of tree as sharp as any needle.'

'All human?'

Zoren shook his head. 'Maybe they were once, but they aren't now.'

'You've seen worse in war.'

'These still spoke.'

CHAPTER TWENTY-EIGHT

Danu slept and Danu dreamt.

In the dream, she saw her sister fight Cernubus in a maelstrom of magic, felt the upwelling of rage that her kin directed at the hunter for his betrayal. She wished her sister well for the first time in a millennium, but that was all she could do. When her sister retreated, bloody and beaten, seeking refuge in the depths of Golgotha, Danu woke.

The goddess rose softly from the ground that had been her only bed since she had been captured, and looked out of the bars of her prison at the blackened thing the glade had become. Her eyes were drawn inevitably to the scattered remains of the lesser gods who had lived with her in the glade. The sight had ceased to make her sick. Now it just made her sad and – when she had the energy – angry. The bars of her cell vibrated with raw magic, dampening her awareness and stopping her seeing the events in the wider forest.

When she had first been caught, she had tried to use the power of the forest, clutching her hands into the restorative earth, but Cernubus had pre-empted her, and the bars that held her extended into the ground. She was totally caged.

Still, she could feel Cernubus return, exultant in his victory over her sister. The moment he set foot on the glade's island, the feeling punched her in the stomach, a fist of nausea at the sheer wrongness of him. His victory had made him stronger. Humans had witnessed some of his deeds from afar, would make up stories, and Cernubus had harnessed the Kurah's nascent belief in him for future use.

Danu fixed her eyes on the sky. The moon hung low. It was not hard for her to tell that the alignment was only one more night away. Time was short. The sound of footsteps did not pull her gaze from the sky.

'I see you're awake,' said Cernubus.

Danu glanced at him. Her view of him wavered in the light, distorted by the heat of the cell, but even so, she could make out the runes he had carved into himself. Cernubus ... he hardly had the right to the name any more ... He was no longer a god ... The bastard creation of a thousand faiths, cults and superstitions.

Yet, weren't they all that? The decayed remains of beliefs so ancient that only a handful of them had any idea where they had come from. Cernubus was virtually impossible to recognise from the being that had once hunted the forest with her. Tall as ever, his scarred skin was red raw from walking in lands hotter than Kurah for millennia. His hair – always a wild tangle – now had a greasy limpness to it. And the robes he had clothed himself in were slack modifications of Kurah religious clothing. All his beauty had been cut away.

'Why?' she asked. 'The alignment is not for another night. I am a prisoner. Why return?'

'I think you know,' said Cernubus. 'Or did you sleep through that?'

'I know, and your addict's return to the Kurah to soak up their belief. But why come to me to gloat?'

'I do not gloat. You have a purpose.'

'Vedic will come for me,' Danu smiled.

'What can a forestal – a made thing – do to me?'

'But he still lives?'

'Not if he sets foot here.'

'He will come,' said Danu, sitting back – her expression a picture of serenity.

'Well, that does rather seem to be the question, doesn't it? Will he throw away the life he hoards so carefully to try to save you? I want to know where he is.'

'You're afraid of him?'

Cernubus drew closer to the cage, his eyes crawling over her skin as if memorising every inch of her. Danu turned her back on him, casting her gaze over at the trees.

'Why do you seek him if you are not afraid? He is just a forestal, barely magical at all.'

'You know damned well why,' said Cernubus, his voice low. 'You see the same patterns I do. You know the girl is with him, and you know what I am trying to achieve. We never settled our argument all those years ago. The disaster can be averted if one of us wields all the power.'

'As long as that is you,' she said, with a thin smile.

Danu could sense he was wound tight and ready to snap – he was beginning to make mistakes. She needed a collection of them to have any chance at all of getting free.

'Your days on this world are drawing to a close, Danu. Provoking me will only make those that remain painful. Tell me where you have hidden them.'

'You still intend to go ahead with the sacrifice?'

'I do.'

'There hasn't been a human sacrifice to us in nearly a thousand years. They are starting to find their own way again. Why encourage them to go back? You know our time is limited, so what can this achieve?'

'They are savage, spiteful and foolish creatures. Look what they have done to the forest that birthed us. They need gods, whether they realise it or not; a strong, powerful and beneficent god can show them the way. I have what they do not – thousands of years spent thinking about the coming time – and I know what we must do to survive.'

'All you care about is your own survival. None of us can prevent what is coming. The universe is bigger than humanity or gods.'

'Blood can. It is the old magic that helped make us strong. We were elevated for a reason.'

'Your memory is failing. We were elevated by accident.'

'Is that so? Look at you now – the mother goddess, the earth goddess, brought low by the Kurah and a smattering of magic. I remember the time when half the known world worshipped your every word. You are the one who has lost your way.'

'Times change.'

'They do. And where once your followers numbered in the millions, now they run in the thousands.'

'Because you have killed them, harangued them and bullied them to the point where they believe in nothing,' she hissed, turning back to him.

'They believe in the terror lurking in the dark. They believe in me.'

'You will fail,' said Danu, 'for you do not understand me or my reasons for doing anything, and in that you have wrought your own doom.'

Danu smiled as Cernubus blinked under her calm gaze. Briefly she felt his consciousness flicker past her, back to the imperial camp, presumably to see if his plan was unfolding as he had hoped. She had needled him. The god's soul returned as fast as it had departed, satisfied – it seemed to Danu – that nothing was awry in the preparations for the sacrifice. She knew herself there were no gods in the immediate area. She'd thought that she sensed Pan, but it had been a fleeting echo over the noise of the small cell that had become her prison. Wishful thinking.

'Everything is nearly ready,' he said. 'Once the alignment is under-way, I will control the forest.'

'Are you sure?' asked Danu.

Cernubus faltered. 'What do you mean?'

'You're bleeding,' said Danu, her fingers outstretched.

Cernubus put his hand to his shoulder, where an ugly welt trickled blood down his chest, matting hair and attracting flies. Danu laughed as he hissed in pain, smirked as he used his good arm to heal the wound, and looked disappointed when the flesh knotted back together. *What was causing that?* Perhaps his hold on the Kurah was not quite as strong as appearance suggested. Danu took a deep breath and twisted the knife.

'Didn't notice that? Interesting. Can you feel anything?'

'Be quiet.'

'You can't, can you?' She peered closer at his self-inflicted tattoos. 'What did you do to yourself?'

'You did this to me,' he said, glaring at her.

Danu folded her arms. 'I did no such thing. I banished you and you deserved it. I did not cut you or turn you into the hateful husk I see before me. You did that all by yourself.'

The god lost control. There was no time to exploit it as she had planned. Cernubus was through the bars of the cell before she could move, his arm connecting with her jaw in the next instant and snapping her head back. The goddess fell to her knees with the shock of it, the copper taste of blood in her mouth. Cernubus stood over her. The bars hummed behind him.

'If it weren't near the alignment ...' he said.

'Then you'd still be in exile,' she said, spitting blood. Her only hope now was to distract him long enough for Vedic to arrive. 'I know the cult that you hoodwinked into returning your power, and the ones you fed off in your search for more. The humans used to have a name for your kind.'

'I didn't just search for more power; I found it,' he answered, kicking her.

Pain flowered in her belly. Gasping for breath, watching her own spit drop to the mud, Danu struggled to move away from the raging god as he landed her with blow after blow. There wasn't the frenzied attack she would have expected but a cold, surgical punishment that had one purpose: to inflict pain without actually killing her before the sacrifice – she still had to look like Danu.

On the edge of the darkness, two eyes stared at her. The creature started towards her, but the goddess stretched out her hand, her silent command stopping the being from coming any closer. She did not need another death in her name, especially not that one, anything but that one.

As the hunter circled her, taunting her, she found the trees were reacting to the presence of the fawn, threatening discovery through their excitement. Danu forced her mind away from the pain she was feeling and concentrated on masking the forest's recognition of her silent guardian. As Cernubus struck again, Danu closed her eyes,

NEIL BEYNON

picturing the woodsman. From there, the memories flowed like the sea, sweeping her into her past and away from the pain of now. When she opened her eyes once more, the small watcher had gone, across the land towards the lake, safe at last. As she rolled onto her back and looked up at the sentinels, she hoped Vedic was near. There wasn't much time, and she could do no more.

'ARE YOU READY?'

Anya looked down at the god as she spoke. Pan was sitting cross-legged by her, his hands implanted into the soil, and Vedic sat on her right. Akyar and Meyr wandered back towards them. The light breeze carried a faint smell of burnt wood as if someone, somewhere, were making camp. All was quiet. You could almost have supposed they were gathering to sing songs round their own campfire, friends meeting again after a time apart rather than on the eve of another fight. *And will you kill again? Here in this world, where it matters?*

Anya no longer knew whose voice she was hearing in her head. She did not know how to answer the question. There was no longer any shaking when she picked up her sword, and she had not seen any ghosts since Golgotha, but the thought of ending someone's life? She knew she might have to kill again, but she had pushed the thought away whenever it popped into her head.

Pan moved from sitting to standing. Anya could not say how. Soil crumbled from his hands, and he appeared only half there, like he was drunk on wine or the leaf her grandfather and Falkirk used to smoke. Akyar and Meyr murmured hello.

'Do you think you will get to the Tream in time?' asked Vedic.

Pan smiled. 'We will get there in time. Whether we can persuade Hogarth is another matter. Can you free Danu?'

Vedic raised an eyebrow. 'You tell me. This is your idea.'

'Hers,' said Pan.

'That's not very reassuring,' snapped Vedic.

'Stop,' said Anya, her voice firm. 'Let us part friends. We have all been through so much, and there is so far yet to go.'

Pan nodded. Vedic glowered. She'd take it.

'Farewell, woodsman,' said Pan, offering his hand.

Vedic stared at the offered hand for a moment. Anya thought he wasn't going to take it, but then he did, grabbing Pan's forearm in the Kurah manner. She flinched. Pan smiled.

'Remember, freeing Danu is more important than killing Cernubus. If you can manage that, we will have a chance.'

Vedic frowned but nodded.

Akyar did not ask permission but clasped Vedic in a bear hug that lifted the woodsman from his feet.

'You gnarly bastard,' he yelped. 'Take that fucking hunter down.'

'Get off me,' said Vedic, although there was the ghost of a laugh in his tone.

Meyr stepped forward, and Vedic bent down so they were at eye level. 'You tell your father to forget about the Morrigan.'

Meyr nodded. He offered his hand not in the Kurah way but the Shaanti, fist extended, and Anya watched as Vedic returned the signal without thinking, knuckle to knuckle. A passing moment, but Anya felt like someone had poured ice down her back. She could not say why. Meyr ran to her and gave her a hug as if he would never see her again. Pan and Akyar joined in.

'Let's get on with this,' growled Vedic. 'We need to get going. It's a long trek to the glade.'

They broke the hug. Pan wandered out into an area of ground that was not covered in broken trees or burnt brush, and began the incantation. He brought his hands together in a loud clap, and power surged down his arms, forming a light between the palms of his hand that fizzed and burned incandescent orange. The air smelt faintly of sulphur. As Anya watched, the light moved away from the god's hands and held position a little ahead of them. Pan observed his work like a potter reviewing clay on the wheel. The god muttered words Anya did not understand, and rotated his hands. The light formed a rectangle the size of a door, splitting away in the centre to form a frame through which the forest looked different from the trees around him. This new section of forest had no felled trees, no sign of fire and looked like the ancient, giant oaks of the Tream city.

'Go now,' said Pan, his voice strained and the cords of his neck standing out like the rigging of a ship. 'I do not know how long I can hold this.'

Akyar put Meyr through first. He glanced back at Vedic and Anya. Anya felt a little pull in her gut as she watched her friend step through the magic and disappear. Pan let out a sigh and dropped his hands. She was about to ask if he was still going when the frame of magic folded in and dragged Pan through it. She stared at the empty space.

'He usually dismounts better than that,' said Vedic.

Anya laughed.

The ghost of a smirk crossed Vedic's face as he looked up at the setting suns casting the forest in the shadows of fires. This made Anya think of pyres. She pushed the thought far away.

'We should get going,' said Vedic. 'It'll be dawn before we reach the glade, and if the wolves are loose again, we may need to take to the trees.'

Anya nodded. She felt tired in her bones and had hoped for a fire at least, but there was no time. The alignment was at most one night away. She trudged off after Vedic.

'So, do you think we can find any other gods who can help us?'

Vedic shook his head. 'The older ones, those who the Shaanti use in everyday language, they may be able to reform, but Cernubus seems to know what he's doing when it comes to killing them.'

Anya clutched her arms round herself, half longing for the moment the walking warmed her up and half dreading the further exhaustion that would come with it. She hadn't slept in ages now, and she was too weary to guard her words.

'What about the stone god?'

Vedic glanced at her. 'I doubt he would be much help, even if he existed.'

'Why?'

'It's hard to imagine a more bloodthirsty creature,' said Vedic. 'The Kurah, when they followed him, they worshipped the stone and the desert. They believed the rock took blood and gave life to those who sacrificed. That is why they do not usually take prisoners.'

'You're from Kurah,' said Anya, 'aren't you?'

Vedic did not look at her. 'Pan. He told you.'

'Yes,' said Anya. 'But it's not just that. The cave, the ghost who spoke, he was from Kurah – that was the accent – and when you swear ... that's Kurah as well, although I don't recognise the dialect.'

Vedic swore in Kurah.

Anya laughed. 'It doesn't matter. You clearly don't agree with them any more.'

Vedic stayed silent. The forest was dark and there was no moon. They had to slow their progress to avoid tripping or being struck by errant branches.

'I thought perhaps you had been the stone god once,' said Anya.

Vedic laughed. A surprisingly good noise despite the fact it was directed at Anya, and she found herself laughing alongside him.

'Oh, lassie, Pan would be rolling on the ground if he heard that.'

Anya pushed her companion gently. 'Come on, forestal. I know what I need to know. Let's get to the glade.'

'Oh, and what's that?'

Anya looked back at him. 'That you're not a nice man.'

Vedic's smile faded.

She added, 'We don't need you to be nice to Cernubus.'

Vedic nodded. 'No chance of that.' He stopped dead. He looked as if he were listening to something.

'What's wrong?'

The woodsman dropped down to his knees, his sword drawn. Anya followed his lead as he moved forward slowly, with his blade ready.

'There is a creature ahead of us.'

In the distance, maybe two hundred yards away, a pair of eyes flickered faint orange with reflected light from the sentinels.

It's got to be a wolf, thought Anya, her hand reaching for her sword.

Vedic gently stopped her and shook his head.

'Not a wolf,' he said. 'Too small.'

'What is it, then?'

'Something else.'

Gripping his sword tighter in one hand, Vedic moved closer to the eyes. The creature was considerably smaller than the wolves. Barely bigger than a medium-sized dog. The animal moved closer on seeing

Vedic approach. The woodsman stopped. This was not the behaviour he expected. The creature continued its slow approach towards them.

'What is it?' asked Anya, making Vedic – who had not heard her – jump. 'Is it a dog?'

'No. It's a ...' said Vedic, leaning closer. 'I'll be damned ...'

Emerging from the bushes was a small, bloodied and bedraggled-looking infant deer. Anya couldn't understand why Vedic was reacting to the fawn like he had seen a ghost, or why he was trying to encourage the creature closer to him. She'd never seen him like this with animals.

'What? It's just a fawn.'

'Anya,' said Vedic, looking up at her as the fawn drew close to his hand. 'You owe this fawn your life.'

Anya looked from Vedic to the fawn and back again.

'I thought you said that was Pan.'

'I was wrong,' he said. The woodsman held out his hand. 'I assumed the curse came from Pan's spell, but I've seen this little chap before on the day you came into my life and this was done to my arm. I think this fellow has come from Danu, or someone who wants to help her. We may have another ally.'

The fawn approached Vedic's outstretched digits, sniffing them suspiciously for a few moments. The deer ran his head along the woodsman's fingers, Vedic scratching the creature behind the ears.

'You seem to have made a new friend,' Anya said.

'Yes,' he said, rubbing the ugly scar on his arm. 'Rather different from our first meeting.'

'Wonder why he's here now,' said Anya, sitting back down.

'Yes,' said Vedic, watching as the fawn looked at Anya. It walked towards her, stopped, stamped his hoof and turned his head towards the darkness. He repeated the movement.

'You want to be alone with Vedic?' asked Anya, confused.

The fawn shook his head. The creature walked towards her, nudged her, came back, nudged Vedic, then turned towards the darkness again, stamping his foot and snorting as best he could.

'He's offering to lead the way,' said Vedic.

'Why?'

'Because Danu must be in danger,' said Vedic, tightening his pack. 'We have to go. Now.'

'Because of a fawn?'

Vedic nodded.

'You're mad,' she said, checking her sword.

They followed the fawn into the inky black of the forest and towards the lake that led to the glade. The lack of wind allowed the sound of the water lapping against the shore to float over the forest to them, growing ever louder as they drew closer. They walked until the suns began to poke over the edge of the world, setting the horizon alight and casting the forest in the first tawny shadows of daylight.

THE MUD WAS soft against Danu's cheek.

The goddess lay, bruised and bleeding, on the ground of her cage while Cernubus watched her from where he sat on a fallen tree. It was hard to say who felt them arrive first. Danu's hands clenched involuntarily as the earth spilled its secrets: the familiar wave of wrongness coupled with the excitement of the woodsman's presence on the island once more. She could feel Vedic's familiar footfall, the belief pouring from him into the ground like the most potent wine.

Cernubus stood, grabbing his spear from the ground.

'It seems your pet is as stupid as he looks.'

Danu did not say anything. She pushed herself to a seated position, cast her hair back from her face as best she could and wiped the blood from her mouth. Cernubus sneered.

'You're preening yourself for him.' He gave her a look of disdain.

'No,' she answered. 'I am not.'

Cernubus removed his outer robe, dropping it to the ground; he stood in a tunic, cut off at the sleeves, and a pair of loose cloth trousers. Gently he swung the spear in a few looping parabolas that terminated in thrusts.

Danu watched, her face a mask. *At least*, she thought, *Vedic is skilled enough to avoid his magic.*

'The Kurah king doesn't know he's still alive, does he?' she said, seeking to draw his attention once more.

'What?' asked Cernubus, ceasing his drills.

'Your friend, the king – he doesn't know that Vedic is alive, does he?'

Cernubus did not reply.

'I thought not,' she said, returning her gaze to the glade.

CHAPTER TWENTY-NINE

'I CAN DO THIS ALONE,' said Vedic. 'If you want.'

Anya flinched. They were crawling through the wasteland of the glade; the lush undergrowth they had walked through on climbing onto shore had quickly dropped away to ashen remains, reminiscent of Golgotha. The fawn was dashing from stump to stump ahead of them, trying to keep itself low and out of sight. Beyond the tangled weave of fallen trees, they could just make out the shimmering light that had been fashioned into a prison cell: magic burned through the shape, creating a haze of heat. Everything smelt of ash and stale wood smoke.

'Dreams,' whispered Anya, stopping. Her mother's voice was as clear now as in Golgotha, though the tone was changing. *Courage, child.*

'What?'

'I've been having nightmares ever since I escaped. I wasn't sure at first what I was seeing, but I think I know now. That bastard's been invading my dreams for weeks. I thought it was just my imagination, and then I thought it might be ... someone else ... but it's him. Cernubus must be the one: torn cities, ritual sacrifice, battles, you name it – he's sent all that shit my way, to try and destroy my mind with what he is doing outside the forest. No, Vedic, I can't sit this one out. You can't imagine what he's done.'

Vedic stared at her. He looked like he was about to speak, but then he changed his mind. She drew her sword. She thought of the warrior she had killed. She thought of Fin.

'And the thing is, I'm not nice either.'

Vedic smiled, although it did not reach his eyes. 'Onwards, then?'

She nodded.

'You might as well come out,' called Cernubus. The god's voice was low. It settled somewhere in the back of Anya's skull and vibrated.

Swords drawn, they stepped into the light.

Cernubus did not bother to raise his spear in any kind of defensive posture. They walked, blinking, weapons raised towards him and with enough distance between them to swing.

The god stood resting against his weapon – his pose as nonchalant as his face. Anya felt his eyes on her briefly in the way a person might glance at an ant before moving on. She sought out the cage, the figure wavering like a mirage beyond, the heat of the magic failing to mask the goddess in its captive grasp.

The Morrigan sat in the cage, staring back at her, except she wasn't the Morrigan. Anya knew that instinctively, despite the striking resemblance, and as her eyes trawled for evidence as to why, she noticed the upturn of the goddess's mouth, a stark contrast to her sister. Danu's dreads fell lower; her chin was narrower; and her clothes had never been black – they were a brown-tinged green or had once been before she'd been beaten. Her left eye was swollen; her lower lip was split; and bruises lined her arms and legs. The goddess smiled at her.

Anya felt herself grin back. Her spine tingled. Anya thought this might be a little like how she had imagined meeting her mother. She had never known her mother – the woman had left long before her first memories began – but that didn't stop her imagining what it would be like. The goddess smiled at her as if nothing else in the forest existed, showing a warmth and love that was meant for no one else but Anya alone, and asking nothing in return. The goddess's gaze was like going home and not realising you'd missed it until the moment you walked in again. Anya's body fizzed with pleasure. Her eyes blinked back tears, and all she wanted to do was to have the goddess put her arms around her and tell her everything would be fine.

Anya watched as the goddess's gaze passed from her to Vedic and her expression changed. Danu took on a strange look: hunger, fear, rapture, all rolled into one, and it reminded her of her grandfather on receiving his first drink of the day. Anya looked away, shamed, as if witnessing a private exchange.

'Laos,' said Cernubus.

'Cernubus,' said Vedic, nodding.

Cernubus dipped his head slightly in acknowledgement. The god's eyes tracked them into the centre of the glade; the pair moved slowly. Anya looked for signs of the wolves or Kurah, but there appeared to be no one else on the island who she could see. She wasn't sure where the fawn was.

'You'll find no one else,' said Cernubus, amusement skirting his face. 'The Morrigan did not leave many of the pack alive, not that I need them.'

Anya ignored him.

'I want Danu,' said Vedic, rolling his neck to loosen the muscles.

'Ah, now,' said Cernubus, circling them. 'I saw her first, long before your ancestors even picked up a rock and cast a word to it.'

'You're going to let her go,' said Vedic, shrugging. 'One way or another.'

'Bold words, old man,' said Cernubus. A smile ghosted his lips but did not touch his eyes. 'Still, I'm surprised, and impressed. Loyalty from someone she's kept in a cage for fifty years, Kurah king after Kurah king, undoing all your work, and you – who commanded millions – reduced to chopping dead wood. I found your bastard god much reduced and easy to crush.'

Anya's eyes flicked uncertainly between Vedic and Cernubus. Her memory was stirring. The woodsman ignored her glances, though his knuckles were now gripping his sword tight enough to turn his skin luminescent white.

Why aren't we attacking? What's Cernubus talking about? This was not going as Anya expected.

'It needed undoing,' said Vedic, his voice cracked. 'I was misguided.'

'I see the rumours are true,' said Cernubus, his laugh soft. 'Danu did unman you.'

Vedic smiled. 'I'm a little old for that barb.'

Cernubus shrugged. 'You may have been mistaken; who's to say? But I promise you, coming here was an error. You should have run long and hard. Lived your life away from here. Instead, you'll help fuel my fire.'

'I know,' he said, letting his sword drop lower.

Anya moved, seeking to flank the god before Vedic killed himself by lowering his guard or worse. She couldn't understand what he was doing.

'Then you're finally ready?' the god asked, surprised but ready to execute the woodsman with his spear. 'You no longer fear the other side?'

'I am prepared,' said Vedic, eyes not moving from the god. 'Why? Are you scared of the dark?'

'Vedic?' asked Anya, her eyes flicking round to get a look at him.

Cernubus examined the woodsman, stepped in closer. 'You give up so easily?'

Vedic brought his head forward in a sharp crack, slamming his forehead into Cernubus's nose.

The god staggered back, more surprised than hurt.

Vedic's sword followed his headbutt in close succession, though Cernubus blocked it.

'I wouldn't go that far,' said Vedic, swinging round for another strike.

HOGARTH STARED out of the window of his throne room across the forest, his jaw knotting and smoothing as if he were chewing his problems.

The king's small entourage watched silently, waiting for him to speak. Weeks had passed since Akyar had left, and no word had been received from his vizier. The men he had sent to watch over them had been found dead near the borderlands with the gods. Now his own wife, Jiana, was preparing to go looking for his lost son, and he was practically under house arrest from the elders.

Jiana entered the room. Hogarth threw a quick glance at her before returning to the window. She had come to say goodbye. She nodded at the king's bodyguard as she walked over to Hogarth and slipped her hand onto her husband's shoulder. The king turned slightly, his cheeks wet.

'You still mean to go?'

Jiana nodded.

'I wish I could leave as well, come with you.'

The guards stepped forward, ready to restrain him if they had to, ready to enforce the elders' ruling themselves and protect the king from himself.

Jiana shook her head, placing her hand on his chest. Her meaning was clear even without her whispering in his mind. The impotence of his position and the stark reality that he might not see his son again brought more angry tears. His wife lifted her hand to her head, then her heart before resting it on Hogarth's chest, the words echoing in his mind.

'As you will be in mine. Be careful, and do not trust the woodsman,' said Hogarth, resting his hand on hers. 'He is more dangerous than he appears. He has done things ... things to rival even the Morrigan. For such a short-lived species, they are capable of such extraordinary destruction.'

'The woodsman isn't evil.'

The voice came from the far side of the room, near the door. The pair froze – they didn't believe what they were hearing.

'Mother?' said Meyr.

Jiana and Hogarth turned. The queen hesitated for a moment, uncertain if he was really standing in the doorway. Hesitation gave way to relief, and she ran to gather her son in her arms. She hugged him, burying her face in his shoulder. The muted sounds of her cries rebounded round the chamber. Hogarth sank slowly onto the step of the dais, his shoulders dropping. His cheeks were still wet, but this time the emotion was welcome.

The king's gaze passed from his son to the figures that had walked with him into the room. Akyar looked a century older than he had when he left, leaning on his sword, covered in dust, his robe tattered, and he was accompanied by a shorter and hooded figure that was neither Vedic nor Anya. His eyes were only noticeable within his hood when they reflected the firelight of the torches.

'Sire,' said Akyar, bowing. 'It is good to see you again.'

'Thank you, old friend,' said the king to Akyar. He turned to the stranger. 'And to you, friend, but you do not look to be one of the party who I sent for my son.'

'You are welcome, Lord Hogarth,' said the stranger, leaving his hood up. 'I come on behalf of the woodsman, and Anya, who must tend to their own business now.'

'It is customary to call me by my correct title in my own hall,' said Hogarth, rising to his feet. 'Who are you, stranger?'

'I'm afraid you will have to forgive me, lord. I am not permitted to call any person king, be they man, Tream or god,' said Pan, drawing back his hood. 'As to who I am, I have had many names, but you can call me Pan.'

Every Tream save Jiana and Hogarth drew their weapons. They surrounded the god and Akyar with steel. Akyar glared at Hogarth. Pan smirked.

'Call your men off. You could not kill me even if you tried. I mean you no harm.'

Looking up from his mother's arms, Meyr addressed the guards. 'Please, put your swords away. This god helped me as much as anyone.'

'He'd be fuel for Cernubus's fire without Pan's help,' said Akyar, his anger barely contained.

'Cernubus?' asked Hogarth.

'Once upon a time, your people called him the hunter,' said Pan. 'As the humans once did. He is an ancient god. He was responsible for your son's kidnapping, not Danu.'

'He used the Morrigan,' said Akyar, 'knowing she resembled Danu and how you would react.'

Hogarth glanced at his son, and at his vizier standing defiantly by the god and surrounded by guardsmen. The Tream guards looked uneasily at Akyar, uncertain what to do, turning as one to the king for his approval.

'I believe my son and the heir to the Tream throne just issued an order. I would have the instruction obeyed as if it were my own.'

'Thank you for your hospitality, Lord Hogarth,' said Pan, stepping forward. 'I come on an urgent errand from my sister Danu, the rightful leader of the Shaanti gods.'

'What do you want, Pan?' asked Hogarth, his gaze lingering on his wife. 'I am not well disposed to gods, regardless of who they are.'

Pan smiled, though the grin did not reach his eyes.

'I understand your wariness in dealing with my kind, and I abhor what my sister and Cernubus did to Meyr. However, the situation is far worse and more complex than you realise.'

'Perhaps you are right,' said Hogarth. 'For I care little about what happens to a goddess of the glade or human children. Where is this Cernubus?'

'Will you listen, Hogarth?' snapped Akyar.

Shock rolled round the chamber like a leaf on a breeze, carried first this way, then that. No one spoke to Hogarth in this way, not even Akyar in private. *Should I put him back in his place?* thought Hogarth. *Perhaps that is the problem. I am not much given to listening to others. I only tolerated the elders' decision not to let me go, because I knew the warriors would side with them.*

'Tread carefully, old friend,' said Hogarth, sitting.

'The god is in league with the Kurah,' said Pan. 'The young king has led his forces onwards, fresh from success with the Delgasians, and used Cernubus's power to shore up his supply lines. As we speak, he controls all of the Shaanti coast and lands between here and Mortone, and he has used his spies and Cernubus to entice the thain from Vikrain in the hope of her people escaping to the ocean – but they will have to fight the Kurah either way.'

'Why?'

Akyar answered. 'Montu wants to control the continent. He believes the Tinaric will invade if he cannot demonstrate his might. Cernubus wants the forest. The wood is the seat of the gods' power, and with that power, he can control all human life.'

'Montu wants to be ruled by a god? I thought the Kurah deposed their priests and abandoned their gods.'

Pan smiled sadly. 'Yes, the stone god is dead. Montu believes he can control Cernubus. He is mistaken.'

'His grandfather managed to control the Priest.'

'Did he?' asked Pan.

Hogarth shrugged. 'What did he want with my son?'

'Blood,' said Pan, closing his eyes for a moment. 'Blood is the most powerful binding agent for the magic we use. The blood of the heir, in the hands of a god and obtained during the most mystical day in front of the largest army in human history ... The fount of belief would be unprecedented.'

'Power enough to attack us?'

'Oh, yes,' said Pan, opening his eyes. 'More than enough.'

'That would mean war,' said Hogarth.

'If you lived – except you wouldn't,' said Pan, shrugging. 'Cernubus is too strong, and while he does not seek the genocide of the Tream, he desires a world ruled by humanity, and humanity ruled by him.'

'You gods,' hissed Hogarth.

'The gods have not done this,' said Akyar. 'Cernubus is a renegade. He has taken dark magic from around the world, and he has cut the words into himself. He is no longer just a god.'

'Cernubus wasn't just after me,' said Meyr, his mother clutching him tight. 'They have captured every child they encountered. All Shaanti children for miles around the forest are to be burned at noon on the day of the alignment.'

'Tomorrow,' added Akyar.

'I know,' said Hogarth, his voice more even than he felt. 'Scouts brought back word the day before yesterday.'

'Do you know that humans believe in a place that you go to after you die?' asked Akyar.

'I am familiar with the concept,' said Hogarth, unable to meet his vizier's stare. 'It is a story told by children unable to face up to reality.'

'Maybe,' said Akyar, shrugging. 'But the underworld exists. It is called Golgotha, where the dead walk on their final journey. That place is worse than the stone of the Kurah and more bereft of hope than the desert where no trees grow. A tree-forsaken hell on our doorstep.'

'You talk as if you have been there,' said Hogarth, his gut churning.

Akyar's eyes flashed angrily. 'We have.'

No, thought Hogarth. *Oh, my son. Oh, my friend. What have I done?*

'Not for long,' said Akyar. 'But Golgotha is where the Morrigan was holding Meyr – and do you know who I met there?'

Hogarth shook his head.

'I met a ferryman,' said Akyar. 'A dead god with blonde hair who was once a god of laughter and tricks like the one standing next to me, and who the Morrigan loved. Do you know who killed him?'

Hogarth did not reply.

'We killed him,' said Akyar. 'I no longer know who started the trouble between the gods and us ... It doesn't matter ... What is at hand is whether we want to sit by and be destroyed by our indifference, or help another species that laugh and cry and care for each other as we do.'

Hogarth closed his eyes. He let the information seep into his brain. When he opened them again, he looked not at his son but at Pan. The god was holding Akyar's hand.

'What do you want, Pan?' asked Hogarth.

At last, thought Pan. He gave a silent prayer of thanks to Danu that Meyr had performed his part so well, placing Hogarth in a position where he would listen to the god.

'I would like you to attack the Kurah,' said Pan, refusing to look away from the king's gaze. Akyar squeezed his hand. 'Preferably as soon as possible. We have little time.'

'This is a human affair. They made your kind; they should have to clean up after themselves,' replied Hogarth, turning his back to Pan.

This was not what Pan wanted to hear.

'No,' said Akyar, letting go of Pan's hand. 'It is not. The Kurah will destroy the Shaanti. Then they will come for us.'

'They will be busy turning on the hunter,' replied Hogarth, without turning round.

'No,' replied Akyar. 'The hunter will kill Montu, and the Kurah will follow him as they once followed the Priest. Can you imagine the horrors they will do to us under his command? To Meyr?'

Pan watched the king look at his son. He did not speak. His hands balled into fists and loosened in response to whatever internal battle was going on behind those dark eyes.

Jiana dropped her arms from Meyr and stepped forward. The king's eyes switched to her scarred face, which was imploring her husband with her thoughts. The king's eyes stopped her feet, and her look was cast aside, falling instead on Pan. The god was confused. He met her gaze, his eyes noting the ruined flesh for the first time. *Oh, please say it isn't so.*

'Why does the Lady Jiana not speak?' asked Pan, his suspicion forming a wave of nausea.

'I see the gods are not all-knowing,' said Hogarth, sounding bitter again.

'No. Neither are we all-powerful, as my lord knows full well.'

'The Morrigan cut her tongue from her mouth as I looked on,' whispered Meyr, his expression flat and his voice muted.

Pan's hands − held together in front of him − dropped to his sides. His face slackened and lost colour as he stepped forward. He was exhausted from the spell that had folded space and brought them to the Tream city. More magic would be risky, he knew, but then the danger was already so large that he didn't know how they would carry the day.

Pan's eyes were wet as the god took the queen's arm, the firelight of the torches flickering in the darkness of his pupils. The guards started forward, but Akyar shook his head, halting them. Hogarth's hand drew his sword a few inches, but Meyr put his small hand on his father's to stop him. The king did not remove it. The god was dimly aware of every person in the room watching him as he led Jiana over to the side of the throne room where saplings lined the wall, placed in a trough of soil.

Pan scooped some of the mud and smeared the dirt over the queen's scars. There were murmurings from the Tream gathered in the room, mutterings of having tried this, but he ignored them. The Tream lore was not as strong as the gods'. They could not speak to the forest as he could. Chanting softly to himself, he embraced the queen, his hands lifting to her ruined cheeks. Keeping her calm with his open look, communicating his intent as he did when using his mind to talk to Akyar, he kissed her, gently. As she responded, the god bit down on his own tongue until he drew blood, the copper salt bitterness of the fluid swilling between Jiana and himself.

In the hushed silence, Pan could hear Hogarth finally draw his sword, but the god was lost now in the cant he was creating; the magic burned through him. The sound of more steel unsheathing was like distant rain as the queen and the god broke slightly apart, both mouths open, an ice–green stream of magic visible between the fingers of the god as he cupped her face. The two drew together again. When they broke apart, the queen was unsteady on her feet, and the god set her standing with a gentle kiss on the brow.

Behind her, the king fumed.

'Go with peace,' said Pan, not moving his focus from the queen. 'It is freely given. There is no obligation to any Tream.'

'You will explain yourself,' said Hogarth, pointing his sword at the weary god. 'You have already corrupted Akyar.'

'Hush, Hogarth,' said Jiana, her voice unsteady from lack of use. 'Pan has corrupted no one. He has undone the Morrigan's work.'

Hogarth turned back to his wife, and his sword dropped to the floor. Jiana smiled back at him from a face untouched by scar tissue. The king embraced her with a fierce hug that extended to enclose his son. The god smiled as he wearily sat himself down on the dais. Akyar made to move to his side, but Pan waved him off. The sensation of wrongness was coming from deep in the forest: he could feel power being drained out of these far distant parts towards the glade.

'Do you have any suggestions where to attack the Kurah?' asked Hogarth, his eyes not leaving his wife.

Pan looked up at the king. 'Are you sure? I did not do this for your favour – I would not have you think I have manipulated you into a battle you do not want.'

Hogarth smiled. 'I know you did not, but if I hear you right, the battle will come whether I want it or not, and only the fool allows his enemy to pick the terms of engagement.'

Pan nodded. 'Time is pressing. I can sense Vedic and Cernubus fighting even as we speak. The Kurah eastern flank is exposed to us, and the thain, if she comes, will come from the west. Should you attack from the east, then we can crush them between you and the Shaanti.'

'What if the woodsman kills Cernubus?' asked Akyar.

'We still have to free the children,' said Pan, shaking his head. 'Do not put too much faith in that one, and don't underestimate the Kurah. They want to control this continent, and they can't do that while there are Shaanti, Tream and gods occupying the land. Cernubus is not the only threat.'

'It will be difficult to get there in time,' said Hogarth.

'Do what you can, my lord,' said Pan. 'I can ask no more than that.'

'The woodsman can defeat Cernubus?' asked Hogarth.

Pan was quiet, then said, 'No, I don't think so.'

'Then why bother,' asked Hogarth, 'when we will lose?'

'He does not have to kill Cernubus,' said Pan. 'You can erode my cousin's power by defeating the Kurah. All Vedic has to do is free Danu. Besides, I might be wrong.'

'There's always hope?' asked Hogarth. 'Is that it?'

Pan nodded. He felt like he was carrying the weight of the forest on his shoulders as he replied.

'Akin to hope. Although I do not speak of that which left this land so long ago. For me, defiance and mischief have always been good substitutes. How we choose to fall can be as meaningful as managing to stay on our feet.'

'Even the fallen tree has its uses,' said Hogarth, with a grim smile.

Pan nodded.

'Summon the warriors,' said Hogarth to his guard. 'We head for the Barrens as soon as they are mustered.'

Pan stood and bowed to the king. The guardsmen finally lowered their swords, sheathing them. The god drank in the sweet smell of the pine wood surrounding them and tried to gather what scraps of energy were left in the ground. Far away, Cernubus was fighting hard and using up the forest like it was a glass of water.

'Thank you, sire,' said Pan. He turned to leave, hoping to make his exit a little way away from the Tream where they would not see the method he planned to use to return. He hoped he had enough energy.

'Are you going somewhere?' asked Hogarth, surprised.

'Yes,' said Pan, looking back. 'I have done what is needed here. Now I must help Vedic as best I can.'

'How can you manage another trip?' asked Akyar, stepping forward, concerned.

'With difficulty,' said Pan, his face gaunt. 'But I'll live.'

The god paused. In looking over at the king and his son, a weapon caught his eye. The blade glinted from the wall: sleek, silver and gold, elegant and deadly, the sword was nearly as long as a man, a wooden sheath hanging just below it. Together they would have looked like a staff, perhaps were even used as such.

It can't be, thought Pan. *Why would he leave the weapon behind if it were?*

'What is that?' asked the god, drawing closer to the sword.

'I think you know,' said Hogarth, following Pan's gaze. 'The Shaanti called it the Eagle's Claw. Not many priests' weapons were as effective as this one. The lives that blade has taken could fill the forest.'

'His tongue was also pretty effective,' said Pan, unable to look away from the sword.

'True.'

'How did you get it?' asked Pan, walking to where the blade hung.

'I found it,' answered Hogarth.

'You know, in Kurah, they even warn their children against this weapon,' said Pan softly, running his hand down the blade. He was surprised that he could smell the oiled wood of the sheath so strongly. He had assumed the weapon would smell of nothing, or of blood. The sword was beautiful in a terribly simplistic way.

'I believe the owner is who they warn against,' said Hogarth, his tone careful and even.

'Yes,' said Pan, shaking his head. 'To be feared as much by your own people as your enemy ... takes a kind of talent.'

'Not one I care to emulate,' said Hogarth, with a slim smile.

'Tried to give it to him, did you?'

Hogarth nodded.

'He did not want it,' said Jiana. She sounded in awe of the weapon. 'He fears it.'

Pan smiled. 'Well, he should, nevertheless. I think we may yet have use for a legend. A blade that even the Kurah fear ... May I take it to him?'

'If you wish,' said Hogarth, frowning. 'I never really cared for it.'

The god lifted the weapon from the wall. The scars of the sword's forging had left swirls down the blade that glinted in the light. The Kurah blacksmith who'd forged it had been talented indeed, copying the Delgasian technique for hardening the steel. Meyr met his gaze as he turned to leave the throne room, extending his hand. Pan smiled, shaking the prince's hand.

'You're going to fight as well,' said Meyr, concerned.

'Yes. Cernubus has slain many already – friends, family and worshippers. I would serve my purpose and teach him the true meaning of chaos.'

'He knows how to kill gods?' asked Meyr.

Pan found himself moved by the boy's concern. 'Yes, I'm afraid he does.'

'Be careful,' said Meyr, hugging the god. 'The world would be a sad place without you.'

'Oh, I'll be back,' said Pan, laughing. 'For now, I go to sow my tricks amongst my cousin's plans.'

Akyar stood in front of him as if determined to stop the god leaving.

'I must,' he whispered to Akyar.

'I know,' said the Tream, gathering Pan to him and kissing him, his body pressed hot against the god. 'Return to me.'

Pan nodded. He could not bring himself to look back at Hogarth. Pan turned and kept on turning, spinning on his heel until he became a blur, faster and faster, until he was no longer solid but a spinning vortex of dust that sped out of the door, knocking pictures from walls.

In the space of the conversation, his mood had changed. He felt more himself, and he decided to work his spell in full view against what he knew to be Danu's wishes. As he spun through the palace and out into the forest, he could feel the Tream eyes on him, their unasked questions hanging over him, and his total absence of answers ringing hollow. In the whirlwind, it sounded like a fool's laugh, but he was happy to play as such. At least he would go down laughing and with enough power to put up a fight.

ANYA CRASHED INTO THE TREE.

The air exploded from her lungs, and she heard her blade snap underneath her as she dropped to the ground. She tried to lift herself up, but the pain in her back was a searing weight that she couldn't shift. She slumped back down, watching from the dirt as Vedic fought on alone.

The woodsman bled from a number of wounds. His thin hair was matted with sweat, but he swung his sword without signs of flagging. The problem with his technique was not that he failed to penetrate the god's defence – he was landing more blows – but that his attacks didn't wound Cernubus. Where steel separated the god's flesh, Cernubus used his own power to heal himself. However, where the god landed wounds on Vedic, they cut and bled, leaving him weaker and weaker. Anya wasn't sure how much longer the woodsman could keep up with the god.

Vedic rolled out of the way of a spear thrust, coming to his feet near Anya.

'I'm impressed, Laos,' said Cernubus, swinging his spear. 'You're not rusty after chopping wood for half a century.'

'It's not a skill you forget,' said Vedic, eyes not leaving the god.

'Tell me, Laos,' said Cernubus, nodding at Anya. 'Have you had her yet?'

'You cast your words like a boy playing at battle, not a god of millennia,' said Vedic, spinning his sword back into a guard position and looking for an opening. 'I left such things behind long ago.'

'Perhaps I should,' said Cernubus, pacing round the woodsman. 'Before I burn her in front of the armies of Kurah. What do you think? How would you do it?'

Anya got to her feet. Ignoring the pain in her back, she limped around, looking for a weapon: a sword, a stone, a stick – anything to help Vedic with. Cernubus ignored her, continuing his assault on the woodsman with renewed speed and ferocity.

'I'm surprised she's with you, really,' said Cernubus, breaking away once more. 'I can smell Pan's stench on her. It wouldn't take much to bring him away from that Tream he is so infatuated with, and to be honest, I'd have thought she'd be eager to be away from the likes of you, Kurah.'

Anya spotted a bow. From the look of the thing, it had been discarded in the bushes by one of the fallen gods. It cost her to draw the bow, but she had found a use for her rage at least.

'Oh, I'm full of surprises,' said Anya.

'Ah,' said Cernubus. 'Back with us, I see. Perhaps – before I kill him – you can tell me how you, a clanswoman, can follow Laos?'

Anya did not blink. 'Laos, Vedic, whatever this warrior's name – Kurah or not – he is true to his word.'

'She doesn't know?' said Cernubus, gently testing the woodsman's guard once more. 'You haven't told her?'

Vedic wheeled around Cernubus's spear thrust. Though the attack missed him, Vedic was grey as he turned to face the god once more, eyes flicking to Anya. She looked for a more serious wound, thinking he must be losing blood, but she couldn't see one. Something twisted in her belly. The movement was coiled like a snake, and she felt the sweat on her own skin as cold as ice.

'His secrets are his own.' Anya unleashed an arrow that slammed into the wood near Cernubus's head.

'Tell her, Laos,' said Cernubus, goading the woodsman with his spear. 'Tell her about *your* word. Tell her, *priest.*'

Anya paused, second arrow strung. *Priest?* Why did it feel like there were cold fingers tightening in her chest? *But the Kurah had no god any more, not since ... No ...*

'What's the matter?' asked Cernubus. 'Are you ashamed of who you are, Laos?'

Vedic did not respond.

'I'll tell her, then. This man you call Vedic, this man whose given name is Laos, was not always a forestal – and never a warrior as you know warriors – he was a Kurah priest. Or rather, the Priest, the definite article, you might say ...'

Anya lowered her bow in disbelief. Vedic. Laos. He had to be over a hundred years old. He had been old when he had fought in the last war. The hand in her chest twisted. *Please don't let it be true.* The blanket memory of the lake had been pulled from the myriad of dreams, and they cycled through the forefront of her brain without pause or mercy. She hadn't been experiencing Cernubus's dreams; she hadn't been a passenger in the god's head at all. Every nightmare had been Vedic's memory.

They faded to her grandfather, Thrace, the once-proud general of the thain, disintegrating into a drunk before her eyes, her grandmother driven into the wilds by what she had seen, crushed by the memories of the massacre at Vremin and the carnage that had been dealt out by the Kurah military commander called the Priest. Her grandmother assassinated by Kurah.

No, she thought, *he can't be.* And yet she knew it was the truth.

'I see you have heard of him,' said Cernubus, circling the woodsman. 'The Butcher of Vremin and the faithful lapdog of the Kurah king. How many people have you sacrificed?'

'The Priest is dead,' said Vedic, swinging his sword. 'I am Vedic.'

'You are Laos, the priest who led the Kurah armies across the continent, the priest who destroyed three cities in three days, the priest who sacrificed the whole of the city of Blumenthal to the stone god, and the priest whose master tried to have him killed in these woods all those years ago.'

'I was mistaken,' said Vedic, attacking.

The woodsman's timing was off. Cernubus belted him in the stomach with the butt of his spear, sending Vedic airborne and his sword into a tree and out of reach. The god smiled as he drew back his spear.

Anya saw all this through a clouded veil of half-held tears. Danu must have kept him alive – why? She felt sick. The weight of Cernubus's words drove her to her knees.

Laos the Priest had responded to his king's command – Montu's grandfather – for a united continent and taken the armies of the Kurah under the banner of the stone god. Only the Shaanti had defeated them. Fifty years ago, within sight of the forest.

My grandfather, my people, she thought. *I have betrayed them all by trusting this Kurah demon, and now we are all dead.*

Anya felt an emotion rise in her. The feeling churned and burned in her gut, and she thought it might engulf her, until she found she could hold the fire, there in the centre of her chest. The emotion made everything sharp and focused. She looked down at her once-shaking hands that were now steady as a rock. She remembered the word her grandfather had taught her for this feeling. *Fury*.

Wind gusted through the glade, lifting the burnt detritus into the air and forcing Anya onto her feet and away from Vedic. She could only just make out Cernubus as the wind lashed her hair against her face, and even the god was forced to raise his hands to protect his eyes from the dust and ash.

The whirlwind emerged at breakneck speed from the forest, shooting over Vedic and striking Cernubus in the chest. The god was slammed to his back, sliding away from the woodsman. The force of the wind pushed everyone else to the ground. The tornado resolved itself into Pan, who stood clutching a long staff, his face lined with effort and his legs buckling into the thick, choking ash.

Vedic lifted his feet over his head and flicked up from the ground, running as best he could to his trapped blade and trying to work the weapon loose.

Anya could not bring herself to move. She found herself retching as Cernubus rolled to his feet again. His eyes, black as Danu's, were fixed on Pan. The two gods seemed as if they were drinking in the light from the glade.

'Priest!' shouted Pan, ignoring the more powerful god in favour of the gnarled woodsman.

Vedic turned.

Pan dropped to his knees, ignoring the advancing Cernubus, and pulled his staff apart to reveal the sword. Anya had been told by Falkirk that this sword had given her grandfather the scar that ran down his face from right to left. Few warriors had survived an encounter with the Butcher of Vremin. Thrace had, driving the Kurah back from Vremin with the fury of what he had seen in the sacked city. Still, it had not been enough. You couldn't undo what had been done.

The trickster threw the blade with the last of his strength, spinning the weapon end over end, describing an arc that Anya watched lead to Vedic. The woodsman stepped to one side, grabbing the hilt as the sword spun past him, his hands sliding onto the weapon with an ease born of a lifetime of practice, and a new man stood where Vedic had been.

Anya thought she had been afraid in the camp; she thought she had been frightened in Golgotha; but she hadn't known the meaning of the word until she saw the look in Vedic's eyes upon holding that weapon once more. It was a look of pure hunger that went beyond what she had seen on Danu, beyond what she had seen on her grandfather's face when he drank, and became as demonic as anything she had seen on Cernubus.

Cernubus's foot connected with Pan's chin, throwing the trickster god into Danu's cell. Caught in the magic field, Pan let go a strangled cry before falling to the ground. He lay still.

Vedic spun the sword from hand to hand; the blade moved from limb to limb as if it were an extension of his arms. Anya thought the woodsman looked taller, like he had been made more real and more present by the weapon. She didn't know any more if that was a good thing or not.

'What of your oath?' said Cernubus, spinning the shaft of his spear with one arm while inviting the woodsman to attack with his other.

'As you keep trying to remind me,' said Vedic, refusing to look at Anya, 'I am Laos. What is a priest without his staff?'

'Dead,' said Cernubus, stabbing the spear again.

The woodsman blocked, twisting his sword as he struck Cernubus's spear from his hand. He rolled past the god, his thick arms pushing the blade into a powerful backhanded thrust that ran through Cernubus from spine to belly.

The god stared down at the blade protruding from his chest. The woodsman turned to face Cernubus and swung his sword again, slicing the god's neck with a powerful stroke that should have beheaded him. Cernubus laughed, a wet, gargling sound that made Anya's stomach flip as she willed the god to fall, but he remained on his feet, wounds healing. Still, the woodsman fought on.

Vedic slammed the blade into the god's chest with all his power. Cernubus grabbed the weapon as the blade went in, holding the sword there, and capitalising on the woodsman's error – Vedic could not remove it. The god smiled, but flecks of blood traced his teeth, and sweat beaded his brow in a way that Vedic's strikes had not incurred moments earlier. He wasn't healing as quickly now. Vedic tried to twist the blade in Cernubus's chest, clearly hoping that the increased pain would force Cernubus to release the blade.

'That may not kill, but it does irritate,' said Cernubus, angry for the first time. 'I'd just as soon you stopped.'

The god raised his hand, sending magic arcing at the woodsman, striking him in the chest and knocking him across the clearing. Vedic fell on the ground, his charred tunic smoking where the spell had struck him. Anya knew he wasn't dead, because his chest was still moving, but she didn't expect him to get up again. Anya struggled to feel sorry for him.

Cernubus withdrew the blade from his torso and tested the weight of the weapon in his own hand. His chest healed as he swung the sword in lazy circles that cut the air with low whooshing noises. To her surprise, Anya watched Vedic as he tried to get to his feet, Cernubus advancing on him with his own sword.

'Now,' said the god. 'I grow bored – let us end this.'

Anya burned with her fury. The feeling lit her up as if she were a golem from one of Falkirk's stories, and she felt rage propel her forward. Anya stepped between Cernubus and the woodsman, her bow drawn. She wasn't sure why.

Cernubus stopped and smirked. 'Bored of you too, little one. Get out of the way.'

'You're not going any further.'

'He's not worth your life.'

Anya paused. 'Maybe not, but he's all I've got.'

'Anya,' said Cernubus, looking fixedly at the bow. 'You have nothing.'

The bow flamed in Anya's hands, forcing her to drop it. She pulled her blistered palms close to her chest instinctively. She sucked in air with painful, ragged gasps before Cernubus raised his free hand, lifting her off the ground as though he were clasping her around her throat, choking the life from her.

Vedic moaned behind her, clutching his scarred sword-arm as he writhed in pain, but it was as if he were far away, the sound muted and distorted.

'Now, little one,' said Cernubus, closing his upraised hand into a fist, 'Golgotha awaits.'

Beads of light shot into Anya's vision; the force of the spell that Cernubus was using to strangle her had tilted her head back, and all she could see was the night sky. The streaks of light looked like the sentinels had begun dancing for her pleasure alone.

'STOP,' said Vedic, clutching his arm, which felt like it was on fire.

His face contorted in agony. He suspected his own death was near and that he had failed, but still – he had to try.

Cernubus did not release Anya, but his gaze dropped to Vedic. The woodsman had managed to pull himself to his knees. His right arm hung limply from his side, and the god suddenly understood the curse that was burned into Vedic's limb.

'This is over, Vedic,' said Cernubus. 'You can't stand; you have no weapon; and this one's lungs are running out of oxygen. I don't have to kill you, do I? If she goes, so do you.'

Vedic smiled. 'I may not be able to stand, but I'm not weaponless. Not while you're doing that.'

Cernubus laughed.

That's better, thought the woodsman. *He doesn't understand.* The scar where the arrow had scored him weeks ago was torn open from the fight, bleeding and angry. The wound throbbed with a pain that shot up his arm and down his spine, growing with intensity as Anya's eyes flickered shut.

'I wonder what happens if you mix two curses,' said Vedic, smiling.

The hunter did not answer but tightened his spell's grip on Anya.

'Let's find out,' said the woodsman as he rolled for Danu.

Cernubus, one hand still controlling the spell choking Anya, threw Vedic's own sword at the woodsman with his other. The missile narrowly missed, piercing the ground by Vedic's feet. The forestal thrust his arm into the magic field trapping Danu and screamed.

All was light.

THE WOODSMAN'S arm shattered the cage.

The forest's power shot through Danu once more and returned her to full consciousness. The forest sang; much of it howled chords of pain as the wounds Cernubus had left on the land bit deep. Behind this, going deeper, was the strength of what remained. The power surged away from where the forest had been chained by Cernubus, and flowed to her – and it was good. Danu stepped over the fallen body of Pan.

Vedic pulled his pain-ravaged body towards his sword.

Danu had watched the fight from her cell. She'd stood as close to the cage as she could without being knocked from her feet by the magic field that trapped her. She had no doubt Cernubus intended to kill her.

The thought was not a welcome one. She did not fear dying for herself, but she would not be the only casualty: there was the forest, the land and the mortals. Cernubus would not be able to sustain humanity if he succeeded: eventually, the humans – even the Kurah – would also pass, crushed under the weight of another despotic god that wanted nothing to change. Cernubus was a fool who thought he could bend the world to his own will and escape the hand fate had dealt him. Cernubus had never understood.

The hunter released Anya. The girl dropped to the ground where she stood, not moving save for the faint rise and fall of her chest. Cernubus stepped back.

'It's too late, Danu. You're too weak.'

'If you're so powerful,' she replied, 'why am I still breathing?'

'Good question,' said Cernubus.

The god sent magic streaming at Danu. The magic arced around her, whipping her hair up around her face but leaving her unharmed. The hunter poured more into the attack. She laughed, sucking in the power, drawing the attack, sputtering to a halt.

'Is it my turn?' Danu asked.

Cernubus looked down at Anya, her eyes now open and looking up at him.

'It's her,' he said. 'She's fuelling your power. Somehow.'

'Wrong again.'

Danu struck. She unfurled her arms, releasing a single burst of power that flared brighter than the suns and lifted Cernubus from his feet, sending him crashing through the trees into the distance, ploughing up the scorched earth as he was shoved through the glade into the lake.

'Damn.'

Danu frowned, dismayed at the power of her own attack. In her mind's eye, she saw Cernubus emerge from the detritus of trees as a stag, limping as fast as he could towards the Kurah camp. The hunter had escaped.

'Am I dead?' asked Anya, looking up at Danu.

'No, child,' said Danu, kneeling. 'Far from it.'

'Good,' said Anya. 'I still have things to do.'

CHAPTER THIRTY

I T I S *the landscape of my childhood.*

The landscape of my escape. The Barrens stretch out as far as my eyes can see, and wherever my eyes fall, I can see there are Kurah warriors. I'm Anya, but in this dream I am Vedic, who is really Laos – the Kurah Butcher of Vremin and the man who nearly killed my grandfather, and who my grandmother spared for no reason I can think of. In my right hand, I am gripping a staff of worn wood, leaning on it, and my left hand is hooked on the breast of my dirt-encrusted, crimson-stained robe. I have a name now to go with the clothes. I cannot tell if the disgust is my own or his. The feeling is total.

From the heaving mass of soldiers, a rider approaches, his cloak swathed in purple and his head flecked with grey. I recognise the old Kurah king. The king's familiar rasp sets my teeth on edge, though I can't understand the words. He points at the forest, his meaning clear, and I shift my feet before replying. I turn to look back at the forest, a dark green monster that could swallow us whole without even blinking. The old king smiles wanly at me – he gestures at his men and shrugs. There is silence for a long while.

Two men detach themselves from the crowd. Archers, both of them, and they walk with reluctance over to where I stand. I speak, loud and clear. The king laughs, as do several warriors in the crowd. The two men do not. In fact, I notice that they do not look at or acknowledge anything, save me. Idly I wonder if they can see me as I actually am, as Anya. I walk towards the forest. I check that the two men are with me, and I wave them further apart, putting us in a loose formation as we enter the woods. The forest is cooler than the Barrens, refreshing in the muted sunlight beneath the canopy.

My companions are quiet now, searching the undergrowth for signs, looking across the trees as if hunting for someone, or perhaps for more than one person. I cannot tell. When the others speak, they do so in low, hissing tones. I find myself moving ahead, my body advancing with a speed that they cannot cope with. Deeper and deeper into the forest we go.

When I emerge into the clearing, I don't recognise it. Not at first. There is no cabin, no area set aside for the chopping of wood and no sign anyone lives there. I blink in the sun. Eyes unable to adjust. I'm knocked from my feet to my belly. Hard pain ignites in my shoulder, agony unlike any I have encountered in my life. As I try to get to my feet, I feel a new sensation over the pain, the thing protruding from my shoulder blade, pushing against the breeze, a new addition to my body. As I face my attacker, my fingers confirm that an arrow has embedded itself there.

The bowman, one of the men who came with me into the forest, has strung another arrow and has it locked on my chest. His aim is true, steady and calm, but his brow is sweating, his face grey with emotions that make my stomach churn with fear. The bowman doesn't just want me dead – he wants the killing to hurt. The wound in my shoulder is on fire, as if this were actually my body. I speak. I raise my arms slowly and insist harder – I do not need to understand my host's – Laos's – language to know he is daring them. I am inviting death. Briefly I wonder – if I die in this dream, will I die in the real world? Am I already dying, and this is just the strange echo of consciousness following a fatal wound? There is a faint memory that I am in trouble back where I was before I fell into this dream, that my neck should be hurting.

I don't see the wolf until she is on the bowman, just as he fires, sending the arrow into my thigh rather than my chest. I don't wait around to see what happens but limp deeper into the forest, staff forgotten, and I hunt around the trees for the other archer. The screams of the mauled bowman go on for a long time.

Eternity must feel like this, *I think. I have been walking for what feels like forever. I am deep in the forest. So deep I do not recognise a single landmark, and the only sound of life is the occasional cricket. But I can hear more. Something I desperately need. Water.*

Somewhere nearby, there is running water. I cannot tell from where, but Laos seems to know as I change direction purposefully. The forest is lighter here, the sun's tendrils penetrating deeper into the canopy as I emerge onto the edge of a small and rocky pool.

I freeze. I am not alone.

There is a woman in the water. She is naked, her skin gleaming in the sunlight, her hair spread in a peacock tail–like fan, black dreadlocks floating round her head. The woman is on her back, looking up at the sky, and as I feel my now-noticeably male body respond to the sight of her, I know this is Danu.

I drop to my knees, exhaling with pain from the arrow embedded in my leg. The undergrowth hides me, although I can still see down to the water. Below, in the pool, Danu pushes her feet under her and scans the edges of the water. She must have heard me. I press further down into the bushes.

She continues bathing, although I note, on the brief occasions I can bring myself to look, that she keeps her back to where I lie. The bathing seems to take her an eternity. My legs feel like rock by the time the goddess emerges from the water. That the pain has subsided is good, but I now feel sick from the loss of blood. When Danu does leave the water, she comes towards me, picking up a simple white robe that wraps round her with ease. Her skin is already dry from an unseen force.

The goddess looks directly at me.

'Master Priest,' she says. 'You're hurt. Please allow me to tend to your wounds.'

I raise myself up from the undergrowth. I hesitate, looking at the goddess for signs of duplicity, but eventually, pain wins out and I stumble down to where she stands.

'That's better,' she says.

Taking my arm, she leads me to a boulder on which to sit. I stumble a few times on the way to the rock, but her firm hand keeps me on my feet, despite my size.

'How do you speak my language?' I ask.

I can understand Laos clearly now.

'I know all tongues,' she says. 'But you are not speaking your language, and neither am I. You're speaking Shaanti.'

'Why?'

'I prefer Shaanti to your language,' she says. 'It sounds better.'

'Blasphemy,' I cough.

Danu laughs.

'Who are you?'

'Don't you know, Laos?' she replies.

'You know my name?'

'I know lots of things,' she replies. 'I know you'll die if I don't treat those wounds.'

'I am prepared,' I reply. 'My god waits for me. I have wrought his will across the land and have nothing to fear. I shall be with him in glory.'

'Are you so sure?'

We nod.

'Well, that's good,' she says, smiling again. 'Faith is good. My own followers do not believe in such things, but I can see it's a great comfort to you. Tell me, what have you done to serve your stone god?'

An image flashes in front of me: a burning city. I stood in its grounds in another dream, and I feel sick as I recall what I did. No. What I witnessed Laos do. This is just a dream. A nightmare. We look away.

'You must know,' I answer. 'You seem to know everything else.'

'You learn quickly,' she replies. 'Do you not want to tell me in your own words?'

'I ... I do not,' I reply. Is it Laos or me? I no longer know. 'Who are you? Are you a queen?'

She laughs. 'If my people had a queen, then I would be it, but they do not. If I told you who I am, then you would not believe me. Worse, you might try to serve your god one last time. That would be disappointing.'

'You're safe from me,' I reply, eyes unblinking. I can feel my stomach flipping over.

I have no idea why Danu would be different from anyone else, but I know my words are true. Perhaps she has bewitched him.

Danu smiles. 'I do believe I am. I am Danu.'

'That's a nice name,' I reply, like a dumb boy.

I am unable to hold her gaze.

'Isn't that the name of the Shaanti god?'

'Goddess, and not the only one. I have many kin,' she replies.

'You're a goddess?' I ask, my face twitching into a frown. 'You're a handsome lady, but you know too much, and I cannot listen to this blasphemy. There is only one real god, the stone god, and he does not walk the lower realms.'

Danu pushes us back onto the boulder, chanting softly under her breath, and she draws the arrow from my thigh – the wound closes as soon as the arrow is withdrawn, and leaves me staring. I paw at where the wound has been, looking for a scar, looking for anything that shows a sign of the injury, but there is nothing.

'How?'

Danu smiles. She leans in to grab the other arrow. I'm no longer aware of the second wound, just her body pressed against my leg, the swell of her breast on my shoulder as she clasps the arrow embedded in me and draws the shaft out in one swift motion. I gasp for air, but again there is no blood, no scar. The goddess looks at the arrow with disdain before casting it aside.

'What are you? A witch?'

'You know,' she replies. 'You just don't like it.'

'But ...' I stand.

I listen, unable to look away or close my eyes. I can hear the moment of clarity in my ... in Laos's voice. I can hear the horror that is so close to what I feel but so much worse when passed through my voice. 'If you're a god ... then ... what of my ... what have I ...?'

I drop to my knees. I am in Laos's memories all at once. His entire past that is not mine collides in my skull. The city screams all about me; the light burns my eyes; the girl falls from the tower; the boy looks at me with eyes falling dull with death; and the ghosts of the dead sing out as one. Laos killed them all. Vedic killed them all.

'All the things I've done in my life!'

Danu does not move to me. She nods. She's enjoying this, and I realise I am also enjoying the woodsman's pain. I want him to feel like this. I want him to feel the weight of the ghosts on his back, of the broken lives, of my grandfather – wysgi-laden breath gagging me as I drag him home after another night of drinking. I want him to hear every scream lest he forgets. I want to hear every scream lest I forget.

'Yes, Laos,' Danu answers. 'All those people, all those innocents. Their blood soaking the ground, their cries circling you like crows wherever you go. All those lives broken, the detritus you left behind. All of it for nothing. Predicated on a lie.'

'I didn't know.'

'Yes, you did,' she says, finally drawing close to me. Grabbing my chin, forcing my eyes to hers. 'You knew.' She looks deep into me. 'You ... are not as I expected. Is that what my sister saw?'

I try to look away. I can't.

'No,' I reply. 'I didn't know.' But my voice sounds hollow.

A beat passes. Gazes lock.

'What should I do?' I ask. 'Should I worship you instead?'

Danu does not turn away. There is hunger in that look, contradicting her words. 'I have no need of fanatics, intoxicating though they are.'

'What should I do?' I plead.

'I could kill you,' she says, tilting her head. 'To tread here is a death sentence to most men.'

'What would happen to me then?'

'You'd be dead – whatever do you mean?'

'You're a goddess,' I reply. 'Surely you know what lies beyond.'

Danu laughs. 'Ah, no, I do not. Beyond the trip across Golgotha, I know little. Perhaps there is a paradise awaiting the just and a hell awaiting the wicked – in which case, you, I fear, are in trouble. I suspect I would be too. Perhaps there is paradise for all. Perhaps there is a hell for all. Perhaps there is nothing. No god knows.'

'But you are immortal?'

'Compared to you? Perhaps, but not in the truest sense. All things die. I am no different, and I don't know the secrets beyond any more than your own god would, if he stood in my place.'

'I will not beg for my life.'

'No, I know you won't, but you're afraid. I can smell it on you. Like all the other apes, you fear the dark. Sometimes I think the universe would be better if you'd remained in the trees and left us in the shadows.'

'I want to make things right,' I reply. 'While there is still time.'

'You can't,' she says. 'What's done is done. There is only now and the choice of what to do. The dead do not come back.'

'Please ... I need to repent ...'

'I know you do, foolish Kurah. Thinking you can do whatever you want and a sorry will make it all right. How many would it take? A hundred? A thousand? To save as many as you took? It is comforting because it abdicates you of responsibility. You can never undo this stain.'

The goddess is glaring at us now.

'Please ...'

She looks away. 'Will you do what I wish?'

'Yes.'

'Whatever I ask?'

'Yes!'

'Then that's a start.'

Danu leads me into the treeline. I try to wake up, to no avail. I am forced to watch, to feel everything. I cannot tell what is me any more and what is Laos. The night is a lone one.

CHAPTER THIRTY-ONE

THE PAIN WAS like the feeling of cold steel in her chest.

The thain had taken a blade through her left lung once when she was in her twenties, in a brief skirmish with the Kurah, before the witch-warrior, Gobaith, became her bodyguard. They had thought she would die. The feeling of the steel when the blade was in her had been almost as painful as the feeling in her chest today. She had sent the healer away, despite his protestations. If she was going to die, there was little he could do now save give her tinctures that would dull her pain and blunt her mind. She would see them safe before she took the long walk across Golgotha.

The rain drove down on them as if it were the third player in the Kurah axis. The weather was bitter and cold, and smelt faintly of magic and left the thain with the feeling that more was happening back at the forest than she could imagine. She had regretted sending Bene as soon as she had done it, and now, slumped in her saddle and soaked to the skin, she wondered if it had been a fatal mistake. He was the only one she could trust, the only one she could conceivably hand over power to now that Jeb was dead. *What if I die before there is another?*

Vort rode back to her. The thain had let herself fall back to the centre of the spearhead formation the army was in – better for her to be seen amongst them than hiding at the front or the back. The former general leant over from her horse to try and make herself understood.

'We must make camp!'

The thain stared at her. She shook her head. 'We must get to the coast.'

'That'll do us no good if everyone dies before we get there,' shouted Vort back. The storm was heavy.

'How many?' asked the thain, mentally totting up the deaths she already knew about.

'Forty,' said Vort. 'And there's a father and child not in a good way at the rear of the convoy.'

The thain nodded. 'You may make camp.'

Vort nodded back, tight-lipped, and the thain had the overwhelming sense, not for the first time, that she did not hold with the thain's habit of talking to everyone as if they were the same. The thain did not care very much what Vort thought. She was far more concerned with where her shadow was, and if she had identified the defector in her midst. She noticed Vort staring at her.

'Is there anything else, Major?'

'Milady,' said Vort. 'The council recognises your long service but is wondering if you might join us for a discussion over the rest of your plan.'

'Major Vort,' she replied, her voice cold. 'The terms of our agreement are clear, and these are war circumstances. I have full control.'

'In your current condition?'

'What condition is that?' she barked back, too weary to mince her words. 'I demoted you. What concern is it of yours?'

Just at that moment, the thain thought she could smell citrus trees, a strange thing to scent in the middle of a storm, and the thought distracted her from Vort. The lady looked confused.

'You're clearly exhausted, milady. You are no longer young, and no one would think any less of you if you shared your burden.'

The thain looked hard at Vort. Someone must have put her up to this, but who? The thain was having trouble thinking in a straight line, and the rain was making it hard to see. She coughed. There was blood in her mouth. The world was bending in peculiar patterns, and it felt like the rain was washing everything.

Vort spoke. The words sounded like she was speaking through her cloak.

The thain tumbled into the soft mud, where the earth swallowed her up.

'IS SHE GOING TO DIE?'

The thain did not know how long she had been unconscious, only that she was lying in her makeshift bed, in her tent, and the sound of rain on canvas was fierce. There were at least three people she could sense in the room from smell alone, but she refused to open her eyes or try to sit up. She had no idea what was going on. Was she a prisoner?

'How many people saw her fall?' asked Vort.

'Only a handful,' replied one of Bene's men who had stayed behind. She couldn't recall his name. That was terrible.

'Is she going to die?' repeated the speaker of the council.

'No,' said Yorg. 'Not today. She has pushed herself too far and has a severe infection in her lungs.'

This was the agreed party line if she had an attack of her fatal condition while in public. Yorg was briefed to give only this information, regardless of her actual condition, and so she had no idea if she had additional injuries. She didn't feel like she had. The aches were just the usual chest pain and the constant faint taste of copper at the back of her throat.

'Are we in charge yet?' asked the speaker.

'No,' said Vort. 'You are not. If this persists, we may need to look at this with the loremasters and determine if the council can take over, but even if there is a precedent, you would not carry the warriors with you yet.'

The thain felt a surge of gratitude towards Vort. She may have been a bit handy with her knife, but she was honest and true. She needed more like her. She opened her eyes.

'How long?' she asked.

'Milady!' said Yorg and the speaker together.

The thain pushed herself up on her elbows. The tent was full of not just the three she had heard but the whole of the council. She attempted a faint smile. 'Am I dead that all my friends and colleagues are spread before me?'

'Milady,' said Vort. 'We feared for your life.'

'Well,' she said. 'My life is fine. You may return to your duties.'

'Milady,' said the speaker. 'We must discuss what we do next. The ports are still a number of days away, and the people are failing.'

'There are no changes to your orders,' said the thain. 'Save that Vort is returned to her rank.'

Vort gave her a nod of appreciation.

The thain did not look away from the council members staring at her as if she had gone mad. Her chest burned, but she did not show any pain.

'Milady,' protested the speaker.

'Are you challenging me?' asked the thain, reaching for her sword.

The speaker raised her hands. 'No, milady.'

'Get out,' hissed the thain. 'All of you.'

The ruler glared, straight-backed, until only the healer remained and she was able to fall back into the pillows, her eyes streaming from the pain. Yorg rushed over to her.

'How long can you buy me?' she gasped as he looked her over.

'You will be dead before the alignment,' said the healer, his voice cracking. 'The disease is in the final stages.'

The thain closed her eyes. The final betrayal. Perhaps all leaders craved just another hour on the stage to get their meaning across. Or maybe this was just a situation that made her feel as if she couldn't go yet.

'I should get the council in again,' said Yorg. 'They're right, we need to make preparations.'

'No,' said the thain, sitting back up. 'The council will not lead.'

'They are the people we chose,' said the healer. 'There is no heir – who else?'

The thain shook her head. 'No. They are the people who desired to rule and have proven themselves unworthy. Bring me parchment and a pen.'

'What will you do?'

The thain smiled. 'It will be random and temporary, save when there is war; then Bene or whoever holds his post will lead.'

Yorg passed the thain pen and parchment.

'Those chosen will not understand what they are dealing with.'

'That's the point.'

MONTU WATCHED as Zoren danced and shuffled his cant.

The mage's body was covered in soil. His eyes shone and his hair was growing white and thin as he expended himself into the glowing gate of energy on the edge of the camp. The battalion shuffled uneasily between the king and the portal. They disliked this display of power, and they feared the return of Cernubus. This irritated Montu in his bones. They should have been talking about how their king was starting to leverage the same power.

'You understand your job, Commander?' asked the king.

The warrior looked at Montu. He nodded. 'Leave enough alive to bring back and witness the god's sacrifice. Kill everyone else.'

Zoren let forth a scream and appeared to fold into himself. A gust of wind blew him to dust, leaving only the portal that looked out on a rain-strewn landscape fifty leagues away.

THE ATTACK STARTED with a trebuchet bolt.

The missile arced through the storm and landed on one of the Shaanti smiths' tents, crushing the occupants and sending confusion through the camp. More hissed down and shook the ground. The Kurah hit the Shaanti line with their full force, and all was chaos.

THE ALARM WAS an insistent ringing of the warning bells.

The thain put the half-finished parchment to one side. She could smell smoke despite the rain and hear screams as people panicked. Cursing, the leader moved as fast as she could from her bed, which was not quickly, and began pulling on her armour. It felt looser than it should. The healer stuck his head through the canvas opening to her tent.

'Do not attempt to fight,' he said. 'We will see them off.'

'It's the Kurah,' said the thain. 'It is my job.'

'Your job is to stay alive,' replied Yorg.

The shadow moved him gently to one side and stepped into the tent.

'Leave us,' she said. 'I will see milady is taken care of.'

The thain did not watch him leave but turned to pick up her sword.

'Do not try to dissuade me,' she said. 'I would go out with steel in my hand.'

The thain attempted to raise her sword. She felt it lift off the chair it was resting on, but the weight pulled the point down and into the soil.

'How is that working for you?' asked the shadow, not unkindly.

The thain felt herself go down to one knee.

'I have so little time left,' she whispered. 'Let me choose how I die.'

The shadow came over to her and knelt by the thain, cupping her head in her hands. 'Why?'

She looked the shadow in her eye. 'Because the Shaanti must go on, or all my life has been a waste.'

'Everything ends,' said the shadow. 'Perhaps it is just our time.'

The thain dropped her sword and put her hands to the shadow's. 'What have you found?'

The shadow took her hands from the thain and pulled the leader into her lap, hugging her as if she were a child.

'You were right, of course. There is another traitor, and she was working with Golan.'

'What did you find?' whispered the thain.

The shadow pulled a bundle from within her cloak, spreading the fabric out on their legs. The ground shook. There was screaming all around, but once again the noise seemed to the thain like it was coming from a vast way away. The cloth contained shards of glass that glittered in the candlelight. She felt cold. The sensation wasn't the disease.

'Is that a signal?'

'It was,' said the shadow. 'I destroyed the signal where I found the cursed device. I doubt she has been foolish enough to use it.'

'Could you tell who the signal belonged to?'

The shadow flinched. Only a mage could trace the origin of the signal. They had never spoken openly of her smattering of magical power. It was just understood that the shadow could get into places others could not, and in the hints of power in the time they spent alone. There was no time left for subtlety.

The shadow nodded.

'Who?'

'Vort,' she replied.

The thain felt the world fall away again. *Vort?* She had lost all her senses. She had taken Vort at her word; she didn't question it – why else would the general disobey her wishes and slay Golan? Vort, who had been her rock since that moment. Vort, who could have quietly knifed her as she fell from her horse. Vort, who even now was leading her forces as the enemy attacked under her invitation.

'I must go. I restored her rank,' she muttered, trying to stand. Finding her legs wouldn't work, she toppled onto her belly.

'What's happening?' she found herself muttering over and over as the shadow clutched her to her chest, crying again and again.

'Muriel,' the shadow whispered. 'Muriel.'

The thain fell quiet at her name. She lifted her hands up to her shadow's eyes and softly said the shadow's true name back. 'Sevlen.'

'I am not as strong as the witch-warrior,' Sevlen replied in low tones. 'But I can try.'

The thain tried to scream for her to stop, but it was too late, and the dark rolled over Muriel like a spring storm.

THEY WERE SCREAMING STILL when she woke.

The thain had no idea how much time had passed. The pain in her chest had subsided to a low ache, and she found she could move her legs again. No one was holding her now. She shifted. Someone was lying next to her. She pushed herself up to her hands and knees to look, and her heart broke into splinters. An old woman lay dead by her side, impossibly ancient, her hair white like bone and her skin wrinkled and cracked like old leather. She was dressed in the shadow's clothes.

'Sevlen,' she said, over and over again. 'Not you. Not you.'

The thain couldn't see. Her eyes were streaming tears. She felt the power that her shadow had poured into her to stave off the illness, and with the magic came knowledge, all that Sevlen, her shadow, had seen in her time and remembered and felt. Sevlen's voice whispered inside Muriel.

Use this.

The thain saw her general concealing the signal. She saw her slaughter Golan. She saw the god fighting Jeb. She felt the anger burning in her like Atos, the brightest of the sentinels. She placed the shadow down gently, covering her with a blanket from her bed, and picked up her sword. She did not bother with her helmet. Looking up at the mirror by her bed, she cut the plait from her hair as a sign of mourning and left the tent.

Vort was standing on high ground, barking orders at the warriors and avoiding any fighting. The thain did not wait for Vort to notice her. There were a few council members nearby, those who did not wish to fight, and most of her best commanders, who were attempting to convince the general to change course. Muriel did not bother with the battle. The first job was the cancer at the heart of her people.

'Vort ab Rain!'

The rabble stopped and turned. Vort looked at her.

'Vort ab Rain,' she yelled. 'You have betrayed me and our people.'

'What is she talking about?' asked the speaker.

Vort shook her head. 'No, madam. You have that honour. You should have surrendered to the Kurah thirty years ago.'

Vort drew her sword and came down to meet her.

'And you should have challenged me if you wanted my seat.'

'But I don't,' she sighed. 'I just want peace.'

'Peace is only possible between equals,' said the thain. 'Montu wants servants.'

'I want us to live.'

The thain gestured around at the burning camp and the fighting. 'How is that working for you?'

'Where are the civilians?'

The thain smiled. She had done something right at least. In the event of an attack, she had asked Bene's remaining warriors to lead the majority of those who couldn't fight and those who were caring for them with Gor-Iven into the catacombs that lined the hidden road. She had told no one else, her dwindling intuition keeping her from trusting anyone outside of her own guard.

'You don't need to worry about that,' she said, and attacked.

Vort parried fast. She spun round and mounted her own attack. She missed with the blade but managed to graze the thain's head with her foot as she kicked up and round. The blow caught the thain by surprise but didn't do much else, and Vort lost her leg below the knee when she tried again. The thain sliced her blade clean through at the point where Vort's shin plate ended for her knee to bend. Vort dropped her blade, falling to the mud and clutching at the wound. The thain did not give her a chance to speak. The thain brought her sword down through Vort's skull. The general shuddered once and fell still.

The thain glared up at her audience. 'General Vort was in league with the Kurah.'

'Thank the gods you are recovered,' said Commander Wobyn, relieved as she embraced the thain. 'The Kurah are trying to trap us in a pincer, attacking both ends of the road.'

'Show me.'

They led her up to the top of the high ground. There were two fronts. One line at the south of the camp where, improbably, the Kurah had attacked from Vikrain. That route had been clear only the day before. It should not have been possible. The thain pushed the conundrum from her mind – they were here regardless. She looked to the second, northern front where another Kurah force was attacking.

'How did they attack the rear?'

Wobyn frowned. 'They appear to have mages, possibly from Delgasia. There is a portal in amongst their trebuchets.'

'Are they using magic now?'

Wobyn shook her head. 'Mercifully, no.'

'There is no mercy in the Kurah,' said the thain. 'If they are not using spells, then they have used up their magic. Our first piece of luck.'

'The Kurah from the north are more tired than those at the south,' said Wobyn. 'The line there is holding better than the north. We wanted to move our forces south and defend the line.'

The thain nodded. This made sense. The threat was from the south – a fresh force was a real danger, whereas the northern force, even though they might have more men, were overextended and tired from the coast. But then what? The coast was gone. Even if they held the southern force, they could not defeat the northern.

'They have us trapped,' said the speaker. 'It is time to parley.'

The thain raised her sword and placed the point at the throat of the speaker. 'Utter another word, and I will end you. I cannot be certain all of Golan and Vort's treachery was accomplished alone.'

Think. What would the witch-warrior have done? There was only one option. The Kurah do not take captives. If there was no escape to the north and no retreat back to Vikrain, there was only one option that would give the civilians a chance to survive. If the civilians headed south-west, up into the hills, they might find unoccupied ports that they could sail from.

'Commanders, Generals,' said the thain. 'Our choices are limited. I feared this betrayal was imminent, hence the measures I took with those who cannot fight – but for them to escape, we must now do the unthinkable. We must take the portal from the Kurah.'

'Why?' asked Wobyn.

'Because then we are going to attack the Kurah at the forest's edge, and we're going to string that Kurah king up by his guts.'

The council went pale. The warriors didn't look much better.

'How are we going to do that?' asked Wobyn. 'We can't even hold the southern force back.'

'We will smash the northern army,' said the thain, 'making it look like we are making a retreat. We will fall away into the catacombs – no one will reveal what they see there on pain of death. We'll loop back and attack the Kurah from their flank, where they will be weakest because they do not know this land. They will not expect it.'

'It might work,' conceded Wobyn. 'But we will not last long against the Kurah at the edge of the forest. Danu cannot help us.'

'We might do better than you think with the element of surprise and the squad I sent under General Bene. They will arrive before us.'

'Any dissenters?'

Some of the council looked ready to speak up, but a quick glance at Vort's body dissuaded them.

'Good. Tell your warriors, when the horn sounds, they are to attack north with everything they have and only defend against the south. When the horn sounds a second time, they are to make for the catacombs.'

The thain dismissed them with a wave of her hand and turned back to review the battle. The battle was not going well, and she wished she could be in any of dozens of places, fighting.

You know this is a trap, came the shadow's voice in her head. *They just want an excuse to bring you to the forest. Montu is not foolish enough for such a basic error.*

Yes, I know. She answered the voice with her own. *I am counting on it.*

CHAPTER THIRTY-TWO

THERE WAS a man looking down at Anya.

The Shaanti's hand floundered for her dagger before she remembered he was not a man at all but a god, Pan, and no threat. The concern and relief that was etched on his face left her guilty. The memories of the fight slammed into the front of her skull and rolled right over that emotion, taking her out the other side to angry. Pan should have told her. Breathing hurt.

'Cernubus?' Anya asked, her voice cold.

'Danu ... she ... he's gone,' said Pan, eyeing her with concern. 'Don't move. You're wounded.'

The god placed his hand on the top of her breastbone and closed his eyes. Anya felt the heat from the magic form under his fingers like a pool of warm water; the spell seeped into her chest and sought out the tributaries of her pain. Where the magic passed, the pain eased. Pan removed his hand.

Anya sat up.

The scars of Danu's attack on Cernubus were obvious: a large person-sized welt in the tangled mess of burnt detritus, scars built upon scars. The goddess stood in the clearing. The fight was almost over.

How long have I been unconscious? Anya thought.

Danu turned to look at Anya. Anya felt her heart pound in her chest as the goddess's eyes passed over her, cheeks flushing with another's memories. Danu's gaze lingered only a moment, seeing all, before moving on over Pan and towards the woodsman.

Anya stood.

Vedic seemed to sense Danu's gaze approaching and raised a bloody head to meet her eyes, the look on his face not dissimilar from those in the crowd Anya had dreamt of in her nightmares. Anya held her breath without realising it. She could kill him. But instead, a little bit of Anya died as she watched the goddess and the Priest, their gaze entwined.

'Come here, Master Priest, so I may tend thy wounds,' Danu said. The look on her face was that of a thirsty woman who had been given water.

Vedic smiled. A tired grin, but unlike others Anya had seen, the smile met his eyes, and there he was, struggling to his feet ... and bowing. Vedic had given everything he had against Cernubus; Anya knew what it meant for him to stand there with the goddess again. Still, she couldn't square the man she saw before her with the leaking nightmares that had invaded her skull for weeks. The toll his deeds had wrought on her family and kin were unforgivable.

'Should I say my line?' he said, spitting a stream of blood to the ground. 'For I cannot regret anything I have done here today.'

He's making a joke. He's joking about the things he did. I will kill him. Anya went to step forward, but Pan put a hand gently on her arm.

'No,' Danu replied, her head dipping in acknowledgement. 'You cannot.'

Vedic's legs buckled.

Anya felt herself flinch towards him in spite of herself. She wanted to catch him, and she only stopped because Danu got there first. *What do I do?* There was no answer from either version of her mother's voice in her mind now. This was just her.

Vedic dropped to the ground, and in the same instant, Danu caught him. She held him up with a strength belying her size and hugged him so tight her hands looked luminescent.

'I did not think to see you again,' whispered Vedic.

'I told you that you would,' answered Danu, the magic flowing from her into him.

Anya blinked. The goddess was staring at her again.

Anya struggled to look at Danu – it hurt Anya's chest to gaze at her too long. There was an energy behind Danu's eyes probing Anya, testing her, demanding something of her, and she wasn't sure what. She was met with the desire not to anger this being who seemed so much older, and more powerful, than any of the strange creatures she had encountered since she ran from the camp. She could not bring herself to look at Vedic at all.

'Now Cernubus is dead,' Anya said, 'time is short – we must get to the camp and free the children before the Kurah realise ...'

Pan was staring at her in shock.

'What?'

Vedic's head was bowed in sorrow. He spoke. 'Cernubus is not dead.'

Danu tilted her head, her gaze not moving from Anya. 'I am afraid he escaped.'

Anya faltered. *Cernubus is still alive.* Suddenly the words she wanted to say to Danu, the plea she wanted to make, foundered amongst the profound sense that she was about to take a step she could not undo, that events would move beyond her control. Pan's hand was on her back. Her body ached. The children seemed a very long way away, and exhaustion so very close. She sat down on a log, unsure what to do or say.

Danu set Vedic on his feet like he weighed less than a toddler. She placed a hand to his face, looking for reassurance that he was now able to stand, and it made Anya want to throw her sword at the Kurah scum. Danu turned to her. She looked half-amused and half-worried, as if she could hear what Anya was thinking. Anya realised she almost certainly could. This made her flush again, and in turn it made her angry.

'Time is short,' said Danu, stepping to Anya. She knelt by the girl. She kissed Anya's forehead. 'What would you ask of me?'

'Will you help me stop him? He's going to kill them all,' asked Anya, her voice hard.

Danu was silent for a moment. 'I cannot interfere directly now he is gone from here: the damage would be worse than if he manages his sacrifice.'

'How is saving the Butcher of Vremin not interfering directly?'

Vedic flushed. Pan flinched.

Danu laughed. 'Oh, you're brave, little one.'

Anya's head dropped, her hands clenched. 'What aid do you offer?'

'I will get you into the camp,' said Danu, placing a warm hand on her shoulder. 'I will do my best to ensure you have the support of the Shaanti and Tream army. Already the Tream have attacked the encampment at the behest of Pan, due in no small part to the way you fought for Meyr.'

Anya blinked. 'There aren't enough of them.'

'She's right,' said Pan, sitting down next to Anya. 'It will take more than just the Tream. The thain is too far away to reach them in time.'

'Come with me,' said Anya, taking Danu's hand without thinking. 'Help me save them. You won't corrupt us. You are good.'

Danu closed her eyes as if Anya's words were blows. 'Oh, child. If I could, I would, but your kind has forgotten what the old times were like. Your ancestors sacrificed to me, to Pan, to the others back when we crawled out of the dark time. You should see how life is in the lands beyond the sea, where our cousins still walk amongst their believers, from engineer to the laughing man. They are not as close to the source as we are, but their power is enough for the humans to slaughter themselves in ever-larger numbers.'

'We're not like that here,' implored Anya, meaning it. The goddess looked torn, as if she might change her mind.

'You don't understand,' said Pan, his eyelids drooping at the memory. 'The blood from the sacrifice ... we were addicted to the belief that flows from spilt blood.'

Anya looked at the trickster. There was no sign of duplicity on his face. The gods had held so much promise, so much hope. Now they were bowing out from confronting their own kind. *How did you kill a god?* She looked at Vedic, who was still staring at Danu as if he were lost in a dream. *How did you kill a forestal?* If there was nothing else she could do, there would be revenge on this man. She drew her sword and pointed the blade at the woodsman.

'What about you?'

Vedic looked at her, confused. He thought Anya meant to fight him there, with the gods present to witness his destruction. The thought had crossed her mind, but she had concluded that there was no way she could get to him without Danu stopping her.

'Will you help save the Shaanti children from your so-called king?'

Vedic looked stunned. 'You would trust me?'

Anya laughed. 'No. I just want to show Danu what you are really like.'

Vedic flinched as if struck.

'Will you help?'

'Why does it have to be me?' he asked.

'It doesn't. I might be able to free them on my own.'

Vedic looked at Pan, who shook his head. The forestal looked up at the black above, the pale moonlight and the two visible sentinels moving into vertical alignment in their slow millennia-long dance above. By dawn, they would be there like a chain of light across the sky, meeting the suns as they rose over the horizon, and the alignment would give Cernubus the power he needed.

'I saved your life more than once, did I not?' asked Anya.

Vedic nodded.

'You owe me a *juren*,' said Anya, using the Kurah word for 'blood debt'.

Vedic held her gaze now. 'I am no longer Kurah.'

'I saw you with that,' said Anya, nodding at his sword, the Eagle's Claw. 'There's plenty of Laos left.'

Vedic looked down. Danu put her hand on his shoulder.

'I will help you,' said Pan.

Danu glared. 'You will not.'

Vedic shook his head, rubbing his left arm as if in pain. 'No.'

They were all looking at him now.

'It has to be me,' said Vedic.

Anya did not know what to say. She had expected him to refuse, to embark on his mantra that he was not a nice man, and for Danu to see him for what he was, a lying butcher. Instead, she saw a gnarled warrior, weary and bloody, lifting himself to offer service to her. She didn't know who disgusted her more – Laos or herself.

'How do you know?' asked Pan of Vedic. The trickster was cross.

Vedic looked at the two gods for the first time without any semblance of shame. 'Because I have seen the coming battle before.'

Anya could feel her sword wavering. Could she trust him? Could she trust any of them?

'I am responsible for my own actions, and you have every right to hate me for what I did to your people ... to your grandfather ... to your grandmother for that matter. Thrace was like many of the warriors on both sides, a brave man in impossible times.'

Anya felt the world spin. She wanted to strike at him; she wanted to ask him about her grandfather; she wanted to ask for his help enlisting Danu – she wanted to run away.

Vedic continued. 'You have no reason to trust me, but if you do, I will help you save those children.'

Danu's eyes closed, and to Anya it looked as if someone had slipped a blade in between her vertebrae. Pan held out his arm for her to steady herself. When Danu looked again, her eyes were wet.

Anya felt her anger flash.

'Are you sure?' Danu asked.

'I am,' said Vedic, turning to Anya. 'If Anya will have me.'

Anya did not answer. She wasn't sure what to think. In her head, she wanted to say no, to say she didn't trust him and would be safer going into the camp on her own than with the likes of him. In her heart, she felt like, for the first time, there was hope of success. Had they not gone into Golgotha together and returned? They made a good team, and she hated herself for it.

'What about Cernubus? We can't kill a god.'

'All things can be killed,' said Pan, picking up the woodsman's sword. 'All things can be defeated, even the hunter. If he can be weakened, he can be destroyed.'

Anya recalled the discussion in the Cordon on how to kill a god. Did the legend of the Priest and the sword have enough belief behind it to counter the hunter's dark magic?

Anya looked at Vedic, staring back at her. 'This doesn't mean I've forgotten.'

Vedic smiled. 'Good. You'll be my conscience and able to stop me, should I go too far.'

Danu spoke. 'It is decided.'

Anya looked at the sentinels above, swimming into the silver light of dawn. 'It is nearly time.'

'Grab the rest of your weapons,' said Vedic. 'We need to move. Do you have armour for her?'

Danu nodded.

Anya frowned as Vedic went to leave the clearing. 'Where are you going?'

Vedic looked back at Anya and then flashed a look at Pan. 'To change. Time for the Priest to return to his flock. I have one last sermon to deliver.'

CHAPTER THIRTY-THREE

Dawn picked at the horizon.

Anya tightened the jerkin that Danu had given her. The clothes were Shaanti warrior uniform, scuffed and worn, but a close enough fit that she only had to use a strip of her old, torn clothes to pull the jerkin in at the waist. The thick leather and light plating on the arms would make it hard for anything other than a direct strike to get through. She checked her movement to ensure no fatal restriction, stretching her arms and legs in a series of slow-motion strikes and kicks. Anya didn't want to know where the armour had come from. Enough of her people had died under the boughs of these trees. Perhaps if her mother had not left, Anya could have worn her grand-mother's armour, but her mother had taken that on her one-way quest.

Slowly Anya stretched out, attempting to keep her muscles loose despite the tension that was creeping up from her gut. The smell of burnt wood and recent death undercut everything, but over the top of the stench, there was a faint scent of pine, ready to push away the damage, promising the forest was stronger. Anya tested the edge of her blade. It felt sharp, but still she took the stone she had been using and continued working the edge.

'Careful,' said Vedic. He must have been standing in the treeline, watching. 'You'll blunt it.'

Anya stopped. She did not look back at him. She could not bring herself to.

'Are you ready?' she asked, her voice flat.

'Yes,' he said, adding, 'Danu is waiting to send us.'

'Why are you doing this?' she asked, still not turning. 'Are you trying to atone for your wrongs?'

He didn't answer right away.

'I'm not sure that is possible,' he said. He sounded tired. 'I'm fairly certain it isn't. No, I'm not trying to atone for anything.'

It had not escaped Anya's notice that she had the chance to kill the woodsman in the coming battle, if she wanted to, and there would be nothing anyone else could do. All such thoughts vanished at her first glimpse of Vedic. She very nearly dropped her sword. Her heart beat so loud in her ears she thought she was going to pass out. She wanted to run, but her legs had ceased to work.

Vedic was standing in a robe that might once have been white but was now a dull shade of pinkish brown, flecked with yellow age spots. His hood was down, and his face looked cold and stern now he was back in his old uniform. The certain knowledge that the robe was stained with the blood of Shaanti didn't help her uneasiness. He was the figure straight out of her childhood nightmares – the Butcher of Vremin, the Kurah king's right hand.

'The Priest once more,' said Anya, her voice cracked, fear giving way to anger.

She held her blade point first at his chest. Vedic did not move.

'I will not,' Anya said, and lowered her blade. 'For the slim chance I will trade with you, demon.'

'Your blade did not shake,' said Vedic, his tone approving.

Anya looked down at her hands. They weren't trembling. The fury she felt towards Vedic, the utter righteousness of her anger, had bound them in steel.

Vedic gestured at his robe. 'This is to help us get through the camp, to weaken Cernubus. They will, at worst, mistake me for one of their own, and at best, they may simply flee before us, thinking me a ghost. Of course, I am neither ghost nor demon, just a man.'

'No more damning words did any demon speak,' said Danu, stepping from the trees.

Anya shifted her gaze to Danu. 'And you, how can you bear to be in his presence, let alone lie with him?'

Danu smiled. 'Ah, little Anya. Do not rush to judge what you do not understand.'

Anya flushed. She looked at the goddess. 'Maybe you and I will have a reckoning when this is said and done.'

'The Shaanti are nearing the Kurah,' said Danu, ignoring the threat. 'You must go soon, or the moment will be lost.'

Danu did not require pipes or chanting to realise her power. The goddess stepped forward from them, sweeping her right arm in a high arc, and where the limb passed, the world folded. The Kurah camp flickered; men ran for the lines; alarm bells rang; fires were spreading; and all around was the sound of people dying. The battle raged.

'Time for me to go home,' said Vedic. 'Sword.'

Danu threw the sword in its scabbard. Sheathed, it looked like a wooden staff to the untrained eye. 'Go with luck, Vedic.'

Vedic dipped his head in acknowledgement. He seemed on the edge of speaking, but Anya was relieved when he appeared to think better of it.

'Remember what I told you,' said Pan.

Vedic nodded.

Anya said nothing to either god. She couldn't trust herself to speak with care, and she felt little in the way of gratitude. Her heart thumped like an angry fist. She could feel the adrenaline pumping through her veins and the whispering of her ghosts at her shoulders. She stepped forward, and together they walked into the camp.

HOGARTH ROLLED under the swinging sword, severing the man's arm with a smooth back-swing, blood hot in his mouth from where the warrior had caught him with his fist.

The king wiped the dead man's blood from his eyes, taking advantage of finding a brief pause to look back across the field at the battle. His men were cutting down more of the enemy to each of their own casualties – their night-time vision was an early advantage over the Kurah. It wasn't enough. The reinforcements weren't panicked: their own king had made his presence known and calmly reorganised the line, the coming dawn lighting the way. The Kurah had begun casting their own arrows at the edge of the forest. He ducked under another swing from an opportunist Kurah who fell to the Tream's riposte, and he was back in the battle: slash, block, kill, step. Slash, block, parry and roll – and kill.

'We must pull back.'

Hogarth looked over at the warrior who had spoken to him. A man he had trusted since boyhood, and for a moment he was Akyar, but Hogarth remembered Akyar was with the archers at the forest's edge. They had barely spoken since his return. Hogarth felt his resolve harden even as his own archers unleashed another volley. Akyar had increased the range to avoid Tream, pushing the archers to the edge of their ability, and the arrows fell with devastating effect on the newly reorganised Kurah line. Hogarth looked back and saw the archers moving out from the trees in order to reach the reinforcements. Akyar's warriors were now exposed to the Kurah's returning fire.

The Kurah king could be heard barking at his own archers to take their Tream counterparts out.

'To me!' shouted Hogarth.

The realisation that the Shaanti had not arrived at the battle had fallen on him like a felled tree, and his only thought was to save his people. They were in danger of being surrounded, of being wiped out completely. Unless ...

'Form up! Wall!'

Hogarth brought his people into his surrounding area, where they began to lock up their shields. The king had steered clear of open-battlefield tactics in order to disrupt the Kurah line, but the time for stealth had passed, and he needed the strength of the shield wall to slow his casualties. This wasn't about breaking the Kurah but about surviving to get back to the forest, and to attack again when they didn't expect it.

'Ready!'

Kurah troops poured towards them, seeking to cut off their route to the forest, but once the shield was in place, they would find the Tream hard to stop. Hogarth signalled to the warriors as Akyar brought the archers forward again, comfortable with a shorter range now their people were protected. The stink of blood mingled with that of bodies and other, more putrescent scents as the flow of death turned the ground to mud that tripped and clung. The initial flurry of swordsmen had given way to larger Kurah pikemen used to standing down Delgasian cavalry. Hogarth cursed. The Kurah pikes were strong enough to break through the Tream shields.

'Hold!' Hogarth hissed as the pikemen broke into a charge, leaving it to the last minute before he let his line break.

Most of the Tream warriors rolled out of the way of the pikes and took many of the Kurah down with swift sword thrusts, but the damage had been done. They were exposed once more. Hogarth saw the Kurah advancing and fancied he saw their king turning his back on the battle, secure in his victory. *We are going to die here. Where are the clans? Have I been betrayed after all?* He grabbed his sword tightly as his anger built in his chest. If they were to die here, then he would make such an end that his people would live on forever in the legends of the Kurah.

The world erupted in light brighter than the rising suns, blinding the Tream king and driving him to his knees. Was this death?

As Hogarth adjusted to the glare, he saw that warriors on both sides were down from the force of this new magic. The light had subsided a little, allowing him to try to look at where it was emanating from. Through the burn, he thought he could see shadows moving – two of them – drawing closer: one tall and one shorter – both armed.

The Kurah cried out, 'Who are you?'

'Do you not recognise me?' came the answering call, in Kurah. The voice was very familiar to Hogarth, but was he coming as friend or foe?

'I, who have returned fifty years after you betrayed me. Do you not recognise Laos, the King's Eagle?'

THE THAIN PULLED her horse from bolting and looked down on the carnage ahead of her. The battle spilled in all directions, appearing out of control to the untrained eye, but she was pleased to see her warriors smashing open the southern line. The brief advantage would not be enough, of course. Even now, in the distance, she could see the Kurah signals going up to bring the northern line, off chasing the phantoms of the 'retreating' Shaanti. It didn't matter. By the time they returned, the Shaanti would be gone.

The Shaanti warriors were forcing their way towards the gateway with the unrelenting fury of people with nothing left to lose. Montu had gambled on the thain running her people to the forest, a prolonged march that would give him plenty of warning and the easy option of mopping them up at a place of his choosing, but if she could take the portal ... Well, a surprise attack was one thing; one in the heart of your own camp was another.

The challenge would be to close the portal after they were through to prevent them being flanked. She wiped the rain from her face in a pointless gesture. The weather was awful, serving as an ally, evening the field of battle and preventing the Kurah, in their heavier armour, from moving with ease. Lightning forked and scorched the ground up ahead, electrocuting one of the Kurah.

The thain looked at the portal and back at the corpse. She laughed. Finally she felt like the world was turning in her favour as she saw a brief glimpse of Atos, one of the sentinels, in the sky.

'To me!' she cried, picking up a spear from her saddle and geeing her horse on for the portal. 'To me!'

The Shaanti formed up ahead and behind her, moving with the seasoned practice of a well-drilled army, and they cut through the bewildered Kurah, who had expected a broken force, with surgical precision. The thain galloped to the edge of the portal and waved her army through. Some of the warriors were wide-eyed as they went into the wavering portal and into the Kurah camp, but most of them were nodding at their leader with grim determination. They understood. This was no longer about survival. This was about revenge.

The thain took a brief look round before wiping the metal spear, and as she stepped through, she drove it into the ground by the portal. On the other side of the magic, all was dry but just as battle-strewn, and far away a Kurah warning horn was ringing. Lightning flashed back on the plains side of the portal, striking the spear.

The magic detonated, throwing the thain through the air as if she weighed nothing. She thought about her mother, the previous thain, throwing her up in the air and catching her again, and she wished someone would catch her now. There was only the cold, painful slap of the mud. Her last thought before she lost consciousness was she hoped the catacombs would keep her people safe.

ON HEARING the woodsman's voice, Akyar lifted his eyes from the mud where he lay hiding from the burst of light that had blinded his warriors.

He looked to see what magic had brought them this distraction at the moment when all seemed lost. Tream and Kurah alike were scattered in confusion, the battle forgotten, all staring at Vedic.

Akyar could see the Shaanti warrior at his side was Anya. Vedic lifted a staff that looked familiar to the vizier, but Akyar had no time to tarry. The Tream were recovering faster, cutting down Kurah where they were able to, despite the mesmeric effect of the woodsman's words on the crowd.

Vedic showed no signs of wanting to leave or attack. Akyar forced himself to face his men and order the archers to line up.

'You're not Laos!' screamed one of the generals from the line. 'You're just another Shaanti warrior. Kill him!'

'I am Laos,' said Vedic. 'How else could I walk through the forest and out here to stand in front of you? Does your new god not control the forest?'

The Kurah responded in their own tongue. The tone was a mocking one that you didn't need to speak the language to understand.

Vedic replied in the same tongue with a tone as cold as the general's. At the end of his diatribe, the woodsman drew his weapon and concluded in Shaanti.

'Who but I could wield this weapon?'

Akyar couldn't understand why the woodsman wasn't getting out of the way. The Tream on the field were trying to form up, but they were still cut off, and Akyar feared that they were going to be massacred, along with Hogarth. For now they had breathing room, thanks to Vedic, but the lull would not last. The vizier racked his brain in search of a solution.

In the distance, the general advanced on Vedic with his own sword drawn. A challenge had been issued; the general couldn't back down and was now attempting to throw the woodsman off by talking at him incessantly.

Akyar ignored it. An idea was forming. He moved the Tream with him into a different position, as close to the battle as he could get without being drawn into the fighting. He turned his attention back to Vedic once they were ready.

'I don't think you need worry about me, General,' said Vedic, smiling. 'But the Tream horde behind. Hogarth, down!'

Akyar was relieved to see the Tream on the field drop to the ground as the woodsman pushed Anya down. This was a moment of pure flow like he had read the ancient scholars talked of, a moment where the vizier was in full control of the field, and he felt his arm fall to his side as he shouted the release command. The archers let their arrows fly. They were close enough to loose their bowstrings at an almost horizontal angle, giving little to no warning. The Kurah fell in droves. The first wave of Tream archers dropped, and the next released in the same way, devastating the Kurah line and causing chaos as they scrambled to pull up a shield wall. Akyar didn't allow himself the time to enjoy the moment: the whole attack had relied on surprise, and that was gone now.

Akyar drew his sword. 'Attack!'

The vizier ignored the instructions the king had given him, and led his force in a charge of the Kurah line. Hogarth looked like he grasped what Akyar was trying to do, and scrambled to his feet, forming up the survivors of his own warriors to join the charge. He couldn't see Vedic or Anya. The Tream prayed to the trees that they were safe as he tightened his grip on his sword and the two lines collided.

All was steel, blood and fire.

In the distance, horns went up in a rapid wave of alarm across the Kurah camp, and the Kurah shield wall broke, lines scattering, and Tream poured into the camp as the battle degenerated into pockets of fighting.

'I can't believe that worked,' said Akyar, looking at the changed field.

His guard looked at him. 'We were lucky. Did you hear the horns?'

'Yes – we frightened them,' said Akyar. 'They will be gathering their reserves to counter. We must withdraw.'

The guard shook his head. 'No, sir, we don't have to withdraw, and we didn't cause the alarm. The Shaanti are here, at last.'

CHAPTER THIRTY-FOUR

'Don't run, you whoresons!'

The Kurah king was not impressed as he arrived at what was left of the northern line. The Tream archers had reversed the tide despite the odds. Hundreds of Kurah lay dead, and in the chaos, his men were either running or lashing out at each other. The generals had lost control, with only one or two calling down for additional troops. Cernubus had returned in a hurry, refusing to see the king, and was hidden away inside his tent, conducting more rituals. Montu didn't care what the god did, as long as he kept his side of the deal, but an attack from the forest had not been part of it. The king grabbed one of the men, pulling him away from the line he had been moving towards. The man blinked in shock.

'You – go get the signallers to move the archers down.'

Men fell all around. The king's thigh burst with sharp, burning pain. A forest of arrows had sprung up all around, and one of them sprouted from his left leg. He cursed, snapping the arrow off and tearing cloth from a less fortunate man to tie off the wound. He felt fizzing in his belly despite the pain. This was his chance: no Kurah king had faced the Tream in several generations, and despite their weaker numbers, they were a sharp, challenging force. If he could defeat them without killing them all, they would make a strong addition to his own forces.

'Sire, you wanted archers?'

The king looked at General Inci, the man who led his bowmen and the larger force beyond. He nodded.

'The Tream are overrunning our line. Deal with them.'

Inci looked confused. 'Our men are in the way—'

'We have allowed the enemy to get a toehold. Now do as I say. People we have in abundance.'

'Yes, sire.'

The king drew his own sword and made his way to the line.

'Form up,' he shouted. 'Three lines. Get me damned cavalry! We need to end this and concentrate on the Shaanti attack.'

THERE WASN'T time to think.

The fury she had trapped in her belly had stopped the shaking of her hands, and her mind was focused on getting to the prisoners. A Kurah burst from the tents, cursing and swinging his blade with rage at spotting Shaanti so far behind their lines. She parried the blow that would have taken her head, and swung round, cutting his legs off. She did not finish him but continued on.

Anya put the next man down with the hilt of her sword, smashing it into his face before he even thought to swing. She ran on. There was no need to check whether Vedic had her back, because she'd realised she had no choice but to trust him. If he wanted to betray her, he could – at any time – and she would die. They were somewhere in the north of the camp, moving amongst tents that looked like they were being used for supplies, and the number of Kurah had fallen to manageable levels.

Five Kurah swarmed at them from different directions. Anya swung her leg round in a sweeping arc, knocking the first unconscious. She sliced off the next man's arm and dropped under the third's swing. She looked up in time to see Vedic break her attacker's neck. The two he had killed lay bleeding behind him. She had not seen how he'd killed them. The woodsman's blade was still in its sheath.

Vedic led them steadily south into the rising sunlight. In the distance, the siege towers were being pulled into new positions; one of them had been toppled by the Shaanti and was now on fire. Anya could see men struggling to load the ballista against her kinsmen, who swamped the camp even as the Tream made their way in behind her. The Kurah were regrouping, but they were taking large losses.

'What is it?' she asked.

Vedic had stopped at the edge of the line of tents they were moving along, his large limbs stretched wide as he pushed his left ear as close to the side of the tent as he could without revealing himself to whoever he was listening to. Anya dropped her bow round, an arrow sliding into the string without conscious thought as she moved to the woodsman's side. He held up a hand to stop her, without looking round.

'I SEE ALL IS GOING WELL.'

The king turned at hearing the voice. Cernubus stood leaning on his spear with casual interest. Fresh blood stained his robe, but he did not appear hurt or worn out. The Kurah ruler turned back to the battle. He would make no attempt to enter the fray: his men were finally holding, and several of his generals were moving amongst the battle, leading by example.

'No thanks to you,' he replied.

'You wanted a battle,' said Cernubus, gesturing at the surrounding carnage. 'I have given you a battle.'

The king shifted. 'Is the thain with the Shaanti forces?'

Cernubus nodded. 'She will be.'

The king remained silent as he watched the battle for signs of Tream mistakes. They began to fall back as the Kurah numbers started to tell, and the Tream moved to form into a wedge. The Kurah cavalry were ready. The battle was turning back in his favour, and he felt his confidence returning. In many ways, this was a much better test of his forces than he had anticipated, closer to what they might face in a Tinaric invasion, where the numbers and weaponry would be much closer to their own.

'You brought two armies down on me,' said the king, tapping the ground with his blade. 'Hardly the actions of an ally.'

'I did what you asked. Why are they ringing that damned bell? We know there's an attack.'

The king tilted his head – he had not noticed the alarm bell still ringing out. This was decidedly odd. The bell was coming not from the northern line but from the southern line, and that wasn't right either unless ... they had taken the portal.

'That's the southern line,' said the king, breaking into a run. 'That's why there are so many of them.'

THE SOUTHERN LINE foundered in the early morning sun. Many men had rushed to the northern line, not realising an attack was imminent, and were unable to hear the call for help over the sound of men dying. The Shaanti cavalry had ridden straight in behind the line and caused a massacre. They burned through the camp, killing Kurah wherever they could find them. The king took all this in from a small ridge that looked down on the southern line. A row of tents hid him from raiders.

'Do something!' said the king, turning to Cernubus.

The god watched the scene without emotion. 'It's all right. They're nowhere near the pyres. You just need to hold them until midday.'

The portal exploded, showering them in dirt and blood, and making the king's ears ring. *Damn this god*, thought the king. He looked up at the morning sky. The alignment had begun, and the celestial dance was impressive: the first stage was underway with the twin suns rising in the south and the sentinels continuing to shine in an almost-perfect line across the sky. By the afternoon, they would be in final formation.

Montu barked at his men. 'Damn you. This is your fault. You, man – get the horsemen from the eastern line. No, don't use the signaller. Run and send another to the northern line. We need a more even distribution of forces. Go.'

Cernubus dropped to the ground. He appeared to be listening again. The king shoved him with his foot.

'Stand and fight, even if you won't use your power to help me.'

Cernubus ignored him, rising a moment later when he had satisfied himself that whatever he had heard was correct. He looked at the king and lifted his hand. A pulse of light burst upon the southern line, sending Shaanti rolling from their horses. The god was no longer smiling. The king felt his stomach flip at the sudden seriousness of the immortal.

'Hold the men until midday,' said Cernubus, turning to the king. He stared at Montu so hard the king felt like his skin was being peeled away.

There was screaming now from the north. Men scattered all around them, running as if the stone god itself was on their heels and ready to take them down to hell. Cernubus lifted his spear in concern, and the king felt his own grip tighten on his sword hilt.

'Now what?'

AKYAR FOUND himself separated from the Tream.

The vizier led as he had always been taught by Hogarth, from the front, and so had cut and bludgeoned his way into the Kurah line as they shattered and panic spread through the forces. He saw the occasional glimpse of Anya and Vedic making their way inexorably towards the scaffolding and the sacrificial prisoners waiting to die. He pushed the thought from his mind. He had another idea.

The Kurah king stood on a small rise, barking orders and talking to someone that the Tream could not see clearly. Who it was didn't matter. The way was clear because the Kurah were already panicking. What if their leader was killed in clear view by one of the 'mythical' Tream? What would that do to their forces? Would that weaken the scarred god? *It would be revenge*, he thought. The Kurah and Cernubus had wrought such pain down on his people, had left him so exposed in front of his peers. He was not given much to rage, but he burned with it as he stepped onto the rise.

'You have come a long way, little prince,' he said. 'But the time has come for you to leave.'

Montu turned. The vizier saw the tall warrior the king had been talking to roll from view, but he thought nothing more of it.

'Who are you?'

'I am the vizier of the Tream,' he replied.

Montu frowned. 'I retreat from no one.'

'I wasn't planning on letting you,' said Akyar, lifting his blade.

Montu drew his own sword. 'You should have stayed in the forest, Tream.'

Akyar had the advantage. He was taller and his arms were longer, allowing him to strike without moving his body in range, but the Kurah king was beyond good with a sword. He did not break a sweat as he parried and swatted aside Akyar's attempts at finishing the duel. *How did a human, practically a child, get so good with a blade?* Akyar asked himself.

In the distance, there was another bright flash and more yelling. Perhaps another god had arrived. Akyar was only dimly aware of the wider battle as he fought for his life on the knoll. Perhaps Cernubus was returning. But no, that couldn't be right, because the scarred god was there already; he knew that.

'Why do it?' asked Akyar. 'Why attack the forest?'

Montu smiled. 'Because we can.'

The Kurah king twisted his blade and flicked the Tream's sword out of his hand and across the grass, running his weapon back across the vizier's stomach in a line of fire. The Tream gasped. His hands went to the wound, even as he could feel his body trying to heal.

'What in the gods ...?' hissed Montu, staring at the Tream.

'No, no, no,' said Cernubus behind Akyar.

The Tream heard a swoop of the spear being drawn back, and then his legs were on fire and folding under him.

Cernubus continued. 'You have to remove their heads to kill them. He'll just heal.'

Oh gods, thought Akyar. *I'm going to—*

Cernubus struck off Akyar's head with his spear.

CHAPTER THIRTY-FIVE

THEY CAME to watch what transpired.

Pan and Danu stepped through a portal they'd created a short way from the battle, behind the treeline, hidden from view. There was little that could be done about the light show that accompanied such magic. Danu folded the portal behind her, and Pan knew there was no way she would risk Kurah warriors making their way deep into the forest. Hooded and cloaked, they made their way onto the field, staying away from the fighting but looking for the pieces they had set on the board.

'Our sister is here,' said Danu, gesturing at the Morrigan.

The goddess stood, unmoving, on the far side of the battle, staring up the small rise at the sacrificial pyre.

'If she tries to involve herself ...' began Pan.

'She won't,' said Danu, her voice cracking. 'She is here for another reason.'

Pan was about to ask what when he felt the connection in the back of his mind, the line that tethered him to Akyar, go slack and vanish. It felt like a spear of ice had been rammed into his skull. His words stopped, and he began to gag as he dropped to his knees.

Danu was at his side. 'What is wrong?'

Pan could feel tears pouring down his face. He felt hollow. He mentally tongued the place in his mind where Akyar had been, and found nothing.

'He's dead.'

Danu frowned. 'Who? Vedic?'

'No,' said Pan, forcing the nausea down. 'Akyar.'

Danu clutched him to her. 'Oh, Pan, I am so sorry.'

Pan pushed her away.

'You're wrong,' he said. 'We cannot sit on the sidelines.'

'This is a battle,' Danu said. 'People die.'

'Cernubus killed him.'

Danu looked at him. Perhaps she was thinking of Vedic. Pan didn't care. He just didn't want to fight her as well.

'I understand,' she replied, refusing to argue.

Pan let power pour to his hands. He set off at a run for the hill and the scarred god, who stood laughing over his friend's still-warm body. He noted Danu did not follow.

TEARS STREAMED DOWN Anya's face at the sight of her fallen friend. Akyar's body lay at the feet of the scarred god as the Kurah king spoke words she could not make out over the storm of her grief. Vedic put his hand on her shoulder. She shrugged his hand off. She felt sick. She was hyperaware of the cold, cloying mud under her feet, of her stomach churning, of the feeling that she had failed another.

'Anya,' Vedic said, his voice gentle. 'The children.'

Anya looked up. The rage pulled at the harness she had built for it. Cernubus was right there for the taking – if he fell, then the army would scatter and all would be safe. She was the daughter of the witch-warrior of the Shaanti; she could do this thing for her people even if the act killed her, and Akyar would be avenged. Anya felt energy flicker under the ground. The movement felt like the presence she had sensed when they had been up in the mountains, seeking refuge from Cernubus. Vedic shifted next to her. Did he sense the power?

'You can't kill him,' said Vedic, not unkindly. 'I'm not sure anyone can.'

Anya knew he was right. Their best chance was to move round the king and his ally. Whether you thought of him as a demon or a god was irrelevant – Cernubus was deadly.

'I know,' she replied.

Vedic nodded. He seemed satisfied that she wasn't going to berserker-charge the pair, and he moved towards the next tent, which would take them out of view, towards the prisoners.

Pan came from nowhere, incinerating the tents all around them. The trickster was making a noise that Anya had never heard in her life. Somewhere between a bellow and a scream, and speaking of pain on the scale of the universe. If Anya had ever wondered how the Morrigan could have razed so much of the forest when Bres had been killed, she had no doubt now. Pan's rage caught even Cernubus by surprise. The scarred god managed to almost turn towards the vengeful god before Pan struck him in the midriff, a vicious spear-like takedown that also sent the Kurah king to the ground. The trickster thrust his hands, burning with magic, into Cernubus's torso. The scarred god cursed.

Montu picked himself up, holding his sword, and looked straight at Vedic and Anya.

'Fuck,' said Vedic, putting himself between Anya and the king. 'Go!'

'But Pan ...' she tried to argue.

Vedic lifted his sword-staff as he looked her straight in the eyes. 'Go!'

Anya flinched. *It doesn't matter if you feel fear*, said her mother's voice. *It's what you do with it that matters.*

Anya turned her back on her friends, though the pain of moving on nearly broke her, and started running for the prisoners even as she heard Vedic's and Montu's swords kiss in the midday sun. But when she closed her eyes, she saw Akyar's body, and the tears were hard to hold back.

'YOU ARE brave to show your face here, priest,' said Montu, holding his sword in a guard position. 'The punishment for that robe is not one I would want to endure.'

Vedic smiled at the Kurah ruler. 'Where else should I be but at my master's side?'

The king's hand tightened on his sword. Vedic noted the boy's knuckles were turning white. 'I thought my grandfather had killed all your kind.'

'Laos is not any priest,' said Vedic, swinging his staff in lazy arcs to loosen up his arms. The woodsman was frightened by how at home the weapon felt in his hands, like renewing a conversation with an old friend. If Vedic let himself, he could almost hear the sword talking to him.

Other Kurah were turning to look at them now.

'Did you hear what he called himself?' was the murmuring cry amongst the men. 'He is the Priest returned.'

But they did not run. The fascination of watching a legend stand in front of their king, the King's Eagle, the Priest, was too much to run away from, and Vedic felt all eyes on him. There was a surge beneath his feet; energy flickered back and forth, as if unsure what to do, and when the thing touched Vedic's feet, it made the world brighter. He had felt this before.

Pan and Cernubus fought in a tangle of magic and heat just a few feet away, oblivious to the confrontation taking place. Akyar's body lay to the woodsman's left, but he would not focus on the corpse. He had to buy Anya time.

'Laos is dead,' said the king, drawing his blade. 'You're being ridiculous, priest. You would be over a hundred if you were him.'

'One hundred and forty-nine to be precise,' said Vedic, spinning his staff from one hand to the other and around his neck before planting it back on the ground in front of him. 'But I've kept in shape. Now, let me guess which of Jeran's boys spawned you. You have Bale's stature and Fen's pride but ... no. Vince would be your father, I think.'

The men around them were pale as ghosts. Yet still they did not run.

'Kill him,' said the Kurah king to his men. 'I am bored of this madman. We have a war to win.'

No man moved.

'I said, kill him. What's wrong with you?'

Vedic could see the king's anger growing at his men's superstition.

'They're scared of me,' said the woodsman, stepping forward. 'They know their history and what your grandfather did to me. They fear what the Butcher of Vremin will do to the family who betrayed him.'

'You were a threat to the kingdom,' said the king, raising his sword to emphasise his words. 'They feared you and your mad faith more than us. You'd have overthrown us if your god willed it.'

'You believe?'

The king positioned his sword in guard. Vedic stopped his approach.

'I believe you think you're Laos,' said the king. 'But your delusion will get you killed. I could not let you live now even if you confessed your deceit.'

'Oh, I think your men would disagree.'

'One in ten of them will die for this disobedience,' said the king. 'But you won't see it.'

Vedic smiled. 'I see they still use my treatise on punishment for disobedience.'

The king smiled. 'Oh, we've moved on quite a bit since then.'

The ruler's attack was swift and strong, but Vedic was faster, rolling clean out of the way and coming to his feet still without striking back. The men looked on but did not try to intercede on the king's behalf; it was as if they were rooted to the ground. The ruler spun round ready for a counter-attack, but Vedic stood leaning on his staff as if worn out. The king smiled.

'Are you defeated already, old man?'

Vedic laughed. 'Are you so eager to die?'

The king's eyes narrowed. 'You are unwilling to defend yourself. And you ask me if I am eager to die?'

Vedic shrugged. 'I have every reason to kill your grandfather, but he is already dead. I would not hold you responsible for your ancestor's sins. You could leave this place and free the children. You could refuse to do the bidding of that thing that was once a god.'

'You would prefer I sacrificed to the stone god, who I – king of the Kurah – destroyed?'

Vedic smiled. 'I doubt you killed that creature, but no, I make no such claim or request, no such boon. Just leave here. Your analysis of history is faulty – if you seek to drive back an invasion force, you must seek willing help.'

The king made another attack.

Vedic blocked the series of blows with his sheathed sword without drawing the blade from the wood. He rolled backwards, out of strike range. Two warriors made a start towards him as his back came within reach, but his staff spun out, knocking out the men, and returned to the ground in front of Vedic before their blades made it from the sheath.

Vedic looked at the warriors surrounding him. If they got over their fear, he would not make it off the knoll alive, and the longer the battle went on, the more likely they would see him not as a ghost but as a man. He could see narrowing eyes on more than one man who thought it odd the Priest would not fight.

In truth, he didn't know why he wasn't fighting the king and cutting down the man who had slaughtered so many. Yet the king's deeds were nothing compared to what he had done himself. Had Montu done anything different from Laos? Who was Vedic to judge?

He has unleashed a second god on his people. He has pushed them into a needless war that may destroy his entire nation's security. How many more will die before he sees the futility, the evil of it all? I have to stop him.

Kill him, said his own, harsher voice, the one he thought of as Laos. The thing under the forest flicked beneath him again.

The king attacked once more.

This time Vedic did not move. He drew the sword from the staff, and the men stepped back as the woodsman moved under the ruler's sweeping strike and spun. The Eagle's Claw bit into the king's arm, cutting through without any difficulty and sending Montu's weapon to the ground. The woodsman's strike followed through into a powerful spinning blow across the whole of the king's body, slicing him in half. The Kurah king fell, in two pieces, to the mud, and all was silent save for the last hiss from Montu's open mouth.

The men stared at Vedic, covered in their leader's blood.

Vedic looked at the men. Beneath him he could still feel that powerful energy flickering. He raised his sword. The thing seemed to hum with the magic Pan had cast and the belief of the warriors.

'Who's next?'

They ran. Alone on the knoll, knee-deep in corpses, Vedic finally noticed that Cernubus and Pan had vanished.

CHAPTER THIRTY-SIX

Anya didn't look back.

She could hear Vedic's low tones but could not make out the words as she ran along the soft path up the hill. The going was hard. The recent rainfall, blood and worse things besides had made the mud slick. The mire sucked at her boots, trying to draw her into a tight embrace from which she would not escape, and for the briefest of moments, she thought she was running across a collection of Kresh. She fell into the cold mud a second time, and her bow nearly broke beneath her. She cursed.

Kurah burst through the tents alongside her but did not pause to attack or even look at her as they ran. She slung the bow back over her shoulder and drew her sword. The climb towards the sacrifice site was causing her to breathe hard, and she was unsure how long she could keep the pace up. Near the edge of the large cleared area of the pyre, she had to face another Kurah, the sole guardsman left behind.

The guard's hands shook as he held out his sword to defend his post. His shaking was nearly as bad as Anya's. She had been able to fool herself that the men she had fought on her way to the prisoners were still alive and just wounded, but she would have to kill this man who wasn't much older than her. The guard's armour was nearly as oversized as the man's she had murdered to escape.

The fear nearly killed her. She felt it slide up her legs like hands rooting her to the spot, and pure instinct lifted the blade to block the guard's clumsy, aggressive strike. Afterwards she felt that she should have struck out in rage, that her confidence should have returned in a shining moment of insight and caused her to hack the bastard to pieces. The reality was, her response was instinctive.

Her boot came right round in a tight snap that knocked the guard to the ground, and her sword sliced down in a continuous smooth spin that severed his head.

The pause felt like a thousand years.

The strike had been a simple move that Falkirk had drilled into her when she was much younger. She had used it without thinking.

Anya looked down at the still-warm body, the shocked face of the guard staring blindly up at the sky, and threw up. She felt the shakes take her; she struggled to hang on to her sword, and for a few moments, she could do nothing but stare at what she had done. This man no longer existed, because of her.

The cries of men drawing closer broke her reverie. The children crowded her mind. She remembered the dead Shaanti. She steadied her hands with the fury still burning in her belly.

Anya emerged into the area around the scaffolding for the sacrifice and looked up at the huge pyre the Kurah had constructed. Above her, the suns were creeping ever higher towards the sentinels. The air buzzed and throbbed with undischarged magic – like in parts of Golgotha, or the deeper areas of the forest – and if she closed her eyes, she fancied she could see the ghosts of all the trees that had once filled the land to the coast.

The children were not crying. They were beyond that.

Anya made a clockwise sweep of the area around the pyre, realising, after a few moments, that they hadn't opted for a single cage as she had dreamt but that they had spread the prison wagons around the pyre, pointing inward on the thing that would eventually kill them. The children lay listless and forlorn. Hope had long since left them. Many of them were malnourished; all of them were traumatised from the things they had seen and the certainty that they would be dead come sunset. Not one of them looked up as she made her way to the first cell.

'Keys?' she demanded.

One of the children, a boy of about eight, looked up. 'Who are you?'

She paused, uncertain what to say. 'Anya, the one who got away.'

The boy blinked. 'They've been looking for you. They are going to kill you if they find you.'

'If you tell me where the key is, they won't kill any of us.'

The boy blinked. He seemed unsure if she was real or in his imagination.

'I came back for you,' she hissed, desperate. 'I came back for all of you.'

There was no answer, but more of the children crawled to the front of their prison cells, trying to get a good look at her as she cursed and tried to smash the lock on the first cell with the base of her sword hilt. This made a loud noise but didn't do anything other than hurt her wrist.

'The guard,' said a little girl who could not have been more than five.

The boy who had spoken moved her behind him.

'Is that right?' Anya asked. The boy stared at her with unblinking eyes. 'Please.'

The boy nodded.

'Damn.' She cursed herself for not checking the body. 'I'll be right back.'

The keys were soaked in blood. Freeing them took her far longer than she would have wished, and she slipped and slid as she tried to make her way back to the makeshift prison. Anya felt like the suns set in that moment. In reality, a storm cloud had just passed overhead, but the sudden drop in light and heat from the suns above made Anya tighten her grip on her sword.

A tall figure bled from the shadows between the tents and moved with warrior-like poise into her path back to the prisoners. He was dragging a body behind him.

'Vedic!' she found herself calling out even as she realised the person was too tall, his hair too thick and wild, the skin emerging from the hood he was drawing back too scarred. Vedic had failed.

Cernubus smiled at her. She could see now it was Pan he was dragging behind him, though she could not tell if he was alive or dead.

'Hello, Anya,' said the hunter. 'How about a kiss?'

THE THAIN HURT ALL OVER.

She did not know how far she had been thrown, or how long she had been unconscious, but she knew she had been lucky. Nothing felt broken. There were the sounds of people fighting and dying all around her, but she must have looked like a corpse, because no one was attacking her. She opened her eyes. It was still daylight. She reached out for her sword and found the weapon nearby, which was a small miracle – she must have held on to the hilt until she hit the ground.

'Milady!'

The thain brought her sword round to defend herself and nearly ran Bene through. Her bodyguard was blood-streaked and sweat-soaked but alive, and here. She could have kissed him.

'You are alive!' he yelled.

'I am,' she said. 'Although I do not feel it.'

'The Kurah are in retreat in places,' said Bene, his voice in wonder. 'How have we done this?'

The thain sat up. 'It's probably a ruse. We can't defeat them on our own.'

Bene shook his head. 'Haven't you seen? The Tream are with us.'

The thain felt the news hit her like a cold hand across the face. *The Tream? That was an unexpected miracle that gave them a chance. No*, she thought. *Bene might be ignorant of the Tream, but I've met Hogarth, years ago when treating with the gods during the last war. There still aren't enough.*

'The prisoners?' she asked.

Bene shook his head. 'The Kurah have dug in and are defending the pyres with everything they've got. They look like they are waiting for a counter-attack to happen.'

'The hunter?'

'There are rumours of two gods duelling,' said Bene. 'But I have not seen them.'

The thain would not let herself think of hope. Any other god on the field couldn't be Danu: she would not intervene so directly, even if she was free. The mud felt cold under her hands, and she could feel the pull of old and fresh injuries as she got to her feet and returned her sword to her hand. She could not see any sign of her horse. Perhaps it had survived and run off.

'Orders, milady?' Bene asked.

The thain took in the battle around her. 'Our generals have things in hand?'

Bene nodded. 'We drilled them well.'

'Then you're with me,' she said. 'We're going to keep an old promise to General Thrace.'

Bene nodded. His men were scattered around the thain and the bodyguard. There were two dozen keeping them safe in the midst of the battle. He whistled. Ten of his warriors took up closer positions around the thain. The squad set off at a run for the prisoners, only fighting where they had to, taking the narrow lanes between tents. They found Hogarth in a razed section of the camp. The tents had been burned away, the ground scorched, and two corpses littered the ground. In front of one of them, holding a head to his own, was Hogarth. The Tream king was crying as if he were a child.

The Shaanti didn't know what to do. They stared with their weapons drawn but not raised at this strange creature from their legends, his mottled skin slick with blood of the Kurah, and his sword next to him on the grass. The thain stepped forward slowly.

'Hogarth,' she said, her voice gentle.

'You are late,' said the king, though his voice lacked true anger. All was sorrow.

'I am sorry,' said the thain. 'We came as soon as we could.'

'He wasn't a warrior,' said Hogarth, still weeping. 'He fought anyway. And your god killed him.'

The thain flinched. She thought of Sevlen and Jeb. 'The hunter is

THE SCARRED GOD

not our god,' she said. 'We fight the same enemy. I have lost people I cared for to this god as well.'

'He was my friend for a thousand years and across countless campaigns. We stood together when your ancestors were still killing each other in the name of gods.'

The thain was close enough now to put her hand on his shoulder, and she did so. The Tream felt hot to the touch. His skin was somewhere between bark and human flesh, and he smelt faintly of pine, despite the smoke and blood all around.

'What was his name?'

'Akyar,' replied Hogarth.

The thain looked at the head. She felt a start. She knew the dead Tream – he had been there with Hogarth when she had passed through their lands all those years ago. The vizier had been a kind and thoughtful man who was the most knowledgeable person she had ever talked to.

'I remember him,' she said. 'I am truly sorry. He was good. If we ever make it out of here, his name will live on amongst the Shaanti as long as one of us draws breath.'

Hogarth placed the head by the body and draped what was left of his only robe over his friend's remains.

'What happened here?' asked Bene, bending over the other body. The fallen man was Kurah. His cloak was once purple but was now sodden with blood, and he had been almost cut in two by someone. 'This wound is too large for a Tream weapon.'

'Akyar didn't kill the Kurah king,' said Hogarth.

The thain looked at the corpse. *Montu dead? That was the miracle they needed!* She went over to Bene, saw the young Kurah she had met only once, when he was a boy, and felt the thrill of a chance. She felt regret and guilt at this feeling. The man ... the boy ... was younger than her own late son. Still, his death was an opportunity.

She turned to Bene. 'Take this body to the highest point and proclaim that Montu has fallen.'

Hogarth nodded. 'Wise. But the god is who they follow, not this one.'

The thain shrugged. 'There is a chance. Who did this?'

Hogarth raised his eyebrow. He moved over to his sword and picked it up. 'You cannot read the ground?'

The thain smiled. 'I could chance to, but time is short.'

'Ah, yes,' Hogarth replied. 'The children.' The king looked up at the sentinels glowing in the daytime sky. 'The alignment is close at hand.'

'Hogarth, you have my friendship for what you have done here today,' she said. 'Please, what happened?'

'Akyar fought Montu, and the scarred god killed him.'

'Montu too?'

Hogarth laughed. 'No, that was Laos.'

The thain went cold. 'I beg your pardon.'

Hogarth walked up to her. 'Oh yes, Laos is here. He fights with us. Shall we?'

The Tream was gesturing towards the pyres and the remaining Kurah line.

The thain stared at him. 'Laos is here?'

Hogarth nodded.

The thain clutched her sword tight. 'Show me.'

Anya slammed into the cage.

There was a muted thud as the impact drove the air from her lungs, closely followed by the cracking of the struts and another thud as she dropped to the ground. The children in the darkness behind her cried out; others whimpered; and a few brave ones put their hands out to touch Anya, to see if she was still alive. She cursed, her voice hoarse and her throat dry from the fighting.

The fire the god had started spread like a noose around the cages until they were almost entirely hemmed in. She spat a globule of blood into the dust in front of her as she struggled to get to her feet. She had lost her sword. She wasn't sure when, but somewhere in the back of her mind, a voice screamed at her that the god had made a mistake. He had thrown her into the door.

One eye was swollen shut; her tunic and leggings were torn in several places from narrow escapes from the god's spear; and she was bleeding from at least three places in addition to her face. Yet Anya got up, raising her fists and shifting her weight to the balls of her feet – ready to fight, the key clutched in one fist. Cernubus had thrown her a fair way. He stood looking at her across the smoke. His laugh made her teeth ache as he made his way forward, her sword in one hand and his spear in the other. She did not have much time.

Anya swung for the door, but Cernubus had already spotted the keys. He threw her sword.

The weapon spun through the air with a low whoop that belied the speed and accuracy of the throw, tattooing Anya to the door of the cage, piercing her through the shoulder. She swore loud and clear. Fire hotter than the one raging only a few feet away burned through her right side. The god stepped towards her, his spear spinning in a lazy rhythm. She tried to pull the sword from her shoulder, but the steel had gone right through and embedded itself in the wood strut of the door behind. Anya could feel the blood seeping from the wound, down her back and dripping onto the ground below.

Anya was dying. Desperate, she tried to reach for the keys that she had dropped on the mud in front of her but couldn't get a grip.

'Your war is over, Anya,' said Cernubus, stepping closer. 'Your fate was written the moment you came back instead of running. Did you really believe you could defeat a god?'

The hunter looked above at the twin suns, which had almost reached their apex, the sentinels trailing behind. He looked back at her with an expression approaching peace. He had succeeded. The alignment was at hand, and all he had to do was toss his victims into the fire. Not even the granddaughter of the witch-warrior had been able to defeat him. She, too, would be killed for the hunter. Anya had done his work for him, she realised, her stomach flipping over. All the while she had been trying to act for Danu, for the children, for the Shaanti, but it had been Cernubus she had really been working for. How was she any different from Vedic?

Whenever we are involved, nothing goes as planned.

Danu's words haunted her as Cernubus raised his spear. She could hear the sound of approaching warriors, Shaanti in all likelihood, but they were too late, because she'd allowed Cernubus to start the fires, and now they were cut off. All because she had been arrogant enough to think she could free the children, because she had dared to think she was a hero – like her grandmother, like her grandfather. Yet her grandfather had also been a drunk. A bitter and broken old man who had struggled to raise his daughter and granddaughter alone while he slowly killed himself with wine bought on his younger self's reputation. And her mother had run away, never completing her mission, whatever the thain had sent her to do. Anya had hoped one day to restore her family's legend where her mother had failed. Anya wasn't sure where her own ego stopped and her desire to do the right thing began.

'I know where to put this,' said Cernubus, looking at his raised spear.

The lance glinted in the sunlight, drawing a perfect arrow to the suns, an alignment all of its own, and Anya wondered – in the brief pause before the strike – if she would feel pain or if she would merely awaken in Golgotha. The light of the suns blinded her, forcing her to close her eyes, and so she heard rather than saw the spear strike. There was no pain.

There was the sound of metal striking on metal. For a moment, Anya thought Cernubus had driven the thing right through her with such ease that she had not felt the blow and – for a moment of brief hope – that the spear had struck and broken the lock behind her. That would have given the children a chance of escape. Something brushed in front of her. There was a grunt and the sound of steel kissing.

Anya was still alive. Blinking, looking away from the light, she saw a familiar figure roll out of the way of a spear thrust and come up in a spinning kick that sent the god onto his back, his weapon clattering away.

Vedic winked at her as he flicked the Eagle's Claw into his guard position, and Cernubus nipped up, pulling his spear to him with a flick of magic that coiled across the ground like a snake.

HOGARTH STARED AT THE FLAMES.

The fire had run almost as fast as the wind. The tents

surrounding the caged children had caught and created a wall of flame that none could pass. Shaanti and Tream mingled, both trying to find a path through the heat to where the children were imprisoned.

Hogarth could see enough to realise that it was futile. There would be no way through. The hunter had been too careful. Sensing the battle had turned, he had set fire to the camp in an attempt to buy himself enough time. If he killed the children, none of this would matter, anyway. He would be strong enough to take them all.

'You, search for something to breach the fire. All of you, look for anything,' shouted Hogarth at the warriors closest to him.

'I'm not sure there is anything that can get through that.'

Hogarth turned to look at the thain. She still didn't look like a ruler to the Tream, but Hogarth recognised his own mannerisms in the woman, and she had steered her people well. The thain smiled, and the ghost of the woman Hogarth had met in the forest decades before was there.

'Well, this is a pretty problem,' said the thain. 'We need a god.'

Hogarth grunted. 'I'm not sure they would be much use in there. I wonder if Laos got here in time.'

'You believe he can be trusted?'

Hogarth paused. 'He is a friend of the Tream. He came to help the children.'

'And Thrace and Gobaith's granddaughter was with him?'

Hogarth nodded. 'Anya. Yes, she was with him. The Tream owe them a great debt.'

Beyond the flames, they could see figures moving in the flickering haze the pyre was producing, although there wasn't enough visibility to make out who they were. The sound of steel on steel spoke of a fight going on within the fire's circle. Shaanti brought water, forming a line from the Kurah stores and passing it along in buckets, but no amount of it was going to be enough. Hogarth looked above at the sentinels; he could feel a presence at the back of his senses, and he had never felt this before in all his time in the forest. The trees were awake. All of them.

He was afraid.

'We need a miracle,' said the thain, sounding more sober. 'And I fear we have already had our fill today.'

Hogarth stared into the flames, trying to make out what was going on beyond. He didn't believe in miracles. Someone was lying on the ground on the other side of the fire. They weren't moving. At first the Tream king thought he was staring at a corpse. Hogarth only realised the man on the ground was a god when his eyes adjusted to the heat. Pan was staring up at the sky.

'Pan,' he said.

'What?' asked the thain, following the Tream's gaze to the prone figure. She blinked. 'You're right! Is he dead?'

Hogarth shook his head. 'His head and heart are intact. Pan!'

The god did not respond.

'Pan,' said the thain, as clearly as she could without shouting. 'You must get us through the fire.'

Pan did not react.

'I wasn't asking,' said the thain, her voice harsh.

Pan glanced at her.

'I believe,' she said.

The god groaned. He rolled to his belly and thrust his right hand into the earth. The spell looked to be draining the god down to a dangerous level, where his hair was turning white and his skin starting to crease. The smell of citrus and sulphur made uncomfortable bedfellows. The Tream found himself gagging as the fire in front of them was eaten by the earth. Pan collapsed back into unseeing paralysis.

They could see the ground on the far side now, and the people fighting in front of the cages. Vedic and Cernubus duelled with the intensity of a deadly ritual dance. Beyond them a girl leant, severely wounded, against one of the cages, from which eyes stared from the shadows. Hogarth barely recognised the bloody thing Anya had become.

'It can't be,' said the thain.

Hogarth turned to look at the Shaanti ruler. He had hoped the old woman wouldn't want to kill Laos. He saw his own feelings writ large across her face, the visceral hate, and there was little comfort that he, too, had felt that way towards the woodsman. The thain had gone grey with the sight of Vedic and was now fumbling for her bow.

'That is Laos,' said Hogarth, placing his hand on the woman's shoulder. 'And he's on your side.'

The thain blinked. 'Why? Because the Kurah king tried to kill him?'

'No. Because of Thrace's girl.' Pan pointed at the woman leaning against the cage.

'I watched that man slaughter more of my kind than I care to remember,' said the thain, still holding her bow as if to draw. 'I saw the aftermath of his *mercy*. I saw the terror he cast amongst his own people. Now you tell me to trust him?'

'Only Laos can do this,' said Pan, trying and failing to lift himself up. 'Look.'

The god was pointing at the Kurah who had been fighting and were now stopping to stare at the duel between the Priest and Cernubus. Pan tried to move again. Slowly the god pushed himself to his hands and knees, drawing breath to stand.

The trickster froze when Cernubus struck. One moment, Hogarth thought the god was able to get to his feet, and the next, the deity couldn't move. The ground fell away from Pan as magic picked him up. In the distance, as if coming from a very long tunnel, was another voice. Only when Pan started to convulse in mid-air did Hogarth realise it was Cernubus who had spoken.

'Stay out of this, goat,' repeated the hunter.

Somewhere beyond, above the sound of the children crying, or the sword colliding with the spear, someone was calling for help.

CHAPTER THIRTY-SEVEN

Vedic did not move fast enough.

The spear head sliced across his thigh, opening a deep tear that he felt in the base of his spine, telling him something important had been severed, and he cursed as he spun away, favouring his injured leg. The woodsman brought his sword round in a high sweep that nearly shattered the god's spear as Cernubus stabbed for another strike. His breath was coming in ragged gasps; his arms felt like lead; he bled from a dozen wounds; and yet he could still feel the fight that had never let him down. He had no room for another strike of his blade, but a well-placed elbow forced Cernubus to drop the spear, and a firm, unexpected headbutt sent the god sprawling away from his weapon.

'You're flagging,' grunted Vedic, kicking the god's spear further away.

He turned in time to see the god nip up and call the spear back to his hands. He noted the way the weapon took a short while to obey, a noticeable lapse, but not long enough to dissuade the god from coming at him again. The attack was clumsy – Vedic wounded him, but before the woodsman had even finished turning for a killing blow, the god had already healed.

'You can't win,' said Cernubus, spinning his spear. 'I am as the mountains compared to you. Timeless and forever.'

'I don't have to win,' answered Vedic, spitting blood.

Cernubus looked up at the sky. They were moments from alignment. Below, Vedic could feel the presence that had been flitting in and around their battle freeze. Moreover, he saw the god flinch from it.

'I do not have time for this,' said Cernubus, extending his hand.

Vedic felt the magic crawl over his skin. The sensation was like cockroaches with sharp metallic limbs crawling over him, trying to pluck him into the air, trying to force his arms under their will and crush him into the ground. It drove him down to one knee.

There was a counter-spell. The magic was cool, like the soothing sensation of water sliding over him, and Cernubus cursed as Vedic opened his eyes. There was a new presence. The power was not underneath them but stood out in the open, stopping his destruction. At first Vedic thought Pan had intervened. How had the god overpowered the vicious Cernubus? How had he made his way over the flames?

Pan had not intervened. He was trapped. Danu had not broken her word and intervened. Instead, Vedic saw the Morrigan staring at them, without words, from just inside the far flames. She wore no expression. She was still caked in dust from wherever she had crawled back from, her arms hugging herself as she watched the unfolding battle. He wasn't sure why she had stopped the hunter.

The god looked momentarily uncertain.

'See, Vedic,' said Cernubus, raising his spear. 'Death has come to find you.'

Vedic laughed. 'I am a little old for baiting.'

The god attacked. There was no joking, no attempt at toying with the woodsman this time as Cernubus made a precise and sustained series of thrusts and strikes. Vedic took a nasty slash along one of his arms as he tried to defend himself. The woodsman's counter was slow but unpredictable, and the Eagle's Claw bit deep across the god's belly. Cernubus spun away, clutching at the wound that did not heal as before.

'That hurts,' said the god, bemused as his hand came away from the wound, still bloody.

'Your power is weakening,' said Vedic, trying to make out what had shifted the tide. He could see figures beyond the flames.

Cernubus raised his spear with his other hand. 'You are deluded. The blood loss has gone to your head.'

Vedic shook his head as he walked closer. 'No, I'm not. Your men have run away. They do not believe in you any more, but they fear me. I have been seen not just by them but by the Shaanti. The priest who survived. They doubt you.'

Cernubus swung, but Vedic blocked and parried.

'You are just a forestal,' said Cernubus. His wound was starting to close, an obvious drain on his energy. 'Belief cannot make you stronger.'

Vedic laughed. 'Many would call me a demon, would they not, Anya?'

But Anya did not answer, lost in whatever darkness the god had consigned her to. Cernubus staggered further away. *Odd*, thought Vedic. *I could have sworn she was watching me.*

'You're dying,' said the woodsman, dropping in pain to one knee. 'And so am I. Look around you. What have you won?'

The hunter's eyes danced across the fire, registering the faces beyond and their eyes reflecting the amber heat of the flames as he tried to stand. Vedic thought he saw a small flicker of a smile; a plan was formulating in the god's head, and he knew he had to press on fast.

'They have seen what I did to the Kurah king,' said Vedic through ragged breaths. 'Your own followers have seen me return when I should be dead, have seen me defy the king and you. They believe in me – Laos the Priest. I am the devil they warn their children against. I am the warrior that the Shaanti clans whisper about in taverns and that old warriors fear when darkness falls. They're more afraid of me than of you.'

'You're just a man,' said Cernubus, spinning in attack. 'I am nearly as old as humanity. People believed in me. People feared me. I am the teeth in the long night.'

'Gods are nothing more than our magnified reflection,' said Vedic, blocking. 'Don't you know that by now? It was not a god, stone or otherwise, who destroyed Vremin. It was me. It was not a god who ordered the Shaanti army spiked at Medusa. It was me. I killed millions, enslaved thousands and took more lands than any general or priest in our history. What do you have? A sacrifice? Who do you really think they're going to believe in?'

The god stared at the woodsman, his face uncertain.

Vedic faltered. The pain in his leg reached a crescendo as he tried to remain standing, his sword blade sinking into the ground as he leant on it. He coughed up blood in gouts onto the mud.

Cernubus straightened, his belly finally healing once more.

'You almost had me,' said the hunter. 'Now, tell me, why do you look forward to Golgotha? What did you see in the darkness that so appealed to you? Did you see the faces of those who you sent before you? Did you see hell?'

Vedic smiled, tired. 'No, you fool. I saw nothing.'

Cernubus smirked.

'Really, I saw nothing,' said Vedic, wiping his beard with his sleeve. 'Void, darkness, everlasting nothingness. This is it.'

Vedic did not feel as confident as he made out. The woodsman could feel the blood loss from his wounds, particularly his leg, starting to take effect; pinpricks of light danced and wove through the air in front of his eyes. It was getting harder to focus on things, but there was a grimly familiar feel to all this. The sight of Anya, stoic in her determination as she pulled the sword from her shoulder with a scream, pulled Vedic back.

Cernubus turned to hurl his spear at the girl, trying to catch her before she got the keys and started freeing the children. Vedic saw his chance. He plunged the blade deep into the god's back, through his heart and out the other side, forcing the god to drop his spear. Cernubus sank to his knees, clutching at the blade protruding from his chest, but the woodsman removed the weapon too fast for the god to gain a purchase.

'It's over.'

'No, it isn't,' said Cernubus, raising his right arm.

Anya was thrown away from the door, rolling to a halt near the edge of the fire. She did not move but lay there, staring at the suns high above. Only her breathing indicated life, and here was Cernubus rising once more with his chest healing in front of Vedic.

'The trickster's magic isn't strong enough for me,' said Cernubus. 'You're dying. Can you feel the blood leaving you? It's trailed all around here. Are you scared? You should be.'

Vedic's head felt light; he wasn't sure if he could stand up any more, let alone fight. He staggered back out of striking range as Cernubus advanced on him. The sense of familiarity was back again, only this time the feeling was far worse; it threatened to choke him, to pull him under into Golgotha.

The Morrigan made a step forward. Her face was still unmoving, but her own dark sword had emerged from the cloak.

'You should not have come,' said Vedic, raising his sword.

'I promised you at the end you would see me again,' said the Morrigan.

'Take him,' said Cernubus, wiping sweat from his brow. 'I grow weary of this.'

The Morrigan looked at Pan and back at the hunter. 'No.'

The word was said simply but brooked no dissent.

Cernubus turned to stare at her with disbelieving eyes, his spear pointed not at Vedic but at his former ally. The area around the scarred god's heart, where Vedic had run him through, was a mess, and the wound was not healing. The Morrigan did not raise her weapon, but Vedic could have sworn he saw a satisfied smirk ghost across her face.

'There will be no stepping back from this, cousin,' said Cernubus, punctuating his words with the spear. 'I will destroy you along with all the others.'

'You cannot destroy death,' said the Morrigan. She pointed at the fire, and the faces grew easier to see beyond. 'You see, your fire grows low.'

Beyond the falling flames, clansmen and Tream lifted their weapons. Vedic saw a nod from an anxious Hogarth, but Pan still hung suspended in the hunter's power. Cernubus was not done yet.

'You're next, hag,' replied Cernubus, bringing his spear up.

Vedic saw Anya roll to her side, clutching at the keys as she did so, and he drew the air from his lungs in a battle cry as he charged, limping, at the god. Vedic struck with a rally of blows in furious succession as he sought the advantage over Cernubus, pushing the god far from Anya. The girl had turned her back on the battle, rotating through each key as systematically as she could as she moved from cage to cage, freeing the children.

Vedic wasn't sure where they could go with the fire looming close, but now at least they had a chance. Cernubus, distracted by the Morrigan, had only just managed to get his spear up in time to block the woodsman, and the impact sent the god in a spiral that presented its own opportunity for a strike. The hunter slashed the spearhead down Vedic's back.

The woodsman felt his trunk erupt in flame, his sword dropping from his hands as he sank to his knees in agony. There was nothing left. He had done all he could, and as the god made his way towards him, he could summon no more strength. Vedic watched in a daze as Anya turned from the last-but-one cage and saw Cernubus going for Vedic. He couldn't get to his feet even as she ran with her sword raised for the god; there was no strength in his legs as Cernubus dodged her strike and brought the butt of his spear up into her jaw, snapping her head back. Anya fell like a puppet with her strings cut, and he could not tell this time if she was breathing. Everything hurt as badly as everything else. He was dying.

The Morrigan turned to look him right in the eyes. Still she did not move to take him but tilted her head in a way that had always reminded him of a crow.

And he remembered why this all seemed so familiar.

CHAPTER THIRTY-EIGHT

I'M DYING, thought Vedic. *This is what I saw in the Mnemosyne.*

He felt like brittle rock. He wondered if that was how the stone god had felt before the scarred god killed him.

Vedic looked round at the mud and the fire and the people-shaped smudges in the distance, and the sense of déjà vu was overwhelming.

Cernubus probed again with his spear, and Vedic parried without thinking. It would be easier to let the hunter end this now, but the alignment was still happening, and the woodsman needed to hang on for the moment to pass. Besides, in his premonition of his death, Cernubus wasn't who he had seen kill him. There was power in that thought. Vedic could feel the heat of the fire all around, even though the flames were dying faster than he was. The receding heat brought the warriors beyond into sharp relief, and they looked like the Shaanti that he spent his youth killing – they appeared as wraiths, impossible ghosts that move of their own accord. Just like he had seen all those years ago on the side of the lakes, with the Morrigan. Might that mean the warrior that wielded the killing weapon was here?

I thought I understood, and I did not.

Cernubus bore down on him with the spear.

I wish Danu was here, thought Vedic.

The forestal did not know where the energy came from to lift the sword in his hands. He thought he could sense Anya in the back of his head, as he had realised she had somehow been during his nightmares of his time as Laos. Perhaps the energy was Danu sending a final burst of power. It didn't matter. The energy allowed him to block the god's blow, though the strike felt like it had enough force to drive his arms out of their sockets and through his back. The Shaanti broke forward and tried to attack, to bring the scarred god down.

The distraction, short-lived, allowed Vedic to regain his feet. Cernubus drove off the Shaanti and grabbed one of the children Anya had managed to free, tossing the boy towards the fire.

Vedic turned from the god, half running, half limping to catch the boy. There was movement behind him. He was expecting the strike of the spear, but a Tream leapt like a shadow come to life and grabbed the boy from mid-air.

The woodsman saw the Tream roll to the ground with the child tucked under him before they disappeared into the dark. The god swung his spear at Vedic. Vedic parried. There was no time for a protracted duel. *How to stop a god?*

The ghosts of the Shaanti stared at Vedic. He was aware that he was near death, because the hallucinations were fast and frequent, and he could no longer tell what was really happening to him.

This will never be enough, whatever I do here today – they will always remember what I did when I was Laos.

The energy unfurled under Vedic just as he tried to block another attack from Cernubus. The god was too fast for him. The pain came like fresh morning dew, slipping the world back into the front focus of the woodsman's mind, colours bright under the midday suns. Vedic could feel the sentinels in the alignment as the god in front of him twisted the spear embedded in Vedic's chest. The wound didn't hurt any more. There was strength left in the forestal yet.

I wish Danu were here.

Vedic remembered that he was still holding his sword. The movement he used to bring the sword up above his head was pure pain as the rock-hard metal in his chest shifted, tearing him more. Nevertheless, Vedic twisted away from the god, breaking the hunter's hold on the spear and giving Vedic more momentum as he swung round, bringing the sword down on Cernubus's skull. The blade bit deep. Cernubus stared at the woodsman in shock. Vedic pulled his weapon free, and the scarred god fell to the ground.

The legend-soaked sword, dripping in belief, did its work well. The god did not heal. Cernubus was lying in the fragments of himself, trying to speak and failing. The god looked smaller to Vedic now as he leant on his sword, looking over the creature. The Shaanti – whether they were ghosts or real – did not move. Vedic thought that was strange.

I do not believe in ghosts, because I know there is nothing once you die. I know there is the sweet, cold, dark and oblivion. There are no such things as gods, not really. This thing before me is a different creature. I do not understand what nature of beast he is, beyond knowing what he is not, and the sky above is broiling with cloud because a storm is coming. The ground is shaking because it is really made up of plates of rock, like all those philosophers I killed once claimed.

There was another creature there though. Vedic could feel the energy unfolding underneath the Barrens, and somehow the creature was in his head, and it was not Anya.

I can help you.

I can help you.

Vedic shook his head, trying to ignore the voice. The scarred god was starting to rise in front of him, and he knew that he still hadn't done enough to end Cernubus. The hunter was trying to heal. Vedic gripped the sword tight in his hands.

Danu was there. He could feel her, beyond the flames. The thing in his head spoke again.

There is a choice to be made in the end, because there always is. There was a choice when you could see again: to open your eyes or to keep them closed. There was a choice when you lifted the knife in the temple: to kill or to spare. There was a choice when you stepped onto the battlefield: to show mercy or not.

Vedic could feel the voice lighting up parts of his mind that he kept locked up. The part of him that he thought of as Laos, the part of him that revelled in the righteous slaughter of the sacrifice, that enjoyed the sacking of the cities and bathed in the glory of it all. That part of him was the kindred of the thing that bubbled below the Barrens, the thing that lived beneath the forest and gave all the gods their power. The energy was the belief surging all around, seeing somewhere to go now that Cernubus was falling, and all the caged power that the god had locked into himself with dark magic was leaking back into the soil.

They were your choices; why regret them? You have another now. Again, you can spare or kill. You are the Priest. You are the Butcher. There is no mercy. There is justice, and it is yours to give.

Vedic lifted the sword. He drove the blade through Cernubus's already-wounded chest and obliterated what was left of the god's heart. Still, the strike was not enough. Vedic dropped to one knee. He was breathing slow and heavy ragged breaths as he pulled the spear from his own chest. His life was leaking away fast now, without the weapon to block the wound. Vedic could feel the world receding from him. But he was not done yet.

I can help you. The voice whispered in his inner ear.

Vedic drove the spear down into the god's chest in desperation. That blow was not enough either.

I can help you. The creature was persistent and seductive. The energy offered more time, and more time was what Vedic needed.

Vedic remembered the god's corpse in the cave. He remembered Pan's words and the warriors looking on. The woodsman needed to kill the belief in Cernubus, to dominate the god utterly as the Priest, and there was one way to do that. Vedic picked up his sword again and forced himself into the ritual Shaanti execution stance – standing over the scarred god with his sword extended. He drew the blade back high over his head and swung, severing Cernubus's head. The killing blow was a small thing. The sky did not split asunder with the death of the god; neither did the ground fall away. The only sign that Vedic had succeeded was the Morrigan stepping up to the god.

The voice started again.

There is still a choice. Let me help you.

You're dying. The blood loss you have sustained is fatal, even without the spear wound, and that has punctured your right lung.

You're not even attempting to staunch the flow of blood. Listen – you can hear your heart beating. It's too loud and too slow. Even for a forestal. There is not long now.

Vedic could hear his own heart thumping in his ears. In the pause between each beat, the sensation felt like a knuckle was being driven into his chest. Breathing felt like someone was squeezing him to death.

I can help you.

You have a choice. I can help you. They all believe in you. She believes in you.

But I am dying, Vedic replied without words. He dropped his sword.

Yes, but that doesn't have to be the end. You can harness my power. You can become a god. You can be better than the hunter, than the trickster or the crow or the mother. You can show them all the way.

Isn't that what you wanted? A life of meaning? To fix the world? You understand now. I am the forest. I am where the power comes from. You comprehend what I am now. You can understand what is being offered, and it is glorious. You have another chance. You can still have a future.

You cannot make gods, Vedic replied. *They are as old as we are.*

You know I am telling the truth. I made them all as much as your kind made them. Plucked them from your kind's confused minds as they crawled across the skin of the desert. They are as old as I made them; they are as old as you made them. You have done what so few before you have done. A whole generation will go forward from this point with your memory on their lips. You are to be reborn a god.

Vedic dropped back to one knee. His right hand tried to staunch the blood in his chest. The thing under the forest was offering him a second chance. The woodsman could recognise the opportunity because nothing he had done that day would ever be enough to restore the upset. He could see the accusation on the thain's face as she moved towards him, her sword in her hand and with a desire to end him as he had ended the god. If he had an eternity ahead of him, that might be different, and unlike the other gods, he had learned the lessons of being the Priest. He would be all-powerful, merciful and just.

Exactly. You know the difference between right and wrong now. You know the risks, and you could serve as a crusader against the injustices of your cousins. In fact, in time, they might listen only to you.

Vedic forced himself to his feet. He staggered over to Anya's prone form and dropped back to his knees, fumbling for a pulse on the girl's neck. Before he could find one, she sighed. She was alive. He knew what Anya's response would be to the voice and that she would never trust him to wield such power. He also knew he could not say no.

ANYA OPENED HER EYES.

Vedic was kneeling over her. His chest was a bloody ruin, and he was as pale as the moon. He was near death, and there was a strange light in his eyes that she thought she recognised from somewhere, though she could not place it. *Cernubus is dead*, she thought. She did not know how she knew, but the information was there in her mind as if she had been wired into the hunter all this time. There was a dark connection in her head. Another creature buzzed up from the Barrens and joined with the woodsman in front of her. At first she thought the power was Danu, but it was not. The creature was neither god nor Tream nor man.

'I can make things right,' said Vedic, his voice ragged like his breathing.

Anya stared at him. She shook her head. The man looking at her was half-Vedic and half-Laos, and so close to the nightmares of her childhood that she wanted to crawl into the ground. She understood now why Danu would not intervene. She understood where the gods had come from and why this always went wrong. *They are us.* People the forest had taken and twisted. The thing burning up into Vedic stretched back from the Barrens to the forest and the trees. Anya had to end this. She knew instinctively what was needed. She knew now that it had been herself she had seen wielding the weapon in the vision of Vedic at the Mnemosyne. She rolled away from him.

The woodsman's sword, the Eagle's Claw, lay on the ground near where the scarred god had fallen. Anya picked up the weapon. The sword was heavy beyond belief, taking all of her strength to lift it. The weapon felt familiar in her hands despite the fact she had only ever picked the blade up in Vedic's nightmares. The sword had power. She could feel the energy whispering from the steel. The power felt similar to the creature she'd sensed underneath in the forest, underneath the Barrens where they stood at that moment, and at the same time whispering in Vedic's ear. The sword was an abomination that she would run from if she could, but instead, Anya locked this fear, along with all the rest of it, inside the rage in her belly and chest. All was fuel to keep going.

The thing spoke to her, pleading with her.

Why won't you let me help him? I know you want this. I can feel it in you. Let my power curl up inside him, forge him into a god that can heal these wounds. You could be glorious together.

'Beware the righteous man,' she said, softly. She could hear her grandfather's ghost echoing the words in her ear.

Vedic was still on his knees. He looked at Anya holding his sword. He did not look afraid. He laughed. Anya sighed. *He doesn't believe I will strike*, she thought. *Or perhaps he wants me to.* She felt herself curl around the fire in her gut, and she used the heat to drive the woodsman's sword home into his heart. People shouted at her. Anya no longer cared.

Vedic looked at her. He seemed calm. Anya tried to hold back tears, failed, and hated herself for weeping for the Butcher of Vremin. The woodsman shook his head at her as if trying to speak to her, but his eyes were already closing. Vedic fell back, his strings finally cut.

Anya watched the forestal fall in a moment that felt like forever. All became light.

CHAPTER THIRTY-NINE

ANYA STOOD on the ash ring that marked the hill of the Barrens.

A month had passed since the battle with the Kurah. There was little breeze that day; the sky was clear; the suns hung in the ruby dawn sky; and the smell of burning had almost disappeared from the air. Her left arm had been strapped up while her shoulder healed. The other gashes had been bound and bandaged by Pan, and after many days sleep, she was nearly feeling human again. She wore no weapon. The war was over. All of the bodies had been removed and buried now.

They had burned the god's corpse in full view to prevent anyone creating rumours of his survival. Anya wasn't sure if a god could resurrect through that kind of thing, but who knew what Cernubus had done to himself during his long exile? None of them wanted to tempt fate. She had them burn Vedic's body for the same reason. There was also the faint hope that the cremation would provoke Danu into coming forth from the forest, but there was no word from any of the gods by then. Anya had not seen Pan since she had woken in the Shaanti camp. The god had been there when she had regained consciousness, cried with her over Akyar and left without saying good-bye. She missed Akyar. To think about what the trickster must be feeling at that loss hurt Anya.

'Strange how little the land remembers after a battle,' said the thain.

Anya turned to the ruler. She sported her own set of bandages from the battle. Her silver hair was worn short, and she wore a simple tunic that was so far from the ostentatious garb of the Kurah king that it made Anya smile. She liked the old ruler. She reminded her of Falkirk on his better days.

'I'm not sure it would have ended that way, if it weren't for Vedic,' said Anya. 'He knew the fight would kill him. In the end, I think he even knew I would wield the blade.'

The thain pursed her lips. 'The enemy of my enemy.'

'What's that?' asked Anya.

'A common threat makes allies of even the most unlikely. Cernubus was as much a threat to him as to us.'

Anya smiled and shook her head. 'No, that wasn't why Vedic killed the hunter.'

'One act of right cannot atone for what he did,' said the thain, softly. 'You weren't there.'

'Yes, I was,' said Anya, sharper than she intended. She moderated her tone. 'You misunderstand. Vedic was a more honest man even when he went by Laos. He had no illusions about the things he had done, the ripples they left in the world, and he didn't want to die. Even at the end, he was tempted. No, he did this for Danu.'

'He worshipped the same gods as us?'

Anya laughed. 'He worshipped Danu, but that's not what I meant. He loved her. He wanted her to see he could make the right choice, that he could forge meaning from the path he took, however pointless, however dark the path might have been. Sometimes, with bad choices, that's all we can do.'

'What about you? He fought alongside you. Might he have not done this to keep you safe?'

Anya frowned. The thought did not sit well with her. Part of Anya felt a little too much satisfaction at wielding the weapon that had killed Vedic.

'I wish he had been the man I thought he was.'

'Yet then we would most likely be dead,' replied the thain. 'Laos was who terrified them, not the woodsman.'

Anya did not reply.

'You should come back to the city with me. Bene is going to replace Golan on the council.'

Anya kicked the ground with her foot. 'You're training him up to take your place.'

The thain laughed. 'No. Maybe. The council will be drawn at random from the people to stop the problems that we experienced, but we still need a defender if the Kurah return, or other tribes from across the water. I was hoping you might take the ink, become his guard as your mother was once mine.'

Anya felt the breeze along her skin. Her scars felt tight and raw against her dressings. 'I don't think so.'

'Why? You've shown yourself more than capable, and you would find the city a welcoming place – the people are already talking about you in the same breath as Gobaith.'

'I am neither my grandmother nor my grandfather,' said Anya, holding her gaze. 'I can fight, but I choose not to. Life is too short.'

'What will you do?'

'I will come to the city,' said Anya, thinking of Akyar. 'But I won't take the ink. I would learn more of my mother, and perhaps, I will find more information on these so-called gods in our archives.'

The thain placed a hand on Anya's good shoulder. 'That is a deal.'

PAN WATCHED the thain leave the girl.

He was on the edge of the treeline, hidden from view. He had been there a while with Danu, standing a few feet away from Anya. Danu was as silent as he had ever known her to be. The smell of the battle was finally dissipating from the edge of the forest, leaving only the soft scent of the trees.

Things had not gone as he had thought they would. Akyar's death still felt like a ragged wound in his mind and heart. It would be time soon for the trickster to head to the desert again. The journey had been delayed, not cancelled. They needed the answers that lay behind the sand. They needed to pull back the memories that were so ancient none of them, not even Danu, could recall them clearly.

'She hates us.'

Danu looked at Pan. 'Yes, perhaps. That may not be a bad thing for now.'

Pan wanted to strike her. 'This wasn't the way this was supposed to happen. You should have told me about Vedic, about what would happen, and I could have—'

'You could have done nothing. You might have changed your behaviour, but that could've stopped Vedic making the choices he did, and things would have been worse. We could not defeat Cernubus while completing our own plans.'

'Maybe we are wrong.'

Danu grabbed Pan by the shoulders. 'Life is not wrong. We know the end is coming, and so we must have a way out.'

Pan stepped out of her grip. 'There is always a chance. We have another alignment in a few years.'

Danu turned back to Anya. 'No, little goat, we do not. That was the last one.'

The trickster didn't know how to respond to that. He didn't have any way of either confirming or denying the goddess's assertion, and he wasn't aware of any archive, anywhere in the forest, where that knowledge could be held.

'During the battle, I felt a presence,' said Pan. 'Under the Barrens, it was ... I've never felt anything like it. What was that?'

Danu did not look at him. 'You have felt that creature before. Long ago.'

'The forest?'

Danu laughed. 'No. The thing that gives the forest life.'

'You?'

Danu stopped laughing. 'I did not give the forest life.'

Pan felt his stomach churn. 'There is another god?'

Danu shook her head as if he had disappointed her. 'Have you learned nothing? There is no true god. The power that birthed the forest is magic, the oldest magic that lives deep below the mud and wakes only when it needs to. The creature is a dangerous thing.'

Pan looked back at the girl. 'You think Anya will succeed where the woodsman did not?'

Danu shrugged. 'I do not know. She is strong, but she knows her own mind in a way that Vedic did not. She may choose another path.'

'You seem at ease with that.'

'The world is as it should be,' said Danu, turning to leave. 'Without freedom, there is no point to life.'

'You would give up?'

'There is always a way,' said Danu, folding her hands into her sleeves. 'When do you leave?'

Pan looked towards Anya. 'I had thought to say goodbye.'

Danu shook her head. 'I don't think so.'

Pan nodded. 'Soon, then.'

ANYA TURNED to look back at the forest.

She was amused that the gods thought she could not sense that they were there, though she herself did not understand how she could. Anya hadn't really expected the gods to try and talk to her after what had happened. You didn't need a god's powers to tell that she had taken her fill of them, even without what she had done to Vedic. She'd still thought that Pan might make the effort to come over to her. Of all of them, he might understand. Instead, they stood at the treeline, staring out as if she couldn't sense them there, ever the manipulators. She looked over at Vedic's ghost. He stared at her with sardonic eyes.

'Don't say it.'

The ghost shrugged. 'I'm not even really here.'

Anya sighed. She'd got used to the idea that she was going to see glimpses of Vedic, her grandfather, Fin and the others wherever she went, although the woodsman was the one who came to her most often now. But the idea that they weren't really there, and that her mind was conjuring them, had taken a little time to understand. In those last moments of the battle, before she had come to, she had been in Vedic's head – not memory fragments, but completely free to roam. She'd seen everything. She'd looked over the edge into the void with him and seen the dark, silent absence beyond.

'They're pathetic,' said Anya, enjoying the breeze on her face.

'They are ancient. Staying alive is habit-forming.'

Anya smiled. She liked this version of Vedic better than the man she had known: he had lost the shadow that was Laos and was closer to the person she had imagined.

'You've decided to hang up your sword, then?'

Anya nodded. 'For now.'

'Your grandfather was right, then.'

'No,' said Anya, sharply.

'But—'

'It's a choice, one of many, and I do what is right.'

'That's a dangerous point of departure, Anya. I should know.'

'Not if you choose to do as little harm as possible in the pursuit of it.'

Vedic folded his arms.

'You don't agree?'

'I think the call of the steel and the way the Shaanti look at you now will be a siren that will be very hard to resist,' said Vedic. 'The Kurah did not invade for fun. There will be another threat, and I think you will take up arms.'

'Perhaps,' conceded Anya. 'But first I will learn how those gods came to play such games with us.'

Vedic smiled.

'You're not even real,' she whispered. 'You never were, and yet I miss your cantankerous face enough to conjure you from my mind.'

Vedic looked at her with an emotion approaching pity.

'I can go if you'd prefer.'

Anya smiled. 'Stay or go as you wish. I do not need a sop to face the night.'

Vedic bowed. 'Indeed, lady, you do not.'

The woodsman faded on the breeze, leaving Anya staring at empty grass. She took one last look around, adjusted her good hand on her belt and set off in the direction of the Shaanti camp. She had the sense of the creature under the ground, angry and petulant, twisting and turning under the mud of the Barrens. The feeling made her smile.

ENJOY THIS BOOK? YOU CAN MAKE A DIFFERENCE.

Word of mouth is still the best way of a book grabbing people's attention and honest reviews help achieve this online.

Much as I hate to admit it, I do not have the resources of a major publishing house and so won't be taking out any tube advertising or television spots.

(Yet).

But I do have an awesome fledgling community of dedicated and loyal readers. An honest review helps bring my stories to the attention of other readers who might like them.

If you enjoyed this book, please could you do me a favour? Take just five minutes and head over to Amazon and leave a review for this book on that site. You can review on Amazon where you bought this book.

Thank you very much.

GET A FREE SHORT STORY

Building a relationship with my readers is the very best thing about writing. I occasionally send newsletters with details on new releases, special offers and other news about my fiction.

And if you sign up to the mailing list you'll get a free copy of my short story, *The Pilgrim*, also set in the world of *The Scarred God*.

You can get the **free** short story by signing up to my mailing list here: https://www.neilbeynon.com/newsletter/.

ACKNOWLEDGMENTS

The Scarred God started life a long time ago and has been through many iterations before release. I am indebted to early readers and supporters for feedback and encouragment. Particularly, my wife, Gemma Beynon; my one-time tutor and friend, Justina Robson; my dear friend and fellow flash fiction alumni, Gareth L Powell; my dear friends Toni Rickenback, Kim Lakin-Smith, Matthew and Laura Harrison. Thank you - you're all superstars.

I've been blessed with some awesome editorial collaborators. Early editorial and development advice was received from my dear friend Donna Scott and I recommend her services to anyone looking for an editor. My copyeditor, Elizabeth Ward, did sterling work when I was up against deadlines. I was very lucky to find a brilliant proofer in Leonora Bulbeck. Thank you all.

Finally, a note of thanks to Mark Stay and Mark Desvaux and the community at the Bestseller Experiment. The podcast got me out of the rut I found myself following the derailment of fledgling writing career in 2013 (AKA the worst year of my life). Keen-eyed observers will note A Significant Passage of Time between that year and the launch of this book. I am indebted to the two Marks, and the community around the show, which kept me sane(ish) on this crazy adventure.

If this book has worked at all, it is due to the help of those above. If it has failed, that's on me.

Neil Beynon
   Wales, 2019.

Printed in Great Britain
by Amazon

24501391R00243